The Two Dianas
Vol. II

by

Alexandre Dumas

Double 9 BOOKS

The Two Dianas

Vol. II

by Alexandre Dumas

ISBN: 978-93-68094-00-5

Published by

DOUBLE 9 BOOKS
2/13-B, Ansari Road
Daryaganj, New Delhi – 110002
info@double9books.com
www.double9books.com
Tel. 011-40042856

ABOUT THE AUTHOR

French author and playwright Alexandre Dumas is best known for his romantic novel La Dame aux Camélias (The Lady of the Camellias), published in 1848. Giuseppe Verdi adapted it into his opera La traviata (The Fallen Woman), which debuted in 1853. Other notable works by Dumas include a number of stage and film adaptations, which are usually titled Camille in English-language adaptations. The playwright Alexandre Dumas père ("father"), the author of classic works including The Three Musketeers and The Count of Monte Cristo, was the father of Dumas. Dumas received the Légion d'honneur (Legion of Honour) in 1894 after being accepted into the Académie française (French Academy) in 1874. The illegitimate child of tailor Marie-Laure-Catherine Labay (1794–1868) and novelist Alexandre Dumas, Dumas was born in Paris, France. His father gave him official recognition in 1831 and made sure the young Dumas attended the Collège Bourbon and the Institution Goubaux for the greatest education available. The elder Dumas was then permitted by law to remove the child from his mother. The younger Dumas was driven to write about sad female characters by her anguish.

CONTENTS

CHAPTER I
IN WHICH DIVERS OCCURRENCES ARTFULLY FALL OUT TOGETHER

Three weeks had elapsed. The last days of September were at hand; and no change of moment had taken place in the respective situations of the different characters represented in this tale.

Jean Peuquoy had paid to Lord Wentworth the trifling sum at which he had shrewdly had his ransom fixed. More than that, he had obtained leave to settle at Calais. We ought to say, however, that he seemed to be in no haste to commence operations. He seemed to be of a very inquisitive and yet careless disposition; in fact, the honest burgher might be seen from morning till night sauntering about on the walls, and talking with the soldiers of the garrison, while apparently thinking no more about the weaver's trade than if he were an abbé or a monk.

Nevertheless, he had either not tried or not been able to induce his cousin Pierre to be his companion in this life of idleness; and the skilful armorer had never turned out more or more finely executed work.

Gabriel's melancholy increased from day to day. He received nothing but general news from Paris. France was beginning to breathe again. The Spaniards and English had wasted too much precious time in besieging and reducing places of no importance; thus the country had had an opportunity to recover its balance, and it seemed as if both France and the king would be saved. This news, to which the heroic defence of St. Quentin had had no small share in imparting such a favorable character, no doubt was cheering to Gabriel; yet he heard not a word of Henri II., of Coligny, of his father, or of Diane! That reflection cast a shadow upon his brow and made it impossible for him to respond, as he might have done at another time, to Lord Wentworth's friendly overtures.

The easy-going and unreserved governor seemed really to have taken a great liking to his prisoner. His ennui, and a little feeling of chagrin during the last few days, had no doubt had their share in arousing this feeling.

The society of a young and clever gentleman of the French court was an invaluable distraction in stupid Calais. Thus it was that Lord Wentworth never allowed two days in succession to go by without calling upon Vicomte d'Exmès, and insisted upon his dining with him three times a week at his own table. This excessive affection was rather oppressive to Gabriel, all things considered; for the governor laughingly swore that he would not release his hold upon his captive till the last extremity; that he would never consent to let him go on parole; and that until the last crown of Gabriel's ransom should be well and truly paid, he would not yield to the cruel necessity of parting from so dear a friend.

After all, this might well be only a refined and courtly way of expressing suspicion of him, so Gabriel did not dare to persist in his excuses; besides, his delicacy led him to suffer uncomplainingly while awaiting the convalescence of his squire, who, it will be remembered, was to go to Paris to procure the sum of money agreed upon as the price of Vicomte d'Exmès's liberty.

But Martin-Guerre—we should say, his substitute Arnauld du Thill—was very deliberate in his convalescence. After a few days, the surgeon who had been called to look after the wound, which the scamp had sustained in a scuffle, had ceased to visit him, announcing that his task was done, and his patient entirely restored to health. A day or two of rest, and the excellent nursing of pretty Babette, Pierre's sister, would be quite sufficient to complete the cure, if indeed it were not already completed.

Upon receiving that assurance, Gabriel had informed his squire that he must start for Paris on the next day but one without fail; but when the morning of that day arrived, Arnauld complained of dizziness and faintness, which made him likely to fall if he took but a few steps without Babette's accustomed support. Thereupon two days' more of delay were asked and granted. At the end of that time a sort of general debility caused poor Arnauld's arms and legs to become perfectly useless; and this new symptom, which was caused doubtless (so he said) by the excessive pain he had suffered, had to be treated with hot baths and a very rigid diet. But this last regimen gave rise to such utter weakness that more delay was considered indispensable, to give the faithful fellow time to build himself up once more with tonics and generous draughts of wine. At least his nurse Babette declared to Gabriel, with tears in her eyes, that if he required Martin-Guerre to set out at once, he would expose him to the danger of dying of inanition on the road.

This extraordinary convalescence was thus prolonged to much greater length than the illness itself, in spite of the tender care of Babette,—a malicious person might say, thanks to that same tender care,—until two weeks had elapsed since the surgeon had pronounced him cured, and it was nearly a month since Gabriel's arrival at Calais.

This could not be allowed to go on forever. Gabriel finally lost his patience; and even Arnauld du Thill, who at first had sought and found all manner of expedients with the best grace in the world, now announced, with a very self-sufficient and triumphant air, to poor broken-hearted Babette, that he could not afford to make his master angry, and that, after all, his best course would be to start at once so that he might the sooner return; but Babette's red eyes and downcast look proved that she hardly understood that kind of reasoning.

The evening before the day when, according to his formal announcement, Arnauld proposed finally to take his departure for Paris, Gabriel took supper with Lord Wentworth.

The governor seemed to have even more melancholy than usual to shake off, for he carried his gayety almost to the point of madness.

When he left Gabriel after escorting him to the courtyard, lighted at that hour only by a lamp which was already flickering, the young man, just as he was wrapping himself in his cloak before going out, saw one of the doors opening into the courtyard partly ajar. A woman, whom Gabriel recognized as one of those employed in the house, glided up to him, with a finger on her lips, and holding a paper toward him with the other hand, said in a low voice,—

"For the French gentleman whom Lord Wentworth entertains so often."

She handed him the folded paper; and before Gabriel had recovered sufficiently from his stupefaction to question her, she was already gone.

The youth, in his perplexity, being naturally of an inquiring mind, and perhaps a little rash, reflected that he had a quarter of an hour's walk to take in the dark before he would be able to read the note at his ease in his own room; and that seemed a long while to wait for the key to a riddle which piqued his curiosity. So without more ado he determined to ascertain at once if anything was required of him. He looked about, and seeing that he was quite alone, drew near the smoking lamp, unfolded the note, and read, not altogether unmoved, the following words:—

> "Monsieur, I do not know you, nor have I ever seen you; but one of the women who wait upon me tells me that you are a Frenchman, and are, as I am, a prisoner. This gives me

> courage to appeal to you in my distress. You are doubtless held for ransom. You will probably soon return to Paris. You can see there my friends, who have no idea what has become of me. You might tell them where I am; that Lord Wentworth is holding me a prisoner without allowing me to communicate with a living, soul, and refusing to name any price for my liberty; and that, shamefully abusing the cruel privilege which my unfortunate position gives him, he has the effrontery every day to speak to me of a passion which I repulse with horror, but which my very scorn and his certainty of impunity may excite to the use of force. A gentleman, and above all, a fellow-countryman, will surely come to my aid in this wretched extremity; but I still have to tell you who I am for whom—"

The letter came to an end there, and was unsigned. Some unexpected interruption or sudden accident had probably caused her to break off thus abruptly, and yet she had chosen to send the letter, even though it were unfinished, so that she might not lose any precious opportunity, and because, although not complete, it still said everything that she wished to say except the name of the lady who was being subjected to such odious restraint.

That name Gabriel did not know, nor could he recognize the trembling, hurried handwriting; and yet a strange feeling of anxiety, an extraordinary presentiment, crept into his heart. Pale with emotion, he drew near the lamp again to read the letter once more, when another door behind him opened, and Lord Wentworth himself came out, preceded by a little page, and crossed the courtyard on his way to his sleeping apartment.

As he recognized Gabriel, to whom he had said good-night some time before, the governor stayed his steps in surprise.

"Are you still here, my friend?" he said, approaching him with his customary friendly manner. "What has detained you? No mishap, I trust, or sudden illness?"

The straightforward young man, without replying, simply held out to Lord Wentworth the letter that had been handed him. The Englishman cast his eye upon it, and became even paler than Gabriel; but he succeeded in maintaining his presence of mind, and while pretending to read it, was really making up his mind how to deal with the matter.

"What an old fool she is!" said he, crumpling the letter in his hand and throwing it on the floor in well-feigned contempt.

No words could have served to throw Gabriel off the scent more quickly or completely, for he was continually absorbed in his own thoughts, and had already begun to lose interest in the unknown. However, he did not abandon his suspicions at once, but responded rather evasively,—

"You don't tell me who this prisoner is whom you are detaining here against her will, my Lord?"

"Against her will, indeed!" said Wentworth, in a perfectly unembarrassed tone. "It is a kinswoman of my wife,—a little crack-brained, if any one ever was,—whom her family wished to send away from England, and who has, much to my disgust, been put in my charge in this place, where it is easier to keep an eye on lunatics as well as on prisoners. However, since you have penetrated this family secret, my dear fellow, I think I might as well tell you the whole story on the spot. The particular mania of Lady Howe, who has read too many of the poems of chivalry, is to imagine, despite her fifty years and her gray hairs, that she is an oppressed and persecuted heroine; and she tries to interest in her behalf, by fables with more or less foundation in fact, every good-looking young cavalier who comes within her reach. Upon my soul, Gabriel, it seems to me as if my old aunt's romancing has enlisted your sympathy for her. Come! confess that her *billet-doux* did cause you a little anxiety, my poor fellow?"

"It's a strange story that you tell me, my Lord, you must agree," said Gabriel, coldly; "you have never spoken to me of your kinswoman that I remember."

"No, to be sure I have not," rejoined Lord Wentworth; "for one does not ordinarily care to admit strangers into one's confidence as to private family matters."

"But how does she come to say that she is French?" asked Gabriel.

"Oh, to arouse your interest more successfully, in all probability," was Wentworth's reply, with a smile which began to be rather forced.

"And this passion which she claims that you inflict upon her, my Lord?"

"The delusion of an old woman who mistakes ancient memories for new hopes," rejoined Wentworth, who was beginning to grow restive.

"Is it to avoid being laughed at, my Lord, that you keep her out of everybody's sight?"

"Ah, how many questions you ask!" exclaimed Lord Wentworth, frowning darkly, but still without any outburst. "I had no idea you were of such an inquiring mind, Gabriel. But it's quarter to nine, and I have your agreement to be in your own quarters before the curfew sounds; for your freedom as a prisoner on parole does not extend so far as to allow any infringement of the police regulations of Calais. If Lady Howe interests you so deeply, we can return to the subject to-morrow. Meanwhile, I beg you will say nothing about these delicate family matters; and I have the honor to wish you good-evening, Monsieur le Vicomte."

Thereupon the governor saluted Gabriel, and re-entered the house. He desired to retain his self-control to the end, and feared that he might become too much excited if the conversation were to continue.

Gabriel, after a moment's hesitation and thought, left the governor's mansion to return to the humble abode of the armorer. But Lord Wentworth had not remained so entirely master of himself to the last as to do away with all suspicion in Gabriel's heart; and the young man's doubts, which were added to by his secret instinct, assailed him anew on his way through the streets.

He determined to say nothing more on the subject to Lord Wentworth, who was not likely to give him any information, but to watch and make inquiries, and to find out if he could whether the fair unknown was really a countrywoman of his own, and the Englishman's prisoner.

"But, *mon Dieu*! even if that is proved to demonstration," thought Gabriel, "what can I do then? Am I not myself a prisoner here? Are not my hands bound, and has not Lord Wentworth a perfect right to call upon me for my sword, which I wear only by his favor and at his pleasure? There must be an end to this state of things; and I must be able to have matters on a different footing, in case of need. Martin-Guerre must absolutely and without more trifling be off to-morrow. I will tell him so myself this very evening."

So when the door had been opened to Gabriel by one of Pierre Peuquoy's apprentices, he went up to the second floor, instead of stopping, as he generally did, at his own room on the first floor. Probably everybody in the house was asleep at that hour, Martin-Guerre no doubt like the others. If so, Gabriel concluded to awaken him and make known to him his firm determination. He noiselessly approached the room occupied by his squire, so that he might disturb nobody's slumbers.

The key was in the outer door, which Gabriel softly opened; but the inner door was closed, and Gabriel could hear through the partition bursts of laughter and the clinking of glasses. Thereupon he knocked with some force, and announced himself in an imperious voice. The noise ceased abruptly; and as Gabriel only called the louder, Arnauld du Thill hurriedly opened the door to his master. In fact, he made too much haste, and failed to allow sufficient time for a fluttering dress, which was vanishing through an opposite door, to disappear completely before Gabriel came in.

He took it to be some little love-making with the housemaid; and as he was not very prudish in his ideas, he could not refrain from smiling as he reprimanded his squire.

"Aha, Martin," said he, "I think you must be much better than you pretend! A table all set, three bottles, and two covers! I seem to have frightened away your companion at the banquet. Never mind! I have seen now very decisive proofs of your recovery, and I am more than ever free from hesitation about ordering you to start to-morrow."

"That was my intention, you know, Monseigneur," said Arnauld, rather abashed; "and I was just saying my adieus—"

"To a friend? Oh, yes!" said Gabriel, "that shows your kind heart; but friendship must not make us forget our duty, and I must insist that you be on your way to Paris before I rise to-morrow. You have the governor's safe-conduct; your outfit has been ready for some days: your horse is as thoroughly rested as yourself; your purse is full, thanks to the confidence of our good host, who has only one regret, worthy man, and that is that he is unable to advance the whole of my ransom. You lack nothing, Martin; and if you start early in the morning you ought to be in Paris in three days. Do you remember what you are to do when you are safely there?"

"Yes, Monseigneur. I am to go at once to the house in the Rue des Jardins de St. Paul, to inform your nurse of your safety; to ask her for the ten thousand crowns required for your ransom, and three thousand more for your expenses and debts here; and as tokens of my authority, I am to show her this line from you, and your ring."

"Useless precautions, Martin, for my good nurse knows you well, my faithful fellow! but I have yielded to your scruples. Remember to see that this money is got together as quickly as possible, do you understand?"

"Never fear, Monseigneur. When I have the money, and have handed your letter to Monsieur l'Amiral, I am to come back even faster than I went away."

"No wretched quarrels on the way, above all things!" "There is no danger, Monseigneur."

"Well, then, adieu, Martin, and good luck to you!"

"In ten days you will see me here again, Monseigneur, and at sunrise to-morrow I shall be a long way from Calais."

On this occasion Arnauld kept his promise. He allowed Babette to go with him next morning to the city walls. He embraced her for the last time, swearing solemnly that she should see him again very soon; then he drove his spurs into his horse, and was off in high spirits like the rascal that he was, and speedily disappeared at a bend in the road.

The poor girl made haste to get back to the house before her terrible brother should have arisen; but she had to send word down that she was ill, so that she might indulge her grief alone in her chamber.

Thereafter it would not be easy to say whether she or Gabriel awaited the squire's return the more impatiently. They were both doomed to wait a long while.

CHAPTER II
HOW ARNAULD DU THILL CAUSED ARNAULD DU THILL TO BE HANGED AT NOYON

During the first day Arnauld du Thill had no unfortunate encounter, and pursued his journey with reasonable celerity. He met parties of the enemy from time to time along the road,—German deserters, disbanded Englishmen, and Spaniards insolent in the pride of conquest; for there were more foreigners than Frenchmen at this time in our poor debased France. But to all questioners Arnauld proudly exhibited Lord Wentworth's safe-conduct; and all of them, not without some regretful grumbling, thought best to respect the signature of the governor of Calais.

Nevertheless, on the second day, in the neighborhood of St. Quentin, a detachment of Spaniards undertook to get the better of him by claiming that his horse was not included in the safe-conduct, and that they might conclude to confiscate him; but the false Martin-Guerre was firm as a rock, and demanded to be taken to their commander, whereupon they released the sharp fellow and his horse without more ado.

However, the adventure served as a useful lesson to him, and he resolved henceforward to avoid as far as possible all meetings with armed bands. But it was a difficult matter; the enemy, although they had gained no decisive advantage by the capture of St. Quentin, nevertheless occupied all the surrounding country. Le Catelet, Ham, Noyon, and Chauny were in their hands; and when Arnauld found himself before Noyon, on the evening of the second day, he made up his mind that his best plan was to avoid the town by a detour, and not put up for the night until he came to the next settlement.

In order to do this he had to leave the high-road. Arnauld, being but little acquainted with the country, lost his way; as he was trying to get back into the right road again, he suddenly found himself at a turn in the path in the midst of a detachment of armed men, who likewise seemed to be in search of something.

It is easier to imagine than describe Arnauld's intense satisfaction when he heard one of them cry out as soon as he caught sight of him,—

"Hallo! If here isn't that miserable Arnauld du Thill now!"

"Arnauld du Thill on horseback?" said another of the party.

"Great Heaven!" said the squire to himself, turning pale, "I seem to be known hereabouts; and if I am really recognized, it's all over with me."

It was too late, however, for him to turn about and make his escape, for the soldiers were all around him. Fortunately it was already pretty dark.

"Who are you, and where are you going?" one of them asked him.

"My name is Martin-Guerre," replied Arnauld, trembling with fear; "I am the squire of Vicomte d'Exmès, now a prisoner at Calais, and I am on my way to Paris to procure the money for his ransom. Here is a safe-conduct signed by Lord Wentworth, governor of Calais."

The leader of the troop called one of his men, who carried a torch, and began with very serious mien to examine Arnauld's pass.

"The seal is all right," said he; "and the pass seems to be genuine. You have told the truth, my friend; and you may go on about your business."

"Thanks," said Arnauld, breathing again.

"One word more, my friend. You have not chanced to meet on your way a man who had the appearance of a fugitive, a rascally gallows-bird, who answers to the name of Arnauld du Thill?"

"I don't know any such man as Arnauld du Thill," was Arnauld du Thill's hasty reply.

"Perhaps you don't know him, my friend; but you might have met him among these by-paths. He is about your height, and as well as one can judge in this darkness, of somewhat the same build. But he is by no means so well dressed as you, I must admit. He wears a brown cape, round hat, and gray leggings, and he should be in hiding somewhere in the direction that you came from. The villain! Oh, if he but fall into our hands just once more, that devilish scoundrel!"

"What has he done, pray?" inquired Arnauld, hesitatingly.

"What has he done? This is the third time that he has escaped from us. He claims that we made his life too hard for him. I think he's right too! When he ran away the first time he carried off his master's light o' love. Surely that deserved punishment. Then he had nothing to pay for his ransom. He has been sold over and over again, and has passed from hand to hand, and was the property of anybody who wanted him. It was no more than fair that since he could be of no value to us, he should entertain us; but that made him proud, and he didn't choose to do it any longer, so he ran away again. Now, this makes the third time that he has done it, and if we catch the blackguard again!"

"What will you do to him?" asked Arnauld, again.

"The first time we beat him; the second time we half killed him; and the third time we will hang him!"

"Hang him!" echoed Arnauld, in alarm.

"To the nearest tree, my good fellow; and without trial. He is ours. To hang him will amuse us, and teach him a lesson. Look to your right, my friend. Do you see that gallows? Well, we shall string up Arnauld du Thill on that very gallows the moment we succeed in capturing him."

"Oh, indeed!" said Arnauld, with rather constrained merriment.

"It's just as I tell you, my friend! so if you meet the rascal, just take him in hand, and bring him to us; we will not forget the service. Until then, farewell."

Thereupon they were leaving him, but he, feeling immensely relieved, called them back.

"Pardon me, masters, but one good turn deserves another! I am completely astray, you see, and have not the slightest idea where I am; so just set my compass right for me, will you?"

"That's very easily done, my friend," said the trooper. "Those walls behind you and the postern-gate that you can just distinguish in the darkness are part of Noyon. You are looking too far to the right, toward the gallows; look more to the left, where you see the pikes of our comrades glistening, for our company is doing guard-duty to-night at that postern. Now, turn about and you have in front of you the road from Paris through the wood. About twenty paces from here the road forks. You may turn to the right or left, as you think best. The roads are of equal length, and come together at the ferry over the Oise about a fourth of a league from here. Having crossed the ferry, bear always to the right. The first village is Auvray, a league from the ferry. Now you know as much as we do, my friend. A pleasant journey to you!"

"Thanks, and good-evening," said Arnauld, putting his horse to a trot.

The directions they had given him were very accurate. Twenty paces away he came to the fork, and left the selection to his horse, who chose the left-hand road.

The night was very dark, and the forest doubly so. However, in about ten minutes Arnauld arrived at a clearing in the woods; and the moon, breaking through the clouds, cast a feeble and uncertain light upon the road.

At that moment the squire was thinking of the fright he had had, and of the strange adventure which had put his *sang-froid* to the test. Though his mind was at ease as to the past, he could not contemplate the future without misgiving.

"This must be the real Martin-Guerre, whom they are hunting under my name," he thought. "But the gallows-bird has got away! I shall find him at Paris as soon as I get there myself, very likely, and a fine contest I shall have on my hands in that case. I know that nothing but impudence can carry me through; but it may be my destruction. Why need the blackguard have escaped h He is getting to be a great nuisance certainly; and it would be a great kindness to me if those brave fellows would hang him. He is decidedly my evil genius."

This edifying monologue was yet unfinished when Arnauld, who had a very keen and practised sight, saw or thought he saw, a hundred paces or so ahead of him, a man, or more properly speaking, a shadow, which, as he drew near, suddenly disappeared in a ditch.

"Hallo! another ill-timed meeting,—an ambush perhaps," thought the prudent Arnauld.

He tried to plunge into the woods, but the ditch was impassable for horseman and horse. He waited a few moments, then ventured to look around. The phantom, which had raised its head, disappeared as quickly as before.

"Can it be that he is as much afraid of me as I am of him?" said Arnauld to himself. "Are we equally anxious to avoid each other? Well, I must do something, since this infernal undergrowth prevents my going across through the woods to the other road. Must I go back to the fork in the road! That would be the surest way. May I not bravely put my horse on the run and pass my man like a flash? That would be the shortest way to do. He is on foot, and unless a shot from an arquebuse—but no, I won't give him time for that."

No sooner resolved than carried out. Arnauld drove both spurs into his horse's sides, and went by the man in ambush or hiding like a streak of lightning.

The man did not stir.

That rather lessened Arnauld's terror; he pulled up his horse, and even went back a few steps, acting upon a thought that had suddenly occurred to him.

Still the man gave no sign of life.

Thereupon all Arnauld's courage came back to him; and now, almost certain that he was right in his conjecture, he rode straight up to the ditch.

But at this juncture, and before he had time even to utter an exclamation, the man gave one leap, and releasing Arnauld' right foot from the stirrup with a sudden movement, and throwing it roughly over the saddle, he cast the squire from his horse, fell to the ground upon him, and seized him by the throat with his knee on his chest.

All this took place in less than twenty seconds.

"Who are you? What do you want?" asked the victor of his fallen foe.

"Let me get up, I beseech you!" said the almost strangled voice of Arnauld, who felt that he had met his master. "I am a Frenchman; but I have a safe-conduct from Lord Wentworth, governor of Calais."

"If you are a Frenchman," said the man,—"and in truth you seem not to have an accent like all these demons of foreigners,—I have no need of your passport. But what made you approach me in such an extraordinary way?"

"I thought that I saw a man in the ditch," said Arnauld, as the pressure on his chest was somewhat relaxed; "and I was coming to see if it wasn't a wounded man, and if there wasn't something I could do for him."

"Your purpose was good," said the man, withdrawing his hand and taking away his knee. "Come, get up, comrade," he added, extending his hand to Arnauld, who was soon on his feet. "I gave you rather a—rather a rough welcome; but you must excuse me, because I have no mind just now to have anybody interfering with my affairs. But you are a fellow-countryman, which is a very different matter; and far from injuring me, you may do me a great service. Let us get to know each other first. My name is Martin-Guerre; and yours?"

"Mine? Mine? It's Bertrand," said Arnauld, with a start; for being alone with him at night, and in that dense forest, this man, whom he ordinarily ruled completely by virtue of his cunning and shrewdness, now quite as completely had him in his power by virtue of his strength and courage.

Fortunately for Arnauld, the darkness assured his remaining unrecognized, and he did his best to disguise his voice.

"Well, friend Bertrand," continued Martin-Guerre, "let me tell you that I am an escaped prisoner, and that I got away this morning for the second time (my captors say for the third) from these Spaniards and English and Germans and Flemings; in short, from this whole catalogue of foes who have settled down upon our poor land like a swarm of locusts. For may I be hanged if France is not at this moment another Tower of Babel! For the last month I have belonged, just as you see me now, to twenty jabberers of different nationalities; and each patois was always harsher and more outlandish to listen to than the last. I was tired to death of being harried from village to village, which was done to me so much that I began to think they were simply making sport of me, and amusing themselves by tormenting me. They were forever blackguarding me about some pretty little witch named Gudule, who was supposed to have fallen in love with me so madly apparently as to have run away with me."

"Aha!" ejaculated Arnauld.

"I am just telling you what they told me. Well, their raillery tired me so much that one fine morning I took to my heels, all alone, however. As bad luck would have it, they caught me, and pounded me so that I had to pity myself. But what was the good of it all? They threatened to hang me if I did it again, but that only made me all the more anxious to attempt it; and this morning, seizing a favorable opportunity while they were arranging their quarters at Noyon, I gave my tyrants the slip again finely. God knows how eagerly they have been hunting for me to hang me! But as I am strongly opposed to that conclusion of the affair, I have been perched up in a tall tree here in the woods all day, waiting for night to come; and I couldn't help laughing, although rather feebly, to see them pass right under my feet, cursing and swearing. When it became dark, I left my observatory. Now, in the first place, I have lost myself in the woods, having never been here before; and in the second place, I am dying of hunger, not having had a morsel between my teeth for twenty-four hours, except a few leaves and roots, which do not make a bountiful meal. That is why I fell down from weakness, as you can easily understand."

"Phew!" said Arnauld. "I didn't understand it that way just now; on the contrary, you seemed to me, I must confess, to be quite vigorous."

"Oh, yes," said Martin, "because I pommelled you a little. However, don't be angry about it. It was the fever of hunger that lent strength to my arm. But now you are my Providence; for you, being a fellow-countryman, surely will not let me fall into the hands of those fellows again, will you?"

"No, to be sure I will not, if I can help you in any way," replied Arnauld du Thill, who was reflecting in his shrewd way upon what Martin had said.

He began to see light on the subject of regaining his advantage, which had been put in some peril by the strong grasp of his double.

"You can do a great deal for me," Martin-Guerre went on ingenuously. "Are you not somewhat acquainted with this neighborhood?"

"I belong in Auvray, a quarter of a league from here," said Arnauld.

"Are you on your way there?"

"No, I am just coming from there," replied the crafty knave, after a moment's hesitation.

"Does Auvray lie in that direction, then?" asked Martin, pointing toward Noyon.

"Exactly so," replied Arnauld; "it is the first village out of Noyon on the road to Paris."

"On the road to Paris!" cried Martin; "well, just see, then, how a man may get turned around in the woods! I fancied that my back was turned to Noyon, whereas I was really coming back to it; that I was going toward Paris, whereas I was really getting farther away. The cursed country is entirely strange to me, as I was just telling you. So it seems that I must travel in the direction from which you came to avoid walking into the wolfs jaws."

"You are quite right, Master! I am going to Noyon; but walk with me a few steps. We shall find at the ferry over the Oise, close by, another road which will take you to Auvray more directly."

"I am very much obliged, friend Bertrand," said Martin; "to be sure, I want to be as sparing of my steps as possible, for I am very tired and very weak, having, as I was telling you, about as little sustenance in me as I well could have. You don't happen to have anything to eat about you, friend Bertrand, do you? If you have, you will have saved me twice over,—once from the English, and again from starvation, which is quite as terrible as they."

"Alas!" was Arnauld's reply, "I haven't a crumb in my haversack! But if you care for a draught of good wine, why, my calash is quite full."

In fact, Babette had taken care to fill her unfaithful swain's calash with *vin de Chypre*,—a very potent wine of the period; and Arnauld up to that time had indulged very sparingly, so as to retain his rather easily upset reasoning powers amid the perils of the road.

"I think I should be more than glad of a drink!" cried Martin-Guerre, enthusiastically. "A draught of wine is sure to enliven me a bit."

"Well, then, take it and drink away, my good fellow!" said Arnauld, offering him his calash.

"Thanks! And may God requite you!" said Martin, who set to work unsuspiciously to drown his sorrows in the wine, which was as treacherous as he who offered it, and whose fumes almost immediately began to work upon his brain, which was easily affected on account of his long abstinence from food.

"Well, well," said he, hilariously, "this light wine of yours doesn't lack fire!"

"Oh, *mon Dieu*! it's quite harmless!" said Arnauld; "I drink two bottles at every meal. But as the evening is very fine, let us sit here on the grass awhile; and do you take a good rest, and drink at your leisure. I have time enough; and I shall be all right if I reach Noyon before ten o'clock, which is the hour for closing the gates. But you, although Auvray still flies the standard of France, are nevertheless likely to meet with troublesome patrolling parties if you follow the high-road so early; while if you leave it, you will lose your way again. The best course will be for us to stay here awhile, and quietly talk matters over. Where were you made prisoner?"

"I don't quite know," said Martin-Guerre, "for there are two contradictory versions of that matter, just as there are of almost the whole of my unfortunate life,—one which I believe myself, and another which I hear from others. For instance, I am assured that it was at the battle of St. Laurent that I surrendered at discretion; while my own idea is that I was not present on that occasion, and that it was somewhat later than that I fell into the hands of a party of the enemy all by myself."

"What do you mean?" asked Arnauld, feigning incredulity. "Have you two histories, pray? Your adventures seem very interesting and instructive, to say the least of them. I must confess that I am extravagantly fond of such tales. Just take a good drink to freshen up your memory, and tell me something of your life. You are not from Picardy?"

"No," replied Martin, after a pause, which he occupied in drinking three fourths of the contents of the calash; "no, I am from the South,—Artigues."

"A fine country, they say. Is your family there?"

"My wife and children, my good friend," replied Martin, who had become very expansive and confidential under the influence of the Chypre.

Being stimulated partly by Arnauld's questions and partly by his constant libations, he began to narrate with great volubility his whole history, even to its least detail,—his youth, his love-affairs, and his marriage; that his wife was a very charming woman, notwithstanding a slight failing in regard to her hand, which was too quick and too heavy at once. In truth, a blow from a woman was no dishonor to a man, although it was rather tiresome in the long run. That was why Martin-Guerre had left his too-emphatic wife. Then followed a circumstantial account of the causes, details, and sequel of the rupture between them. However, he loved her still at heart,—his dear Bertrande! He still wore on his finger his iron marriage-ring, and over his heart the two or three letters which Bertrande had written the first time they ever were separated. As he told of this, the honest fellow wept. It was decidedly tender-hearted wine. He would have liked to go on with the details of everything that had happened to him since he entered the service of Vicomte d'Exmès; that a demon had pursued him; that he, Martin-Guerre, was double, and did not recognize himself at all in his other existence. But this portion of his narrative seemed less interesting to Arnauld du Thill, who kept luring him back to talk of his childhood and his father's house, of his friends and kinsfolk at Artigues, and of Bertrande's charms and failings.

In less than two hours the treacherous Arnauld, by dint of skilful and persistent questioning, knew all that he cared to know about the former habits and the most private concerns of poor Martin-Guerre.

At the end of two hours Martin, with his head on fire, rose, or rather tried to rise; for as soon as he moved, he stumbled and fell heavily back onto his seat.

"Well, well, what's the matter?" said he, with a loud laugh which was a long while dying out. "Upon my soul, your saucy wine has done its work! Give me your hand, pray, my friend, so that I may be able to stand up."

Arnauld courageously went about hoisting him up, and at last succeeded in getting him on his legs, but not in a posture of classical equilibrium.

"Hallo, there! what a number of lanterns!" cried Martin. "Oh, what a fool I am! I took the stars for lanterns."

Then he began to sing at the top of his voice,—

"Par ta foy, envoyras-tu pas
Au vin, pour fournir le repas
Du meilleur cabaret d'enfer
Le vieil ravasseur Lucifer?" [1]

"Don't make such an infernal noise!" cried Arnauld; "suppose some party of the enemy should be passing near, and hear you?"

"*Basta*! I'm not afraid of them," said Martin; "what could they do to me? Hang me? It must be very fine to be hanged. You have made me drink too much, comrade. I, who am commonly as sober as a judge, don't know how to fight against drunkenness, and then, besides, I had been fasting, and I was almost starved; now I am thirsty."

"'Par ta foy, envoyras-tu pas—'"

"Be still!" said Arnauld. "Come, try to walk. Don't you mean to put up for the night at Auvray?"

"Oh, yes, I want to put up for the night," said Martin, "but not at Auvray; down here on the grass, beneath God's lanterns."

"Yes," retorted Arnauld; "and to-morrow morning some Spanish patrol will come along and discover you, and send you to take up your quarters with the Devil."

"With Lucifer, the old rake?" said Martin. "No, I prefer to pull myself together a bit, and drag myself as far as Auvray. It's this way, isn't it? Well, I'm off."

But it was absurd for him to talk about pulling himself together: for he described such marvellous zigzags that Arnauld saw clearly that without some help from him, Martin would speedily lose his way again,—that is to say, he would very likely be safe for the time; and that was just what the villain did not want.

"Come," said he to poor, drunken Martin; "I have a kind heart, and Auvray is not so very far away. I will go there with you. Just let me unhitch my horse; then I can lead him by the bridle, and give you my arm."

"*Ma foi*! I gladly accept," rejoined Martin; "I am not proud, and between ourselves I confess that I believe I am a little tipsy. I am still of the opinion that light wine of yours does not lack strength. I am very happy, but just a little tipsy."

"Well, let's be off; it's getting late," said Arnauld du Thill, starting off on the road by which he had come, with his double leaning on his arm, and heading straight for the postern gate of Noyon. "But to beguile the time," he added, "are you not going to tell me another amusing story about Artigues?"

"Shall I tell you the story of Papotte?" said Martin-Guerre. "Ah, poor Papotte!"

The epic of Papotte was rather too incoherent for us to undertake to reproduce here. It was almost finished when these two Dromios of the sixteenth century arrived in rather indifferent trim before the Noyon gate.

"There!" said Arnauld; "I have no need to go any farther. Do you see that gate h Well, that is the gate of Auvray. Knock there, and the watchman will open for you; you tell him that you are a friend of mine, and he will point out to you my house, only two steps from the gate. Go there, and my brother will welcome you and give you a good supper and a good bed. Now, comrade, let me shake your hand once more, and adieu!"

"Adieu! and many thanks," said Martin. "I am only a poor devil, and in no condition to realize all that you have done for me. But never fear, the good Lord, who is a just God, will know how to requite you. Adieu, my friend."

Strangely enough, these drunken predictions made Arnauld shudder, though superstition was not among his faults; and for a moment he thought of calling Martin back. But he was already knocking lustily at the postern.

"Poor devil, he is knocking at the door of his tomb!" thought Arnauld; "but, bah! this is childishness."

Meanwhile Martin, with no suspicion that his fellow-traveller was spying him from a distance, was shouting at the top of his voice,—

"Hallo there, watchman! Hallo, Cerberus! open the gate, blockhead! It is Bertrand, worthy Bertrand, who has sent me."

"Who goes there?" demanded the sentinel from within. "It's too late to come in. Who are you to be making such an uproar?"

"Who am I? You drunkard, I am Martin-Guerre, or Arnauld du Thill, if you please; or the friend of Bertrand, if you like that better. I am several people all at once, especially when I am in liquor. I am twenty rakes or so, who are going to give you a good sound drubbing if you don't open the gate for me at once."

"Arnauld du Thill! You are Arnauld du Thill?" asked the sentinel.

"Yes, I am Arnauld du Thill, twenty thousand cartloads of devils!" said Martin-Guerre, hammering away at the gate with feet as well as fists.

Then there was a noise behind the gate as of troops assembling at the call of the sentinel.

A man with a lantern opened the gate; and Arnauld du Thill, crouching behind the trees at a little distance, heard several voices crying out together in surprise,—

"Upon my word, it's he! It's he indeed, upon my soul!"

Poor Martin-Guerre, recognizing his tyrants, uttered a cry of despair, which struck upon Arnauld's heart in his hiding-place like a malediction.

Then he judged from the trampling and yelling that brave Martin, seeing that everything was lost, was making a stout fight for liberty; but he had only two fists against twenty swords. The noise grew less, then died gradually away until it ceased altogether. They had dragged Martin away, blaspheming and cursing.

"If he expects to smooth matters over with insults and blows—" said Arnauld, rubbing his hands.

When he could hear nothing more, he gave himself up to reflection for a quarter of an hour; for he was a very deep rascal, this same Arnauld du Thill. The result of his meditation was that he penetrated three or four hundred paces into the woods, tied his horse to a tree, laid his saddle and blanket upon the dead leaves, wrapped himself in his cloak, and in a few minutes was sleeping the deep sleep which God makes much easier for, the hardened villain than for the innocent.

He slept eight hours without stirring.

Nevertheless, when he awoke it was still dark; and he knew from the position of the stars that it must be about four o'clock in the morning. He rose and shook himself, and without disturbing his horse, crept softly out toward the high-road.

On the gallows which they had pointed out to him the night before, the body of poor Martin-Guerre was swinging gently to and fro.

A hideous smile flickered upon Arnauld's lips.

He approached the body without a quiver; but it was hanging too high for him to touch. Then he climbed up the gallows-post, sword in hand, and when he had reached the necessary height, cut the cord with his sword.

The body fell to the ground.

Arnauld came down again, removed an iron ring hardly worth the taking from the dead man's finger, searched in his breast and there found some papers which he carefully put away, put his cloak on again, and coolly walked away, without a look, without a prayer for the poor wretch whom he had worried so during his life, and whom he thus robbed in death.

He found his horse in the underbrush, saddled him, and started off at full speed toward Aulnay. He was well satisfied, villain that he was, for Martin no longer was an object of fear to him.

A half-hour later, just as the first glimmer of day began to appear in the east, a wood-cutter, chancing to pass that way, saw the gallows-cord cut, and the body lying on the ground. He drew near, fearful and curious at the same time, to the dead man, whose clothes were in disorder, and the cord loose around his neck; he was wondering whether the weight of the body had broken the cord, or if some friend had cut it, too late, no doubt. He even ventured to touch the body to make sure that it was really lifeless.

To his unbounded alarm, the body moved its head and hands, and raised itself upon its knees; and the terrified wood-cutter fled into the woods, crossing himself over and over again, and commending his soul to God and the saints.

[1] "Old Lucifer, thou libertine,
Wilt thou not send some wine
From Acheron's best cabaret
To grace this feast of mine?"

CHAPTER III
ARNAULD DU THILL'S BUCOLIC DREAMS

The Constable de Montmorency, who had only returned to Paris the night before, after paying a royal sum by way of ransom, had presented himself at the Louvre to ascertain how the land lay; but Henri had received him with forbidding coolness, and had indulged himself in the highest encomiums upon the administration of the Duc de Guise, who had so arranged matters, he said, as to diminish, if not altogether to amend, the misfortunes of the kingdom.

The constable, pale with anger and jealousy, thought that he might at least hope to find some comfort from Diane de Poitiers. But the favorite also received him very coldly; and when Montmorency complained of such a reception, and gave voice to his fear that his absence had been a very bad thing for him, and that some more fortunate man than he had succeeded him in the good graces of the duchess, Madame de Poitiers rejoined impertinently,—

"*Dame*! of course you know the new by-word of the Parisian populace?"

"I arrived but now, Madame; and I do not know," the constable began hesitatingly.

"Oh, well! they say now, this scandal-loving populace, 'This is the motto of St. Laurent: he who forsakes his post, loses it.'"

The constable, with a blanched face, saluted the duchess, and left the Louvre with death at his heart.

When he reached his hotel and was alone in his own room, he cast his hat violently on the floor.

"Oh, these kings and these women!" he cried. "An ungrateful lot they are! They care for nothing but success."

"Monseigneur," said his valet, "there is a man asking leave to speak to you."

"Let him go to the devil!" retorted the constable. "I am in fine condition to receive visitors! Send him to Monsieur de Guise."

"Monseigneur, this man begged me to tell you his name, which he says is Arnauld du Thill."

"Arnauld du Thill!" exclaimed the constable, "that's a different matter. Show him in."

The valet bowed and withdrew.

"This fellow Arnauld," the constable reflected, "is clever, cunning, and avaricious,—more than that, he has no scruples and conscience. Oh, if he could only help me to be revenged on all these people! To be revenged, do I say? But what should I gain by that? He might possibly help me to make my way back into favor! He knows many things. It has already occurred to me to make use of my knowledge of this Montgommery affair; but it would be much better if I might learn something from Arnauld which would enable me to dispense with doing that."

At this moment Arnauld du Thill was ushered into the room.

Joy and impudence were struggling for the mastery in the rascal's expression. He bowed to the ground before the constable.

"I thought you were a prisoner," said Montmorency.

"So I was, Monseigneur, just as you were."

"But you seem to have got out of the difficulty," rejoined the constable.

"Yes, Monseigneur; I paid them in my money,—that is to say, I laughed at them instead. You used your money and I used my wits; and here we are both at liberty."

"Ah, you are an impudent scoundrel," said the constable.

"No, Monseigneur," rejoined Arnauld, "it was just my modest way of saying that I am out of money, that's all."

"Hum!" grumbled Montmorency; "what do you want of me?"

"Money, since I have none, Monseigneur."

"And why should I give you money?"

"Why, to pay me, Monseigneur," replied the spy.

"Pay you for what, pray?"

"For the intelligence I bring you."

"Tell me your news."

"Let me see your crowns."

"Villain! suppose I were to have you hanged?"

"A most contemptible way that of loosening my tongue, Monseigneur, to stretch my neck."

"He is so very audacious," thought the constable, "that he must know that I can't do without him."

"Well, fellow," he said, aloud, "I have no objection to making some slight further advance to you."

"Monseigneur is very kind," said Arnauld; "and I will not fail to remind him of his generous promise when he has settled up his outstanding debt to me."

"What debt?" asked the constable.

"Here is my account, Monseigneur," said Arnauld, producing the famous document which we have seen him at work on so often.

Anne de Montmorency cast his eyes over it.

"Yes," said he, "this paper contains, besides services which are entirely fanciful and imaginary, others which might have been very useful to me at the time when you rendered them, considering my situation at that time, but which at present serve no purpose except to make my regrets all the more poignant."

"Bah, Monseigneur! it may be that you exaggerate the extent of your disgrace," said Arnauld.

"What's that?" said the constable. "Do you know, then, pray, does everybody already know, that I am in disgrace?"

"People suspect as much; and so do I, Monseigneur."

"Very well, then, Arnauld," Montmorency rejoined bitterly; "you may very well suspect too that it is of no use to me at present that Vicomte d'Exmès and Diane de Castro were separated at St. Quentin, since in all probability the king and the grande sénéchale are no longer willing to give their daughter to my son."

"*Mon Dieu*, Monseigneur!" was Arnauld's response. "I imagine that the king would very gladly consent to give her to you if you could give her back to him."

"What do you mean?"

"I say, Monseigneur, that our sire, Henri II., ought to be very sad at heart at this moment, not only because of the loss of St. Quentin and the battle of St. Laurent, but also because of the loss of his dearly loved daughter Diane de Castro, who disappeared after the siege of St. Quentin without leaving any traces by which it is possible to tell what has become of her; for there have been twenty contradictory and inconsistent reports about her disappearance. Having only returned yesterday, of course you know nothing of all this, Monseigneur; I didn't know it myself until this morning."

"I had so many other things to think of," said the constable, "it was quite natural that I should be thinking of my present disgrace rather than of my past favor."

"Very true!" said Arnauld; "but would not that favor how back in your direction if you should say to the king something like this, for instance: 'Sire, you are sorrowing for your daughter, and searching for her everywhere, and asking news of her from every one you see; but I alone know where she is, Sire?'"

"Do you mean to say that you know, Arnauld?" asked Montmorency, eagerly.

"My trade is to know things," said the spy. "I told you that I had news to sell; and you see that my goods are not of poor quality. You should reflect on that, Monseigneur."

"I reflect," said the constable, "that kings have a way of remembering the defeats of their servants, but not their merits. When I have restored Henri's daughter to him, he will be beside himself with delight at first; all the wealth and all the honors in his whole realm would not be enough to requite me in the first flush of his gratitude. Then Diane will weep, and say that she would rather die than give her hand to any but her dear Vicomte d'Exmès; and the king, being entirely under her control, and dominated by my bitter foes, will remember the battle that I lost, and forget the child I have restored to him. So all my efforts will be pushed out of sight to accomplish the happiness of Vicomte d'Exmès."

"In that case it will be necessary," said Arnauld, with a smile of sinister meaning, "that Vicomte d'Exmès should disappear at the moment that Madame de Castro reappears. Ah, that would be a fine game, eh?"

"Yes; but I am reluctant to resort to such extreme measures," said the constable. "I know that your hand is sure, and your tongue discreet; but—"

"Oh, Monseigneur entirely mistakes my intention!" cried Arnauld, assuming an air of injured innocence. "Monseigneur does me great injustice! Monseigneur believed that I wished to get rid of this youth by a—violent process." (He made an expressive gesture.) "No, a thousand times no! I have a much better plan than that."

"What is it, pray?" asked the constable, with unfeigned interest.

"Let us first arrange our own little matters, Monseigneur. Suppose that I tell you the place where the lost damsel is to be found. I insure the absence and silence of your son's dangerous rival, at least for the length of time necessary to conclude his marriage. These are two notable services, Monseigneur. Now, in return, what will you do for me?"

"What do you ask?"

"You are reasonable, and I will be the same," rejoined Arnauld. "In the first place, you will settle, will you not, without haggling, the little account for past services, which I had the honor to present to you just now?"

"Very well," replied the constable.

"I knew that we should have no difficulty on this first point, Monseigneur. The total is an insignificant sum, and the whole amount is hardly enough to cover the expenses of my journey, and for certain gifts which I expect to buy before I leave Paris. But then, money isn't the only thing in the world."

"What!" said the astonished and almost alarmed constable, "can it really be Arnauld du Thill who says that money isn't the only thing in the world?"

"Even Arnauld du Thill, Monseigneur, but no longer the needy and avaricious Arnauld du Thill whom you formerly knew. No; another Arnauld, content with the moderate fortune he has—earned, and no longer desirous, alas! of anything except to pass the rest of his life in peace in the country where he was born, under his paternal roof-tree, and amid the friends of his childhood, in the bosom of his family. That was always my dream, Monseigneur; and I have ever looked forward to that as the peaceful and delightful termination of my—troubled life."

"Yes," said Montmorency, "if it is necessary to go through the tempest in order to enjoy calm weather, you will surely be happy, Arnauld. But have you made your fortune?"

"Only a moderate one, Monseigneur,—only a moderate one. Ten thousand crowns is a fortune for a poor devil like me, especially in my humble village, and in the bosom of my modest family."

"Your family! your village!" rejoined the constable; "you whom I supposed to be without home or kinsfolk, and to be living on your wits in a second-hand coat, and under an assumed name."

"My real name is Martin-Guerre, Monseigneur, and Arnauld du Thill an assumed one, in truth. I was born at the village of Artigues, near Rieux, where my wife and children now live."

"Your wife!" echoed old Montmorency, more and more bewildered. "Your children!"

"Yes, Monseigneur," replied Arnauld, in the most comically sentimental tone imaginable; "and I ought to notify you, Monseigneur, not to count upon any further services from me, and that these two suggestions which I have just made will be the very last I can undertake to carry out. I am going to withdraw from business, and lead an honest life henceforth, surrounded by the affectionate regard of my people, and the esteem of my fellow-citizens."

"That's all very fine!" said the constable; "but if you have become so modest and pastoral that you don't care to talk about money any more, what price do you ask for these secrets which you say that you possess?"

"I ask for something more, and yet less, than money, Monseigneur," replied Arnauld, this time in his natural tone; "I ask for an honor,—not for honors, of course, but just a little honor, of which I am very much in need, I confess."

"Explain yourself," said Montmorency, "for you are speaking in enigmas."

"Well, then, Monseigneur, here it is: I have had a writing prepared which attests that I, Martin-Guerre, have been in your service for so many years as—as squire (we must draw on our imagination a bit); that during all that time I have conducted myself as a trusty and faithful and most devoted servant; and that this devotion, Monseigneur, you have desired to repay by giving me a sufficient sum to enable me to pass the rest of my life in comfort. Place your seal and your signature at the foot of that document, Monseigneur, and we shall be quits."

"Impossible!" was the constable's response. "I should render myself liable to a charge of forgery—that is to say, to be branded as a forger and a felon—if I signed such a mass of lies."

"They are no lies, Monseigneur, for I have always served you faithfully, according to my own lights; and I assure you that if I had saved all the money I have obtained from you heretofore, it would amount now to more than ten thousand crowns. So you do not expose yourself to any charge of falsifying; and besides, do you think that I don't render myself liable to very grave penalties in order to bring about the happy result of which you have only to reap the fruits?"

"Wretch! Such a comparison—"

"Is perfectly fair, Monseigneur," Arnauld retorted. "Each of us is in need of the other, and equality is the daughter of necessity. The spy restores you your credit, so you must do as much for the spy. Come, no one hears us, Monseigneur, so no false shame! Ratify the bargain; it is a good one for me, but even better for you. Give and take, you know. Sign, Monseigneur!"

"No, not till afterward," rejoined Montmorency. "Give and take, as you say. In the first place, I must know the means you propose to use to arrive at this twofold result which you promise me. I must know what has become of Diane de Castro, and what will become of Vicomte d'Exmès."

"Very well! Except as to some minor details, I am ready to satisfy you on these two points, Monseigneur; and you will be forced to agree that chance and myself together have arranged things excellently well for your interest."

"Go on!" said the constable; "I am listening."

"As far as Madame de Castro is concerned, she was neither slain nor carried away, but simply made prisoner at St. Quentin, being included among the fifty notable persons who were to be held to ransom. Now, why has not the one into whose hands she has fallen made public his capture? How is it that Madame de Castro herself has not sent any information of her whereabouts? As to that, I am entirely in the dark. To tell the truth, I thought she was already free, and expected to find her here in Paris when I arrived. It was only this morning that I learned from the public reports that nothing was known at court of her whereabouts, and that this fact was by no means the least of Henri's causes of anxiety. It may be that in these troublous times Madame Diane's messages may have been misdirected or gone astray; or perhaps some other mystery may be hidden under this delay. But at all events, I can put at rest all doubt, and say positively where, and in whose hands, Madame de Castro is."

"That information would indeed be very valuable," said the constable. "Where is the place, and who is the man?"

"Wait a moment, pray, Monseigneur!" said Arnauld. "Have you no wish to be equally well informed as to Vicomte d'Exmès? For although it is a good thing to know the whereabouts of our friends, it is even more advantageous to be posted as to those of our enemies."

"Oh, a truce to your proverbs!" said Montmorency. "Where is this D'Exmès?"

"Also a prisoner, Monseigneur," replied Arnauld. "Who is there who hasn't been a prisoner more or less in these times? It has been quite the fashion. Well, Vicomte d'Exmès has followed the fashion, and he is a prisoner."

"But he surely will be at no loss to let his whereabouts be known," was the rejoinder of the constable. "He must have friends and plenty of money; no doubt he will procure the wherewithal to pay his ransom, and will be down upon us very soon."

"You are quite right in your conjectures, Monseigneur. Yes, Vicomte d'Exmès has money; and he is very impatient to be at liberty, and proposes to pay his ransom at the earliest possible moment. In fact, he has already sent a messenger to Paris to procure the price of his freedom and hasten back to him with it."

"What can we do, then?" asked Montmorency.

"Fortunately for us, though unfortunately for him," Arnauld continued, "the person whom he has sent to Paris in such hot haste is myself, Monseigneur,—no other than myself, who am in Vicomte d'Exmès's service as squire, under my real name of Martin-Guerre. You see that you can call me a squire without falsehood."

"And have you not executed your commission, you blackguard?" said the constable. "Have you not your pretended master's ransom already in your pocket?"

"Indeed I have, Monseigneur, you may be quite sure, for one doesn't leave such things on the ground. Consider, too, that not to take the money would be to arouse suspicion. I took it to the last crown,—for the good of the undertaking. But don't be alarmed! I shall put off taking it to him for a long while, on one pretext or another. These ten thousand crowns are just what I need to help me to pass the rest of my life piously and honestly; and I should be supposed to owe them to your generosity, Monseigneur, on the strength of the paper you are going to sign."

"I will not sign it, you villain!" cried Montmorency. "I will not knowingly become the accomplice of a thief."

"Oh, Monseigneur," said Arnauld, "what a harsh name that is to apply to a stern necessity, which I submit to so that I may do you a service! What! I allow my devotion to you to stifle the voice of my conscience, and you recompense me thus for it? Oh, well, so be it! Let us send Vicomte d'Exmès this sum of money, and he will be here as soon as Madame Diane, if not before her. Whereas, if he should not receive it—"

"Well, if he should not receive it?" said the constable.

"We should gain so much time, Monseigneur. In the first place, Monsieur d'Exmès will wait patiently a fortnight for my return. There is naturally some delay about procuring ten thousand crowns; in fact, his nurse didn't hand them to me till this morning."

"Did that poor creature trust you, then?"

"She trusted me, supported as I was by the viscount's ring and handwriting, Monseigneur. Besides, she knew me perfectly well. Well, then, we will say a fortnight of patient waiting, a week of anxious waiting, and another week of hopeless waiting. It will be a month, or a month and a half, before Vicomte d'Exmès will send another messenger in search of the first. But the first will be hard to find; and if it is not easy to get together ten thousand crowns, it will be almost impossible to get ten thousand more. Thus you will have ample time to marry your daughter twenty times over, Monseigneur; for Vicomte d'Exmès will be as completely out of sight as if he were dead for more than two months, and will not reappear, living and furious with rage, before the beginning of the new year."

"Yes, but he will come back!" said Montmorency; "and the very first day he will set about finding out what has become of his good squire, Martin-Guerre, will he not?"

"Alas, Monseigneur," rejoined Arnauld, piteously, "the answer to be made to him, I regret to inform you, will be that faithful Martin-Guerre, on his way back to his master with the ransom which he had been sent after, unluckily fell into the hands of a party of Spaniards, who, having probably rifled his pockets and robbed him, cruelly hanged him at the gates of Noyon to assure his silence."

"What's that? Do you mean to be hanged, Arnauld?"

"I have been, Monseigneur; see how zealous I am in your service. It will only be as to the date of the execution that the various versions of the story will differ somewhat. But can one believe plundering soldiers who are interested in concealing the truth? Come, Monseigneur!" continued the audacious fellow, gayly but with determination in his tone; "believe that my precautions have been very carefully taken, and that with an experienced blade like myself there is not the slightest danger that your Excellency will ever be compromised. If prudence were banished from earth, it would take refuge in the heart of a hanged man. Besides, I say again, you will only be declaring what is true. I have served you for a long while, as a number of your people can bear witness as well as yourself; and you have given me quite ten thousand crowns in all, be sure of that. Do you want me to give you a receipt for it?" added the scamp, magnificently.

The constable could not restrain a smile.

"Yes," said he, "I do, varlet; if at the end of the account—"

Arnauld interrupted.

"Come, come, Monseigneur," said he; "you are only quibbling about the form now, and what do superior minds like ours care for form? Just sign without any more ado."

He spread out upon the table before Montmorency the document which needed only his signature.

"But in the first place, the name of the city where Diane de Castro is confined, and of the man whose prisoner she is?"

"Name for name, Monseigneur; put yours at the foot of this paper, and you shall have the others."

"Very good," said Montmorency.

He dashed off the bold scrawl which served him for a signature.

"And the seal, Monseigneur?"

"There it is; now are you satisfied?"

"As thoroughly as if Monseigneur had given me the ten thousand crowns."

"Well, then, where is Diane?"

"In the hands of Lord Wentworth at Calais," replied Arnauld, trying to grasp the document from the hand of the constable, who still held on to it.

"One moment," said he; "and Vicomte d'Exmès?"

"At Calais, in the hands of Lord Wentworth."

"Then he and Diane see each other?"

"No, Monseigneur; he lives at the house of an armorer, one Pierre Peuquoy, while she is an inmate of the governor's house. Vicomte d'Exmès has no more idea than you, I am willing to swear, that she is so near him."

"I must hasten to the Louvre," said the constable, relaxing his hold on the paper.

"And I to Artigues," cried Arnauld, in triumph. "Good luck, Monseigneur! Try not to be a constable who is laughed at again."

"Good luck, blackguard! and try not to be hung for good."

Thereupon each went his way.

CHAPTER IV
THE ARMS OF PIERRE PEUQUOY, THE ROPES OF JEAN PEUQUOY, AND THE TEARS OF BABETTE PEUQUOY

Nearly a month elapsed at Calais without bringing about any change in the situation of those whom we left there to their great regret. Pierre Peuquoy was always working away diligently at his armor; Jean Peuquoy had begun to weave again, and in his leisure moments finished some ropes of extraordinary length; Babette Peuquoy was always weeping.

Gabriel's waiting had gone through the various phases sketched by Arnauld du Thill to the constable. He had waited patiently the first fortnight, but had begun then to grow impatient.

He now visited Lord Wentworth only on very rare occasions; and his calls were always very brief. There had been coolness between them ever since Gabriel had rashly interfered in the fictitious family affairs of the governor.

The latter too, we take great pleasure in saying, grew more and more gloomy from day to day; but the cause of his uneasiness was not the three messages which had been sent at short intervals since Arnauld's departure, from the King of France. All three made, as may well be imagined, the same demand,—the first politely, the second sharply, and the third with threats: they demanded the liberty of Madame de Castro for such ransom as the governor of Calais chose to name. But to all three he had made the same reply,—that he proposed to keep Madame de Castro as an hostage to be exchanged in case of need during the war for some prisoner of importance, or to be returned to the king without ransom when peace should be concluded. He was strictly within his rights; and intrenched behind his strong walls, he defied Henri's anger.

So it was not the royal anger which worried him, although he could but ask himself how the king had learned of Diane's captivity; the real source of his anxiety was the indifference, every day more contemptuous, of his fair prisoner. Neither humility nor assiduous attention had availed to lower the proud and disdainful spirit of Madame de Castro. She was always the same—calm and sad and dignified—before the passionate governor; and whenever he ventured to utter a word of his love (although it must in justice be said that he never violated the bounds which his title as a gentleman imposed upon him), an expression, at once mournful and haughty, broke poor Lord Wentworth's heart and wounded his pride. He did not dare to speak to Diane either of the letter she had written to Gabriel or of the attempts made by the king to procure his daughter's liberty, so much did he dread a bitter word or a satirical reproof from those lovely but cruel lips.

Diane had noticed that the servant who had dared to undertake to deliver her billet was no longer to be seen about the house, and fully understood that desperate chance had failed her. However, she did not lose her courage, the pure and noble girl waited and prayed. She trusted in God, and in death, in case of need.

On the last day of October, which Gabriel had fixed on in his own mind as the limit to his term of waiting for Martin-Guerre's return, he determined to call upon Lord Wentworth and ask, as a favor, his leave to send another messenger to Paris.

About two o'clock he left the Peuquoy house, where Pierre was polishing a sword, Jean weaving one of his enormous ropes, and w here for several days past, Babette, with eyes red from weeping, had been wandering from room to room, unable to speak, and betook himself straight to the governor's mansion.

Lord Wentworth was busy about something or other at the moment, and sent word to Gabriel begging him to wait five minutes, when he would be entirely at his service.

The hall to which Gabriel had been shown looked out upon an interior courtyard. Gabriel drew near the window to look out into the court, and mechanically ran his fingers back and forth over the panes. Suddenly, beneath his very fingers, his attention was attracted by letters drawn upon the glass with a diamond ring. He looked at them more closely, and was able to make out with perfect distinctness these words: *Diane de Castro*.

It was the signature which was missing at the end of the mysterious letter he had received the month before.

A film came over Gabriel's eyes, and he had to lean against the wall to avoid falling. His presentiments had not lied, then! Diane! It was indeed Diane, his *fiancée* or his sister, whom this dissolute Wentworth actually had in his power! It was to her, the pure and lovely creature, that he dared to speak of his passion.

With an involuntary gesture Gabriel carried his hand to the hilt of his missing sword.

At that moment Lord Wentworth came in.

As he had done on the first occasion, Gabriel, without uttering a word, led him to the window, and pointed out to him the accusing signature.

At first Lord Wentworth turned pale; then asserting that mastery over himself which he possessed in an eminent degree,—

"Well," said he, "what is it?"

"Is that not the name of the mad kinswoman whom you are obliged to hold under restraint here, my Lord?" said Gabriel.

"It may be so; what then?" retorted Lord Wentworth, haughtily.

"If it be the case, my Lord, I know this kinswoman of yours,—a very distant relative, no doubt. I have seen her very often at the Louvre. I am her devoted slave, as every French gentleman should be of a daughter of the house of France."

"And then?" said Lord Wentworth.

"Then, my Lord, I demand of you an explanation of your reason for retaining and treating as you do a prisoner of her station?"

"And suppose I refuse, Monsieur, to oblige you with an explanation, as I have already refused the King of France?"

"Refused the King of France!" echoed Gabriel, in amazement.

"To be sure," replied Lord Wentworth, with unfailing self-possession. "An Englishman, it seems to me, owes no explanation of his actions to a foreign monarch, especially when his own nation is at war with that monarch. So, Monsieur d'Exmès, what if I decline to be called to account by you as well?"

"I should demand that you give me satisfaction, my Lord," cried Gabriel.

"And you would hope to kill me, no doubt," replied the governor, "with the sword which you only wear by my leave, and which I have the right to demand of you at this moment."

"Oh, my Lord! my Lord!" cried Gabriel, in a fury of passion, "you shall pay me for this too."

"So be it, Monsieur," replied Lord Wentworth; "and I will not deny my debt when you have settled yours."

"Powerless!" fairly shrieked Gabriel, wringing his hands,—"powerless at the very moment when I should like the strength of ten thousand men!"

"It is really pretty hard for you," Lord Wentworth continued, "that propriety and law alike bind your hands; but you must confess that it would be altogether too convenient a way for a prisoner of war and a debtor to obtain his freedom and discharge his debt simply by cutting the throat of his creditor and his foe."

"My Lord," said Gabriel, struggling to recover his self-control, "you know that I sent my squire to Paris a month since to procure the sum of money which causes you so much anxiety. Can Martin-Guerre have been wounded or slain on the road, in spite of your safe-conduct? Has he been robbed of the money he was bringing me? That is what I cannot say. The sad fact is that he does not return; and I had just come to beg you to let me send another messenger to Paris, since you have no faith in the word of a gentleman, and have never offered to let me go myself to procure my ransom. Now, my Lord, you no longer have the right to refuse me what I ask, or rather I have the right now to say that you fear to have me at liberty and that you don't dare to give me back my sword."

"To whom would you say that, pray," said Lord Wentworth, "in an English city under my immediate authority, and where you should be looked upon in no other light than as a prisoner and an enemy?"

"I would cry it aloud, my Lord, to every man who has sense and feeling; to every man who has a noble heart or a noble name; to your officers, who understand affairs in which honor is involved; to your workmen even, whom their instinct would enlighten. And all would agree with me against you, my Lord, that in not granting me the means of leaving this place, you have shown your unfitness to be the commander of gallant soldiers."

"But you don't reflect, Monsieur," was Lord Wentworth's cold response, "that rather than let you spread the spirit of mutiny among my men, I have only to say the word, only to raise my hand, to have you cast into a dungeon where you could accuse me only to the deaf and speechless walls."

"Alas! that is too true, ten thousand tempests!" muttered Gabriel, with compressed lips and clinched fists.

The man of sensibility and emotion was being shattered against the impassibility of the man of iron and brass.

But a single word changed the whole face of affairs, and at once put Gabriel and Wentworth on an equal footing again.

"Dear Diane! dear Diane!" said the younger man, in his anguish; "to be able to do nothing for you in your hour of need!"

"What did you say, Monsieur?" asked Lord Wentworth, trembling. "You said, I think, 'dear Diane!' Did you say it, or did I misunderstand you? Can it be that you too love Madame de Castro?"

"Well, then, if I must say it, I do indeed love her!" cried Gabriel. "You love her too, you say! But my love is as pure and devoted as yours is base and cruel. Yes, before God and His angels I love her to adoration."

"What was all that you said, then, about the daughter of France, and the protection that every French gentleman owed to such an one in misfortune?" rejoined Lord Wentworth, quite beside himself. "Ah! you love her, do you? And you are the man whom she loves, no doubt; and whose memory she invokes when she wishes to torment me. You are the man for love of whom she despises mine! the man without whom she might love me perhaps! Ah! are you the man whom she loves?"

Lord Wentworth, but a short time before so mocking and disdainful, now regarded the man who was honored by Diane's affection with a sort of respectful terror; while Gabriel, on hearing his rival's words, raised his glad and triumphant face ever higher and higher.

"Ah, indeed she does love me, then!" cried he; "she still thinks of me! She calls for me, you say? Oh, well, if she calls for me, why, I will go to her,—yes, help her and rescue her. Come, my Lord, take my sword, gag me, bind me, imprison me, and I shall still find a way to help her and save her, since she still loves me, my saintly Diane! Since she still loves me, I dare you and defy you; and though you have arms in your hands and I am unarmed, I am sure of overcoming you, with Diane's love for my buckler."

"True, true; I can well believe it," muttered Lord Wentworth, overwhelmed.

"Thus it would no longer be generous in me to challenge you to single combat," said Gabriel; "so call your guards and tell them to confine me, if you choose. To be in prison near her and at the same time would be of itself a sort of happiness."

A long silence ensued.

At last Lord Wentworth said, with much apparent hesitation, "You asked me, I believe, to allow a second messenger to set out for Paris to procure your ransom?"

"Such was my purpose, my Lord, when I called upon you."

"In your discourse you seem to have reproached me," continued the governor, "for not having had faith in your honor as a gentleman, and for refusing to allow you to go yourself to procure your money, with your word for my security?"

"Very true, my Lord."

"Well, Monsieur," said Wentworth, "you may set out to-day; the gates of Calais will be opened to you; your request is granted."

"I understand," said Gabriel, bitterly,—"you wish to separate me from her. But suppose I refuse to leave Calais now?"

"I am master here, Monsieur," was Lord Wentworth's reply; "and it is not for you to refuse or to accept my commands, but to submit to them."

"Very well, then," said Gabriel, "I will go, my Lord, but without any especial gratitude for your generosity, I warn you."

"Nor have I any need of your thanks, Monsieur."

"I will go," said Gabriel; "but be sure that I shall not long remain your debtor, and that I shall soon come back, my Lord, to pay all my debts at once. Then I shall no longer be your prisoner, nor will you be my creditor, and there will no longer be any reason why the sword which I wear should not cross with yours."

"I might refuse this combat, Monsieur," said Lord Wentworth, rather gloomily; "for the chances between us would not be equal. If I should kill you, she would hate me all the more bitterly; whereas if you should kill me, the result would be to make her love you the more dearly. But no matter, I must and do accept. But are you not afraid," he added sombrely, "of driving me to extremities? When almost all the advantage is with you, might I not be justified in making an unfair use of those which I can still call my own?"

"God on high and the nobility of every country on earth would be your judges, my Lord," said Gabriel, shuddering, "if you should be such a coward as to wreak your vengeance upon those whom you are unable to vanquish, by oppressing those who are unable to defend themselves."

After a pause, Lord Wentworth said,—

"It is three o'clock, Monsieur, and you have until seven—the hour when the inner gates are closed—to make your preparations and leave the town. I will meanwhile give my orders that you be allowed to pass free."

"At seven o'clock, my Lord, I shall have left Calais."

"And be sure," resumed Wentworth, "that you shall never re-enter it again alive, and that even if you should succeed in slaying me in single combat without the walls, my precautions will be taken, and well taken (you may trust my jealousy for that), so that you shall never possess—nay, you shall never even see Madame de Castro again."

Gabriel had already taken some steps on his way from the room; he stopped at the door on hearing these last words.

"What you say is quite impossible, my Lord," he rejoined; "for it is very necessary that I should see Diane again, sooner or later."

"However, it shall not be, Monsieur, I swear to you, if the will of the governor of a city or the last words of a dying man are to be respected."

"It *shall* be, my Lord,—I know not how, but I am sure of it."

"In that case, Monsieur," said Wentworth, with a scornful smile, "you will have to take Calais by assault."

Gabriel reflected a moment.

"I will take Calais by assault, my Lord," said he. "*Au revoir*!"

He saluted and left the room, leaving Lord Wentworth as if turned to stone, and in doubt as to whether he ought to smile or be alarmed.

Gabriel returned at once to the house of Pierre Peuquoy.

He found Pierre polishing the hilt of his sword, Jean making knots in his rope, and Babette sighing.

He repeated to his friends the conversation he had had with the governor, and announced his approaching departure. Not even did he conceal from them the possibly reckless remark with which he had taken leave of Lord Wentworth.

Then he said,—

"Now I am going to my room to make my preparations, and I leave you to your swords, Pierre; you, Jean, to your ropes; and you to your sighs, Babette."

He went, as he had said, to put everything in order for his departure in all haste. Now that he was free, time seemed to creep along until he could get to Paris to rescue his father, and return to Calais to rescue Diane.

When he left his room half an hour later, he found Babette on the landing.

"Are you going, Monsieur le Vicomte?" she asked. "Shall you no more ask me why I weep so much?"

"No, my child; for I hope that when I come back you will have ceased to weep."

"I hope so too, Monseigneur," said Babette, "You expect to come back, then, do you, in spite of the governor's threats?"

"I promise you that I will, Babette."

"And your squire, Martin-Guerre, too, I suppose?"

"Yes, to be sure."

"Are you sure that you will find Martin-Guerre at Paris, however, Monsieur d'Exmès?" rejoined the young girl. "He is not a dishonest man, is he? Of course he hasn't appropriated your ransom? He is not capable of an act of—infidelity?"

"I would be willing to take my oath to his loyalty," said Gabriel, rather surprised at these questions. "Martin has an uncertain disposition, especially since a short time ago; and it is as if there were two different men in his body,—one simple-minded, and very quiet in his ways; the other crafty and noisy. But aside from this variable character, he is a trusty and faithful servant."

"And no more likely to betray a woman than to deceive his master, is he?"

"Oh, that is another matter," said Gabriel; "and I confess that I would not answer for him there."

"Well, then, Monseigneur," said poor Babette, turning pale, "will you be kind enough to hand him this ring? He will know from whom it comes and what it means."

"I will give it to him, Babette," said Gabriel, recalling the last evening before his squire's departure,—"I will give it to him; but the person who sends it knows, I presume, that Martin-Guerre is married."

"Married!" shrieked Babette. "Then, Monseigneur, keep the ring,—throw it away, do anything with it, rather than give it to him."

"But, Babette—"

"Thanks, Monseigneur, and adieu!" whispered the poor child.

She made her escape to the second floor, and had hardly got to her chamber and fallen upon a chair when she fainted.

Gabriel, grieved and anxious over the suspicion which then first crossed his mind, descended the staircase of the old house, deep in thought.

At the foot of the stairs he met Jean Peuquoy, who came up to him with a very mysterious air.

"Monsieur le Vicomte," said the burgher, in a low voice, "you are continually asking me why I am making ropes of such length. I cannot allow you to depart, after your admirably worded farewell to Lord Wentworth, without imparting to you the key to the riddle. By joining together with small transverse cords two long, strong ropes, as the one I am making, Monseigneur, one obtains a ladder of great length and strength. This ladder, when one is a member of the civic guard, as Pierre has been for twenty years, and I for three days, can easily be conveyed in sections and placed under the sentry-box on the platform of the Octagonal Tower. Then, some dark morning in December or January, just for curiosity's sake, we might when on sentry duty attach an end of each rope firmly to these pieces of iron when they are cemented into the battlements, and let the other ends drop into the sea, some three hundred feet below, where some hardy boatman might chance to find himself at that moment."

"But, my dear Jean—" interrupted Gabriel.

"Never mind that, Monsieur le Vicomte," rejoined the weaver. "But if you will excuse me, I should like before you leave to give you something as a souvenir of your devoted servant, Jean Peuquoy. Here is a sort of plan of the walls and fortifications of Calais. I have made it for my own amusement, during those everlasting walks that have surprised you so. Hide it under your doublet, and when you are at Paris look at it now and then for my sake, I beg you."

Gabriel tried to interrupt again, but Jean gave him no time; pressing the hand which the young man held out to him, he took his leave with these words:—

"*Au revoir*, Monsieur d'Exmès. You will find Pierre waiting at the door to pay his respects to you; they will supplement mine."

Pierre was standing in front of his house, holding Gabriel's horse by the bridle.

"Thanks for your kind hospitality, Master," said the viscount. "I shall very soon send you, even if I do not bring it myself, the money which you have been polite enough to advance me. I will add to it, if you please, a slight gratuity for your people. Meanwhile, be good enough to offer your dear sister this little brilliant on my behalf."

"I accept it for her," said the armorer, "on the condition that you will accept in return something in my line,—this horn which I have hung to your saddle-bow. I made it with my own hands; and I should recognize its blast even over the roaring of the stormy ocean,—for instance, on any of the mornings of the 5th of each month, when I am on guard from four o'clock to six, on the Octagonal Tower, which faces the sea."

"Thanks!" said Gabriel, pressing Pierre's hand in a way which showed that he understood him.

"As to these arms, which you have wondered to see me making in such great quantities," continued Pierre, "I am inclined to be sorry that I have such a large stock on hand; for if Calais should be besieged some day, the faction among us which still sympathizes with France might get possession of these arms, and make a dangerous diversion in the very heart of the city."

"Very true!" cried Gabriel, pressing the brave citizen's hand with still greater warmth.

"With this I wish you a pleasant journey and good luck, Monsieur d'Exmès," said Pierre. "Adieu, and to our speedy meeting!"

"To our speedy meeting!" said Gabriel.

He turned and waved a last farewell to Pierre as he stood upon his threshold; to Jean, who had his head out of a window on the first floor; and to Babette too, who was watching his departure from behind a curtain on the second floor.

Then he put spurs to his horse, and was off at a gallop.

Orders had been sent to the city gate by Lord Wentworth, and no objection was made to the departure of the prisoner, who soon found himself well on the road to Paris, alone with his anxiety and his hopes.

Would he be able to effect his father's deliverance on his arrival at Paris; or Diane de Castro's on his return to Calais?

CHAPTER V
SEQUEL TO THE MISFORTUNES OF MARTIN-GUERRE

The roads of France were no safer for Gabriel than for his squire; and he was obliged to exert all his wit and quickness of intellect to avoid obstacles and delays. In fact, it was not till the fourth day after leaving Calais, notwithstanding all his haste, that he finally reached Paris.

But the dangers of the journey caused Gabriel less anxiety, on the whole, than his uneasiness with regard to its termination. Although he was not naturally much addicted to dreaming, his lonely journey almost forced him to think unceasingly of his father's captivity and Diane's, of his means of rescuing those dear and cherished beings, of the king's promise, and of what he must do if Henri failed to keep it. But no! It was not to such an end that Henri II. was the first gentleman of Christendom. The fulfilment of his oath was, no doubt, painful to him; very likely he was awaiting Gabriel's return to remind him of it before issuing his pardon to the old count; but surely he would pardon him. And if he did not?

Gabriel, whenever that desolating thought crossed his mind, felt as if a sword were piercing his heart. He would drive his spurs into his horse, and put his hand to his sword; and generally it was the sad and sweet thought of Diane de Castro which would remove his anger and soothe his troubled soul.

It was with a mind harrowed by doubt and anguish that he at last reached the gates of Paris on the morning of the fourth day. He had travelled all night; and the pale light of dawn was just beginning to break as he rode through the streets in the neighborhood of the Louvre.

He drew rein before the royal mansion, still closed and silent, and asked himself whether he should wait there or go on; but his impatience made him loathe the thought of doing nothing. He determined to go at once to his own house, Rue des Jardins St. Paul, where he might at least hope to hear some tidings of what he feared at the same time that he longed to know.

His road thither took him by the frowning turrets of the Châtelet.

He stopped for a moment before the sinister portal. A cold perspiration bedewed his forehead. His past and his future lay hidden behind those humid walls; but Gabriel was not the man to allow his feelings to monopolize much time which he might usefully devote to action. He therefore shook off his gloomy thoughts, and went on his way, saying simply, "*Allons*!"

When he reached his home, which he had not seen for so long a time, a light was shining through the windows of the lower hall. The zealous Aloyse was already astir.

Gabriel knocked, uttering his name at the same time. Two minutes after he was in the arms of the worthy soul who had been like a mother to him.

"Ah! is it really you, Monseigneur? Is it really you, my own dear boy?"

She could find strength to say no more than that. Gabriel, having embraced her most affectionately, drew back a step or two, the better to look at her.

There was in his look an unspoken question clearer than words could make it.

Aloyse understood, and yet she hung her head, and made no reply.

"Is there no news from the court, then!" the viscount asked at length, as if not content with the answer implied by her silence.

"Nothing, Monseigneur," replied the nurse.

"Oh, I expected as much! If anything had occurred, good or bad, you would not have failed to tell me at the first kiss. Do you know nothing!"

"Alas! no."

"I see how it is," rejoined the young man, bitterly. "I was a prisoner,—dead perhaps! One does not pay his indebtedness to a prisoner, much less to a dead man. But I am here now, alive and free, and there must be a reckoning with me: whether willingly or by force, it must and shall be!"

"Oh, be careful, Monseigneur!" cried Aloyse.

"Have no fear, nurse. Is Monsieur l'Amiral at Paris!"

"Yes, Monseigneur. He has called and sent here ten times to learn if you had returned."

"Good! And Monsieur de Guise?"

"He also has returned. It is to him that the people are looking to repair the misfortunes of France and the suffering of the citizens."

"God grant," said Gabriel, "that he find no sufferings for which there is no remedy!"

"As to Madame de Castro, who was supposed to be dead," continued Aloyse, hurriedly, "Monsieur le Connétable has discovered that she is a prisoner at Calais; and they hope soon to effect her release."

"I knew it, and, like them, I hope so," said Gabriel, meaningly. "But," he resumed, "you say nothing of the reason why my captivity has been so prolonged,—nothing of Martin-Guerre and his delayed return. What has become of Martin, pray?"

"He is here, Monseigneur, the sluggard, the dolt!"

"What! Here? How long has he been here? What is he doing?"

"He is upstairs, in bed and asleep," said Aloyse, who seemed to speak of Martin with some bitterness. "He says that he is not very well, pretending that he has been hanged!"

"Hanged!" cried Gabriel. "For stealing the money for my ransom,—is that it?"

"The money for your ransom, Monseigneur? You just say a word to that threefold idiot about the money for your ransom! You will see what answer he will make. He will not know what you mean. Just imagine, Monseigneur, he arrived here, very eager, and in great haste; and after reading your letter, I counted out to him ten thousand beautiful crowns. Away he went again, without losing a moment. A few days later whom should I see coming back but Martin-Guerre, crestfallen and with a most pitiful expression. He claimed that he had not received a sou from me. Having been taken prisoner himself some time before the fall of St. Quentin, he had no idea, he said, of your whereabouts for three months past. You had intrusted no mission to him. He had been beaten and hung! He had succeeded in making his escape, and had just returned to Paris for the first time since the war. Such are the romances with which Martin-Guerre entertains us from morning till night when your ransom is mentioned."

"Explain yourself, nurse," said Gabriel. "Martin-Guerre could not have appropriated that money, I would take my oath. He surely is not a dishonest man, and he is loyally devoted to me."

"No, Monseigneur, he is not dishonest; but he is mad, I am afraid,—so mad that he hasn't an idea or a memory; sufficiently insane to require care, believe me. Although he may not be vicious yet, he is dangerous, to say the least. I am not the only one who saw him here either, for all your people overwhelm him with their testimony. He really received the ten thousand crowns, which Master Elyot had some difficulty in getting together for me at such short notice."

"Nevertheless," said Gabriel, "Master Elyot must get together as much more, and even more quickly; indeed, I must have a still larger sum. But we need not worry about that at present. It is broad daylight at last. I am going to the Louvre now to speak with the king."

"What, Monseigneur! without a moment's rest?" said Aloyse. "Besides, you forget that it is only seven o'clock and that you would find the doors closed; they are barely opened at nine."

"That's true," said Gabriel,—"two hours more to wait! Give me the patience to wait two hours, O Lord, as I have already waited two months! At all events, I shall be able to find Monsieur de Coligny and Monsieur de Guise," he continued.

"No, for in all likelihood they are at the Louvre," said Aloyse. "Besides, the king doesn't receive before noon, and you cannot see him earlier than that, I fear. So you will have three hours to converse with Monsieur l'Amiral, and Monsieur le Lieutenant-Général of the kingdom,—that, you know, is the new title with which the king at the present grave crisis has clothed Monsieur de Guise. Meanwhile, Monsieur, you surely will not refuse to eat something, and to receive your old and faithful servants, who have so long wished in vain for your return."

Just at this moment—as if to occupy the young man's mind and effectually beguile his weary waiting—Martin-Guerre, apprised doubtless of his master's arrival, burst into the room, paler even from joy than from the suffering he had undergone.

"What! Is it you? Is it really yourself, Monseigneur?" he cried. "Oh, what happiness!"

But Gabriel gave a very cold reception to the poor squire's transports of delight.

"If by good luck I am here at last, Martin," said he, "you must agree that it is not by your efforts: for you did your very best to leave me a prisoner forever."

"What! you too, Monseigneur!" said Martin, in consternation. "You too, instead of putting me right at the first word, as I hoped, accuse me of having had those ten thousand crowns. Who knows what will come next? Perhaps you will even go so far as to say that you commissioned me to receive them and bring them to you?"

"Of course I did," said Gabriel, quite stupefied with surprise.

"So, then," rejoined the poor squire, in a dull voice, "you believe me, Martin-Guerre, to be capable of basely appropriating money which did not belong to me,—money designed to procure my master's liberty?"

"No, Martin, no," replied Gabriel, earnestly, touched by the tone in which his faithful servant spoke. "My suspicions have never, I swear, led me to suspect your honesty; and Aloyse and I were just saying that very thing. But the money was stolen from you or you lost it on the road when you were coming back to me."

"Coming back to you!" echoed Martin. "But where, Monseigneur? Since we left St. Quentin together may God strike me dead if I know where you have been! Where was I to come back to you?"

"At Calais. Martin. However light and foolish your brain may be, you surely can't have forgotten Calais!"

"How in the world could I forget what I never knew?" said Martin-Guerre, calmly.

"Why, you miserable wretch, do you mean to perjure yourself in that matter?" cried Gabriel.

He said in a low voice a few words to the nurse, who thereupon left the room. Then he approached Martin.

"How about Babette, ingrate?" said he.

"Babette! What Babette?" asked the wondering squire.

"The one you ruined, villain."

"Oh, yes!—Gudule!" said Martin. "You are wrong about the name. It is Gudule, Monseigneur, not Babette. Oh, yes, poor girl! But I tell you honestly that I did not lead her astray; she had fallen before. I swear to that."

"What! still another?" rejoined Gabriel. "But this last one I know nothing about; and whoever she may be, she can have no such cause of complaint as Babette Peuquoy."

Martin-Guerre did not dare to lose his patience; but if he had been of equal rank with the viscount, he would not have kept himself so well in hand.

"One moment, Monseigneur," said he. "They all say here that I am mad; and by Saint Martin! I verily believe I shall go mad just from hearing myself called so. However, I still have my reason and my memory, or the deuce take me! And in case of need, Monseigneur, although I have had to undergo harsh treatment and misery sufficient for two,—still, in case of need, I will narrate to you faithfully from point to point everything that has befallen me during the three months that have elapsed since I parted from you. At least," he hastened to add, "so much of it as I remember in my own person."

"To tell the truth, I should be very glad to hear how you account for your extraordinary conduct," said Gabriel.

"Very well! Monseigneur, after we left St. Quentin together to join Monsieur de Vaulpergues's relieving party, and after we had separated, each to take a different road (as you must remember), events happened just as you had foreseen. I fell into the hands of the enemy. I tried, as you had enjoined upon me, to pay my way with impudence; but a most extraordinary thing occurred,—the soldiers claimed to recognize me as having been their prisoner before!"

"Come, come!" said Gabriel, interrupting him; "see how you are wandering already!"

"Oh, Monseigneur," resumed Martin, "in the name of mercy, let me tell my story as I know it! It is difficult for me to understand matters myself. You may criticise when I am done. As soon as the enemy recognized me, Monseigneur, I confess that I resigned myself to my fate; for I knew—and in reality you yourself know as well as I, Monseigneur—that there are two of me, and that very often, and without giving me any warning whatever, my other self makes me do his pleasure. Perhaps I should say, then, '*We* accepted *our* fate;' for hereafter I shall speak of myself—of *us*, that is—in the plural. Gudule—a pretty little Flemish girl, whom we had carried off—also recognized us, which cost us, I may say parenthetically, a perfect hailstorm of blows. Truly, we ourselves alone failed to recognize ourselves. To tell you all the misery which followed, and into the hands of how many different masters, all endowed with different dialects, your unfortunate squire fell, one after the other, would take too long, Monseigneur."

"Yes; pray shorten your self-condolence."

"I pass over these and worse sufferings. My number two, I was informed, had already escaped once; and they beat me almost to a jelly for his fault. My number one—whose conscience I have in my keeping, and whose martyrdom I am relating to you—succeeded in escaping once more, but was foolish enough to allow himself to be caught, and was left for dead on the spot, notwithstanding which I ran away a third time; but being entrapped a third time, by the double treason of too much wine and a chance acquaintance, I showed fight, and laid about me with all the fury of despair and drunkenness. In short, after having mocked me and tortured me most of the night in most barbarous fashion, my executioners hanged me toward morning."

"Hanged you!" exclaimed Gabriel, believing that the squire's mania was surely becoming hopeless. "They hanged you, Martin! What do you mean by that?"

"I mean, Monseigneur, that they hoisted me up between earth and sky at the end of a hempen cord, which was firmly attached to a gibbet, otherwise called a gallows; and in all the tongues and patois with which they have belabored my ears that is commonly called being hanged, Monseigneur. Do I make myself clear?"

"None too clear, Martin; for to tell the truth, for a man that has been hanged—"

"I am in pretty good condition now, Monseigneur,—that's a fact; but you have not heard the end of the story yet. My suffering and my rage, when I saw myself being hanged, almost made me lose my consciousness. When I came to myself, I was stretched on the fresh grass, with the cord, which had been cut, still about my neck. Had some soft-hearted passer-by, moved by my plight, chosen to relieve the gallows of its human fruit? My misanthropy actually forbade my thinking that. I am more inclined to believe that some thief must have longed to plunder me, and cut the cord so that he might go through my pockets at his ease. The fact that my wedding-ring and my papers had been stolen justify me, I think, in making that assertion without doing injustice to the human race. However, I had been cut down in time; and despite a slight dislocation of my neck, I succeeded in escaping a fourth time, through woods and across the fields, hiding all day, and travelling with the greatest care at night, living on roots and wild herbs,—a most unsatisfactory diet, to which even the poor cattle must find great difficulty in getting accustomed. At last, after losing my way a hundred times, I succeeded in reaching Paris at the end of a fortnight, and in finding this house, where I arrived twelve days since, and where I have received rather a less hearty welcome than I expected, after such a rough experience. There is my story, Monseigneur."

"Well, now," said Gabriel, "as an offset to this story of yours, I can tell you quite a different one (entirely different, in fact), the details of which I have seen you perform with my own eyes."

"Is it the story of my number two, Monseigneur?" asked Martin, coolly. "Upon my word, if I may make so bold, and if you would be so kind as to tell it to me in a few words, I should be only too glad to hear it."

"Do you mock me, scoundrel?" said Gabriel.

"Oh, Monseigneur knows my profound respect for him! But, strangely enough, this double of mine has caused me a vast deal of trouble, has he not? He has led me into some cruel plights. Well, in spite of all that, I don't know why, but I am greatly interested in him. I believe, upon my word of honor, that in the end I shall be weak enough to love the blackguard!"

"Blackguard indeed!" said Gabriel.

The viscount may have been about to enter upon a catalogue of Arnauld du Thill's misdeeds; but he was interrupted by his nurse, who returned to the room, followed by a man in the garb of a peasant.

"Well, what does *this* mean?" said Aloyse. "Here is a man who claims that he was sent here to announce your death, Martin-Guerre!"

CHAPTER VI
IN WHICH MARTIN-GUERRE'S CHARACTER BEGINS TO BE REHABILITATED

"My death!" ejaculated Martin, turning pale at Dame Aloyse's terrible words.

"Oh, God be merciful unto me!" cried the peasant, as soon as he cast his eye upon the squire.

"Can it be that my other self is dead? God be praised!" said Martin. "Am I at last relieved from this continual changing back and forth? Bah! On the whole, upon reflection, I should be a little sorry if it is so, but still reasonably satisfied. Why don't you speak, friend? Speak!" he added, addressing himself to the bewildered peasant.

"Ah, Master," replied the latter, when he had looked closely at Martin and touched him with his hands, "how does it happen that you are here before me? I swear to you, Master, that I came as quickly as a man could come to do your errand, and earn the ten crowns; and unless you came in the saddle, Master, it is absolutely impossible for you to have passed me on the road, and in that case I must have seen you."

"To be sure; but, my good fellow, I never saw you before," said Martin-Guerre; "and yet you talk as if you knew me!"

"As if I knew you!" said the stupefied peasant. "Do you mean to say that you didn't send me here to say that Martin-Guerre had been hanged and was dead?"

"What! Martin-Guerre! Why, I am Martin-Guerre."

"You? Impossible! How could you have told of your own hanging?" rejoined the peasant.

"But why, where, and when did I tell you of such an atrocity?" asked Martin.

"Must I tell you the precise facts now?" said the peasant.

"Yes, everything."

"Notwithstanding the fact that you made up a story for me to tell."

"Yes; never mind that now."

"Well, then, since your memory is so short, I will tell you everything. So much the worse for you if you force me to do it! Six days ago, in the morning, I was at work hoeing my field—"

"Before you go any further, where is your field?" asked Martin.

"Do you want me to tell you the real truth, Master?" said the peasant.

"Why, of course I do, you beast!"

"Well, then, my field is behind Montargis! I was at work when you came along the road, with a travelling-bag on your back."

"'Well, well, my friend," said you, 'what are you doing? Come, why don't you speak?'

"'I am hoeing, Master. I am ready to answer your questions.'

"'How much does this work of yours pay you?'

"'Year in and year out, about four sous a day.'

"'Would you like to earn twenty crowns in two weeks?'

"'Oh, oh!'

"'Say yes or no.'

"'Yes, indeed, I should.'

"'Well, you must go at once to Paris. By making good speed, you will arrive in five or six days, at the latest. Ask your way to Rue des Jardins St. Paul, and find the house of Vicomte d'Exmès. It is to that house that I want you to go. The viscount will not be there; but you will find a good old soul called Aloyse, his nurse; and this is what you must say to her. Now, listen carefully! You will say: "I am from Noyon" (Noyon, you understand, not Montargis),—"I am from Noyon, where one of your acquaintances was hanged a fortnight since. His name was Martin-Guerre." (Be sure to remember that name Martin-Guerre). "Martin-Guerre has been hanged, after being robbed of the money he had about him, so that he might not complain of the robbery. But before he was taken to the gallows Martin-Guerre had time to beg me to come and let you know of his ill-fortune, so that, as he said, you might provide a new supply of money for his master's ransom. He promised me that you would give me ten crowns for my trouble. I waited until he was hanged, and then I came away."

"'There, that is what you are to say to the good woman. Do you understand?' you asked me.

"'Yes, Master," I replied; 'only you said twenty crowns in the first place, and now you only speak of ten.'

"'Fool!' said you, 'here are the other ten in advance.'

"'Very good,' I rejoined. 'But suppose this Aloyse asks me to describe the appearance of Martin-Guerre, for I never saw him, and I ought to be able to tell how he looks.'

"'Look at me.'

"I looked at you.

"'Very well; now you can describe Martin-Guerre, as if it were myself.'"

"How strange!" muttered Gabriel, who had been listening to this narration with most profound attention.

"Now," continued the peasant, "I am here, Master, ready to repeat the lesson you taught me (for you said it to me twice, and I know it by heart), and I find you here before me! It is very true that I loitered on the road, and drank up your ten crowns in the roadside cabarets, because I expected soon to have the other ten in my pocket; but at all events I am within the time you fixed. You gave me six days, and it was just six days ago that I left Montargis."

"Six days!" said Martin-Guerre, sadly and thoughtfully. "I came through Montargis six days ago! I was on the road to my own province six days ago! Your story is extremely probable, my friend," he continued, "and I believe it implicitly."

"But no!" Aloyse eagerly interposed, "this man is evidently a liar, when he claims to have talked with you at Montargis six days ago, for you have not been out of these doors for twelve days."

"Very true," said Martin; "but my number two—"

"Then again," continued the nurse, "he says that it is only a fortnight since you were hanged at Noyon; while according to your own words it was a month ago."

"Yes, it certainly was," said the squire; "I was thinking when I woke this morning that it was just a month to-day. However, my other self—"

"Oh, nonsense!" cried the nurse.

"It seems to me," Gabriel interposed, "that this man has finally put us upon the right track."

"Oh, indeed you are not mistaken, kind sir," said the peasant. "Shall I receive my ten crowns?"

"Yes," said Gabriel; "but you must leave your name and address with us. We may have need of your testimony some day. I begin to detect some very evil doings, although my suspicions are not yet clearly defined."

"But, Monseigneur—" Martin began to remonstrate. Gabriel interrupted him sharply. "Enough of that!" said he. "Do you see to it, good Aloyse, that this man goes his way content. This matter shall be attended to in due time. But, do you know," he added, lowering his voice, "that I may perhaps have to take my revenge for treachery to the master before I deal with the treachery to the squire."

"Alas!" muttered Aloyse.

"It is now eight o'clock," continued Gabriel. "I shall not see my good people until my return; for I must be at the doors of the Louvre when they are opened. Even though I may not be able to obtain an audience of the king until noon, I can at least have some conversation with the admiral and Monsieur de Guise."

"And when you have seen the king, you will return here at once, will you not?" asked Aloyse.

"At once; don't you be anxious about me, my good nurse. Something seems to tell me that I shall come out victoriously from all these dark plots which intrigue and impudence are weaving around me."

"Indeed you will, if God heeds my earnest prayer," said Aloyse.

"I go," rejoined Gabriel. "You remain here, Martin, for I must go alone. Come, come, my good fellow, we shall justify you and deliver you from your other self in good time; but you see I have another justification and another deliverance to accomplish first of all. To our speedy meeting, Martin! *au revoir*, nurse!"

Each kissed the hand which the young man extended. Then he left the house, alone and on foot, wrapped in a great cloak, and with a grave and haughty mien directed his steps toward the Louvre.

"Alas!" thought the nurse, "even so I once saw his father depart, and he never returned."

Just as Gabriel, after crossing the Pont au Change, was walking through the Place de Grève, he noticed a man, enveloped like himself in a cloak, which was however of coarser material, and more carefully held in place than his own. More than that, this man was evidently trying to conceal his features beneath the broad brim of his hat.

Gabriel, although he thought at first that he recognized the figure and carriage of a friend, nevertheless pursued his way; but the unknown, as soon as he saw Vicomte d'Exmès, gave a sudden start, and after seeming to hesitate for a moment, stopped suddenly and said very cautiously, "Gabriel, my friend!"

At the same time he half disclosed his face, and Gabriel saw that he had not been mistaken.

"Monsieur de Coligny!" he exclaimed, without however raising his voice. "You here! and at this hour!"

"Hush!" said the admiral. "I confess that just at this moment I have no desire to be recognized and spied upon and followed. But when I saw you, my dear friend, after so long a separation, and so much anxiety on your account, I could not resist the temptation to accost you and grasp your hand. How long have you been in Paris?"

"Only since this morning," said Gabriel; "and I was on my way to see you at the Louvre first of all."

"Oh, well," said the admiral, "if you are not in too great haste, just walk a few steps with me. You must tell me what you have been about during your long absence."

"I will tell you all that I can tell the most loyal and devoted of friends," Gabriel responded. "But first, Monsieur l'Amiral, I know you will allow me to ask you a question on a subject which is of more interest to me than anything else in the world."

"I can imagine what that question will be," said the admiral. "But ought you not to be quite as well able to forecast my reply to it, my dear friend? You propose to ask me, do you not, whether I kept my promise to you,—whether I told the king of the glorious and indispensable part which you had in the defence of St. Quentin?"

"No, Monsieur l'Amiral," Gabriel replied; "really that is not what I was about to ask you; for I know, and have learned to trust in your word, and I am perfectly certain that your first thought on your return to Paris was to fulfil your promise, and to declare generously to the king, and to the king alone, that my efforts counted for something in St. Quentin's long resistance. In fact, I have no doubt that you exaggerated my small services in your narration to his Majesty. Yes, Monsieur, I know all that without asking. But what I do not know, and what it is of the greatest moment that I should know, is the reply of Henri II. to your kind words."

"Alas! Gabriel," said the admiral, "Henri made no other reply than to ask me what had become of you. I was very much puzzled what to tell him. The letter you left for me on your departure from St. Quentin was very far from explicit, and only reminded me of my promise. I told the king that I knew you had not fallen, but that you had been made prisoner in all probability, and from a feeling of delicacy had not wanted to inform me of it."

"And to that the king—?" asked Gabriel, eagerly.

"The king said, my dear friend: 'That is well!' and a smile of satisfaction hovered upon his lips. Then, when I was enlarging upon the magnificence of your feats of arms, and upon the obligations which you had laid upon France and her king, 'Enough of that!' Henri interposed, and haughtily changing the subject of conversation, compelled me to speak of something else."

"Yes, that is just as I supposed it would be," said Gabriel, with bitter irony.

"Courage, my friend!" rejoined the admiral. "Do you not remember that at St. Quentin I warned you that it was not safe to rely upon the gratitude of the great ones of the world?"

"Oh, yes!" said Gabriel, threateningly; "it was all very well for the king to choose to forget when he hoped that I was dead or in prison; but when I remind him of my rights, as I propose to do very soon, he will find that he has got to remember."

"And suppose his memory persists in being defective?" asked Monsieur de Coligny.

"Monsieur l'Amiral," said Gabriel, "when one has undergone an insult, one applies to the king to see justice done. When the king himself offers the insult, one has no resource but to apply to God for vengeance."

"I imagine, too," the admiral rejoined, "that if it should be necessary, you would constitute yourself the instrument of the divine vengeance."

"You have said it, Monsieur."

"In that case," Coligny resumed, "there is no better place nor time than the present to remind you of a conversation we once had on the subject of the persecuted religion, when I spoke to you of a sure means of punishing kings, while serving the cause of truth at the same time."

"Oh, yes! our conversation was just in my mind," said Gabriel. "My memory does not fail me, you see. I may at some time resort to your means, Monsieur,—against Henri's successors perhaps, if not against himself, since your remedy is equally efficacious against all kings."

"That being so," the admiral continued, "can you give me an hour of your time now?"

"The king does not receive till noon; my time belongs to you until that hour."

"Come with me where I am going, then," said the admiral. "You are of gentle birth, and I have seen your character put to the proof, so I will demand no oath from you. Promise me simply that you will preserve absolute silence as to the people you are about to see, and the things that you hear."

"I promise not to lisp a word," said Gabriel.

"Follow me, then," said the admiral, "and if you meet with injustice at the Louvre, you will at least have your revenge in your own hands in advance; follow me."

Coligny and Gabriel crossed the Pont au Change and the Cité, and were swallowed up in the labyrinth of lanes and alleys which then existed in the neighborhood of Rue St. Jacques.

CHAPTER VII
A PHILOSOPHER AND A SOLDIER

Coligny stopped at the beginning of Rue St. Jacques, before the low door of a house of mean exterior. He knocked: first a wicket in the door was opened, and then the door itself, when the invisible sentinel had recognized the admiral.

Gabriel, following in the steps of his noble guide, passed through a long dark passage-way, and ascended three flights of worm-eaten stairs. When they were almost under the roof, Coligny knocked three times with his foot at the door of the highest and most wretched-looking apartment in the whole house. The door opened, and they went in.

They found themselves in a room of considerable size, but gloomy, and quite bare. Two narrow windows—one looking upon Rue St. Jacques, and the other upon a back alley—admitted only a very uncertain light. There was no furniture save four stools and an oak table with twisted legs.

At the admiral's entrance, two men, who seemed to be expecting him, rose to greet him; a third remained discreetly apart, standing at the front window, and merely bowed low to Coligny from that distance.

"Theodore," said the admiral to the two men who had welcomed him, "and you, Captain, I have brought with me to present to you a friend, who is at all events to be your friend—our friend—hereafter, if he cannot yet be so called."

The two strangers bowed silently to Vicomte d'Exmès. Then the younger, he who was called Theodore, began to talk with Coligny in a low tone, and with much animation. Gabriel walked away a few steps to leave them more at liberty, and was thus able to scrutinize at his leisure the men to whom the admiral had presented him, but whose names even he did not know.

The captain had the strongly marked features and determined bearing of a man of resolution and action. He was tall and dark and sinewy. One needed not to be a keen observer to read audacity in his expression; eager, burning zeal, in the fire of his eyes; and an energetic, forceful will, in his sternly compressed lips.

The companion of this haughty adventurer was rather more like a courtier; he was a graceful cavalier with a well-formed and jolly face, a keen glance, and refined and easy bearing. His dress, which was strictly in accord with the latest fashion, was in strong contrast with the garb of the captain, which was simple almost to the point of austerity.

As for the third individual, who had remained standing at some distance from the others, his striking countenance could but attract notice despite his attitude of reserve; his broad forehead and the piercing keenness of his eye were enough to indicate to the least observant the man of thought, and, let us say at once, the man of genius.

Coligny, having exchanged a few words with his friend, drew near Gabriel.

"I beg your pardon," said he; "but I am not the only master here, and I had to consult my associates before disclosing to you where and in whose company you are."

"Am I to know now!" asked Gabriel.

"If you wish, my friend."

"Where am I, pray?"

"In the poor chamber where the son of the cooper of Noyon, Jean Calvin, held the first secret meetings of those of the Reformed religion, and whence he almost had to march to the stake. But to-day he is at Geneva, triumphant and almost omnipotent; the crowned heads of the world have to reckon with him; and the memory of him alone is enough to make the damp walls of this wretched hole more glorious than the golden arabesques of the Louvre."

At the mention of the great name of Calvin, Gabriel bared his head. Although the impetuous youth had hardly concerned himself hitherto about matters of religion or morals, yet he would have been far behind his age if the austere and toilsome life, the sublime and awe-inspiring character, the bold and imperious doctrines of the law-maker of the Reformed religion had not more than once engrossed his thoughts.

However, he rejoined calmly,—

"And who are these whom I see around me in the venerated master's chamber?"

"His disciples," was the admiral's reply,—"Theodore de Bèze, his pen; La Renaudie, his sword."

Gabriel saluted the charming writer who was to be the historian of the Reformed Church, and the adventurous soldier who was to be the abettor of the Tumulte d'Amboise.

Theodore de Bèze returned Gabriel's salutation with the courteous grace which was natural to him, and said with a pleasant smile,—

"Monsieur le Vicomte d'Exmès, although your introduction here has been accompanied with so many precautions, pray do not look upon us as very dark and dangerous conspirators. I hasten to assure you that if the leaders of our sect meet secretly here three times a week, it is only to exchange information as to the religion, and to receive, it may be, a neophyte, who, as he believes in our principles, asks to share our perils; or some man whom on account of his personal qualities we are anxious to win over to our cause. We are obliged to the admiral for bringing you hither, Monsieur le Vicomte, for you are surely one of the latter class."

"And I, gentlemen, am of the former," said the stranger, who had thus far stood aloof; and as he spoke, he came forward rather shyly and modestly. "I am one of those humble dreamers upon whom the light of your principles has fallen in his darkness, and who longs for a closer view of them."

"But it will not be long, Ambroise, ere you will be numbered among the most illustrious of our brotherhood," said La Renaudie, speaking for the first time. "Yes, gentlemen," he continued, turning to Coligny and De Bèze, "he whom I now present to you, still an humble practitioner, it is true, and still young, as you see, will nevertheless be in due time, I will answer for it, one of the bright and shining lights of the religion, for he is a great worker and a profound thinker; and we may well exult that he has sought us out of his own will, for we shall point with pride to the name on our rolls of the surgeon Ambroise Paré."

"Oh, Monsieur le Capitaine!" exclaimed Ambroise.

"By whom has Master Ambroise Paré been instructed in our principles?" asked Théodore de Bèze.

"By Chaudieu the minister, who introduced me to Monsieur de la Renaudie," Ambroise replied.

"And have you already made the solemn abjuration?"

"Not yet," replied the surgeon. "I desire to be entirely sincere, and not to take any vows except upon thorough acquaintance with the matter. I confess that I still have some doubts; and certain points are still too obscure forme to be able to join you irrevocably and without reservation. It is to have these cleared away that I have longed to meet the leading men of the religion, and have made up my mind to go, if necessary, to Calvin himself; for truth and liberty are the ruling passions of my life."

"Well said!" cried the admiral; "and be assured, Master, that no one of us could ever wish to strike a blow at your rare and proud independence of thought."

"What did I tell you?" rejoined La Renaudie, triumphantly. "Will he not be an invaluable conquest for our faith? I have seen Ambroise Paré in his library; I have seen him at the bedside of the sick (yes, I have seen him too on the battlefield); and everywhere, whether combating error and prejudice, or caring for the wounds and sufferings of his fellow-creatures, he is always thus,—calm, cool, superior to the vicissitudes of fortune, always master of others and of himself."

Gabriel here interposed, much moved by what he saw and heard.

"May I be allowed one word? I know now where I am; and I can imagine what motive induced my generous friend, Monsieur de Coligny, to bring me to this house, where are met those whom King Henri calls his heretics, and looks upon as his mortal enemies. But I have certainly more need to be educated in the faith than has Master Ambroise Paré. Like him, I have been a man of action; but, alas! I have done but little thinking, and he would be doing a great service to a new inquirer into all these new ideas, if he would consent to enlighten me as to the reasons or motives which have inclined his noble intellect to the Reformed sect."

"No interested motive at all," replied Ambroise Paré; "for to succeed in my profession it would be for my interest to conform to the belief of the court and the princes. So it is not interested motives, but the force of reason, Monsieur le Vicomte, as you suggest: and if the illustrious persons before whom I am now speaking authorize me so to do, I will try to set forth my reasons in a few words."

"Go on! go on!" cried Coligny, La Renaudie, and Theodore de Bèze at once.

"I will be brief," rejoined Ambroise, "for my time does not belong to me. In the first place, I tried to disentangle the leading idea of the Reform from all theories and formulas. The brushwood once cut away, these are the principles which I laid bare, for which I would most assuredly submit to persecution in every form."

Gabriel was listening with admiration which he made no attempt to conceal, to this disinterested expounder of the truth.

Ambroise Paré continued.

"Religious and political domination, the Church and royalty, have hitherto substituted their regulations and their laws for the will and reasoning of the individual. The priest says to every man, 'Believe this;' and the prince, 'Do thus and so.' Now, matters have gone on in this way so long that men's minds remained as the minds of babes, and had perforce to lean upon this double discipline to make their way through life. But now we *feel* that we are strong, and hence we *are*. Nevertheless the prince and the priest, the Church and the king, are unwilling to lay down one jot of the authority which has become a principle of existence with them. It is against this anachronism of iniquity that the Reformed religion *protests*, in my view. Hereafter let every soul examine carefully its belief, and reason out its submission to this domination; and then I believe we shall see the regeneration to which our efforts are devoted. Am I wrong, gentlemen?"

"No, but you go too far and too fast," said Theodore de Bèze; "in this bold way of mingling politics and moral questions—"

"Ah! it is that very boldness which attracts me," Gabriel interrupted.

"But it is not boldness; it is logic!" rejoined Ambroise Paré. "How can that which is fair and just in the Church not be equally so in the State? How can you disavow as a rule of action that which you admit as a rule of thought?"

"There is the spirit of revolution in the bold words you have uttered, Master," cried Coligny, thoughtfully.

"Of revolution?" Ambroise coolly rejoined. "Why, I am talking about revolution."

The three leaders looked at one another in surprise. Their looks seemed to say, "This man is much stronger even than we supposed."

Gabriel did not forget for a moment the engrossing anxiety of his whole life; but he was now applying to it what he had just heard, and was lost in thought.

Theodore de Bèze said most earnestly to the outspoken surgeon,—

"It is absolutely necessary that you should join us. What do you ask?"

"Nothing more than the privilege of conversing with you now and then, and of submitting to your intelligence and knowledge such difficulties as I still encounter."

"You shall have more than that," said Theodore de Bèze; "you shall correspond directly with Calvin."

"Such an honor for me!" cried Ambroise Paré, flushing with delight.

"Yes, it is essential that you should know him, and he you," rejoined the admiral. "Such a disciple as you are deserves a master like him. You hand your letters to your friend La Renaudie, and we will see that they reach Geneva. We will also hand you his replies. They will not be long in coming. You have heard of Calvin's extraordinary powers of application; and you will be satisfied."

"Ah," said Ambroise Paré, "you give me my reward before I have done anything to merit it. How have I deserved so great a favor?"

"By being what you are, my friend," said La Renaudie. "I knew that you would win their hearts at the first stroke."

"Oh, thank you, thank you a thousand times!" Ambroise responded. "But," he added, "I regret to say that I must leave you, there are so many patients awaiting me."

"Go, go!" said Théodore de Bèze; "your reasons are too sacred for us to try to keep you. Go! Do what is right as you believe what is true."

"But as you leave us," Coligny interposed, "rest assured that you leave none behind you but friends, or, as we say of those of our religion, 'brothers.'"

Thus they took leave of him heartily and cordially; and Gabriel, warmly pressing his hand, was not behindhand in this friendly parting.

Ambroise Paré went his way, with joy and pride in his heart.

"Truly one of the elect!" cried Théodore de Bèze.

"What scorn for the commonplace!" said La Renaudie.

"What uncalculating, unreserved devotion to the cause of humanity!" said Coligny.

"Alas!" rejoined Gabriel, "how paltry must my selfishness appear beside such self-abnegation, Monsieur l'Amiral! I do not, like Ambroise Paré, subordinate facts and persons to ideas and principles; but on the contrary, ideas and principles to facts and persons. The Reformed religion will be for me, as you know too well, not an end, but a means. In your noble, unselfish struggle I should take part to serve my own purposes. I feel that my motives are too personal and selfish for me to dare to defend so pure and holy a cause, and you would do very well at this moment to spurn me from your ranks as unworthy to serve therein."

"Surely you traduce yourself, Monsieur d'Exmès," said Theodore de Bèze. "Even though you should obey less exalted impulses than those of

Ambroise Paré, still the ways of the Lord are many, and one does not find the truth by travelling on one road to the exclusion of all others."

"Yes," said La Renaudie, "we very seldom listen to such professions of faith as that you have just heard, when we address to those whom we wish to enlist in our cause the question, 'What do you ask?'"

"Oh, well," Gabriel responded with a sad smile; "to that question Ambroise Paré answered: 'I ask whether justice and right are really on your side.' Do you know what my reply would be?"

"No," Théodore de Bèze replied; "but we are ready to answer you on every point."

"I should ask," Gabriel rejoined, "'Are you sure that you have on your side sufficient material power and sufficient members to make a good fight, even if not to conquer?'"

Once more the three enthusiasts exchanged looks of wonder. But their wonder had not the same meaning as before.

Gabriel looked at them in gloomy silence. Theodore de Bèze, after a pause, replied,—

"Whatever may be the feeling that prompts that inquiry, Monsieur d'Exmès, I agreed in advance to answer you on every point, and I will keep my promise. We have with us not only common-sense, but strength as well, thank God! The progress of our principles has been rapid and undeniable. Three years ago a Reformed church was founded at Paris; and the great cities of the kingdom—Blois, Tours, Poitiers, Marseilles, and Rouen—all have churches of their own. You can see for yourself, Monsieur d'Exmès, the enormous crowds which are attracted by our meetings at the Pré-aux-Clercs. People, nobility, and courtiers give up their pleasure-making to come and sing with us Clement Marot's French hymns. We intend next year to determine our numbers by a public procession; but at the present time, I venture to say that we have a fifth of the population with us. We may therefore without presumption call ourselves a party, and may reckon, I think, upon inspiring our friends with confidence, our enemies with dismay."

"That being so," said Gabriel, coolly, "I may very possibly before long enrol myself among the former and assist you to combat the latter."

"But suppose you had found us not so strong?" asked La Renaudie.

"Then I confess that I should have sought other allies," replied Gabriel, still firmly and calmly.

La Renaudie and Theodore de Bèze both made a movement of astonishment.

"Ah!" cried Coligny, "do not judge him, my friends, too hastily or too harshly. I have seen him at work at the siege of St. Quentin; and when one puts his life in peril, as he did there, it bespeaks no ordinary soul. But I know that he has a holy and terrible duty to perform, which leaves no part of his devotion at his own disposal."

"And in default of my devotion, I would like to offer you at least my sincerest aid," said Gabriel. "But in very truth I cannot give myself up to your service absolutely and without consideration; for I am devoted to a necessary and formidable task, which has been imposed upon me by the wrath of God and the wickedness of man, and while that task remains unfinished, I beg you to pardon me, for I am not the arbiter of my own fate. The destiny of another takes precedence of mine at all times, and wherever I may be."

"One may devote oneself to a man as well as to an idea," said Theodore de Bèze.

"And in such a case," added Coligny, "we shall be happy, my friend, to serve you, just as we shall be proud to avail ourselves of your services."

"Our good wishes will go with you; and we will stand ready to assist you in case of need," said La Renaudie.

"Ah! you are heroes and saints as well," cried Gabriel.

"But take care, young man," said the stern La Renaudie, in his familiar and yet noble language,—"take care, when once we have called you our brother, to be worthy of the name. We may admit a private devotion into our ranks; but the heart sometimes deceives itself. Are you perfectly certain, young man, that when you believe yourself to be entirely devoted to thoughts of another, no personal consideration whatever has its influence on your actions? In the object which you are striving to accomplish, are you absolutely and truly disinterested? Are you, in short, urged on by no passion of your own, though it may be the most generous and worthy of passions?"

"Yes," added Theodore de Bèze, "we do not ask for your secrets; but search your heart, and tell us that if you were justified in revealing to us all its feelings and all its plans, you would not feel the least embarrassment in so doing, and we will believe your word."

"In speaking thus, my dear friend," said the admiral, in his turn, "it is to impress upon you that a pure cause must be upheld with clean hands; otherwise one would only bring misfortune upon his cause and himself."

Gabriel listened to and looked at the three men one after another, who were as stern to others as to themselves, and who, standing around with keen, serious mien, were questioning him as friends and judges at once.

At their words he turned pale and red by turns.

He questioned his own conscience. Being a man of impulse and action, he was doubtless too little accustomed to reflect and inquire into his own motives. At this moment he asked himself in alarm, whether in his filial devotion his love for Madame de Castro was not an element of very great weight; whether he was not at heart as anxious to learn the secret of Diane's birth as to procure the old count's liberty; whether, in short, in this matter of life or death he was really as unselfish as he must be according to Coligny to deserve God's favor.

Fearful doubt!—whether by some selfish mental reservation he might not compromise his father's welfare in the sight of God.

He shuddered in anxious uncertainty. A circumstance, seemingly unimportant, awoke his nature to action once more.

Eleven o'clock struck from the church of St. Severin.

In an hour he would be in the king's presence.

With a firm voice he said to the leaders of the Reformed sect:—

"You are men of the Golden Age; and those who are most irreproachable in their own sight find their self-esteem debased and saddened when they compare themselves with your ideal. Yet it is not possible that all of your party should be such as you are. That you, who are the head and the heart of the religion, should keep a close and strict watch upon your purposes and your acts is necessary and beneficial; but if I throw myself into your cause, it will not be as a leader, but as a common soldier simply. Stains upon the soul only are indelible; those upon the hand may be washed away. I will be your hand,—that's all. I venture to ask, Have you the right to refuse the aid of this bold and daring hand?"

"No," said Coligny; "and we accept it here and now, my friend."

"And I will stake my life that it will rest upon the hilt of your sword as pure and unstained as it is valiant," added Theodore de Bèze.

"The very hesitation," said La Renaudie, "which our rather rough and exacting words caused in your scrupulous heart is our sufficient guarantee. We know how to judge men's characters."

"Thanks, gentlemen," said Gabriel,—"thanks from my heart for not depriving me of the confidence of which I am so much in need in the hard task which I have before me; thanks to you especially, Monsieur l'Amiral, who have thus, as you promised, furnished me in advance with the means of punishing a breach of faith, even if committed by an anointed king. Now I am obliged to leave you, gentlemen, and I will say, not adieu, but *au revoir*. Although I may be of those who obey the course of events rather than abstract ideas, I believe, nevertheless, that the seeds you have sown to-day will bear fruit hereafter."

"We hope so, for our own sakes," said Theodore de Bèze.

"I must not hope so for my sake," rejoined Gabriel; "for, as I have avowed, it will be only bitter misfortune which will drive me to adopt your cause. Adieu once more, gentlemen; I must now go to the Louvre."

"I will go with you," said Coligny. "I must repeat to Henri II. in your presence what I have already told him once in your absence. Kings have but short memories; and we must not allow this one to forget or to deny. I will go with you."

"I should not have ventured to ask this favor of you, Monsieur l'Amiral," cried Gabriel; "but I accept your offer most gratefully."

"Let us go, then," said Coligny.

As soon as they had left Calvin's chamber, Theodore took his tablets, and wrote these names:—

Ambroise Paré,

Gabriel, Vicomte d'Exmès.

"It seems to me," said La Renaudie, "that you are a little hasty in enrolling these two men among us. They have made no promises whatever."

"They are ours," replied De Bèze. "One is in search of the truth, and the other fleeing from injustice. I tell you they are ours, and I shall write Calvin to that effect."

"This will have been a great day for the religion, then."

"Indeed it will," said Theodore; "we shall have made the conquest of a profound philosopher and a valiant soldier,—a mighty brain and a strong arm, a winner of battles and a sower of ideas. You are right; it is really a great day."

CHAPTER VIII
WHEREIN MARY STUART'S LOVELINESS FLITS ACROSS THE COURSE OF THE STORY WITH AS TRANSIENT A GLEAM AS IT CASTS UPON THE HISTORY OF FRANCE

When Gabriel, accompanied by Coligny, reached the portals of the Louvre, he was overwhelmed by the first words that reached his ears.

The king did not receive that day!

The admiral, notwithstanding he held that high rank and was the nephew of Montmorency, was too gravely suspected of heresy to have much credit at court. As for Gabriel d'Exmès, the captain of the Guards, the ushers of the royal suite had had ample time to forget his face and his name. The two friends were rewarded for their trouble only by being permitted to pass beyond the outer doors.

Within it was still worse. They wasted more than an hour in parleying and bribing and threatening. As rapidly as they succeeded in inducing one halberdier to allow them to pass, another barred their way. All the varieties of dragon, more or less formidable, which watch over the safety of kings seemed to be multiplied tenfold to impede their passage.

But when by sheer persistence they had succeeded in penetrating as far as the great gallery which led to the king's closet, they found it impossible to go farther; the orders were too strict. The king, closeted with the constable and Madame de Poitiers, had given express instructions that he was not to be disturbed on any pretext.

It was necessary that Gabriel should wait till evening if he wished for an audience.

Waiting, weary waiting, when he believed that he was about to reach the goal which he had been striving for through so much difficulty and suffering! The few hours still to be passed seemed to Gabriel more terrible and more to be dreaded than all the perils which he had hitherto defied and overcome.

Without listening to the kind words with which the admiral sought to console him, and to urge patience upon him, he stood at the window looking gloomily at the rain which had begun to fall from the sombre sky, a prey to anger and anguish, restlessly feeling the point of his sword.

How to overturn and pass by the stupid guards who prevented him from making his way to the king's apartment, and perhaps to his father's liberty? Such thoughts filled his brain, when suddenly the curtain before the door of the royal antechamber was lifted, and a fair and blooming figure seemed to the saddened youth to light up the gray, rainy atmosphere.

The little queen-dauphine, Mary Stuart, was passing through the gallery.

Gabriel, as if by instinct, uttered a cry, and stretched out his arms toward her.

"Oh, Madame!" he said, hardly conscious of what he was doing.

Mary Stuart turned, recognized Gabriel and the admiral, and came up to them with her ever-ready smile.

"So you have returned at last, Monsieur le Vicomte d'Exmès," said she. "I am very glad to see you again; I have heard much talk about you of late. But what are you doing at the Louvre at this early hour, and what is your wish?"

"To speak to the king! to speak to the king, Madame!" Gabriel replied in a stifled voice.

"Monsieur d'Exmès," it was the admiral who spoke, "has really much need to speak to the king without delay. It is a very serious matter for him, and for the king as well; but all these guards prevent his entering, and attempt to put him off till this evening."

"As if I could wait till evening!" cried Gabriel.

"I believe," said Mary Stuart, "that his Majesty is just finishing some important despatches. Monsieur le Connétable de Montmorency is still with the king, and really I am afraid—"

A piteous glance from Gabriel prevented Mary from finishing her sentence.

"Well, we will see," she resumed. "I will take the risk."

She made a sign with her little hand. The guards respectfully fell back, and Gabriel and the admiral were at liberty to pass.

"Oh, thanks, Madame!" said the eager youth. "Thank you, who, in every respect like an angel, always appear to comfort or to aid me in my suffering."

"The way is clear," responded Mary Stuart, smiling. "If his Majesty is very angry, do not betray the angel's share in your entrance, except at the last extremity, I beg of you."

She inclined her head graciously to Gabriel and his companion, and was gone.

Gabriel was already at the door of the king's cabinet. There was in the last antechamber one more usher who undertook to oppose their entrance. But just then the door opened; and Henri himself appeared on the threshold, just giving some last instructions to the constable.

The king's distinguishing characteristic was not resolution. At the sudden appearance of Vicomte d'Exmès, he recoiled, and even forgot to be angry.

Gabriel's great virtue was firmness. He bowed low before the king in the first place.

"Sire," said he, "deign to accept my most respectful homage."

Then turning to Monsieur de Coligny, who was following him, and whom he wished to relieve from the embarrassment of speaking first,—

"Come, Monsieur l'Amiral," said he, "and in accordance with the kind promise you made me, be kind enough to remind his Majesty of the part that I took in the defence of St. Quentin."

"What is all this, Monsieur?" cried Henri, beginning to recover his self-control. "How is it that you intrude yourself thus upon us, without authorization or announcement? How do you dare to call upon Monsieur l'Amiral in our presence?"

Gabriel, who was as bold at such momentous crises as he was before the enemy, and who well understood that it was no time to lose his courage, replied in a perfectly respectful but determined tone,—

"I thought, Sire, that your Majesty was always ready when justice was to be done, even to the meanest of your subjects."

He had taken advantage of the king's backward movement to walk boldly into the cabinet, where Diane de Poitiers, pale as death, and half reclining upon her couch of carved oak, watched the actions and words of the audacious young man, without power to speak a word, so great was her anger and surprise.

Coligny had entered also upon the heels of his impetuous friend, and Montmorency, as much stupefied as the others, had followed his example.

There was a moment of silence. Henri turned to his mistress with an inquiring look; but before he had resolved upon any course for himself or she had had time to suggest one to him, Gabriel, who knew well that at that moment he held a very advantageous position, said again to Coligny with an imploring and at the same time dignified accent,—

"I beseech you to speak, Monsieur l'Amiral!" Montmorency quickly shook his head at his nephew, but brave Gaspard took no note of it.

"Indeed I will speak," said he, "for both my duty and my promise require me to do so.

"Sire," he resumed, addressing the king, "I here repeat to you, in brief, and in presence of Monsieur le Vicomte d'Exmès, what I thought it my duty to tell you in greater detail before his return. It is to him, and to him alone, that we owe the prolonged defence of St. Quentin, even beyond the time fixed by your Majesty."

The constable made a meaning movement. But Coligny, looking steadily at him, nevertheless went calmly on,—

"Yes, Sire, three times and more Monsieur d'Exmès saved the town, and had it not been for his courage and energy, France, beyond a doubt, would not have been at this hour on the road to safety, in which we may hope that she may henceforth be able to maintain herself."

"Come, come! you are too modest or too obliging, my nephew!" cried Monsieur de Montmorency, utterly unable to restrain his impatience any longer.

"No, Monsieur, I am just and truthful," said Coligny, "nothing more. I contributed my own share and with all my strength to the defence of the town which was intrusted to me. But Vicomte d'Exmès rekindled the courage of the people, which I looked upon as already dead beyond redemption; he succeeded in throwing into the town reinforcements which I had no idea were in the neighborhood; last of all, he frustrated a surprise

"I remember it all," he said to Gabriel.

"Ah, Sire, thanks!" cried Gabriel, with eyes shining with delight.

But Madame de Poitiers at this moment calmly interposed,—

"Doubtless the king remembers it all, Monsieur d'Exmès; but you yourself seem to have forgotten."

A flash of lightning from a cloudless sky could not have terrified Gabriel more than these words.

"What have I forgotten, Madame, pray?" the young man murmured.

"One half of your task, Monsieur," Diane replied. "You said to his ajesty,—and if these are not your exact words, I at least give their sense,— e, to purchase the freedom of the Comte de Montgommery, I will arrest enemy in his triumphal march toward the heart of France.'"

"Well, did I not do it?" asked the bewildered Gabriel.

"Oh, yes!" replied Diane, "but you added: 'And even, if it be necessary, ssailed shall become the aggressor, and I will seize one of the towns ich the enemy is in possession.' That is what you said, Monsieur. ore it seems to me that you have done but half of what you agreed What answer have you to that? You held St. Quentin for a certain of days; it was well done, I do not deny. You have shown us the fended as you promised; but where is the town taken?"

mon Dieu, mon Dieu!" It was all Gabriel in his utter despair could gth to say.

see," Diane resumed with the same *sang-froid*, "that my memory tter and more at my command than yours. Yet I venture to hope ou remember."

is true, I do remember now!" cried Gabriel, in bitterness of spirit. said that, I meant simply to say that in case of need I would he impossible; for is it possible at this time to take any town ds of the Spaniards or the English? Is it, Sire? Your Majesty, by o go, tacitly accepted the first of my offers, without giving me that after such an heroic effort and a long term of captivity led upon to carry out the second. Sire, it is to you—to you— ne town for the freedom of one man,—is not that enough? content with such a ransom; and must it be that on account h word which escaped me in the exaltation of my spirit, upon me, a weak human Hercules, another task a hundred

attempted by the enemy, which I had not foreseen. I say nothing of the way in which he bore himself in the mêlée; we all did our best. But what he did with his own hand and brain, the enormous share of glory that he won for himself on that occasion, may well lessen or even render vain and illusory all of mine,—that I proclaim aloud."

Turning to Gabriel, the brave admiral added,—

"Is it thus that I ought to speak, my friend? Have I carried out my agreement to your satisfaction? Are you content with me?"

"Oh, I thank and bless you from the bottom of my heart, Monsieur l'Amiral, for your loyalty and virtue," said Gabriel, deeply touched, and pressing Coligny's hands. "I expected no less of you. But look upon me, I beg, as bound to you forever. Yes, from this hour, your creditor has become your debtor, and will remember his debt, I swear to you."

Meanwhile the king, frowning and with downcast eyes, was beating his foot impatiently on the floor, and seemed deeply vexed.

The constable gradually approached Madame de Poitiers, and exchanged a few words with her in an undertone.

They seemed to have come to some decision, for Diane began to smile; and her diabolical and feminine grimace made Gabriel shudder, as he happened to be looking at the beautiful duchess at that moment.

However, Gabriel found strength to add,—

"I will keep you no longer, Monsieur l'Amiral. You have done more than your duty toward me; and if his Majesty will deign now to grant, as my first reward, the favor of a private interview—"

"Later, Monsieur, later; I do not say no," said Henri, quickly, "but just now it is impossible."

"Impossible!" cried Gabriel, sorrowfully.

"Why impossible, Sire?" Diane interrupted pleasantly, to Gabriel's great surprise, and the king's as well.

"What! do you think, Madame—?" stammered Henri.

"I think, Sire, that a king's most pressing duty is to render to each one of his subjects that which is his due. Now, your debt to Monsieur d'Exmès is one of the most well-founded and sacred of all debts in my opinion."

"No doubt, no doubt!" said Henri, who began to read the signals in the favorite's eyes; "and I wish—"

"To hear at once what Monsieur d'Exmès has to say," Diane finished his sentence. "That is right, Sire, and no more than justice."

"But his Majesty knows," said Gabriel, more and more lost in amazement, "that it is essential that I should speak with him alone?"

"Monsieur de Montmorency was just about to retire as you came in, Monsieur," rejoined Madame de Poitiers; "and you have yourself taken the trouble to tell Monsieur l'Amiral that you would detain him no longer. As for myself, as I was a witness of the contract the king made with you, and can even, if need be, remind his Majesty of its exact terms, perhaps you will allow me to remain."

"Most assuredly, Madame; I ask you to do so," murmured Gabriel.

"My nephew and myself will take our leave, then, of his Majesty and of you, Madame," said Montmorency.

He made a sign of encouragement, as he passed, to Diane, of which she seemed in no need, however.

For his part Coligny ventured to press Gabriel's hand; then he followed his uncle from the room.

The king and the favorite remained alone with Gabriel, who was in a state of alarm at the unexpected and mysterious protection accorded to him by Diane de Castro's mother.

CHAPTER IX
THE OTHER DIANE

In spite of his marvellous self-control, Gabriel could not blood from leaving his cheeks nor his voice from quivering moment's pause he said to the king,—

"Sire, it is in fear and trembling, and yet with implicit co kingly word, that I venture, having only yesterday escape to recall to your Majesty's mind the solemn engagement th enter into with me. The Comte de Montgommery still li you would long ago have stayed my voice."

He stopped with a terrible oppression at his hear motionless and mute. Gabriel resumed:

"Well, then, Sire, since the Comte de Montgomm according to Monsieur l'Amiral's testimony, I did St. Quentin beyond the limit fixed by your Majes my promise; now I beg you to keep yours. Sire,

"Monsieur!" said Henri, hesitatingly.

He looked anxiously at Diane de Poitiers possession seemed to be quite undisturbed.

Nevertheless, it was a difficult positio used to thinking of Gabriel as dead or in himself with a reply to his terrible demar

In the face of this hesitation Gabrie

"Sire," he continued, in an almo that your Majesty has forgotten! You interview; what I undertook to d Majesty's reciprocal undertaking w

The king was touched in spi noble youth; the generous instin

times harder than the first,—yes, Sire, even impossible, and understood to be so?"

The king made a motion of his lips, as if to speak, but the grande sénéchale made haste to forestall him.

"Is it, pray, any easier and more practicable, is there any less of danger or of madness, despite your promises, in setting free a dangerous prisoner, who was guilty of the crime of *lèse-majesté*? You offered to do the impossible in order to obtain the impossible, Monsieur d'Exmès; and it is not fair that you should demand the fulfilment of the king's word when you have not kept your own promise in full. The duties of a sovereign are no less weighty than those of a son; enormous, nay, superhuman services rendered the State can alone produce such a condition of things as would justify his Majesty in nullifying the laws of the State. You have a father to save,—very well; but the king has France to protect."

And with a look which was a fit commentary to her words, Diane reminded Henri of the great danger of allowing the old Comte de Montgommery and his secret to rise from the tomb.

But Gabriel, making a last effort, stretched out his hands to the king, and cried,—

"Sire, it is to you—to your sense of right, to your kind heart—that I appeal. Sire, hereafter, aided by time and circumstance, I bind myself to win back a town for my country, or to die in the attempt. But meanwhile, Sire, for very pity's sake, let me see my father!"

Henri, taking counsel from the penetrating gaze of Diane and her whole demeanor, responded, steadying his voice,—

"Keep your promise to the end, Monsieur; and I swear before God that then, and then only, will I fulfil mine. My word is worth as much as yours."

"That is your last word, Sire?" asked Gabriel.

"That is my last word."

Gabriel bent his head for a moment, overwhelmed and vanquished, and altogether beside himself from his fearful repulse.

In one moment he revolved in his mind a whole world of thoughts.

He would be revenged upon the ungrateful king and his perfidious favorite; he would throw in his lot with those of the Reformed religion; he would accomplish the destiny of the Montgommeries; he would strike

Henri a mortal blow, even as Henri had struck the old count; he would cause Diane de Poitiers to be banished from court in disgrace, and bereft of all her honors. Henceforth that should be the one aim of his will and his life; and far removed and impossible as its accomplishment might seem to be for a simple gentleman, he would find a way to accomplish it.

And yet his father meanwhile might die twenty times over. The avenger was very well; but the savior was better. In his position, it was hardly more difficult to capture a town than to punish a king; but the former end was holy and glorious, the other criminal and impious: in the one case he would lose Diane de Castro forever; in the other who could say that he might not win her?

Everything that had happened since the fall of St. Quentin passed before Gabriel's eyes like a flash.

In one tenth of the time that it takes us to write all this the gallant and ever-ready heart of the young man had begun to throw off its depression. He had made a resolution, formed his plan, and thought that he could see in the distance a favorable result.

The king and his mistress marvelled, and were almost afraid, as they saw him raise once more his pallid but tranquil face.

"So be it," was all he said.

"You are resigned, are you?" asked Henri.

"I have made my decision," Gabriel replied.

"How? Explain yourself," said the king.

"Listen to me, Sire. Any attempt that I should make to put into your hands a town to pay for the one which the Spaniards have taken from you would seem to you hopeless, impossible, the act of a madman, would it not? Be frank with me, Sire, and you too, Madame,—is not this really your opinion?"

"It is true," Henri replied.

"I fear so," added Diane.

"In all probability this attempt will cost me my life, and produce no other result than to cause me to be looked upon as an absurd fool," Gabriel continued.

"It was not I who proposed it to you," said the king.

"Doubtless, your wisest course would be to give it up," Diane rejoined.

"I have told you, however, that I have resolved upon it," said Gabriel.

Neither Henri nor Diane could restrain an admiring exclamation.

"Oh, be careful!" cried the king.

"Of what?—of my life?" retorted Gabriel, laughing aloud. "I sacrificed that long, long ago. But, Sire, there must be no misunderstanding and no subterfuges this time. The terms of the bargain we are making together before God are now clear and precise. I, Gabriel, Vicomte d'Exmès, Vicomte de Montgommery, will bear myself in such fashion that by my means some town which is to-day in the power of the Spaniards or the English shall fall into your hands. This town shall be no paltry village or hamlet, but a strong place, of as much importance as you can desire. There is no ambiguity there, I think."

"No, truly not," said the king, uneasily.

"And you," Gabriel resumed, "Henri II., King of France, do also on your part bind yourself to open the doors of my father's dungeon, at my first demand, and to give up to me the Comte de Montgommery. Do you so bind yourself? Is it done?"

The king noticed Diane's incredulous smile, and said,—

"I give you my word."

"Thanks, your Majesty. This is not all, however. You can well afford to give one guarantee more to this poor maniac, who is hurling himself into the abyss before your very eyes. You must be indulgent to those who are about to die. I ask of you no signed writing, which might compromise you,—doubtless, you would refuse it; but here is a Bible, Sire; place your royal hand upon it, and take this oath: 'In exchange for a town of the first class, the recovery of which I shall owe to Gabriel de Montgommery alone, I pledge myself upon the holy gospels to restore Vicomte d'Exmès's father to liberty; and I declare in advance that if I prove false to this oath, said viscount is freed from all allegiance to me and mine. I say that whatever he may do to punish me for my false swearing will be well done, and absolve him before God and man for any crime against my person.' Take that oath, Sire."

"By what right do you ask it of me?" said Henri.

"I told you, Sire, by the right of one who is soon to die."

The king still hesitated; but the duchess with her disdainful smile made a sign to him that he might take the required oath without fear.

She really believed that for the moment Gabriel had lost his reason; and she shrugged her shoulders in pity.

"Very well; I consent," said Henri, with a fatal impulse.

With his hand on the gospel, he repeated the words of the oath which Gabriel dictated.

"At least," said the young man, when the king had done, "this will suffice to spare your remorse. Madame Diane is not the only witness to our new contract, for God also has witnessed it. Now, I have no more time to lose. Adieu, Sire. In two months from now I shall be no longer among the living, or my father will be in my arms."

He bowed low before the king and the duchess, and left the room in haste.

Henri, in spite of himself, remained for a moment thoughtful and grave; but Diane laughed merrily.

"Come, why don't you laugh, Sire?" said she. "Surely you see that this madman is lost, and that his father will die in prison. You may safely laugh, Sire."

"I am laughing," said the king, suiting the action to the word.

CHAPTER X
A GRAND SCHEME FOR A GREAT MAN

The Duc de Guise, since he had borne the title of Lieutenant-General of the kingdom, occupied apartments in the Louvre itself. The ambitious chief of the house of Lorraine thus slept, or rather lay awake, every night in the royal dwelling of the kings of France.

What waking dreams did he have beneath that chimera-haunted roof? His dreams had taken a great stride forward since the day when he confided to Gabriel, in his tent before Civitella, his designs upon the throne of Naples. Would he be content now? Being a guest in the royal palace, would he not say to himself that before long he might well become its master? Did he not already feel vaguely the pressure of a crown about his temples? Did he not with a complacent smile contemplate the good sword which, more powerful than the magician's wand, might transform his hopes to reality?

We may imagine that even as early as this, François de Lorraine did harbor such thoughts; for consider! Did not the king himself, by calling him to his assistance in his distress, justify his wildest ambition? To intrust to him the welfare of France at such a time was to recognize him as the first captain of his age! François I. would not have been so modest! No, he would have girded on the sword of Marignan. But Henri II., although of great personal courage, lacked the will to command and the force to execute.

The Duc de Guise said all this to himself; but he also told himself that it was not enough to be able to justify his rash hopes in his own eyes, but that he must justify them in the eyes of France; that he must by glorious services and signal success purchase his right and carve out his own destiny.

The fortunate general who had had the opportunity to arrest the second invasion of Charles V. at Metz knew very well that he had not yet accomplished so much that he could venture to try for the whole. Even when at this time he had driven back to the frontier the Spanish and the English, still it was not enough. In order that France might throw herself into his hands, or allow him to take her to himself, he must not only repair her losses, but must make conquests for her.

Such were the-reflections which had preoccupied the great mind of the Duc de Guise since his return from Italy.

He was going over them again on this very day when Gabriel de Montgommery was concluding his new, apparently insane, yet sublime agreement with Henri II.

Alone in his room, François de Guise, standing at the window, was looking into the courtyard with eyes that saw not, and mechanically thrumming upon the glass with his fingers.

One of his people knocked softly at the door, and upon receiving the duke's permission to enter, announced Vicomte d'Exmès.

"Vicomte d'Exmès!" said the Duc de Guise, who had a memory like Cæsar's, and who also had the best of reasons for remembering Gabriel. "Vicomte d'Exmès! My young companion in arms of Metz and Renty and Valenza! Show him in, Thibault; show him in at once!"

The valet; bowed and left the room to introduce Gabriel.

Our hero (we surely have the right to give him that name) had not hesitated. With the instinct which illuminates the brain at critical moments, and which if it shines throughout the ordinary extent of one's life is called genius, Gabriel, on leaving the king, as if he had foreseen the secret thoughts which the Duc de Guise was fondling in his mind at that moment, betook himself at once to the apartments of the lieutenant-general.

He was perhaps the only living man who could understand and assist him.

Gabriel might well have been touched by the reception which he met with from his former commander.

The Duc de Guise went quite to the door to meet him, and folded him in his arms.

"Ah, you are here at last, my hero!" he said effusively. "Whence have you come h What has become of you since St. Quentin? Ah, how often I have thought of you and spoken of you, Gabriel!"

"Have I really kept any place in your memory, Monseigneur?"

"*Pardieu*! he has the assurance to ask me such a question!" cried the duke. "As if you hadn't ways of your own of making yourself remembered by people. Coligny, who is worth more alone than all the rest of the Montmorencys together, has told me (but in very ambiguous terms, for some unknown reason) a part of your exploits at St. Quentin; nevertheless, from what he did say, I should judge that he said nothing regarding the greater portion of them."

"Yet I did too little!" said Gabriel, with a sad smile.

"Ambitious boy!" said the duke.

"Indeed I am ambitious!" was Gabriel's response, with a mournful shake of the head.

"But, thank God, you have returned!" rejoined the Duc de Guise. "Once more we are together, my friend; you remember what plans we made together in Italy! Ah, poor Gabriel, France needs your valor more than ever now. To what dire extremity have they reduced our country!"

"All that I am, and all that I have," said Gabriel, "is consecrated to her support; I only await your signal, Monseigneur."

"Thanks, my friend," the duke responded; "be sure that I will avail myself of your offer, and you will not have long to wait for my signal."

"Then it will be for me to thank you, Monseigneur," cried Gabriel.

"To tell the truth, however," the duke continued, "the more I look around me, the more embarrassing and serious do I find the situation. I had to hasten at first to the point where the greatest urgency existed, to organize effective means of resistance in the neighborhood of Paris, and to present a formidable defensive front to the enemy,—to stop his progress, in short. But all that amounts to nothing. He has St. Quentin; he has the North! I ought to be at work, and I long to be. But in what direction?"

He stopped, as if to consult Gabriel. He knew the young man's breadth of view, and he had on more than one occasion found his advice worth following; but now Vicomte d'Exmès spoke not a word, carefully watching the duke, and letting him approach the subject in his own way, so to speak.

François de Lorraine thereupon continued:—

"Do not reprove me for my sloth, my dear friend. I am not one of those who hesitate, as you know; but I am of those who reflect. You will not blame me for it; for you are like me,—determined and cautious at the same time. The pensiveness of your young face," the duke added, "seems to me of a severer cast than formerly. I hardly dare to ask you about yourself. You had stern duties to perform, I remember, and formidable foes to discover. Have you other misfortunes to deplore than those of your country? I fear so; for when I last saw you, you were only serious, and now I find you sad."

"Let us not speak of myself, Monseigneur, I beg," said Gabriel. "Let us speak of France, and then we shall be speaking of my hopes."

"So be it," rejoined the duke. "I will tell you with perfect frankness my thoughts and my anxiety. It seems to me that the most essential thing at this moment is to raise the spirits of our people, and restore our former glorious reputation by some striking blow; to change our defensive attitude to an offensive one; and, finally, not to content ourselves with repairing our defeats, but to atone for them by some glorious success."

"That is precisely my opinion, Monseigneur," cried Gabriel, eagerly, surprised and delighted at a coincidence so in line with his own schemes.

"That being your opinion," resumed the Duc de Guise, "doubtless, you have thought more than once of our country's peril and of the means of extricating her from it?"

"Indeed, I have often thought of it," said Gabriel.

"Well, then," continued François de Lorraine, "have you, my friend, gone any further than I? Have you looked this serious difficulty in the face? Where, when, and how to attempt so brilliant a stroke, which we both deem so essential?"

"Monseigneur, I think I know."

"Can it be?" cried the duke. "Oh, speak, speak, my friend!"

"*Mon Dieu*! perhaps I have spoken too soon, after all," said Gabriel. "The proposition I have to make is one of those which will certainly require long preparation. You are very powerful, Monseigneur; but the project I have to suggest may seem impracticable even to you."

"I am not generally subject to vertigo," said the duke, smiling.

"Never mind, Monseigneur," rejoined Gabriel. "At first sight, my plan will—I fear, and I forewarn you—seem extraordinary, insensate, nay, even impossible; really, however, it is only difficult and dangerous."

"But that only makes it more attractive," said François de Lorraine.

"Well, Monseigneur, it is agreed, then, that you will not, in the first place, be horrified. I say again, there will be great risks to be run; but the means of success are in my power, and when I have unfolded them, you yourself will agree with me."

"If that be so, I beg you to speak, Gabriel," said the duke. "But who comes to interrupt us now?" he added impatiently. "Is that you knocking, Thibault?"

"Yes, Monseigneur," said the valet, entering the room. "Monseigneur ordered me to let him know when the hour for the council to assemble had arrived, and it is now striking two. Monsieur de Saint-Remy and the other gentlemen will call for Monseigneur directly."

"True, true," rejoined the duke; "there is a council-meeting to be held now, and an important one too. It is indispensable that I should be present. Very well, Thibault. Leave us; show the gentlemen in when they arrive. You see, Gabriel, that my duty calls me to the king's side. This evening you can unfold your plan to me at your leisure,—and it must be a noble one, since it comes from your brain; meanwhile I beseech you to satisfy my curiosity and my impatience in a few words. What do you mean to do, Gabriel?"

"In two words, Monseigneur, *take Calais*," said Gabriel, calmly.

"Take Calais!" almost shouted the Duc de Guise, falling back in surprise.

"You forget, Monseigneur," said Gabriel, with the same tranquil air, "that you promised me not to be horrified at the first impression."

"Oh, but have you considered this carefully?" said the duke. "Take Calais, defended by a strong garrison, by impregnable fortifications, and by the sea!—Calais, which has been in the power of England more than two centuries! Calais, guarded as carefully as the very key of France! I love an audacious scheme; but will this not be a rash one?"

"Yes, Monseigneur," Gabriel replied; "but it is just because it is such a rash undertaking that no one would ever dream of it or suspect it that it has a better chance of success."

"In truth, that is very possible," said the duke, thoughtfully.

"When you have listened to me, Monseigneur, you will say, 'It is certain!' The rule of conduct to be observed is clearly marked out for us in advance,—to keep it in most absolute secrecy, to throw the enemy off the scent by some false manœuvre, and to appear before the town unexpectedly. In a fortnight Calais will be ours."

"But," the duke rejoined earnestly, "these general indications are not sufficient. Your plan, Gabriel,—you have a plan?"

"Yes, Monseigneur; it is simple, but sure—"

Gabriel had not time to conclude, for at that moment the door opened and the Comte de Saint-Remy entered, attended by a number of nobles attached to the Guise party.

"His Majesty awaits the lieutenant-general of the kingdom at the council-board," said Saint-Remy.

"I am at your service, gentlemen," rejoined the duke, saluting the new-comers.

Then turning quickly to Gabriel, he said in a low voice,—

"I must leave you now, my friend, as you see; but the unspeakably magnificent scheme which you have thrown into my brain will not leave me the whole day, I promise you. If you really think such a project can be executed, I believe I am capable of understanding you. Can you return here this evening at eight? We shall have the whole night to ourselves without fear of interruption."

"I will be prompt to the hour," said Gabriel, "and I will make good use of my time meanwhile."

"I make bold to remind Monseigneur that it is now after two," said the Comte de Saint-Remy.

"I am here; I am quite ready!" the duke responded.

He took a few steps toward the door, then turned and looked at Gabriel, and approaching him once more, as if to be sure that he had understood him aright,—

"Take Calais?" he said again in a low voice, and with a sort of questioning inflection.

And Gabriel, bowing his head affirmatively, replied with his sweet, calm smile,—

"Yes, take Calais."

The Duc de Guise went to attend the council, and Gabriel followed him from the room and left the Louvre.

CHAPTER XI
GLIMPSES AT DIVERS MEN OF THE SWORD

Aloyse was standing at the lower window of the house anxiously awaiting Gabriel's return. When she finally espied him, she raised to heaven her eyes filled with tears; but tears of happiness and gratitude they were this time.

She ran and opened the door with her own hands to her beloved master.

"God be praised that I see you once more, Monseigneur!" she cried. "Do you come from the Louvre? Have you seen the king?"

"Yes, I have seen him," Gabriel replied.

"Well?"

"Well, my good nurse, once more I have to wait."

"More waiting!" Aloyse exclaimed, wringing her hands. "Holy Virgin! it is very hard and very sad to wait."

"It would be impossible," said Gabriel, "if I had not work to do meanwhile. But I will work with a will, and thank God, I can beguile the tedium of the journey by thinking steadfastly of the goal."

He entered the parlor, and threw his mantle over the back of a couch.

He did not see Martin-Guerre, who was sitting in a corner plunged in deep reflections.

"Come, come, Martin, you sluggard, what are you about?" cried Dame Aloyse to the squire. "Can't you even help Monseigneur to take off his cloak?"

"Oh, pardon! pardon!" Martin exclaimed, rousing himself from his revery, and leaping from his seat.

"All right, Martin, don't disturb yourself," said Gabriel. "Aloyse, I wish you would not trouble poor Martin; his zeal and devotion are more necessary to me than ever at this moment, and I have some very serious matters to talk over with him."

Vicomte d'Exmès's slightest wish was sacred to Aloyse. She favored the squire with her sweetest smile, now that he was restored to grace, and discreetly left the room, to leave Gabriel more at liberty to say what was in his mind.

"Martin," said he, when they were alone, "what were you doing there? What were you thinking about so deeply?"

"Monseigneur," Martin-Guerre replied, "I was cudgelling my brain to solve in some degree the enigma of our friend this morning."

"Well, how have you succeeded?" asked Gabriel, smiling.

"Very indifferently, alas! Monseigneur. If I must confess it, I have been able to see nothing but darkness, however widely I have opened my eyes."

"But I told you, Martin, that I thought I could see something better than that."

"What is it, Monseigneur? I am almost dead trying to find out."

"The time has not come to tell you," said Gabriel.

"You are still devoted to me, Martin?"

"Does Monseigneur put that as a question?"

"No, Martin, I say it by way of commendation. Now I appeal to this devotion of which I speak. You must for a time forget yourself, forget the shadow which darkens your life, and which we will drive away hereafter. I promise you. But at present I need you, Martin."

"So much the better! so much the better! so much the better!" cried Martin-Guerre.

"But let us have no misunderstanding," said Gabriel. "I have need of your whole being, of your whole life, and all your manhood; are you willing to place yourself in my hands, to postpone your private troubles, and devote yourself solely to my fortunes?"

"Am I willing!" cried Martin; "why, Monseigneur, it is not only my duty to do so, but will be my greatest pleasure. By Saint Martin! I have been separated from you only too long, and I long to make up for lost time! Though there be a legion of Martin-Guerres inside my clothes, never fear, Monseigneur, I will laugh at them all. So long as you are standing there in front of me, I will see nobody but you in the world."

"Brave heart!" said Gabriel. "But you must consider, Martin, that the enterprise in which I ask you to engage is full of danger and pitfalls."

"*Basta*! I will leap over them!" said Martin, snapping his fingers carelessly.

"We shall hazard our lives a hundred times over, Martin."

"The higher the stake, the better the sport, Monseigneur."

"But this terrible game, once we engage in it, my friend, cannot be laid aside until it is finished."

"Then none but a fine player should take part in it," rejoined the squire, proudly.

"Not so fast!" said Gabriel; "despite all your resolution, you do not appreciate the formidable and extraordinary peril which may attend the almost superhuman conflict into which you and I are about to plunge; and after all, our efforts may be unrewarded,—remember that! Martin, consider all this carefully; the plan which I must carry out almost makes me afraid myself, when I examine it."

"Very good! Danger and I are old acquaintances," said Martin, with a very self-sufficient air; "and when one has had the honor of being hanged—"

"Martin," Gabriel interrupted, "we must defy the elements, exult in the tempest, laugh at the impossible!"

"Indeed we will!" said Martin-Guerre. "To tell the truth, Monseigneur, since my hanging, the days which have passed over my head have seemed to me like days of grace; and I am not inclined to find fault with the good Lord for that portion of the surplus which He has seen fit to allot to me. Whatever the merchant lets you have over and above the bargain, there is no need to account for; if you do, you are either an ingrate or a fool."

"Well, then, Martin, it's agreed, is it?" said Vicomte d'Exmès; "you will go with me and share my lot?"

"To hell itself, Monseigneur! so long as you don't ask me to set Satan at defiance, for I am a good Catholic."

"Have no fear on that score," said Gabriel. "By going with me you may perhaps endanger your welfare in this world, but not in the next."

"That is all that I care to know," rejoined Martin. "But is there nothing else than my life, Monseigneur, that you ask of me?"

"Yes," said Gabriel, smiling at the heroic ingenuousness of that question; "yes, indeed, Martin-Guerre, there is another great service that you must render me."

"What is it, Monseigneur?"

"I want you, as soon as possible,—this very day, if you can,—to find me a dozen or so companions of your mettle, daring and strong and resolute, who fear neither fire nor sword, who can endure hunger and thirst, heat and cold, who will obey like angels, and fight like devils. Can you do it?"

"That depends. Will they be well paid?" asked Martin.

"A piece of gold for every drop of their blood," said Gabriel. "My fortune causes me the least concern, alas! in the holy but perilous task which I must carry through to the end."

"At that price, Monseigneur," said the squire, "I will get together in two hours that number of dare-devils, who will not complain of their wounds, I assure you. In France, and in Paris especially, the supply of that sort of blackguard never fails. But in whose service are they to be?"

"In my own," said Vicomte d'Exmès. "I am going to make the campaign which I now have in mind as a volunteer, and not as captain of the Guards; so I need to have retainers of my own."

"Oh! if that is so, Monseigneur," said Martin, "I have right at my call, and ready at any moment, five or six of my old comrades in the Lorraine war. They are pining away, poor devils, since you dismissed them. How glad they will be to be under fire again with you for their leader! And so it is for yourself that I am to enlist recruits? Oh, well, then, I will present the full complement to you this evening."

"Very good," said Gabriel. "You must make it an essential condition of their employment that they be ready to leave Paris immediately, and to follow me wherever I go, without question or comment, and without even looking to see whether we are marching north or south."

"They will march toward glory and wealth, Monseigneur, with bandaged eyes."

"Well, then, I will reckon upon them and upon you, Martin. As for yourself, I will give you—"

"Let us not speak of that, Monseigneur," Martin interposed.

"On the contrary, we will speak of it. If we survive the fray, my brave fellow, I bind myself solemnly, here and now, to do for you what you will then have done for me, and in my turn to assist you against your enemies, never fear. Meanwhile, your hand, my faithful friend."

"Oh, Monseigneur!" Martin-Guerre exclaimed, respectfully kissing his master's extended hand.

"Come, now, Martin," continued Gabriel, "set about your quest at once. Discretion and courage! Now I must be alone for a time."

"Pardon! but will Monseigneur remain in the house?" asked Martin.

"Yes, until seven o'clock. I am not to go to the Louvre until eight."

"In that case," rejoined the squire, "I hope to be able to show you, before you leave, some specimens of the make up of your troop."

He saluted and left the room, as proud as a peacock, and already absorbed in his important commission.

Gabriel remained alone the rest of the day, studying the plan which Jean Peuquoy had handed him, making notes, and pacing thoughtfully up and down his apartment.

It was essential that he should be able to answer satisfactorily every objection that the Duc de Guise might raise.

He only broke the silence from time to time by repeating, with a firm voice and eager heart,—

"I will save you, dear father! My own Diane, I will save you!"

About six o'clock, Gabriel, yielding to the insistence of Aloyse, was just taking a little food, when Martin-Guerre entered, very serious and stately.

"Monseigneur," said he, "will it please you to receive six or seven of those who aspire to the honor of serving France and the king under your orders?"

"What! six or seven already?" cried Gabriel.

"Yes, six or seven who are strangers to you. Our old Metz companions will make up the twelve. They are all delighted to risk their necks for such a master as you, and accept any conditions that you choose to impose upon them."

"Upon my word, you have lost no time," said Vicomte d'Exmès. "Well, let me see the men; show them in."

"One at a time, shall I not?" rejoined Martin. "Monseigneur can form a better opinion of them then."

"Very well, one at a time," said Gabriel.

"One word more," added the squire. "I need not tell Monsieur le Vicomte that all these men are known to me either personally or through reliable information. Their dispositions and their peculiarities are varied; but they have one characteristic in common,—namely, a well-proved courage. I can answer to Monseigneur for that essential quality, if he will only be indulgent toward some little peccadilloes of no consequence."

After this preliminary discourse, Martin-Guerre left the room a moment, and returned almost immediately, followed by a tall fellow with a swarthy complexion, a reckless, clever face, and very quick of movement.

"Ambrosio," said Martin, introducing him.

"Ambrosio! that's a foreign name. Is he not a Frenchman?" asked Gabriel.

"Who knows?" said Ambrosio. "I was a foundling; and since I grew up, I have lived in the Pyrenees, one foot in France and the other in Spain; and, upon my word! I have, with a good heart, taken advantage of my double bar-sinister, without any ill feeling either against God or my mother."

"And how have you lived?" Gabriel asked.

"Well, it's just like this," said Ambrosio. "Being entirely impartial as between my two countries, I have always tried, to the best of my poor ability, to break down the barriers between them, and to open to each the advantages of the other, and by this free exchange of the gifts which each of them owes to Providence, to contribute, like a pious son, with all my power to their mutual prosperity."

"In a word," put in Martin-Guerre, "Ambrosio does a little smuggling."

"But," Ambrosio continued, "being a marked man by the Spanish as well as the French authorities, and unappreciated and hunted by my fellow-citizens on both sides of the Pyrenees at once, I concluded to evacuate the neighborhood, and come to Paris, the city which is overflowing with means of livelihood for brave men."

"Where Ambrosio will be happy," interjected Martin, "to place at the disposal of Vicomte d'Exmès his daring, his address, and his long experience of fatigue and danger."

"Ambrosio the smuggler, accepted!" said Gabriel. "Another!"

Ambrosio took his leave in great delight, giving place to a man of ascetic appearance and reserved manners, clad in a long dark cape, and with a rosary of great beads around his neck.

Martin-Guerre introduced him under the name of Lactance.

"Lactance," he added, "has already served under the orders of Monsieur de Coligny, who was sorry to lose him, and will give Monseigneur a very favorable account of him. But Lactance is a devout Catholic, and was very averse to serving under a commander who is tainted with heresy."

Lactance, without a word, signified his assent by motions of his head and hands to what Martin had said, who thereupon continued:—

"This pious veteran will, as his duty requires, put forth his best efforts to give satisfaction to Vicomte d'Exmès; but he asks that every facility may be granted him for the unrestricted and rigorous practice of those religious observances which his eternal welfare demands. Being compelled by the profession of arms which he has adopted and by his natural inclination to fight against his brothers in Jesus Christ, and to slay as many of them as possible, Lactance wisely considers it essential to atone for these unavoidable deeds of blood by stern self-chastisement. The more ferocious Lactance is in battle the more devout is he at Mass; and he despairs of counting the number of fasts and penances which have been imposed upon him for the dead and wounded whom he has sent before their time to the foot of the Lord's throne."

"Lactance the devotee, accepted!" said Gabriel, with a smile.

Lactance, still silent, bowed low, and went out, mumbling a grateful prayer to the Most High for having granted him the favor of being employed by so valiant a warrior.

After Lactance, Martin-Guerre brought forward, under the name of Yvonnet, a young man of medium height, of refined and distinguished features, and with small, well-cared-for hands. From his ruffles to his boots, his attire was not only scrupulously clean and neat, but even rather jaunty. He made a most courteous salutation to Gabriel, and stood before him in a position as graceful as it was elegant, lightly brushing off with his hand a few grains of dust from his right sleeve.

"This, Monseigneur, is the most determined fellow of them all," said Martin-Guerre. "Yvonnet, in a hand-to-hand contest, is like an unchained lion, whose course nothing can arrest; he will cut and thrust in a sort of frenzy. But he shines especially in an assault; he must always be the first to put his foot on the first ladder, and plant the first French banner on the enemy's walls."

"Why, he is a real hero, then!" said Gabriel.

"I do my best," rejoined Yvonnet, modestly; "and Monsieur Martin-Guerre, doubtless, rates my feeble efforts somewhat above their real worth."

"No; I only do you justice," said Martin, "and I will prove it by calling attention to your faults, now that I have praised your virtues.

Yvonnet, Monseigneur, is the fearless devil that I have described only on the battlefield. To arouse his courage he must hear drums beating, arrows whistling, and cannon thundering; without those stimulants and in every-day life Yvonnet is retiring, easily moved, and nervous as a young girl. His sensitiveness demands the greatest delicacy; he doesn't like to remain alone in the darkness, he has a horror of mice and spiders, and frequently swoons for a mere scratch. His bellicose ardor, in fact, shows itself only when the smell of powder and the sight of blood intoxicate him."

"Never mind," said Gabriel; "as we propose to escort him to scenes of carnage, and not to a ball, Yvonnet the scrupulous is accepted."

Yvonnet saluted Vicomte d'Exmès according to all the rules of good-breeding, and took his leave, smiling and twirling the ends of his fine black mustache with his white hand.

Two huge blonds succeeded him, of quiet demeanor, and stiff as ramrods. One appeared to be about forty; the other could scarcely have passed his twenty-fifth year.

"Heinrich Scharfenstein, and Frantz Scharfenstein, his nephew," Martin-Guerre announced.

"The deuce! Who are these?" said Gabriel, in amazement. "Who are you, my good fellows?"

"Wir versteen nur ein wenig das franzosich" ("We only understand French a little"), said the elder of the giants.

"What?" asked Gabriel.

"We understand French poorly," the younger Colossus replied.

"They are German *reîtres*," said Martin-Guerre,—"in Italian, *condottieri*; in French, *soldats*. They sell their arms to the highest bidder, and hold their courage at a fair price. They have already served the Spaniards and the English; but the Spaniard didn't pay promptly enough, and the Briton haggled too much. Buy them, Monseigneur, and you will find you have made a great acquisition. They will never discuss an order, and will march up to the mouth of a cannon with unalterable *sang-froid*. Courage is with them a matter of bargain and sale; and provided that they receive their wages promptly, they will submit without a word of complaint to the dangerous, it may be fatal, chances of their kind of business."

"Well, I will retain these mechanics of glory," said Gabriel; "and for greater security I will pay them a month's wages in advance. But time presses; let me see the others."

Glimpses at Divers Men of the Sword.

The two German Goliaths, carrying their hands to their hats in soldierly style and as if mechanically, withdrew together, keeping step with perfect precision.

"The next is named Pilletrousse," said Martin; "here he is."

A sort of brigand, with a wild look about him and torn clothes, came in, swaying from side to side in an embarrassed way, eying Gabriel as if he were his judge.

"What makes you look so ashamed, Pilletrousse?" asked Martin, encouragingly. "Monseigneur here asked me to find some men of brave heart for him. You are a little more pronounced than the others; but really you have nothing to blush for."

Then he continued, addressing his master, in a serious tone:—

"Pilletrousse, Monseigneur, is what we call a *routier*. In the general war against the Spaniards and English he has up to this time fought on his own account. Pilletrousse haunts the high-roads, which are crowded nowadays with foreign robbers, and, in brief, he robs the robbers. As for his fellow-countrymen, he not only respects but protects them. Then, too, Pilletrousse fights and wins; he does not steal,—he lives on prize-money, not by theft. Nevertheless he has felt the necessity of confining his roving profession within more definite limits, and of harrying the enemies of France in less arbitrary fashion. Therefore he has eagerly accepted my suggestion that he should enrol himself under the banner of Vicomte d'Exmès."

"And I," said Gabriel, "will receive him on your statement, Martin-Guerre, on condition that he will no longer make the high-roads and by-ways the scene of his exploits, but will transfer it to fortified towns and the battle-field."

"Thank Monseigneur, blackguard! you are one of us," said Martin-Guerre to the *routier*, for whom, scamp though he was, he seemed to have a sort of weakness.

"Oh, yes, thank you, Monseigneur," said Pilletrousse, effusively. "I promise never again to fight single-handed against two or three, but always not less than ten."

"Very well," said Gabriel.

He who came after Pilletrousse was a pale fellow, of sad and careworn appearance, who seemed to look upon things in general with melancholy and discouragement. The finishing touch was put to the gloomy cast of his face by the seams and scars with which it was abundantly ornamented.

Martin-Guerre brought forward this the seventh and last of his recruits under the name of Malemort.

"Monseigneur le Vicomte d'Exmès," said he, "will be truly culpable if he rejects poor Malemort. He is, in truth, the victim of a sincere and profound passion for Bellona, to speak in mythological phrase. But this passion has heretofore been very unlucky. The poor fellow has a very pronounced and well-educated taste for war; he takes no pleasure except in fighting, and is only happy in the midst of great slaughter; but so far, alas! he has tasted happiness only with his lips. He has a way of plunging so blindly and madly into the thickest of the fray that he is always sure to receive some cut or slash at the first leap, which puts him *hors de combat*, and sends him to the hospital, where he lies during the remainder of the battle, groaning more over his enforced absence than from the pain of his wound. His body is one great scar; but he is vigorous yet, thank God!—he always gets well promptly. But he has to wait then for another opportunity. His long unsatisfied desire wears more upon him than the loss of all the blood he has so gloriously shed. Monseigneur, you must see that you ought not to deprive this melancholy warrior of a pleasure which may be productive of mutual benefit."

"Well, I accept Malemort very gladly, my dear Martin," said Gabriel.

A smile of satisfaction passed across Malemort's pale face. Hope caused his dull eyes to glisten; and he hastened to join his comrades with a much quicker step than when he entered the room.

"Are these all whom you have to present?" Gabriel asked his squire.

"Yes, Monseigneur; I have no others to offer at this moment. I hardly dared to hope that Monseigneur would accept them all."

"I should have been hard to suit indeed, had I not," said Gabriel; "your judgment is good and sure, Martin. Accept my congratulations upon your excellent selections."

"Well," said Martin-Guerre, modestly, "I do like to think that Malemort, Pilletrousse, the two Scharfensteins, Lactance, Yvonnet, and Ambrosio are not just the sort of fellows to be looked upon with contempt."

"I should think not!" said Gabriel. "What rough diamonds they are!"

"If Monseigneur," Martin continued, "should be willing to add to their number Landry, Chesnel, Aubriot, Contamine, and Balu, veterans of the war in Lorraine, I rather think that with Monseigneur at our head, and four or five of our people from here to wait upon us, we should have a pretty fine party to show to our friends, and better still, to our enemies."

"Yes, to be sure," said Gabriel; "arms and heads of iron! You must arm and equip these fine fellows with the least possible delay, Martin. But you have done enough for to-day. You have made good use of your time, my friend, and I thank you for it. My day, although it has been an active and painful one, is not yet ended."

"Where is Monseigneur going this evening?" asked Martin-Guerre.

"To the Louvre, to wait upon Monsieur de Guise, who expects me at eight o'clock," said Gabriel, rising. "But thanks to your prompt zeal, Martin, I hope that some of the difficulties which might have arisen in my interview with the duke are removed beforehand."

"Oh, I am very happy to know it, Monseigneur!"

"And so am I, Martin. You can't dream how necessary it is that I should succeed! Oh, I will succeed!"

The noble youth repeated in his heart as he walked to the door to take his way to the Louvre,—

"Yes, I will save you, dear father; my own Diane, I will save you!"

CHAPTER XII
THE CLEVERNESS OF STUPIDITY

Let us in imagination pass over sixty leagues of space and two weeks of time, and return to Calais toward the close of November, 1557.

Twenty-five days had not elapsed since Vicomte d'Exmès's departure when a messenger from him presented himself at the gates of the English city.

This man asked to be taken to the governor, Lord Wentworth, that he might place in his hands the ransom of his former prisoner.

This messenger seemed to be extremely awkward, and very imprudent; for it was of no use to show him which way to go. Twenty times he passed without entering the great gate which they almost split their throats in their endeavors to point out to him, and he stupidly persisted in knocking at disused posterns and gates; so that the idiot actually made almost the complete circuit of the exterior fortifications of the place.

At last, by dint of directions, each more exact than the last, he consented to allow himself to be put upon the right course; and so great was the power, even in those far-off days, of the magic words, "I have ten thorn sand crowns for the governor," that as soon as rigorous precautions had been observed, and the man had been searched, and Lord Wentworth's orders taken, the bearer of so considerable a sum was readily allowed to enter the city.

Decidedly the Golden Age is the only one in history that was not an age of money!

This stupid envoy of Gabriel lost his way again more than once in the streets of Calais before he succeeded in finding the governor's mansion, which was pointed out to him, however, every hundred paces by some compassionate soul. He seemed to have an idea that he ought to ask every party of guards that he met where he could find Lord Wentworth, and then he would hasten in the direction indicated.

After wasting an hour in traversing a space which should have occupied ten minutes at most, he succeeded at last in reaching the governor's residence.

He was ushered almost immediately into the presence of Lord Wentworth, who received him with his air of accustomed gravity, which seemed almost to be positively gloomy on this occasion.

When he had explained the purpose of his mission and had placed a bag filled with gold upon the table, the Englishman asked,—

"Did Vicomte d'Exmès simply instruct you to hand me this money, and add no message for me?"

Pierre (so the messenger was called) looked at Lord Wentworth with an open-mouthed astonishment which did little credit to his natural talents.

"My Lord," said he at last, "I have no commission to execute with you except to hand you the ransom. At least my master gave me no further instructions; and I do not understand—"

"Oh, it's all right!" Lord Wentworth interposed with a disdainful smile. "I see that Monsieur le Vicomte d'Exmès has become more reasonable since I last saw him. I congratulate him that such is the case. The air of the court of France induces forgetfulness! so much the better for those who breathe it!"

He muttered beneath his breath as if speaking to himself,—

"Indeed, the power to forget is often the better half of happiness!"

"Has my Lord any message to send to my master?" rejoined the messenger, who seemed to listen with a very careless and stupid air to these melancholy asides of the Briton.

"I have nothing to say to Monsieur d'Exmès, since he sends no word to me," retorted Lord Wentworth, dryly. "You may say to him, however, if you choose, that for another month—that is, until January 1, do you understand-I shall be at his service in both my capacities, as a gentleman and as governor of Calais. He will understand."

"Until January 1?" Pierre repeated. "I will tell him, my Lord."

"Very good! here is your receipt, my friend, and a trifle besides, as a slight recompense for the tedium of your long journey. Take it, pray!"

The man, who seemed at first to have some scruples, thought better of them, and accepted the purse that Lord Wentworth offered him.

"Thanks, my Lord," said he. "Will my Lord grant me still another favor?"

"What is that?" asked the governor.

"Vicomte d'Exmès contracted another debt during his stay here, to one of the citizens of the town, named—what was his name?—Pierre Peuquoy, whose guest he was."

"Well?" said Lord Wentworth.

"Will my Lord allow me to seek out this Pierre Peuquoy presently, to repay the amount he advanced?"

"To be sure," said the governor. "I will send some one to show you his house. Here is your passport to leave Calais. I should be glad to allow you to remain here a few days; but the regulations strictly forbid our entertaining a stranger, especially a Frenchman. Adieu, then, my friend, and a pleasant journey to you!"

"Adieu, my Lord, with many thanks."

On leaving the governor's house, the messenger, not without going astray a dozen times, made his way to Rue du Martroi, where our readers may remember that Pierre Peuquoy the armorer dwelt.

Gabriel's envoy found Pierre Peuquoy in his workshop more cast down even than Lord Wentworth in his palace. He was received with marked indifference by the armorer, who mistook him at first for a mechanic.

But when the new-comer announced himself as having come on behalf of Vicomte d'Exmès, the good burgher's face suddenly brightened up.

"From Vicomte d'Exmès!" he cried.

Then turning to one of his apprentices, who was within hearing, putting things to rights in the shop, he said carelessly,—

"Quentin, leave us and tell my cousin Jean that a messenger from Vicomte d'Exmès has arrived."

The discomfited apprentice left the room to obey his master's orders.

"Now you can speak, my friend," rejoined Pierre Peuquoy, eagerly. "Oh, we were sure that the noble lord would not forget us! Speak at once, I beg! What do you bring us from him?"

"His compliments and gratitude, this purse of gold, and these words, 'Remember the 5th!' which he said you would understand."

"Is that all?" asked Pierre Peuquoy.

"Everything, Master. They are very exacting in this neighborhood," thought the messenger. "They scarcely seem to care for good golden crowns; but they have some mysterious secrets which the Devil himself could not understand."

"There are three of us in this house," continued the armorer; "my cousin Jean and my sister Babette as well as myself. You have executed your commission so far as I am concerned; but have you no other for Babette or Jean?"

Jean Peuquoy the weaver entered the shop just in time to hear Gabriel's messenger reply,—

"I have nothing to say to anybody but you, Master Pierre Peuquoy, and to you I have said all that I was commanded to say."

"Very well! You see, brother," said Pierre, turning to Jean, "Monsieur le Vicomte d'Exmès is grateful to us; he returns our money with all due promptitude. Monsieur le Vicomte d'Exmès sends this message to us, 'Remember!' but he himself does not remember!"

"Alas!" sighed a weak, piteous voice behind the curtain.

It was poor Babette, who had heard all.

"One moment," rejoined Jean, who persisted in hoping against hope. "My friend," he continued, addressing the messenger, "if you are of Monsieur d'Exmès's household, you must know one of his retainers and your fellow-servant named Martin-Guerre?"

"Martin-Guerre? Yes, to be sure, Martin-Guerre, the squire. Yes, I know him, Master."

"Is he still in Monsieur d'Exmès's service?"

"He is."

"Did he know that you were coming to Calais?"

"He did know it," the man replied. "He was present, I remember, when I left Monsieur d'Exmès's house. He accompanied me with his—with our master as far as the city-gate, and saw me well on my way."

"And did he give you no message for me, or for any one in this house?"

"Nothing at all, I tell you again."

"Now don't lose your patience, Pierre," continued Jean. "My friend, perhaps Martin-Guerre enjoined upon you to deliver your message privately? But you may as well understand that all precautions are of no avail. We know the truth now. The suffering of—the person to whom Martin-Guerre owes reparation has opened our eyes to everything; so you may speak freely before us. And yet if you still have some doubts upon this point, we will withdraw; and the person to whom I alluded, and whom Martin-Guerre indicated to you, will come and talk with you privately at once."

"By my faith!" said the messenger, "I swear to you that I don't understand one word of all your talk."

"That is enough, and you may as well be content, Jean," cried Pierre Peuquoy, whose eyes were inflamed with anger. "By the memory of my father, Jean! I cannot conceive what pleasure you can take in dwelling upon the insult which has been put upon us."

Jean sadly bowed his head without speaking, for there was only too much reason in what his cousin said.

"Will you be kind enough to count this money?" asked the messenger, who was rather ill at ease in the part he was playing.

"It is not worth the trouble," said Jean, who was more composed, though no less depressed than Pierre. "Take this for yourself, my friend. I will bring you food and drink as well."

"Thanks for the money," returned the envoy, who seemed, nevertheless, decidedly loath to take it. "As for eating and drinking, I am neither hungry nor thirsty, for I breakfasted at Nieullay. I must take my leave at once, for your governor has forbidden my making a long stay in the city."

"We will not detain you, then, my friend," said Jean. "Adieu! Say to Martin-Guerre—but no! we have nought to say to him. Say to Monsieur d'Exmès that we are grateful to him, and that we will remember the 5th. But we hope that he, as well, will remember."

"Listen to me a moment," added Pierre Peuquoy, emerging for the time from his gloomy meditation. "You may also say to your master that we will continue to await him for another month. In that space of time you will be able to return to Paris, and he to send some one hither; but if the present year comes to an end without our hearing from him, we shall believe that his heart has ceased to remember, and we shall be as sorry for him as for ourselves. An upright and honorable gentleman, who is so sure in his memory of money loaned, ought to remember still more tenaciously secrets intrusted to him. With that, my friend, adieu."

"May God keep you!" said Gabriel's messenger, as he rose to depart. "All your questions and all your messages shall be faithfully reported to my master."

Jean Peuquoy accompanied the man to the door, while Pierre remained despondently in his corner.

The lounging messenger, after making many a détour, and losing his way many more times in this perplexing city of Calais, where he had so much difficulty in finding his way about, at last reached the principal gate, showed his passport, and was allowed to pass through after being carefully searched.

He walked for three quarters of an hour at a quick pace without a halt, and did not slacken his gait until he was fully a league from the city.

Then he permitted himself a short rest, and sitting on a patch of turf, seemed to be lost in thought, while a satisfied smile shone in his eyes and lurked about his lips.

"I don't know what there is in that city of Calais," he mused, "to make each man more melancholy than his neighbor, and more mysterious. Wentworth seemed to have an account to settle with Monsieur d'Exmès, and the Peuquoys surely have some grudge against Martin-Guerre. But what have I to do with that? I am not sad, by any means! I have what I want and what I need! Not a stroke of the pen, and not a scrap of paper, it is true; but everything is impressed upon my memory, and with the aid of Monsieur d'Exmès's plan I can easily reproduce the whole place, which has such a depressing effect upon others, but the memory of which makes me equally light-hearted."

In his imagination he ran over all the streets and boulevards and fortified positions, to which his affected stupidity had led him so conveniently.

"It is all there," said he, "as plain and clear as though I had it before my eyes at this moment. The Duc de Guise will be well pleased. Thanks to this little expedition, and to the invaluable suggestions of the captain of his Majesty's Guards, we may bring our dear Vicomte d'Exmès, also his squire, and with a strong force at their back, to the rendezvous appointed by Lord Wentworth and Pierre Peuquoy for a month hence. In six weeks, with the help of God, and favorable circumstances, we shall be masters of Calais, or I will lose my name there!"

And our readers will agree that the latter alternative would indeed have been calamitous, when they learn that this name was that of Maréchal Pierre Strozzi, one of the most celebrated and skilful engineers of the sixteenth century.

After a few moments' rest, Pierre Strozzi resumed his journey, as if he were in great haste to be back at Paris. He thought much about Calais, but very little about its inhabitants.

CHAPTER XIII
DECEMBER 31, 1557

Our readers doubtless have divined why Pierre Strozzi had found Lord Wentworth in such bitter and angry mood, and why the governor of Calais spoke so haughtily and ironically of Vicomte d'Exmès.

It was because Madame de Castro's detestation of him seemed to increase from day to day.

When he would send to ask her leave to call upon her, she would always try to find an excuse for putting him off. But if she were sometimes compelled to submit to the infliction of his presence, her cold and formal reception betrayed only too plainly her feeling toward him, and left him more despairing on each successive occasion.

However, he had not yet grown weary in his love for her. With nothing to hope for, he still did not despair. He desired, at least, to comport himself toward Diane as became the perfect gentleman who had left behind at the court of Mary of England a reputation for most exquisite refinement and courtesy. He overwhelmed his fair captive with his attentions. She was waited upon with the utmost consideration and regal luxury. He had given her a French page, and had engaged for her one of those Italian musicians who were in such high repute at the period of the Renaissance. Sometimes Diane would find in her apartments dresses and ornaments of enormous value, which Lord Wentworth had caused to be sent from London for her; but she never noticed them.

On one occasion he gave a great fête in her honor at which he assembled all the notable English there were in Calais or in France. His invitations even crossed the channel; but Madame de Castro obstinately refused to appear.

Lord Wentworth, being repulsed with such coldness and disdain, said to himself day after day that it would surely be much better for his peace of mind to accept the princely ransom which Henri II. offered, and give Diane her freedom.

But by doing so he would give her up to the welcome embraces of Gabriel d'Exmès, and the Briton could never find in his heart sufficient strength and courage to make so great a sacrifice possible.

"No! no!" he would say to himself, "if she will not be mine, at all events she shall belong to nobody else!"

While he was thus irresolute and suffering, the days and weeks rolled away.

On the 31st of December, 1557, Lord Wentworth had succeeded in making his way into Madame de Castro's apartments. We have said before that he could scarcely breathe elsewhere, although he always left her more melancholy and more in love than ever; but to see Diane, stern though her glance might be, and to hear her voice, however ironical its tones, had become the most imperious necessity for him.

He remained standing while they talked, and she sat before the high chimney-piece.

They talked upon the one harrowing subject which united them and kept them asunder at the same time.

"Suppose, Madame," said the passionate governor, "that at last, beside myself on account of your cruelty, and enraged by your contempt, I should forget that I am a gentleman and your host?"

"You would dishonor yourself, my Lord, but would cast no stain upon me," Diane replied firmly.

"We shall be dishonored together," Lord Wentworth retorted. "You are in my power! Where will you find shelter?"

"*Mon Dieu*! in death," she calmly replied.

Lord Wentworth turned pale and shuddered. That he should cause the death of such as Diane!

"Such obstinacy is not natural," he added, shaking his head. "In reality you would be afraid to drive me to extremities, if you did not still cling to some insane hope, Madame. You are always dwelling upon the happening of some impossible event. Come, tell me, from whom can you be expecting succor at this hour?"

"From God, from the king—" Diane replied.

There was a sort of rising inflection in her voice and in her thought as well,—a hesitation which Lord Wentworth knew only too well how to interpret.

"She is doubtless thinking of that d'Exmès," he said to himself.

But it was a dangerous memory which he did not dare to touch upon or to arouse.

He contented himself with the bitter rejoinder,—

"Yes, count upon the king and upon God! But if God had thought fit to help you, Madame. He would have come to your rescue the very first day, I should think! and here a year has passed away, ending to-day, during which you have not felt the benefit of His protection."

"Then I will rest my hopes on the year which begins to-morrow," replied Diane, raising her lovely eyes to heaven, as if imploring aid from on high.

"As for the King of France, your father," Lord Wentworth continued, "I imagine that he has on hand matters of sufficient moment to occupy all his power and engross the whole of his thoughts. France is in even greater peril than his daughter."

"Ah, it is you who say that!" Diane retorted in a tone of doubt.

"Lord Wentworth does not lie, Madame. Do you know in what condition your august father's affairs are?"

"How can I know in this prison?" Diane replied, who nevertheless could not forbear a movement which betokened interest.

"You have only to ask me," Lord Wentworth rejoined, delighted to be listened to willingly for a moment, even as the bearer of evil tidings. "Well, then, you must know that the return of the Duc de Guise to Paris has in no way ameliorated the situation of France as yet. Some troops have been recruited, and a few places reinforced,—nothing more. At the present moment there is hesitation and uncertainty everywhere. Their full military strength, concentrated on the northern frontier, has succeeded in stopping the triumphant progress of the Spaniards; but the French generals are undertaking nothing on their own account. Will they attack Luxembourg? Will they make a descent on Picardy? Nobody knows. Will they try to retake St. Quentin, or Ham—?"

"Or Calais," Diane interposed, fixing her eyes keenly upon the governor, to note the effect upon his features of this chance shot.

But Lord Wentworth did not even frown; he said with a proud smile,—

"Oh, Madame, allow me to lay that question aside without considering it. One who has any idea at all of warfare will not admit for a moment such an insane supposition; and Monsieur le Duc de Guise has had too much experience to expose himself by such an extraordinary and impracticable undertaking to the ridicule of every man in Europe who wears a sword."

At that moment there was some confusion at the door, and an archer rushed in without ceremony.

Lord Wentworth went to meet him, much irritated.

"What is the meaning of your daring to interrupt me thus?" he demanded.

"Pardon me, my Lord," the archer replied. "Lord Derby sent me to you in all haste."

"And for what pressing reason? Come, explain yourself!"

"Information has been received by Lord Derby that an advance-guard of two thousand French arquebusiers was seen yesterday two leagues from Calais, and his Lordship sent me to notify my Lord at once."

"Aha!" cried Diane, who made no attempt to conceal her satisfaction.

But Lord Wentworth coolly said to the archer,—

"And was it for this only that you have had the impudence to follow me here, villain?"

"My Lord," said the poor devil, in his stupefaction, "Lord Derby—"

"Lord Derby," the governor interposed, "is a short-sighted individual, who takes mounds of earth for mountains. Go and tell him so from me."

"How about the guards, my Lord, which Lord Derby ordered doubled as quickly as possible?"

"Let them remain as they are, and bother me no more with these ridiculous phantoms!"

The archer bowed respectfully and left the room.

"Nevertheless, my Lord," said Diane de Castro, "you see that in the opinion of one of your ablest lieutenants, my insane prevision is capable of being realized to the full."

"I feel more than ever constrained to undeceive you upon this point," Lord Wentworth responded with imperturbable coolness. "I can give you the explanation of this false alarm in two words, nor can I conceive how Lord Derby allowed himself to be deceived by it."

"Let us see," said Madame de Castro, intensely eager for light upon a subject upon which her whole life seemed to be concentrated.

"Very well, Madame," continued Lord Wentworth; "one of two things has happened: either Messieurs de Guise and de Nevers, who are, I admit, skilful and prudent commanders, mean to revictual Ardres and Boulogne, and are on their way thither with the troops whose presence has been announced, or else they are making a feint against Calais for the purpose of calming the fears of Ham and St. Quentin, and mean to try to take one of those towns by surprise, by suddenly retracing their steps."

"But how do you know, Monsieur," rejoined Madame de Castro, with more rashness than discretion,—"how do you know, pray, that their feint has not been made against Ham or St. Quentin, in order to surprise Calais more effectually?"

Fortunately she had to deal with an immovable conviction, rooted upon national and personal pride as well.

"I have already had the honor of assuring you, Madame," said Lord Wentworth, disdainfully, "that Calais is one of those places that cannot possibly be surprised or taken; before it can even be approached, Fort Ste. Agathe must be carried, and the fort of Nieullay as well. To carry all these posts would take a fortnight at least of unvarying success; and during those fifteen days England would be warned of the danger, and would have ample time—yes, fifteen times what would be necessary—to pour forth all her might to rescue her precious city. Take Calais! Ah, I cannot help laughing at the bare idea!"

Madame de Castro, wounded to the quick, bitterly retorted,—

"The source of my sorrow is to you a source of delight. How can you suppose that our souls could ever understand each other?"

"But, Madame," cried Lord Wentworth, growing pale, "I only wished to destroy those delusive imaginings of yours which keep us asunder. I wished to prove to you as clearly as the sun shines that you are feeding upon chimeras, and that the French court must have gone mad before such an attempt as you are dreaming of could ever be imagined there."

"There is such a thing as heroic madness, my Lord," said Diane, proudly; "and I am sure that there are great-souled men too, whose love of glory—nay, whose simple devotion would prevent them from drawing back from such sublime extravagance."

"Oh, yes!—Monsieur d'Exmès, for example!" cried Wentworth, carried away by jealous fury which he could no longer restrain.

"Who told you of that name?" asked Madame de Castro, in amazement.

"Confess, Madame," the governor rejoined, "that you have had that name upon your lips ever since the beginning of this interview, and that in your inmost heart when you were invoking the aid of God and your father you were also thinking of this third liberator."

"Am I obliged to render an account of my thoughts to you?" said Diane.

"You need render no account to me, for I know all," replied the governor. "I know some things of which you have no idea, Madame, and which it suits my pleasure to tell you to-day, to show you how little you can build upon the ecstatic passion of these romantic lovers. Notably, I know that Vicomte d'Exmès was made a prisoner at St. Quentin when you were, and was brought here to Calais at the same time with you."

"Can it be?" cried Diane, astounded beyond measure.

"Oh, there is more than that, Madame! Otherwise I should have told you nothing. For two months Monsieur d'Exmès has been at liberty."

"And I never knew that a friend was suffering with me, and so near me!" said Diane.

"You did not know it, but he did, Madame," said the governor. "I must confess that when he first learned the fact he exhausted himself in terrible threats against me. Not only did he challenge me to single combat, but—as you foresaw, with a charming sympathy—carrying his love to the point of madness, he declared to my face his determination to take Calais."

"My hopes are greater than ever, then," said Diane.

"Don't hope for too much, Madame," said Lord Wentworth; "for once more I tell you, since Monsieur d'Exmès addressed his appalling farewell to me six months have passed. To be sure, I have had news from my aggressor in that time. At the end of November he sent me, with scrupulous promptness, the amount of his ransom; but not a word of his haughty defiance."

"Wait, my Lord," Diane retorted. "Monsieur d'Exmès will find a way to pay his debts of every description."

"I doubt it, Madame, for the day of maturity will soon be past."

"What do you mean?" asked Madame de Castro.

"I sent word, Madame, to Vicomte d'Exmès, by the messenger who came to me from him, that I would await the fulfilment of his double challenge until the 1st of January, 1558. It is now Dec. 31, 1557."

"Well, then," Diane interrupted him, "he has twelve hours still."

"True, Madame," responded Wentworth; "but if I hear nothing from him by to-morrow at this hour—"

He did not finish his sentence. Lord Derby at this moment burst into the room in terror.

"My Lord," he cried, "I was right! It was the French, and they are marching upon Calais!"

"Nonsense!" rejoined Wentworth, changing color in spite of himself,—"nonsense! It is impossible! Who says it is so? More rumors and gossip and fanciful alarms?"

"Alas! no, but facts, unfortunately," Lord Derby replied.

"Not so loud, Derby; don't speak so loud," said the governor, approaching his lieutenant. "Come, come, be cool! What do you mean by your facts?"

Lord Derby replied in a low voice, in accordance with the request of his superior officer, who did not choose to show any signs of weakness before Diane.

"The French attacked Fort Ste. Agathe unexpectedly. Nothing was in readiness to resist their assault,—neither walls nor men; and I am much afraid that they are by this time masters of the first line of fortifications of Calais."

"They will still be a long way off from us," said Lord Wentworth, eagerly.

"Yes," rejoined Lord Derby; "but they will meet with no obstacle after that until they reach the bridge of Nieullay; and the bridge of Nieullay is two miles from this place."

"Have you sent reinforcements to our outposts, Derby?"

"Yes, my Lord, pardon me, without your orders,—nay, in spite of your orders."

"You have done well," said Lord Wentworth.

"Bub the reinforcements will have arrived too late."

"Who knows? Let us not be alarmed. You must go with me at once to Nieullay. We will make these rash rascals pay dear for their audacity; and if they already hold Ste. Agathe, why, we shall be free to drive them out of it."

"God grant it!" said Lord Derby; "but they have begun the game manfully."

"We will have our revenge!" replied Wentworth. "Who commands them, do you know?"

"It is not known,—probably Monsieur de Guise, or Monsieur de Nevers, at least. The ensign who rode here at full speed to bring the almost incredible news of their sudden appearance told me only that he recognized at a distance, in the front rank, your former prisoner, you remember, Vicomte d'Exmès—"

"Damnation!" cried the governor, clinching his fists. "Come, Derby, come quickly!"

Madame de Castro, with her senses sharpened, as they are apt to be at important crises, had heard almost all of Lord Derby's report, although made in a low voice.

When Lord Wentworth took leave of her, he said—

"You will excuse me, Madame; I must leave you, as business of importance—"

"Go, my Lord," she interrupted, not without a tinge of malice in her tone; "go, and try to re-establish your supremacy, which is cruelly threatened. But remember, meanwhile, two things: first, that the greatest delusions are just the ones that are not doubtful; and in the second place, that you can always rely upon the word of a French gentleman. It is not yet the 1st of January, my Lord."

Lord Wentworth, in a fury of rage, left the room without replying.

CHAPTER XIV
DURING THE BOMBARDMENT

Lord Derby was quite right in his conjectures. This is what had happened:—

The troops of Monsieur de Nevers, having made a rapid junction during the night with those of the Duc de Guise, had arrived unexpectedly by forced marches before Fort Ste. Agathe. Three thousand arquebusiers, supported by twenty-five or thirty horsemen, had carried the fort in less than an hour.

Lord Wentworth and Lord Derby reached the fort of Nieullay only in time to see their forces fleeing across the bridge to seek shelter behind the second, stronger line of fortifications of Calais.

But when the first moment of bewilderment had passed, we must admit that Lord Wentworth bore himself valiantly and well. After all, his was a noble soul, in which the pride for which his race was noted had implanted marvellous vigor.

"These Frenchmen must indeed be mad!" he said in perfect seriousness to Lord Derby. "But we will make them pay dear for their madness. Two centuries ago Calais held out a year against the English, and in their hands maintained a siege of ten years. However, we shall have no need to put forth such endurance as that. Before the end of the week, Derby, you will see the enemy beating an inglorious retreat. He has taken everything that he can carry by surprise. Now we are on our guard. So be reassured, and laugh with me at this blunder on the part of Monsieur de Guise."

"Do you mean to send to England for reinforcements?" asked Lord Derby.

"What need is there of doing so?" was the governor's proud reply. "If our reckless foes persist in their rash undertaking, in less than three days, and while Nieullay still holds them in check, all the Spanish and English forces in France will come to our assistance of their own motion. And if these haughty invaders seem to be hopelessly obstinate, why, a message sent to Dover will bring us ten thousand men in twenty-four hours. But until then let us not do them too much honor by showing too much alarm. Our nine hundred soldiers and our strong walls will give them all the work they want. They will not penetrate beyond the bridge of Nieullay!"

Nevertheless, on the following day, January 1, 1558, the French were already masters of that bridge which Lord Wentworth had designated as the utmost limit of their advance. They had opened trenches during the night, and before noon they were battering the bridge to pieces.

It was to the terrible and regular accompaniment of the double cannonading that a solemn and gloomy family drama was being enacted in the old Peuquoy dwelling.

As the urgent questions addressed by Pierre Peuquoy to Gabriel's messenger have doubtless given the reader to understand, Babette had not been able long to hide from her brother and her cousin her tears and their moving cause.

Misery did not indeed come to her by halves, poor child! The reparation which the false Martin-Guerre owed her was due not to herself alone, but to her child as well; for Babette was about to become a mother.

However, when she confessed her fault and its bitter consequences, she did not dare to tell Pierre and Jean that her future was without hope because Martin-Guerre was married.

She hardly admitted it even to her own heart. She would say to herself that it was impossible; that Monsieur d'Exmès must have been mistaken; and that God, who is kind and merciful, would not thus overwhelm and leave without resource a poor, wretched creature whose only fault had been that she had loved too well! She would artlessly repeat this childish reasoning to herself day after day, and would thus still retain some hope. She relied on Martin-Guerre; she relied on Vicomte d'Exmès. Why? Alas! she knew not; but still she hoped on.

Nevertheless, the absolute silence of both master and servant during those never-ending two months had been a fearful blow to her.

She waited with restless impatience, not unmixed with terror, for the 1st of January, which was the extreme limit of time allowed to Vicomte d'Exmès by Pierre Peuquoy.

So it was that the report, vague at first, and afterward indubitable, which spread through the city on December 31, that the French were marching upon Calais, caused her heart to leap with joy unspeakable.

She heard her brother and her cousin say that Vicomte d'Exmès would surely be among the assailants. Then of course Martin-Guerre would be there too; so Babette was justified in her hopes.

Nevertheless, she received with anguish at her heart Pierre Peuquoy's request, on the 1st of January, to come down into the parlor on the first floor, to have some conversation with Jean and himself as to what was best to be done under existing circumstances.

She made her appearance, pale and trembling, before this domestic tribunal, so to speak, which was, however, constituted of only those two men, who had an almost paternal fondness for her.

"My dear cousin, dear brother," she said with faltering voice, "here I am at your commands."

"Be seated, Babette," said Pierre, pointing to a chair which he had placed for her near his own.

Then he continued gently but very gravely,—

"At the beginning of our trouble, Babette, when our urgent questions and our alarm induced you to confess the sad truth to us, I am ashamed to remember that I had not sufficient control of myself to restrain my first impulse of anger and sorrow: I insulted you, I even threatened you; but fortunately for us both, Jean interposed."

"May God bless him for his kindness and his indulgence!" said Babette, turning to her cousin, with her eyes swimming in tears.

"Say no more about it, Babette; say no more about it," rejoined Jean, more moved than he cared to show. "I did very little indeed; and after all, the way to remedy your suffering was not to give you new cause for grief."

"So I finally realized," said Pierre. "Your repentance and your tears touched me too, Babette; my rage melted into pity, and my pity into tenderness; and I forgave you for staining our hitherto stainless name."

"Jesus will be merciful to you as you have been to me, my brother."

"Then, too," continued Pierre, "Jean reminded me that your misery might perhaps not be irreparable, and that he who had led you into error was bound legally and morally to extricate you from it."

Babette held her crimson face still lower. Singularly enough, when another than herself seemed to believe in the possibility of reparation, she herself lost all hope.

Pierre continued,—

"Despite that hope, which I welcomed with delight, of seeing your honor and ours re-established, Martin-Guerre has said never a word, and the messenger sent to Calais by Monsieur d'Exmès a month since brought no news of your seducer. But now the French are before our walls, I presume Vicomte d'Exmès and his squire are among them."

"You may be perfectly sure of that, Pierre," interposed Jean.

"I shall not contradict you, Jean. Let us assume that Monsieur d'Exmès and his squire are at this moment separated from us only by the walls and moats which protect us, or which protect the English, I should say. In that event, if we do see them again, Babette, how do you think that we ought to receive them,—as friends or foes?"

"Whatever you do will be well done, my brother," said Babette, in great alarm at the turn the conversation was taking.

"But, Babette," said her brother, "can you form no idea as to their intentions?"

"Indeed I cannot, God help me! I am simply waiting,—that's all."

"So, then, you don't know whether they are coming to save our honor, or to abandon us to our shame; whether the cannon which are playing an accompaniment to my words announce to us the approach of benefactors whom we ought to bless in our hearts, or treacherous villains who must be punished? Can you not tell me that, Babette?"

"Alas!" said Babette, "why do you ask such questions of me, poor wretched girl that I am, who know nothing except that I must pray and resign myself to my fate?"

"Why do I ask you that question, Babette? You remember what sentiments with regard to France and the French nation were instilled into us by our father. We have never looked upon the English as our fellow-countrymen, but as oppressors; and three months since, no music would have sounded more sweetly in my ears than that which fills them at this moment."

"Ah!" cried Jean, "to me it still sounds like the voice of my country calling me."

"Jean," rejoined Pierre, "the fatherland is nothing more than home on a grand scale; it is an enlargement of the family, an extension of the ties of blood. Ought we to sacrifice to it the lesser ties, the lesser family, the lesser home?"

"*Mon Dieu*! Pierre, what do you mean?" asked Babette.

"I mean this," Pierre replied: "in the rough plebeian work-stained hands of your brother, Babette, the fate of the city of Calais rests at this moment in all probability. Yes, these poor hands, blackened by my daily toil, have it in their power to deliver the key of France to her king."

"And can they hesitate?" cried Babette, who had imbibed with her mother's milk bitter hatred of the foreign yoke.

"Ah, my noble girl," said Jean, "truly you are deserving of our confidence!"

"Neither my heart nor my hands would hesitate for one moment," Pierre rejoined, "if I had it in my power to restore this fair city to King Henri's own hands, or to his representative, Monsieur le Duc de Guise. But the circumstances are such that we shall be compelled to use Monsieur d'Exmès as intermediary."

"Well, why not?" asked Babette, amazed at receiving such a reason for hesitation.

"Well," said Pierre, "however proud and happy I might be to be associated in so grand an achievement with him who was once our guest, it would be quite as distasteful to me to share the honor with a gentleman lacking bowels of compassion, who has helped to tarnish the honor of our name."

"What! you don't mean Monsieur d'Exmès, who is so kind-hearted and so loyal?"

"It is nevertheless true," said Pierre, "that your confidence in Monsieur d'Exmès, and Martin-Guerre's lack of conscience, have brought about your ruin; and yet you see that they both keep silent."

"But what *could* Monsieur d'Exmès do or say?" asked Babette.

"He could have sent Martin-Guerre here as soon as he returned to Paris, my sister, and have ordered him to bestow his name upon you! He could have sent his squire here instead of that stranger, and thus have paid the debt due your heart and the money owed to me at the same time."

"No, no; he could not have done that," said honest Babette, sadly shaking her head.

"What! he was not at liberty to give an order to his own servant?"

"What good would have been done by that order?" said Babette.

"What good?" cried Pierre. "Is there no good in atoning fora crime, or in saving a fair name from shame? Are you losing your wits, Babette?"

"Alas! no, unfortunately!" said the poor girl, weeping bitterly. "Those who lose their wits forget."

"Well, then," continued Pierre, "how, if you are in full possession of your reason, can you say that Monsieur d'Exmès has done right in not using his authority to compel your seducer to marry you?"

"To marry me! to marry me! Oh, how could he do so?" said Babette, in despair.

"What is to prevent him, pray?" exclaimed Jean and Pierre, with one voice.

Both had risen by an irresistible impulse. Babette fell upon her knees.

"Oh," she cried in her despair, "forgive me once more, dear brother! I wanted to conceal it from you. I concealed it even from my own heart! But now that you speak of our blighted honor, of France, and Monsieur d'Exmès, and unworthy Martin-Guerre, what can I do? Oh, my brain is in a whirl! You ask me if I am losing my wits. Truly I believe that I am. Come, you, who are calmer than I, tell me if I am mistaken, tell me if I was dreaming, or if what Monsieur d'Exmès told me was really true!"

"What Monsieur d'Exmès told you!" echoed Pierre, in alarm.

"Yes, in his room, the day of his departure, when I asked him to return the ring to Martin. I did not dare confess my fault to him, being a stranger. And yet he ought to have understood me; and if he did understand, how could he have told me?"

"What—what did he tell you? Go on!" cried Pierre.

"Alas! that Martin-Guerre was already married!" said Babette.

"Miserable wretch!" ejaculated Pierre Peuquoy, beside himself, and springing at his sister with uplifted hand.

"Ah! it is true, then!" said the poor child, in a faint voice; "I feel now that it is true."

She fell fainting upon the floor.

Jean had had time to seize Pierre around the waist and hold him back.

"What are you doing, Pierre?" said he, sternly. "It is not the unfortunate victim that you should strike, but the villain who caused her ruin."

"You are right," Pierre responded, already ashamed of his blind rage.

He stepped apart, stern and gloomy, while Jean, leaning over Babette, tried to resuscitate her. There was a long silence.

At last Babette opened her eyes, and seemed to be trying to remember.

"What has happened?" she asked.

She looked up with a wandering expression into the kind face of Jean Peuquoy bending over her.

Strangely enough, Jean seemed not to be very melancholy. There even was to be seen upon his pleasant face, mingled with deep pity, a sort of secret satisfaction.

"My good cousin!" said Babette, giving him her hand.

Jean Peuquoy's first words to the beloved sufferer were,—

"Don't give up hope, Babette; don't give up hope!"

But Babette's eyes fell at this moment upon the sombre and desolate figure of her brother, and she gave a convulsive start, for everything came back to her memory at once.

"Oh, Pierre, forgive me!" she cried.

As Jean made him an appealing gesture to urge him to be pitiful, Pierre advanced to his sister, raised her from the floor, and led her to a seat.

"Don't be alarmed," said he. "I have no ill-will against you. You have suffered too much. Don't be alarmed. I will say to you as Jean did, don't give up hope."

"Ah, what have I to hope for now?" she said.

"No reparation, to be sure, but vengeance, at all events," Pierre replied, frowning.

"And I," whispered Jean,—"I say to you, vengeance and reparation at the same time."

She looked at him in amazement. But before she could question him, Pierre resumed,—

"Once more, my poor sister, I forgive you. Your fault is surely no greater because a cowardly villain has deceived you twice. I love you, Babette, as I have always loved you."

Babette, happy even in her grief, threw herself into her brother's arms.

"However," continued Pierre, when he had embraced her, "my anger is by no means burned out; it is only shifted to other shoulders than yours. I repeat, I would like now to have under my foot that villanous perjurer and scoundrel Martin-Guerre!"

"Dear brother!" Babette interposed piteously.

"No! no pity for him!" cried the stern burgher. "But I owe an apology to his master, Monsieur d'Exmès; frankly, I must admit that."

"I told you so. Pierre," rejoined Jean.

"Yes, Jean, you were right, as you always are, and I was very unjust to a loyal gentleman. Now everything is explained. Nay, more, his very silence shows his delicate tact. Why should he have cruelly reminded us of an irreparable misfortune? I was wrong! And to think that I was almost on the point of allowing myself, through a grievous mistake, to give the lie to all the convictions and instincts of my whole life, and to make my beloved country, which is so dear to my heart, pay the penalty for an offence which never existed!"

"On what slight contingencies do the great events of the world turn!" was Jean Peuquoy's philosophical comment. "However, no harm has been done," he added; "and thanks to what Babette has told us, we know now that Vicomte d'Exmès has done nothing to make him unworthy of our friendship. Oh, I knew his noble heart; for I have never seen aught in him that did not compel my admiration, except his first hesitation when we broached the subject of taking our revenge for the capture of St. Quentin. But that very hesitation, in my opinion, he is endeavoring at this very moment to make amends for in most brilliant fashion."

The brave weaver raised his hand to call their attention to the loud booming of the cannon, which seemed to sound nearer every moment.

"Jean," said Pierre, "do you know what that bombardment is saying to us?"

"It tells us that Monsieur d'Exmès is there," Jean replied.

"Yes; but," he added in his cousin's ear, "it also tells us to 'remember the 5th!'"

"And we will remember it, Pierre, will we not?"

These whispered confidences alarmed Babette, who, with her mind still engrossed with the one thought, murmured,—

"What are they plotting together? Holy Virgin! If Monsieur d'Exmès is there, may God grant that Martin-Guerre be not with him!"

"Martin-Guerre?" Jean rejoined, having overheard her. "Oh, Monsieur d'Exmès must have dismissed the miserable scamp in disgrace! And he will have done well, even from the blackguard's own standpoint; for we would have challenged him and slain him the moment he set foot in Calais, would we not, Pierre?"

"I shall do that in any case," the brother replied in a tone of inflexible determination; "if not at Calais, then at Paris! I certainly shall kill him!"

"Oh," cried Babette, "this retaliation is just what I dreaded! Not for him whom I no longer love, nay, whom I despise, but for you, Pierre, and you, Jean, both so fraternally kind and so devoted to me!"

"So, Babette," said Jean Peuquoy, with emotion, "in a contest between him and me, your prayers would be offered up for me and not for him?"

"Ah," Babette replied, "that one question, Jean, is the most cruel punishment for my fault that you could inflict upon me. How could I hesitate for one instant to-day between you, who are so kind and indulgent to me, and him, so treacherous and so vile?"

"Thanks!" cried Jean. "It does me good to have you say so to me, Babette, and be sure that God will reward you for it."

"For my own part," Pierre rejoined, "I am sure that God will punish the culprit. But let us think no more about him, my cousin," he said to Jean; "for we have much else to do now, and only three days in which to make our preparations. We must go about, notify our friends, get our arms together—"

In a low voice he said once more,—

"Jean, we must remember the 5th!"

A quarter of an hour later, while Babette, in the solitude of her own chamber, was offering her thanks to God, without a clear idea of her reasons for doing so, the armorer and weaver were going about the city, intent upon the business they had in hand.

They seemed to have forgotten Martin-Guerre, who at that moment, we may say in passing, was in utter ignorance of the warm reception which awaited him in the good city of Calais, where he had never before set foot.

Meanwhile the cannon were thundering away incessantly; as Rabutin says, "charging and discharging, with fury inconceivable, their tempest of artillery."

CHAPTER XV
WITHIN THE TENT

Three days after the scene we have just described, on the 4th of January, in the evening, the French, despite Lord Wentworth's confident predictions, had made a great advance.

They had passed not only the bridge of Nieullay, but also the fort of the same name, of which they had been in possession since the morning, as well as of all the arms and stores which it contained.

From that strong position they could effectually bar the way against any Spanish or English reinforcements coming by land.

Such important results were surely well worth the three days of furious and mortal combat which they had cost.

"Is this a dream?" cried the haughty governor of Calais, when he saw his troops fleeing in disorder toward the city, despite his brave struggle to induce them to return to their posts.

To put the finishing touch to his humiliation, he had to follow them; for his duty required him to be the last to withdraw.

"Fortunately," remarked Lord Derby to him when they were safely within the walls,—"fortunately, Calais and the Old Château will be able to hold out two or three days longer, even with the few troops still at our disposal. The Risbank fort and the harbor are still open, and England is not far a way."

Lord Wentworth's council were unanimously of the opinion that their safety lay in that direction, and it was no longer time to heed the voice of pride. An express must be despatched at once to Dover. On the following day, at the latest, strong reinforcements would arrive, and Calais would be saved.

Lord Wentworth realized the situation, and decided to adopt this course. A vessel set sail at once, carrying an urgent message to the governor of Dover.

Then the council took measures to concentrate all their energies upon the defence of the Old Château, which was the vulnerable side of Calais, inasmuch as the sea, the sand-dunes, and a handful of the civic guard would be more than sufficient to protect the Risbank fort.

While the besieged were thus preparing to make a brave resistance at the probable points of attack, let us glance for a moment at the camp of the besieging army outside the city, and see particularly how Vicomte d'Exmès, Martin-Guerre, and their gallant recruits were employing themselves on this evening of January 4.

Being soldiers, not sappers and miners, and having no duties in connection with the digging of trenches or siege works, but serving only when there was fighting to be done or an assault to be made, they were now taking their well-earned rest. We need only draw aside the door of a tent pitched a little apart on the right of the camp to find Gabriel and his troop of volunteers. The tableau thus presented to view was picturesque and varied.

Gabriel, with bowed head, was sitting in a corner upon the only stool which the establishment could boast, apparently plunged in profound abstraction.

At his feet Martin-Guerre was fitting the buckle of a sword-belt. He looked anxiously at his master from time to time, but did not presume to interrupt the silent meditation in which he was absorbed.

Not far from them, on a sort of couch made of cloaks, a wounded man lay moaning. Alas! the sufferer was no other than the ill-fated Malemort.

At the other end of the tent the pious Lactance was telling his beads with great animation and fervency. Lactance had been unfortunate enough at the storming of Fort Nieullay that morning to knock on the head three of his brothers in Jesus Christ; for that he owed his conscience three hundred *Paters* and as many *Aves*. That was the ordinary penance which his confessor had laid upon him for those he killed; wounded men counted only for half.

Near him, Yvonnet, after having carefully cleaned and brushed his clothes, which were stained with mud and powder, was looking about to find some corner where the ground was not too damp, so that he might stretch himself and take a little rest, for the prolonged watching and toil were not well suited to his delicate constitution.

Two paces from Yvonnet, the two Scharfensteins, uncle and nephew, were making complicated calculations on their enormous fingers. They were figuring out the probable value of their morning's booty. The nephew had been fortunate enough to lay his hand upon a valuable suit of armor; and the worthy Teutons, with beaming countenances, were dividing in advance the money which they expected to receive for their rich prize.

The veterans, in a group in the centre of the tent, were playing at dice; and the players and bystanders alike were following with much interest the varying chances of the game.

A huge smoking torch fixed in the earth lighted up the pleased or disappointed faces, and cast an uncertain, flickering light upon the features of the others, with their contrasted expressions, which we have tried to describe and sketch in the half-darkness.

Gabriel raised his head, as poor Malemort uttered a more dolorous groan than usual, and said to his squire,—

"Martin-Guerre, what time is it now?"

"Monseigneur, I can't tell very accurately," Martin replied, for this stormy night has put out all the stars; "but I imagine that it is not far from six o'clock, for it has been dark more than an hour."

"The surgeon promised to come at six o'clock, did he not?"

"At six precisely, Monseigneur. See, some one raises the curtain; yes, there he is."

Vicomte d'Exmès cast his eyes upon the new arrival, and recognized him at the first glance. He had seen him but once before; but the surgeon's face was one of those which when once seen are never forgotten.

"Master Ambroise Paré!" cried Gabriel, rising.

"Monsieur le Vicomte d'Exmès!" said Paré, with a low bow.

"Ah, Master, I had no idea you were in camp, and so near us!" said Gabriel.

"I try always to be where I can be of the most service," the surgeon responded.

"Oh, I recognize your noble heart in that! and I am doubly glad that you are here to-day, for I need to avail myself of your knowledge and skill."

"Not for yourself, I trust," said Ambroise Paré. "Of whom do you speak?"

"It is one of my people," said Gabriel. "This morning, while charging in a sort of frenzy upon the retreating English, he received a lance-thrust in the shoulder from one of them."

"In the shoulder? It may not be a very serious matter, then," said the surgeon.

"I am afraid it is, however," said Gabriel, in a lower tone; "for one of the wounded man's comrades, Scharfenstein there, tried in such a rough and awkward fashion to pull out the lance-head that he broke it off, and the iron remained in the wound."

Ambroise Paré's face for a moment assumed an expression which augured ill for the sufferer.

"Let me see him," he said, with his accustomed calmness.

He was conducted to the patient's bed. All the veterans had risen and surrounded the surgeon, each one abandoning his game or his reckoning or whatever he was engaged in. Lactance alone continued to mumble his beads in his corner; for when doing penance for his doughty deeds he never allowed himself to be interrupted except to perform others.

Ambroise Paré removed the bandages in which Malemort's shoulder was enveloped, and examined the wound very carefully. He shook his head doubtfully, as if in dissatisfaction, but said aloud,—

"This is nothing."

"Ho, ho!" grumbled Malemort. "If it is nothing, can I go and fight again to-morrow?"

"I don't think so," said Ambroise Paré, probing the wound.

"Ah! you hurt me a bit, did you know it?" said Malemort.

"Yes, I suppose I do," was the surgeon's reply; "but courage, my friend!"

"Oh, I am brave enough," said Malemort. "After all, this has been tolerable so far. Will it be much worse when you have to extract that infernal piece of iron?"

"No, for here it is," said Ambroise Paré, triumphant, holding up, so that Malemort could see, the lance-head he had succeeded in removing.

"I am very much obliged, Monsieur le Chirurgien," said Malemort, courteously.

A murmur of admiring wonder welcomed the masterly skill of Ambroise Paré.

"What! is it all over?" said Gabriel. "Why, it's perfectly marvellous."

"We must agree too," rejoined Ambroise, smiling, "that the wounded man was not afraid of pain."

"Nor the operator unskilful, by the Mass!" cried a new-comer behind the soldiers, whose entrance nobody had noticed amid the general anxiety.

But at the well-known voice all stood aside respectfully.

"Monsieur le Duc de Guise!" said Paré, recognizing the features of the commander-in-chief.

"Yes, Master," rejoined the new-comer, "Monsieur de Guise; and I am amazed and delighted with your superb skill. By my patron, Saint François, I have just been watching at the hospital some downright blockheads of doctors, who have done more harm to our soldiers with their instruments, I swear, than the English with their weapons. But you extracted this iron stake, upon my word, as easily and gently as if it had been a gray hair. And I do not know you! What is your name, Master?"

"Ambroise Paré, Monseigneur," said the surgeon.

"Well, Master Ambroise Paré," said the duke, "I promise you that your fortune is made,—on one condition, however."

"And may I know what the condition is, Monseigneur?"

"That if I get wounded or bruised, which is very possible, especially in these days, you will take charge of me and treat me with as little ceremony as you showed this poor devil."

"Monseigneur, I will do it," said Ambroise, bowing. "All men are equal in suffering."

"Hum!" rejoined François de Lorraine, "you will try, in the case I have mentioned to you, that they may be equal also in the matter of being cured."

"Will Monseigneur permit me now," said the surgeon, "to close and bandage this man's wound? There are many other wounded men who are in need of my services to-day."

"Do so, Master Ambroise Paré," the duke replied. "Go on without paying any more heed to me. I am in haste to see you on your way to deliver as many patients as possible from the hands of our cursed bunglers. Besides, I must speak with Monsieur d'Exmès."

Ambroise Paré at once set about dressing Malemort's wound.

"Monsieur le Chirurgien, I thank you again," said the patient; "but if you will excuse me, I have still another favor to ask of you."

"What is that, my fine fellow?" asked Ambroise.

"Well, it's like this, Monsieur le Chirurgien," said Malemort. "Now that I can no longer feel that horrible stump in my flesh, it seems to me as if I were almost well."

"Yes, almost," said Ambroise, pressing the ligatures together.

"Well, then," said Malemort, in a modest but unembarrassed tone, "will you be kind enough to say to my master, Monsieur d'Exmès, that if there is any fighting to-morrow, I am in perfectly fit condition to take part in it!"

"You fight to-morrow!" cried Ambroise Paré. "Ah! you must not think of it!"

"Oh, I beg your pardon, but I can't help thinking of it," rejoined Malemort, sadly.

"My poor fellow," said the surgeon, "just remember that I order a week of perfect rest,—at least a week in bed, and a week of light diet!"

"Light diet, so far as food is concerned, if you please," said Malemort, "but not abstinence from battle, I beg you."

"You are insane!" resumed Ambroise Paré; "if you but raise your head, the fever will seize you, and you will be a dead man. I said a week, and I will not take off an hour."

"Oh!" roared Malemort, "in a week the siege will be at an end. I shall never get my fill of fighting."

"What a blood-thirsty fellow he is!" said the Duc de Guise, who had been listening to this singular dialogue.

"That is Malemort all over," said Gabriel, smiling; "and I beg you, Monseigneur, to give orders to have him taken to the hospital, and carefully watched there; for if he hears the noise of a mêlée, he is quite capable of trying to get out of bed, in spite of everything."

"Oh, well, that's a very simple matter," said the Duc de Guise. "Give orders yourself to his comrades to carry him there."

"But, Monseigneur," Gabriel rejoined with some embarrassment, "it is quite possible that I shall have work for my brave fellows to do to-night."

"Oho!" said the duke, looking in surprise at Vicomte d'Exmès.

"If Monsieur d'Exmès wishes," said Ambroise Paré, who had drawn near them after he had dressed the wound, "I will send two of my assistants with a litter to take this wounded fire-eater away."

"I am very much obliged to you, and gladly accept your offer; I commend him to your most watchful care," said Gabriel.

Malemort gave vent to another despairing roar.

Ambroise Paré withdrew, having taken leave of the Duc de Guise. At a sign from Martin-Guerre, all but Monsieur d'Exmès retired to the farther end of the tent, and Gabriel was left tête-a-tête with the general directing the siege.

CHAPTER XVI
SMALL CRAFT SOMETIMES SAVE LARGE MEN-OF-WAR

When Vicomte d'Exmès was left alone with the Duc de Guise, he began the conversation thus,—

"Well, Monseigneur, are you content?"

"Yes, my friend," François de Lorraine replied,—"yes, I am content with the results so far attained, but I confess I am very anxious as to the future. It was this anxiety which drove me out of my tent to-night to wander about the camp, and come to you for encouragement and advice."

"But what is there new?" asked Gabriel. "I should imagine that the result so far has surpassed all your anticipations, has it not? In four days you have made yourself master of two of the outworks of Calais; besides, the defenders of the city itself and the Old Château cannot hold out more than forty-eight hours longer."

"Very true," said the duke; "but they can hold out that length of time, and that will be quite long enough to foil all our plans, and save themselves."

"Oh, Monseigneur must allow me to express my doubts of that," said Gabriel.

"No, my friend, my long experience does not mislead me," rejoined the Duc de Guise; "except for some unexpected piece of good fortune, or some occurrence beyond human foresight, our undertaking has failed. Believe me when I say this."

"But why?" asked Gabriel, with a smile, which contrasted strangely with the gloomy prognostications of the duke.

"I will tell you in two words, upon the basis of your own plan. Listen carefully to what I say."

"I am all attention," said Gabriel.

"The extraordinarily hazardous experiment into which your youthful enthusiasm seduced my more cautious ambition," continued the duke, "had no possible chance of success except in the isolation and complete surprise of the English garrison. Calais was impregnable, we were agreed, but might be taken by surprise. We reasoned out our insane enterprise along that line, did we not?"

"And up to the present moment," was Gabriel's reply, "the facts have borne us out in our reasoning."

"They have indeed," said the duke; "and you have demonstrated, Gabriel, that your judgment of men is as keen and far-seeing as your perception of facts; and that you had studied the disposition and character of the governor of Calais as carefully as the interior plan of his seat of government. Lord Wentworth has not belied a single one of your conjectures. He believed that his nine hundred men and his formidable outposts would suffice to make us repent of our reckless freak. He despised us too much to be alarmed, and did not deign to call a single company to his assistance, either from any other part of the continent or from England."

"I did indeed succeed in conjecturing how his arrogant pride would comport itself under such circumstances."

"Thanks to his overweening self-conceit," resumed the Duc de Guise, "we carried Fort Ste. Agathe almost without striking a blow, and the Nieullay fort after three days of successful fighting."

"So that at this moment," said Gabriel, cheerfully, "any bodies of English or Spaniards, coming by land to the rescue of their countrymen or their allies, will find the batteries of the Duc de Guise ready to exterminate them, instead of Lord Wentworth's cannon to second their assault."

"They will be on their guard, and will not approach very near," said the duke, smiling; for the young man's buoyant hopefulness was beginning to infect him.

"Well, then, have we not gained an important point?" said Gabriel.

"No doubt, no doubt," replied the duke; "but unfortunately it is not all, nor is it even the most important part. We have closed one of the roads by which outside reinforcements might enter Calais, and one of the gates of the city. But another gate and another road are still open."

"What one, pray, Monseigneur?" asked Gabriel, pretending to be in doubt.

"Cast your eye upon this map, drawn by Maréchal Strozzi, from the plan you furnished him," said the commander-in-chief. "Calais may be relieved at these two opposite points,—by the Nieullay fort, which covers the approaches on the landward side—"

"But which covers them for our benefit now," Gabriel interrupted.

"Very true," rejoined the duke; "but here on the ocean side, protected by the sea itself, by the marshes and sand-dunes, is the Risbank fort, do you see?—or if you choose to call it so, the Octagonal Tower,—a fort which commands the whole harbor, and makes it impossible for attacking vessels to enter. Let an express be sent to Dover, and in a few hours the English ships will transport hither enough troops and supplies to enable the place to hold out for years. Thus the Risbank fort protects the city, and the sea protects the Risbank fort. Now, Gabriel, do you know what Lord Wentworth has done since his last misfortune?"

"Perfectly well," rejoined Vicomte d'Exmès, calmly. "Lord Wentworth, acting upon the unanimous opinion of his council, has sent an express in hot haste to Dover, to make up for his culpable delay, and expects to receive by this time to-morrow the reinforcements of which he has at last admitted the need."

"Well, you have not finished?" said Monsieur de Guise.

"I confess, Monseigneur, that I cannot look ahead much further," replied Gabriel. "I have not the prescience of God."

"No more than human prescience is needed here," said François de Lorraine; "but since yours stops halfway, I will finish for you."

"I should be glad if Monseigneur would condescend to tell me what will ensue, in his opinion," said Gabriel, bowing respectfully.

"It is very simple," said Monsieur de Guise. "The besieged, reinforced, if need be, by all England, will be enabled after to-morrow to face us at the Old Château with a superior force, if not an absolutely invincible one. If, notwithstanding, we still maintain our position, every Spaniard and Englishman in France will come down upon us here in the suburbs of Calais like the winter's snow from Ardres and Ham and St. Quentin; and when they decide that their numbers are sufficient, they will take their turn at besieging us. I agree that they will not be able to take the Nieullay fort without some difficulty; but they will easily repossess themselves of Fort Ste. Agathe, and then they will have us at their mercy between two fires."

"Such a catastrophe would indeed be terrible," said Gabriel, coolly.

"Yet it is only too likely to happen," rejoined the duke, passing his hand despondently over his brow.

"But surely, Monseigneur," said Gabriel, "you have not failed to consider the means of preventing such a disaster?"

"I am thinking of nothing else, upon my soul!" said the Duc de Guise.

"Well?" asked Gabriel, carelessly.

"Well, our only chance,—and a very precarious and hopeless chance it is, alas!—is, in my opinion, to make a desperate assault upon the Old Château to-morrow, under any circumstances. Nothing will be in readiness, I am aware, even though we were to pass the whole night in most assiduous and unremitting labor. But there is no other course for us to take; and it is less foolhardy than it would be for us to await the arrival of reinforcements from England. The 'French fury,' as they call it in Italy, may possibly succeed, by dint of its extraordinary impetuosity, in storming these inaccessible walls."

"No, it will be helplessly shattered against them," rejoined Gabriel, coldly. "Pardon me, Monseigneur, but it seems to me that at this moment the French army is neither sufficiently strong nor sufficiently weak thus to attempt the impossible. A fearful responsibility rests upon you, Monseigneur. It is probable that we should be finally beaten back after we had lost half of our force. What does the Duc de Guise mean to do in that event?"

"Not to expose himself to total ruin, to a complete overthrow, at all events," said François de Lorraine, gloomily; "but to withdraw from before these cursed walls with such troops as I have left, and save them until better days dawn for our king and country."

"What, the victor of Metz and Renty retreat!" cried Gabriel.

"That is certainly much better than not knowing when one is beaten, as was the case with the constable on the day of St. Laurent," said the Duc de Guise.

"And yet," continued Gabriel, "it would be a disastrous blow to the glory of France, as well as to Monseigneur's reputation."

"Alas! who knows that so well as I?" exclaimed the duke. "See upon what slender threads depend success and fortune! If I had succeeded, I should have been a hero, a transcendent genius, a demigod; I fail, and I shall be henceforth only a vain and presumptuous fool, who well deserved the disgrace of his fall. The self-same undertaking which would have been called magnificent and marvellous, had it turned out happily, will draw upon me the ridicule of all Europe, and postpone if it does not destroy in the germ all my plans and hopes. To what do the paltry ambitions of this world lead!"

The duke ceased to speak, apparently a prey to bitter chagrin. There was a long silence, which Gabriel was very careful not to break.

He desired to give Monsieur de Guise ample opportunity to gauge the terrible difficulties of the crisis with his experienced eye.

When he considered that the duke must have probed them to the bottom, he said,—

"I see, Monseigneur, that you are at present involved in one of those periods of doubt and anxiety which come to the greatest of men in the midst of their greatest works. One word, however: Surely no such lofty genius, no such consummate general, as he to whom I have the honor of speaking, could have lightly engaged in so momentous an enterprise as this, unless the smallest details, the most unlikely contingencies, had all been discussed at the Louvre. You must have worked out in advance favorable results for all possible sudden changes of fortune, and remedies for all possible ills. How does it happen, then, that you are hesitating and seeking anew for them now?"

"*Mon Dieu*!" said the Duc de Guise, "your youthful enthusiasm and confidence fascinated and blinded me, I believe, Gabriel."

"Monseigneur!" said Gabriel, reproachfully.

"Oh, don't feel wounded, I beg, for I bear you no ill-will for it, my friend! I still admire your design, which was both a grand and a patriotic one. But stern reality is very fond of destroying our fairest dreams. Nevertheless, I remember distinctly that I laid before you certain objections, founded upon the possibility of this very extremity to which we are now reduced, and that you removed my scruples."

"And how, Monseigneur, please?"

"You promised me," said the Duc de Guise, "that if we succeeded in a few days in gaining possession of the two forts of Ste. Agathe and Nieullay, the secret arrangement that you had with persons in the town would place the Risbank fort in our hands, and thus Calais might be shut off from all hope of reinforcement by sea or land. Yes, Gabriel, I remember, and you must remember yourself, that you gave me that assurance."

"Very well!" said Gabriel, without the least symptom of anxiety or embarrassment.

"Well," rejoined the duke, "your hopes deceived you, did they not? Your friends in Calais have failed to keep their word, as was to be expected. They are evidently not yet certain of our success, and are timid; consequently they will not show themselves until it is too late to do us any good."

"Pardon me, Monseigneur, but who told you that?" asked Gabriel.

"Why, your very silence, my dear fellow. The time has come when our secret allies ought to come to our assistance, in which event they might perhaps save us. They give no sign, and your lips are sealed; therefore I conclude that you no longer rely upon them, and that we must renounce all hope of succor from that quarter."

"If you knew me better, Monseigneur," was Gabriel's response, "you would know that I never like to talk when I can act."

"What's that? Do you still have hopes?" asked the Duc de Guise.

"Yes, Monseigneur, since I am still living," Gabriel replied, in a grave and melancholy tone.

"And the Risbank fort?"

"Shall be in your hands when necessary, unless I am dead."

"But, Gabriel, it will be necessary to-morrow,—to-morrow morning!"

"Then we shall have it to-morrow morning!" replied Gabriel, calmly,—"that is, I say again, unless I fall; but in that event you cannot reproach one who has given his life in the attempt for his failure to keep his word."

"Gabriel," said the Duc de Guise, "what is it that you have in mind to do? Is it to face some mortal peril or to hazard some insane chance? I do not wish it; I do not wish it! France is only too much in need of such men as you."

"Be not at all alarmed, Monseigneur," rejoined Gabriel. "Though the danger be great, the end to be attained is even greater, and the enterprise is well worth the risk which attends it. You need only think how to profit by the result, and leave the means to me. I am only responsible for myself; but you are responsible for every man in the army."

"At least tell me what I can do to second your plan?" said the duke. "What part have you assigned to me?"

"Monseigneur," Gabriel replied, "if you had not done me the honor to come to my tent this evening, it was my intention to seek you in your own quarters, and to make a request."

"Go on,—speak!" said the duke, earnestly.

"To-morrow, the 5th of the month, at daybreak, Monseigneur,—that is to say, about eight o'clock, the nights being very long in January,—I ask you to station a look-out with keen sight on the promontory from which the Risbank fort can be seen. If the English flag is still waving there at that time, take the chances of the desperate assault you have resolved upon, for I shall have failed; in other words, I shall be dead."

"Dead!" cried the duke. "You see, Gabriel, that you are fearing your own destruction."

"In that event, waste no time in vain regrets for me, Monseigneur," said the youth; "only let everything be in readiness, and devote all your energy to your last effort; and I pray God to give you means of success! Let every man share in the attack! The reinforcements from England cannot possibly arrive before noon; therefore you will have jour hours of heroism before you in which to prove, ere you beat the retreat, that the French are as fearless as they are prudent."

"But, Gabriel, assure me again that you have some chance of success."

"Yes, indeed I have; be sure of that, Monseigneur. Therefore wait calmly and patiently, like the strong man that you are. Do not give the word too quickly for a headlong assault; I beg of you not to stake all upon that cast until it is actually necessary. Last of all, you need only keep Maréchal Strozzi and the miners quietly at work on the siege lines; and let your soldiers and artillerymen await the favorable moment for an assault, if at eight o'clock you are informed that the standard of France is flying over the Risbank fort."

"The standard of France over the Risbank fort!" cried the duke.

"A glance at it in such position," rejoined Gabriel, "will cause the ships on their way from England to retrace their steps without loss of time."

"I agree with you there," said Monsieur de Guise. "But, my dear friend, how will you do it?"

"Let me keep my secret, I implore you, Monseigneur," said Gabriel. "If you knew my extraordinary design, you might perhaps try to dissuade me from it. But it is no longer time to reflect and hesitate. Moreover, in all this I neither compromise the army nor yourself. These men here, the only ones whom I propose to employ, are all my own volunteers, and you agreed to leave me free to do as I would with them. I propose to accomplish my purpose unaided, or to die in the attempt."

"But why this pride?" asked the duke.

"It is not pride, Monseigneur; but I wish to requite as well as I can the priceless favor which you were good enough to promise me at Paris, and which I trust you remember."

"What priceless favor are you talking about, Gabriel?" said the duke. "I am supposed to have a good memory, especially where my friends are concerned; but I am ashamed to confess that in this instance I do not remember."

"Alas! Monseigneur," Gabriel rejoined, "it is a very important matter for me, however! This is what I asked of you: if it should be proved to your satisfaction that in the execution as well as the conception of the project, the taking of Calais was due to me, and to me alone, I begged you not to give me the credit in public, for that credit would belong to you, as leader of the expedition, but simply to announce to King Henri II. the share which I had had under your orders in the conquest. You then graciously allowed me to hope that reward would be accorded me."

"What! Is that the invaluable favor to which you allude, Gabriel?" asked the duke. "The deuce take me if I thought of that! But, my dear fellow, that will be no reward whatever, but a simple act of justice; and in secret or in public, as you choose, I shall be ever ready and willing to recognize and bear witness as I ought to your services and your deserts."

"My ambition does not go beyond what I have asked, Monseigneur," said Gabriel. "If the king be informed of my efforts, he has it in his power to bestow upon me a reward which would be worth more to me than all the honor and good fortune in the world."

"The king shall know all that you may have done for him, Gabriel. But can I do nothing more for you!"

"Indeed, Monseigneur, I have one or two other demands to make upon your good-will."

"Tell me," said the duke.

"In the first place," said Gabriel, "I must have the countersign, so that I may be able to leave camp with my people at any hour of the night I choose."

"You have only to say 'Calais and Charles,' and the sentinels will allow you to pass."

"Then, Monseigneur," said Gabriel, "if I fall, and your assault succeeds, I venture to remind you that Madame Diane de Castro, the king's daughter, is Lord Wentworth's prisoner, and has an indisputable claim upon your courteous protection."

"I will remember my duty as a man and a gentleman," rejoined the duke. "And then?"

"Lastly, Monseigneur, I am about to contract to-night a considerable debt to a fisherman of this coast, named Anselme. If Anselme dies with me, I have written to Master Elyot, who has charge of my property, to provide for the maintenance and well-being of his family, deprived as they will be of his support. But for greater security, Monseigneur, I would be deeply obliged if you would see that my orders are executed."

"It shall be done," said the duke. "Is that all?"

"It is, Monseigneur," Gabriel replied. "But if you never see me again, think of me sometimes, I beg, with a little regret, and speak of me as one for whom you had some esteem, whether it be to the king, who will surely be glad to hear of my death, or to Madame de Castro, who may perhaps be grieved. Now I will detain you no longer, but will bid you hire well, Monseigneur."

The Duc de Guise rose to go.

"Pray banish your gloomy thoughts, my friend," said he. "I leave you, so that you may be perfectly free to go on with your mysterious project; but I confess that until eight o'clock to-morrow, I shall be very anxious and shall find it hard to sleep. But it will be principally because of the obscurity which hides your operations from me. Something tells me that I shall see you again; therefore I will not say adieu."

"Thanks for the augury, Monseigneur," said Gabriel; "for if you see me again, it will be in Calais when it shall have become a French city."

"And in that event," said the duke, "you can fairly boast of having rescued the honor of France, and mine as well, from bitter peril."

"Small craft, Monseigneur, sometimes save large men-of-war," said Gabriel, bowing.

The Duc de Guise, at the door of the tent, gave Gabriel's hand a cordial grasp, and withdrew in deep thought to his headquarters.

CHAPTER XVII
OBSCURI SOLA SUB NOCTE

When Gabriel returned to his seat after escorting Monsieur de Guise to the door, he made a sign to Martin-Guerre, who at once left his occupation and went out, seeming to need no further instructions.

The squire came back after about fifteen minutes, accompanied by a pale, emaciated individual, whose clothes were almost falling from his body.

Martin approached his master, who was again absorbed in thought. The other occupants of the tent were playing or sleeping, as their fancy dictated.

"Monseigneur," said Martin-Guerre, "this is our man."

"Oh, yes!" said Gabriel; "so you are Anselme the fisherman, of whom Martin-Guerre has spoken to me?" he added, turning to the new-comer.

"Yes, Monseigneur, I am Anselme the fisherman," was the reply.

"Do you know the service in which we desire your aid?" asked Vicomte d'Exmès.

"Your squire has told me, Monseigneur; and I am ready."

"Martin-Guerre ought also to have told you," continued Gabriel, "that in this expedition your life will be in danger as will our own."

"Oh," rejoined the fisherman, "he had no need to tell me that; for I knew it as well as he, or even better."

"And still you came?" said Gabriel.

"Here I am, at your service," Anselme replied.

"Very good, my friend; it is the deed of a noble heart."

"Or of a hopeless existence," was the response.

"What do you mean by that?" asked Gabriel.

"Why, by our Lady!" said Anselme. "Every day I take my life in my hand for the sake of bringing home a few fish, and very often I come home empty-handed. So there is very little merit in risking my tanned skin for you to-day, when you promise, whether I live or die, to care for the future welfare of my wife and my three children."

"Very true," said Gabriel; "but the danger that you face every day is uncertain, and hidden from you in a measure. You never go to sea during a gale. But this time the risk is perceptible and unmistakable."

"Indeed," replied the fisherman, "it is perfectly certain that one must be a madman or a saint, to venture upon the water on such a night as this. But that is your affair; and it is not for me to find fault, if you choose to do it. You have paid me in advance for my boat and my body. But you will owe the Holy Virgin a fine candle of pure wax if we arrive safe and sound."

"Even when we have arrived, Anselme," Gabriel resumed, "your labors are not at an end. Having rowed us safely across, you will be called upon to fight, and do a soldier's work after having done duty as a sailor. Don't forget that you are about to incur dangers of two sorts."

"It's all right," said Anselme; "but don't be too discouraging in what you say. Your orders shall be obeyed. You guarantee the lives of those who are dear to me, and I give you mine. The bargain is struck, and let us say no more about it."

"You are a brave fellow!" said Gabriel. "As to your wife and children, let your mind be quite easy; for they shall want for nothing. I have written to my agent Elyot my wishes on that point; and Monsieur le Duc de Guise will himself see that they are carried out."

"That is more than you were called upon to do," said the fisherman; "and you are more generous than a king. I will play no tricks with you. You need only have given me sufficient money to relieve me from embarrassment during these hard times, and I would have expected nothing further. But if I am satisfied with you, I hope that you will not be disappointed in me."

"Let us see," said Gabriel; "will your boat hold fourteen?"

"She has held twenty, Monseigneur."

"You will need strong arms to help you row, will you not?"

"Yes, indeed," said Anselme; "for I shall have my hands full with the helm and the sail, if we can carry sail."

"We have three men," said Martin-Guerre,—"Ambrosio, Pilletrousse, and Landry,—who can row as if they had never done anything else in their lives, and I myself can swim with a pair of oars as easily as with my arms."

"Well, well," said Anselme, joyously, "I shall quite have the appearance of a smart sea-captain with so many fine fellows in my crew! There is one point on which Master Martin has thus far left me in ignorance, and that is the precise spot where we are to land."

"The Risbank fort," Gabriel replied.

"The Risbank fort! Did you say the Risbank fort?" cried the stupefied fisherman.

"Certainly I did," said Gabriel; "what objection have you to offer to that?"

"Oh, nothing," rejoined Anselme, "except that it is hardly possible to land at that point, and that I personally have never cast anchor there. It's nothing but rocks."

"Do you refuse to guide us?" asked Gabriel.

"My faith! no; I will do my best, though I am but little acquainted with that part of the coast. My father, who like myself was born a fisherman, used to say; 'We must not try to lord it over fish or customers.' I will take you to the Risbank fort if I can. A nice little trip we shall have!"

"At what hour must we be ready to start?" asked Gabriel.

"You want to reach there at four, I believe?" returned Anselme.

"Between four and five; no later."

"Very well! from the point where we must embark so as not to be seen and arouse suspicion, we must reckon upon two hours of sailing; the most important thing is not to tire ourselves unnecessarily on the water. From here to the creek is about an hour's march."

"Then we should leave the camp about one hour after midnight?" said Gabriel.

"That will be about right," Anselme replied.

"Well, then, I will go and tell my men," said Gabriel. "Do so, Monseigneur," said the fisherman. "I will ask your leave to lie down with them and sleep until one o'clock. I have said farewell at home; the boat is already carefully hidden and safely moored, so that I have nothing to call me away."

"You are quite right, Anselme," said Gabriel; "lie down for awhile, for you will have enough to tire you before this night is over. Martin-Guerre, you may tell your companions now."

"Ho, there, you fellows! You gamblers and sleepy heads!" cried Martin-Guerre.

"What is it? What's the matter?" they cried, rising and drawing near.

"Thank Monseigneur; for there is a special expedition on foot for one o'clock," said Martin.

"Good! very good! splendid!" was the hearty chorus of the veterans.

Even Malemort added his joyful shout to these unequivocal demonstrations of satisfaction.

But at that very moment four of Ambroise Paré's assistants appeared to carry the wounded man to the hospital.

Malemort was loud in his protestations.

But notwithstanding his cries and struggles, they put him upon a litter and held him there. In vain did he pour most bitter reproaches upon his comrades, even calling them deserters and traitors, since they were despicable enough to go into battle without him. No notice was taken of his epithets; and he was carried off cursing and swearing.

"How," said Martin-Guerre, "we must make our final arrangements, and assign to every man the part he is to play and his position."

"What sort of job have we on hand?" asked Pilletrousse.

"Oh, a sort of assault," replied Martin.

"Then I will be the first one to scale the wall!" cried Yvonnet.

"Very well," said the squire.

"No, that isn't fair!" exclaimed Ambrosio. "Yvonnet always monopolizes the first place in times of danger. Really, it seems as if he thinks of nobody but himself."

"Let him have his way," said Gabriel, interposing. "In the hazardous ascent that we are about to make, the foremost will be the least exposed, I imagine. As a proof of my belief, I propose myself to be the last to ascend."

"Then Yvonnet will be cheated," cried Ambrosio, laughing.

Martin-Guerre assigned to each man his place in the order of march, as well as his number in the boat and in the assault. Ambrosio, Pilletrousse, and Landry were notified that they would have to row. In fact, everything that could be was arranged beforehand, so as to avoid confusion and misunderstanding as far as possible.

Lactance took Martin-Guerre aside for a moment.

"Pardon me," said he; "but do you imagine there is any killing to be done?"

"I am not sure; but it is very possible," Martin replied.

"Thanks," returned Lactance; "in that case I think I will say my prayers and do penance in advance for three or four dead men and as many wounded."

When everything was settled, Gabriel advised his men to obtain an hour or two of sleep. He undertook to awaken them himself when it was time.

"Yes, I shall be glad to get a little sleep," said Yvonnet; "for my poor nerves are terribly excited this evening, and I need above all things to be cool and fresh when I am fighting."

In a few moments not a sound was to be heard within the tent save the regular breathing of the veterans and the monotonous *Pater nosters* of Lactance.

Soon the last-mentioned noise also ceased, for drowsiness had at last overcome Lactance, and he too was asleep.

Gabriel alone was awake and deep in thought.

Toward one o'clock he awoke his men one by one. They all rose and equipped themselves in silence. Then they went softly from the tent and left the camp.

At the words, 'Calais and Charles,' uttered in a low voice by Gabriel, the sentinels allowed them to pass unquestioned.

The little band, under the guidance of Anselme the fisherman, took its way through the fields, along the shore. Not a word was uttered. Nothing was to be heard save the moaning of the wind, and the melancholy voice of the sea in the distance.

It was a dark and stormy night. Not a soul was to be seen along the road traversed by our adventurers. Even if they had met any one, it was more than probable that they would have passed unnoticed; but had they been seen, they would certainly have been mistaken for phantoms at that hour and in such darkness.

Within the city, there was also one man who at that hour was still awake.

It was Lord Wentworth, the governor, although, relying upon the reinforcements for which he had sent to Dover as being sure to arrive on the morrow, he had retired to his own house, hoping to obtain some rest.

He had not slept, in truth, for three days, exposing himself continually, it must be said, at the points of greatest danger with untiring gallantry, and was always to be found wherever his presence was required.

On the evening of January 4 he had paid a visit to the breach of the Old Château, had personally posted the sentinels, and had reviewed the civic militia, who were intrusted with the simple duty of defending the Risbank fort.

But notwithstanding his intense weariness, and although everything was secure and quiet, he could not sleep.

A vague dread, absurd but not to be driven away, kept his eyes wide open as he lay on his bed.

Yet all his precautions were well taken; the enemy could not possibly venture upon a night attack, rèlying upon so trifling a breach as that in the Old Château. As for the other points, they would protect themselves with the aid of the swamp and the ocean.

Lord Wentworth said all this to himself a thousand times, and yet he could not sleep.

He seemed to feel something floating in the night air about the city which told him of a terrible danger from an invisible foe.

In his disordered fancy that enemy was not Maréchal Strozzi, nor the Duc de Nevers; it was not even the great François do Guise.

What! Could it be that it was his former prisoner, whom his bitter enmity had enabled him to recognize several times in the distance from the summit of the fortifications? Was it really that madman. Vicomte d'Exmès, Madame de Castro's lover?

What a ridiculous adversary for the governor of Calais in his strong city, still so impregnably guarded!

However, Lord Wentworth, whatever the reason may have been, could neither overcome this indefinable dread nor explain it.

But he felt its presence, and he could not sleep.

CHAPTERXVIII
BETWEEN TWO CHASMS

The Risbank fort, which on account of its eight faces was also called the Octagonal Tower, was built, as we have said, at the entrance of Calais Harbor, in front of the sand-dunes; and its black and frowning mass of granite towered aloft upon another mass, as forbidding and quite as colossal, of solid cliff.

The sea, when the tide was high, broke against the cliff, but never touched the lowest courses of the stone walls of the fort.

Now, the sea was running very high and very threateningly on the night of the 4th of January, 1558, and toward four o'clock in the morning of the 5th it gave forth that resounding but mournful moaning which makes it resemble an ever restless and despairing soul.

Suddenly, a short time after the sentinel who was stationed upon the platform of the tower from two o'clock to four had been relieved by him whose tour of duty ran from four to six, a sound like a human cry, as if uttered by lungs of brass, made itself distinctly heard amid the tempest, over the moaning of the sea.

Then the newly arrived sentry might have been seen to start, listen attentively, and lean his cross-bow against the wall, after he had made sure of the source of this strange sound. Next, when he had satisfied himself that no eye was upon him, he lifted, with a mighty arm, his sentry-box from the rock, and drew from beneath it a pile of rope which assumed the shape of a long knotted ladder, which he securely fastened to the pieces of iron fixed in the battlements.

Finally he attached the various pieces of rope firmly together, and lowered them over the walls, when two heavy pieces of lead quickly carried the ends down upon the rock on which the fort was built.

The ladder was two hundred and twelve feet long, and the fort two hundred and fifteen feet high.

Scarcely had he completed his mysterious operation when the night patrol appeared at the top of the steps leading to the platform. As the sentinel was standing near his box, the patrol asked and received the countersign, and passed on without noticing anything out of the regular course.

The sentinel, much relieved in his mind, anxiously awaited what was to follow. It was already quarter past four.

At the foot of the cliff was a boat manned by fourteen men, who, after more than two hours of hard and almost superhuman labor, had succeeded in reaching the Risbank fort. A wooden ladder was placed against the cliff. It reached up to a sort of excavation in the rock, were five or six men might stand at once.

One by one, and in absolute silence, the bold adventurers mounted the ladder from the boat, and without stopping at the excavation, continued clambering up the cliff, using both their feet and hands, and taking advantage of every inequality in the face of the rock.

Their purpose was to reach the foot of the tower. But the darkness was intense, and the rock slippery; their fingers were torn and bleeding, and one of them lost his footing, and rolled helplessly down until he fell into the sea.

Luckily the last of the fourteen men was still in the boat, trying vainly to make her fast before trusting himself to the ladder.

The man who had fallen, and who had had the forethought and courage not to utter a cry as he fell, swam vigorously toward the boat. The other lent him a hand, and despite the pitching of the boat under his feet, had the satisfaction of rescuing him safe and sound.

"What! is it you, Martin-Guerre?" said he, thinking that he recognized him in the darkness.

"It is myself, I admit, Monseigneur," said the squire.

"How came you to slip, bungler?" asked Gabriel.

"It was much better that it should have happened to me than to another," said Martin.

"Why?"

"Because anybody else would have made an outcry," replied Martin.

"Well, since you are here," said Gabriel, "help me pass this rope around that great root. I very foolishly sent Anselme ahead with the others."

"The root will not hold, Monseigneur," said Martin: "the least shock will pull it up, and the boat will be destroyed and we shall be carried away with it."

"There is nothing else to be done," rejoined Gabriel; "so let us set about it without more ado."

When they had made the boat fast as well as they could, Gabriel said to his squire,—

"Come, up with you!"

"After you, Monseigneur; otherwise who will hold the ladder?"

"Go up, I tell you!" repeated Gabriel, stamping his foot impatiently.

The time was not propitious for argument or formality. Martin-Guerre mounted as far as the excavation in the cliff, and from that elevation held the uprights of the ladder with all his strength while Gabriel ascended in his turn.

His foot was on the topmost round when a powerful wave struck the boat, broke the rope, and carried ladder and skiff out to sea.

Gabriel would have been lost save for Martin, who, at the risk of dying with him, leaned over the abyss with a motion quicker than thought, and seized his master by the collar of his doublet; then, with all the energy of despair, the brave fellow drew Gabriel up to where he was standing on the rock, as unharmed as himself.

"Now you have saved my life, my gallant Martin," said Gabriel.

"Yes; but the boat has gone," returned the squire.

"Bah! As Anselme says, it is paid for," said Gabriel, with a carelessness assumed to hide his anxiety.

"That's very well!" said the cautious Martin-Guerre, shaking his head; "but if your friend doesn't happen to be doing his turn of duty up there, or if the ladder isn't hanging from the tower, or if it breaks under our weight, or if the platform is occupied by a force stronger than ours,—why, then all chance of retreat, all hope of safety, has gone from us with that cursed boat."

"Well, so much the better," said Gabriel; "for now we must succeed or die."

"So be it!" said Martin, with heroic simplicity.

"Come!" Gabriel rejoined; "our companions ought already to be at the foot of the tower, for I can no longer hear them. Be careful about your footing this time, Martin, and never let go with one hand until you have a firm hold with the other."

"Never fear; I will do my best," said Martin.

They began the perilous ascent; and after the lapse of ten minutes, during which they had overcome innumerable difficulties and dangers, they rejoined their twelve companions, who were anxiously awaiting them, grouped together on the cliff at the foot of the Risbank fort.

The third quarter past four had come and gone. Gabriel, with inexpressible joy, spied the rope ladder hanging against the wall.

"Do you see that, my friends?" he said, in a whisper, to his little party. "We are expected up there. Thank God for it, for we can no longer look behind; the sea has carried away our boat. So, forward, my brave fellows; and may God protect us!"

"Amen!" said Lactance, solemnly.

Indeed it was necessary that these should be determined and resolute men who stood around Gabriel at this crisis; for the enterprise, which had been rash enough up to that point, seemed to become almost insane, and yet not a man stirred at the terrible news that all hope of retreat had been cut off.

Gabriel, in the gloomy light which falls even from the darkest sky, scanned their hardy features, and found them quite devoid of emotion.

They all repeated after him,—

"Forward!"

"You remember the order agreed upon," said Gabriel: "you are to go first, Yvonnet; then Martin-Guerre; then each one in his proper order until it comes my turn; and I shall be the last to mount the ladder. The ropes and knots are firmly fastened, I trust!"

"The ropes are as strong as iron, Monseigneur," said Ambrosio; "we have tried them, and they will bear thirty as safely as fourteen."

"Go on, then, brave Yvonnet!" continued Gabriel; "you have by no means the least dangerous part of the enterprise. Off you go, and be of good heart!"

"My courage never fails, Monseigneur," said Yvonnet, "especially when the drums are beating and the guns roaring; but I confess that I am no better accustomed to noiseless assaults than to swaying cordage; therefore I am very glad to go first, so as to have the others behind me."

"A very modest reason for making sure of the post of honor!" said Gabriel, who did not choose to enter upon a dangerous discussion. "Come, no more excuses! Although the wind and sea drown our words, we must act and not talk. Forward, Yvonnet! and remember that you must not stop to rest until you reach the one hundred and fiftieth round. Are you ready,—musket on your back and sword between your teeth? Look up, not down; and think of God, and not of the danger. Forward!"

Yvonnet put his foot upon the first round.

Five o'clock struck; a second night patrol passed the sentinel on the platform as he made his rounds.

Then, slowly and silently, the fourteen gallant men ventured one after the other upon that frail ladder shaking in the wind.

It was nothing so long as Gabriel, who was the last in the procession, remained within a few steps of the ground; but as they went on, and the living cluster shook from side to side more and more, the danger assumed unspeakable proportions.

It must have been a magnificent yet appalling sight to witness in the darkness and storm these fourteen apparently dumb creatures, like so many demons, scaling the black wall, at whose summit was possible death, while sure destruction awaited them at its base.

At the one hundred and fiftieth round Yvonnet stopped, and all the others did the same. It was agreed beforehand that they should halt at that point long enough for each to say two *Paters* and two *Aves*.

When Martin-Guerre had finished his devotions, he was amazed to see that Yvonnet did not stir. He thought he must have missed his count, and reproving himself for his haste, he began conscientiously a third *Pater* and a third *Ave*.

But still Yvonnet remained motionless. Then—although they were only about a hundred feet from the platform, and it was dangerous to speak—Martin-Guerre struck Yvonnet's legs, and said to him,—

"Go on, pray."

"No, I cannot," said Yvonnet, in a stifled voice.

"You can't, villain! Why not?" asked Martin, shuddering.

"I am dizzy," said Yvonnet.

A cold perspiration broke out in beads on Martin's forehead.

It was a moment before he could make up his mind what to do. If Yvonnet should have the vertigo and fall, they would all be carried down with him; to descend was no less hazardous. Martin felt himself to be incapable of assuming any responsibility whatever at such a terrible crisis. He leaned over to Anselme, who was next behind him, and said,—

"Yvonnet is dizzy."

Anselme shuddered as Martin had done, and repeated the same words to his neighbor, Scharfenstein; and so the word was passed down the ladder, each one in turn removing his sword from between his teeth long enough to say to the man next below,—

"Yvonnet is dizzy."

At last the dreadful intelligence reached the ears of Gabriel, who turned pale and trembled as the others had done when he heard it.

CHAPTER XIX
ARNAULD DU THILL, THOUGH ABSENT, CONTINUES TO EXERT A FATAL INFLUENCE ON THE DESTINY OF POOR MARTIN-GUERRE

It was a moment of fearful suffering,—a supreme crisis. Gabriel saw that he was threatened by three distinct dangers. Beneath his feet, the roaring sea seemed to be calling to its prey with its mighty voice. Before him twelve terrified men, unable to move either forward or back, barred the road to the third source of danger,—the English pikes and arquebuses which were perhaps waiting for them to show their heads above the battlements.

On all sides, terror and death seemed to threaten the poor beings upon that vibrating ladder.

Fortunately, Gabriel was not the man to waste precious time in hesitating even between two formidable perils, and he made up his mind in an instant.

He never stopped to wonder whether his grasp might not fail, and his brains be dashed out on the rocks below. Clinging closely to the rope that formed one side of the ladder, he raised himself by his hands alone, and passed by the twelve men in front of him one after another.

Thanks to his enormous strength of muscle, as well as of soul, he reached Yvonnet without accident, and was at last able to place his feet beside those of Martin-Guerre.

"Will you go on or not?" said he to Yvonnet, in sharp and commanding tones.

"I am—dizzy," replied the poor wretch, whose teeth were chattering and his hair standing on end.

"Will you go on?" repeated Gabriel.

"Impossible!" said Yvonnet. "I feel as if my feet and hands were leaving the rounds to which they are clinging. I am going to fall."

"We will see," said Gabriel.

He pulled himself up as far as Yvonnet's waist, and pricked him in the back with the point of his sword.

"Can you feel the point of my sword?" he asked.

"Yes, Monseigneur! Oh, mercy! I am afraid. Mercy!"

"The blade is sharp and keen," continued Gabriel, with marvellous *sang-froid*. "At the least backward movement on your part it will bury itself in your body. Now listen, Yvonnet; Martin-Guerre will pass in front of you and I shall remain behind. If you do not follow Martin-Guerre,—mark well what I say: if you show one symptom of flinching, I swear by God above that you shall not fall and drag others down with you, for I will nail you to the wall with my sword, and hold you there until they have all passed over your body."

"Oh, mercy, Monseigneur! I will obey!" cried Yvonnet, cured of one fright by a greater one.

"Martin," said Vicomte d'Exmès, "you heard what I said. Pass him and go on."

Martin-Guerre in his turn executed the evolution which he had seen his master perform, and assumed the first place.

"Forward!" said Gabriel.

Martin went bravely up, and Yvonnet, menaced by Gabriel, who carried his sword in his right hand and used only his left to assist his feet in the ascent, forgot his vertigo, and followed the squire.

Thus the fourteen men ascended the last one hundred and fifty rounds of the ladder. "*Parbleu*!" thought Martin-Guerre, whose good humor came back to him as he saw the space which separated him from the summit of the tower growing ever less. "*Parbleu*! Monseigneur discovered a sovereign cure for the vertigo."

He had just finished that pleasant reflection, when his head reached the level of the edge of the platform.

"Is it you?" asked a voice unknown to Martin.

"*Parbleu*!" the squire replied in an unembarrassed tone.

"It is quite time," rejoined the sentinel, "In less than five minutes the patrol will be making their third round."

"Good! we will be ready for them," said Martin-Guerre.

As he spoke he triumphantly placed one knee upon the ledge of stone.

"Ah!" cried the sentinel, suddenly, trying to get a better view of him in the darkness; "what is your name?"

"Why! Martin-Guerre—"

He did not finish what he was saying, for Pierre Peuquoy (it was no other than he) gave him no time to put the other knee beside its fellow, but giving him a violent push with both hands, hurled him headlong into the abyss.

"Holy Jesus!" was all that poor Martin-Guerre said.

Then he fell without a sound, concentrating all his energies in a sublime effort to change the course of his fall so as not to endanger the safety of his companions and his master.

Yvonnet, who followed him, and who recovered all his courage and boldness as soon as he felt the solid rock beneath his feet, leaped upon the platform, followed by Gabriel and all the others.

Pierre Peuquoy made no further opposition. He remained standing as if turned to stone, and unconscious of what was passing.

"Wretch!" cried Gabriel, seizing him by the arm, and shaking him; what insane fury has taken possession of you "What has Martin-Guerre done to you?"

"To me, nothing," replied the armorer in a dull voice. "But to Babette, my sister!"

"Ah, I had forgotten!" cried Gabriel in alarm. "Poor Martin! But it was not he! May he not be saved even yet?"

"Be saved after a fall of more than two hundred and fifty feet upon a rock!" exclaimed Pierre Peuquoy with a harsh laugh. "Come, Monsieur le Vicomte, you would be better employed just now in thinking about taking measures to save yourself and your companions."

"My companions, yes, and my father and Diane," said the young man to himself, recalled by these words to the duties and the risks of his situation; "but still," he continued aloud, "my poor Martin!"

"This is no time to bemoan the villain's fate," Pierre Peuquoy interposed.

"Villain! he was innocent, I tell you, and I will prove it to you. But this is not the time; you are right. Are you still inclined to aid us?" Gabriel asked the armorer, rather bluntly.

"I am devoted to France and to you," replied Pierre. "Very well," said Gabriel. "What remains for us to do now?"

"The night patrol will soon pass," replied the burgher; "we must choke and gag the four men who compose it. But," he added hurriedly, "it is too late to surprise them. Here they are!"

Just as Pierre spoke, the urban patrol actually came out upon the platform by an interior staircase. If they gave the alarm, all might be lost.

Luckily the two Scharfensteins, uncle and nephew, who were of a very inquisitive and prying nature, were prowling around on that side. The men of the patrol had no time to utter a sound. An enormous hand closing the mouth of each one of them from behind, threw them violently upon their backs as well.

Pilletrousse and two others ran to them, and the four bewildered militiamen were easily gagged and disarmed.

"Well done!" said Pierre Peuquoy. "Now, Monseigneur, we must make sure of the other sentinels, and then make a bold descent upon the guard-house. We have two posts to carry. But have no fear of being overborne by numbers. More than half of the city militia, having been influenced by Jean and myself, are for the French cause heart and soul, and only await the proper moment to show their devotion. I will go down first to notify our friends of your success; meanwhile you can look after the sentinels. When I return, my words will already have accomplished three fourths of the task."

"Ah, I would thank you, Peuquoy," said Gabriel, "if Martin-Guerre's death,—and yet from your standpoint you did only what was just."

"Once more, Monsieur d'Exmès, I beg you to leave that to God and my conscience," replied the stern burgher. "I acquit you of blame. Now act your part while I fulfil mine."

Everything happened almost precisely as Pierre had foreseen. The sentinels belonged to the French faction in a large majority of instances. One who undertook to resist was soon bound and rendered incapable of doing any harm. When the armorer returned, accompanied by Jean Peuquoy and a few sure friends, the whole summit of the Risbank fort was already in Vicomte d'Exmès hands.

It remained now to overthrow the *corps-de-garde* with the reinforcement brought by the Peuquoys. Gabriel did not hesitate to go down at once.

Advantage was skilfully taken of the first moment of surprise and uncertainty.

At that early hour, most of those who remained firm in the cause of England, either by birth or interest, were still asleep in perfect security upon their camp beds. Before they were fairly awake, so to speak, hands were at their throats.

The tumult, for it was not a battle, lasted only a few moments. The friends of Peuquoy shouted, "Vive la France! Vive Henri II.!" The non-combatants, and those who were indifferent, lost no time in arraying themselves, as they always do, under the successful banner. Those who made a show of resistance were soon compelled to yield to superior numbers. There were, in all, only two men killed and five wounded, and only three shots were fired. The devout Lactance was unfortunate enough to have two of the wounded and one of the slain to his credit. Luckily he had time to spare!

It was not six o'clock when every part of the Risbank fort was in the power of the French. The disaffected and the suspected were securely confined, and all the rest of the city guard surrounded Gabriel and hailed him as a liberator.

Thus was carried, almost without a blow, and in less than an hour, by an extraordinary and superhuman achievement, this fort which the English had never dreamed of fortifying, because the sea alone seemed to be such an impregnable defence to it,—a fort, which was nevertheless the key to the harbor of Calais, yes, to Calais itself.

The whole transaction was accomplished so quickly and quietly that the entire fort was taken, and new sentinels stationed by Gabriel, and a new countersign given out, before anything of it was known in the city.

"However, so long as Calais itself has not surrendered," said Pierre Peuquoy to Gabriel, "I do not consider that our task is done. So, Monsieur d'Exmès. I am of opinion that you had best keep Jean and half of our men here to make good the fort, and leave me and the other half to go into the city. We may do the French better service there than here, in case of need, by some useful diversion. After Jean's ropes, it will be well to make use of Pierre's arms."

"Are you not afraid," said Gabriel, "that Lord Wentworth, in his rage, may do you an ill turn?"

"Never fear," replied Pierre; "I will resort to a little artifice, which will be justifiable warfare with those who have been our oppressors for two centuries. If necessary, I will accuse Jean of having betrayed us. We were surprised by a superior force, and compelled, in spite of our resistance, to surrender at discretion. Those of us who refused to recognize your victory were driven out of the fort. Lord Wentworth's affairs are at so serious a pass that he must at least pretend to believe us, and be grateful to us."

"So be it! Go down into Calais," rejoined Gabriel, "for I see that you are as clever as you are brave. And it is certain that you can assist me, if I should decide to make a sortie."

"Oh, don't risk that, I beg you!" said Pierre, "you are not in sufficient numbers, and you have little to gain and everything to lose by a sortie. Here in your tower, behind these good walls, you occupy an impregnable position. Pray remain here. If you take the offensive, Lord Wentworth may very possibly retake the fort; and after having accomplished so much it would be a great shame to lose its manifest advantages."

"But do you propose," rejoined Gabriel, "that I should remain idle here with my sword in its scabbard while Monsieur de Guise and all our troops are fighting and risking their lives?"

"Their lives are their own, Monseigneur, but the Risbank fort belongs to France," replied the prudent burgher. "But listen; when I consider that the favorable moment has arrived, and that only one last decisive blow is needed to tear Calais from the hands of the English, I will cause those whom I have with me, and all the inhabitants who share my opinions, to rise as one man. Then, when everything is ripe for victory, you may make a sortie, to give the finishing blow and open the city to the Duc de Guise."

"But who will let me know when I may venture?" asked Gabriel.

"Give me the horn which I presented to you," said Pierre, "whose note served to make your coming known to me. When you hear its sound once more, go forth without fear, and share in the triumph you have so nobly prepared."

Gabriel thanked Pierre heartily, helped him select the men who were to go with him into the city to assist the French troops in case of need, and graciously accompanied them as far as the gate of the fort, out of which they were to pretend they had been driven in disgrace.

By the time this was done it was half past seven, and the first streaks of dawn were visible in the sky.

Gabriel desired to make sure personally that the French standards which were to bring peace to the mind of Monsieur de Guise and strike terror to the English men-of-war were hoisted over the fort. Consequently he ascended to the platform which had been the scene of the main events of that glorious but fateful morning.

With pallid cheeks he drew near the spot at which the rope ladder had been attached, and whence poor Martin-Guerre had been hurled, the victim of a fatal mistake.

Shudderingly he leaned over the abyss, expecting to see the mutilated corpse of his faithful squire on the rocks below.

At first he failed to espy him, and his eye glanced hither and thither in surprise, mingled with a faint hope.

A leaden spout, by which the rain-water from the tower was carried off, had stopped the body midway in its terrible fall; and there Gabriel saw it hanging, motionless and doubled up over the spout.

At first sight he thought that life was extinct, but he desired to pay the last tokens of respect in any event.

Pilletrousse, whom Martin-Guerre had always been fond of, was looking on weeping, and his devotion to his friend seconded his master's pious reflections. He fastened himself securely to the rope ladder, and ventured down into the abyss.

When he reascended, bringing with him, after much labor, the body of his friend, they saw that Martin was still breathing.

A surgeon who was at hand announced that life was not extinct; in fact, Martin regained consciousness to some extent.

But he came back to greater suffering, for he was in a sad plight. He had a broken arm and a crushed thigh.

The surgeon could set the arm without difficulty, but he judged it necessary to amputate the leg, and did not dare to undertake so difficult an operation alone.

More than ever Gabriel deplored that though a victor, he was confined to the Risbank fort. The delay, which had been trying enough before, now became almost intolerable.

If only he could get word to expert Ambroise Paré, Martin-Guerre might be saved.

CHAPTER XX
LORD WENTWORTH AT BAY

The Duc de Guise, upon reflection, could not bring himself to believe in the success of so foolhardy an enterprise; nevertheless, he determined to see with his own eyes whether Vicomte d'Exmès had or had not achieved his end. In such straits as those to which he was reduced, one can but hope even for the impossible.

So, before eight o'clock, with but very few attendants, he was already on the cliff Gabriel had pointed out to him, from which the Risbank fort could be seen with a telescope.

At the first glance that he cast in the direction of the fort he uttered a triumphant cry.

He could not be mistaken; he clearly recognized the standard of France. His companions agreed that it was no delusion, and shared his delight.

"My brave Gabriel!" he cried. "He has really been successful in his prodigious undertaking. Has he not shown himself to be a greater man than I, who doubted its practicability? Now, thanks to him, we can prepare for the capture of Calais, and make sure of it at our leisure. Let the reinforcements come from England, and Gabriel will take it upon himself to give them a hearty welcome."

"Monseigneur, it is as if your words had summoned them," said one of the duke's aids, who turned the glass seaward at this moment. "Look, Monseigneur, are not those English sail on the horizon?"

The duke took the glass, and carefully scanned the wide expanse of the channel.

"Yes; our English friends are really there," he said. "The deuce take me! they have not lost any time; I hardly expected them so soon. Do you know that if we had made our contemplated attack upon the Old Château at this time, the sudden arrival of these reinforcements would have been an extremely bad thing for us? So much the more cause have we for gratitude to Monsieur d'Exmès. Not only does he put victory within our power, but he has saved us from the disgrace of defeat as well. However, we have no need to hurry now; so let us see how the new-comers will act, and, on the other hand, how the young governor of the Risbank fort will behave toward them."

It was broad daylight by the time the English ships arrived within range of the fort.

The French flag burst upon their sight in the first rays of dawn like a menacing apparition; and as if to impress the unexpected sight the more forcibly upon them, Gabriel saluted them with three or four cannon balls.

That removed every shadow of doubt. It was really the standard of France which was floating over the English fort. Of course, then, the city as well as the tower must be in the power of the besiegers; and the reinforcements, though despatched in all haste, had arrived too late.

After a few moments of surprised irresolution, the English ships were seen to be standing off toward Dover again.

They had on board a sufficient force to relieve Calais, but not to recapture the city.

"Thank God!" cried the Duc de Guise, in an ecstasy of delight. "Think of this Gabriel! He knows how to maintain his conquests as well as to conquer; he has put Calais in our grasp, and it only remains for us to close our hands upon the fair city."

He leaped upon his horse, and galloped joyfully back to camp to urge on the siege-operations.

Human events have almost invariably two sides; and the very same occurrences which bring laughter and delight to the hearts of some, make others weep. At the moment when the Duc de Guise was thus clapping his hands for joy, Lord Wentworth was tearing his hair.

After a sleepless night, as we have seen, and excited by presentiments of evil, Lord Wentworth had finally fallen asleep toward morning, and was just leaving his bed-chamber when the pretended fugitives from the Risbank fort were bringing the fatal news into the city, Pierre Peuquoy at their head.

The governor was almost the last person to hear it.

In his pain and indignation he could not believe his ears, and ordered that the leader of the fugitives should be brought before him.

Pierre Peuquoy was at once escorted into the governor's presence; he came in looking decidedly chopfallen, and with a bearing well suited to the occasion.

The cunning burgher, as if still under the influence of the fright he had had, told of the night assault, and described the *three hundred* savage adventurers who had scaled the Risbank fort, assisted, no doubt, by treachery within the walls, which he, Pierre Peuquoy, had not had time to unearth.

"Who commanded these three hundred men?" asked Lord Wentworth.

"*Mon Dieu*! Your late prisoner, Monsieur d'Exmès," was the armorer's ingenuous reply.

"Oh, my dreams have come true!" cried the governor.

Then, with a threatening frown, suddenly remembering what he was not likely to forget,—

"Why, this Monsieur d'Exmès," said he to Pierre, "was your guest, if I mistake not, during his stay in Calais?"

"Yes, Monseigneur," replied Pierre, without embarrassment. "In fact I have reason to believe—why should I conceal it?—that my cousin Jean, the weaver, has had a larger share in this business than he ought to have had."

Lord Wentworth fixed a piercing glance upon the sturdy burgher; but he looked Lord Wentworth fearlessly in the eye.

As Pierre had imagined would be the case, the governor was too sensible of his own weakness, and too well aware of Peuquoy's influence in the city, to allow his suspicions to appear.

After having put some few questions to him, the governor dismissed him with gloomy but friendly words.

Left alone, Lord Wentworth gave way to overwhelming despondency.

What could he do? The city, defended only by its weak garrison, henceforth shut off from all hope of succor by land or sea, and hemmed in between the Nieullay fort on one side and the Risbank fort on the other, both of which threatened instead of defending it,—the city could hold out but very few days longer; in fact, it might be only a few hours.

A terrible state of affairs, indeed, for the haughty pride of Lord Wentworth!

"No matter!" he said beneath his breath, still pale with astonishment and rage,—"no matter! I will make them pay dear for their triumph. Calais is theirs now only too inevitably; but I will at all events hold out to the bitter end, and will sell them their priceless conquest at the price of as many dead bodies as possible. And as for the lover of beauteous Diane de Castro—"

He checked himself, while a hellish thought caused his sombre features to light up with a joyous gleam.

"As for the lover of the fair Diane," he resumed, with a sort of satisfaction, "if I bury myself, as I ought and will, under the ruins of Calais, we will try and see to it, at least, that he has not any reason to rejoice too heartily at our death; his suffering and vanquished rival has in store for him a fearful surprise, and let him beware!"

Thereupon he rushed from the house to encourage his troops and make his dispositions.

Soothed and hardened at once in a measure by reflecting on some evil project, he exhibited such imperturbable *sang-froid* that his very despair inspired hope in more than one doubting heart.

It is no part of the plan of this book to relate the story of the siege of Calais in all its details. François de Rabutin, in his "Guerres de Belgique," gives them in all their prolixity.

The days of the 5th and 6th of January were passed in equally energetic efforts on the one side and the other. Miners and soldiers on both sides did their duty with like courage and heroic obstinacy.

But the superb resistance of Lord Wentworth was rendered hopeless by the great superiority of the force opposed to him; Maréchal Strozzi, who had charge of the operations, seemed to divine all the means of defence and every movement of the English as if the ramparts of Calais had been transparent.

"The enemy must have a plan of the city in their possession," thought Lord Wentworth.

We know who had furnished the Duc de Guise with that plan.

Thus it was that Vicomte d'Exmès, though he was absent, though he was unemployed at the moment, was still useful to his associates; and as Monsieur de Guise remarked in his just gratitude, his beneficial influence had its due effect even from afar.

Nevertheless, the inactive and helpless part that he was forced to play weighed heavily upon the fiery youth. Practically imprisoned in the stronghold he had conquered, he had to occupy his energy in the duty of keeping watch, which was altogether too simple a matter and too easily performed for him.

When he had made the rounds every hour with the watchful vigilance which he had learned during the defence of St. Quentin, he would generally take his place by Martin-Guerre's bedside to comfort and encourage him.

The brave squire endured his suffering with marvellous patience and steadfastness, but he could not get over his surprise and sorrowful indignation at the wicked treatment which Pierre Peuquoy had felt called upon to inflict upon him.

The perfect candor of his anger and his surprise when he talked upon that obscure subject, was in itself sufficient to have scattered any suspicions that Gabriel might still have retained as to Martin's good faith.

Thereupon he decided to tell Martin-Guerre his own story, according to what he presumed to be the true state of the case, judging from appearances and from his conjectures. It was now very evident to him that some villain had availed himself of a marvellous resemblance to Martin, to commit in his name all sorts of scandalous and infamous deeds, of which he was not anxious to accept the consequences, and also, doubtless, to reap the full benefit of all the advantages and privileges which he had been able to divert from his double to himself.

This revelation Gabriel took care to make in presence of Jean Peuquoy. Jean was grieved and terrified in his honest heart at the consequences of the fatal error. But he was especially disturbed as to the person who was guilty of all these crimes. Who was the miserable wretch? Was he married also? Where was he hiding himself?

Martin-Guerre, for his part, was terribly alarmed at the mere idea of such an entanglement. While he was more than overjoyed to have his conscience relieved of such a load of misdeeds of which he had borne the blame so long, he was in despair at the thought that his name had been assumed, and his good fame dragged in the mire by such a villain. And then who could tell to what lengths the scoundrel might still be going under cover of that name, even at the very moment when Martin was lying helpless on his bed of suffering!

The episode of Babette Peuquoy especially caused poor Martin's heart to overflow with sorrow and compassion. Oh, indeed, now he could find excuses for Pierre's seeming brutality! He not only forgave him, but applauded him for what he did. Certainly, it was very well of him thus to avenge his honor so basely outraged! It was Martin-Guerre's turn now to console and reassure poor bewildered Jean Peuquoy.

The good squire, in his applause of Babette's brother, forgot only one thing,—that it was he who was suffering instead of the real culprit. When Gabriel smilingly reminded him of that, "Oh, well, never mind!" said Martin-Guerre. "I am still thankful for my accident; for if I survive, my poor lame leg, or better still, its stump, will serve to distinguish me from the impostor and traitor."

But alas! this doubtful consolation with which Martin buoyed up his hopes was very problematical; for would he survive? The surgeon of the city guard would not promise it; speedy assistance from a master hand was of the utmost importance, and two days would soon have passed, during which poor Martin-Guerre's alarming state had been relieved only by inadequate dressing.

This was by no means the least of Gabriel's reasons for impatience; and many a time, both night and day, he rose and listened intently for that blast of the horn which was at last to relieve him from his enforced idleness.

It was not till the evening of January 6th that Gabriel, who had already been in possession of the Risbank fort for thirty-six hours, thought that he could distinguish a greater uproar than usual in the direction of the city, and unaccustomed shrieks of triumph or distress.

The French, after a most bitter struggle, had made their way victoriously into the Old Château.

Calais could not now hold out more than twenty-four hours.

Nevertheless, the whole of the seventh was passed in superhuman efforts on the part of the English to retake so vital a position, and to maintain themselves in the last posts which they still possessed.

But Monsieur de Guise, far from allowing the enemy to regain an inch of ground, was gaining slowly but surely upon him; so that it soon became clear that the morrow would see Calais no longer under English rule.

It was three in the afternoon. Lord Wentworth, who had taken no heed to himself for seven days, and who had been always in the front rank, dealing out death and defying it, considered that the physical strength and moral courage of his men would hardly hold out two hours longer.

Then he summoned Lord Derby.

"How long do you think," he asked, "that we can still hold out?"

"Not more than three hours, I fear," said Lord Derby, sadly.

"But you can promise that it will be two, can you not?" rejoined the governor.

"Except for some unforeseen occurrence, I can," said Lord Derby, measuring with his eye the distance still to be passed by the French.

"Very well, my friend," said Lord Wentworth, "I place the command in your hands and withdraw. If the English, two hours hence,—but not a moment sooner, you understand,—if, two hours hence, our people have no longer any possible hope, as is only too probable, then I allow you, nay, I command you, the better to relieve you from responsibility, to sound the retreat and capitulate."

"In two hours; very well, my Lord," said Lord Derby.

Lord Wentworth then advised his lieutenant as to the terms he might demand, which would doubtless be granted by the Duc de Guise.

"But," said Lord Derby, "you have forgotten yourself in these conditions, my Lord. Shall I not also ask Monsieur de Guise to hold you to ransom?"

A dull light shone on Lord Wentworth's gloomy features.

"No, no," he replied, with a peculiar smile; "do not worry about me, my friend. I have assured myself of all that I need,—yes, of all that I desire even."

"But—" Lord Derby was beginning to remonstrate.

"Enough!" said the governor, authoritatively. "Do only what I tell you, nothing more. Adieu. You will bear witness for me in England that I did all that human mind and hand could do to defend my city, and yielded only to fate? And now it is for you to hold out till the last moment, but be sparing of English honor and English blood, Derby. This is my last word. Adieu."

Without staying to say or hear more, Lord Wentworth, having grasped Lord Derby's hand, left the field of battle, and withdrew alone to his own deserted house, giving the most strict and explicit orders that no one should be allowed to follow him on any pretext.

He was sure that he had at least two hours before him.

CHAPTER XXI
LOVE DISDAINED

Lord Wentworth believed himself to be sure of two things: in the first place, that two full hours would elapse before Calais would capitulate, and that Lord Derby would demand at least five hours before delivering up the city; in the second place, he was confident that he should find his house entirely unoccupied, for he had taken the precaution to send off all his people to the breach in the morning. André, Madame de Castro's French page, had been imprisoned by his orders; so that Diane must be alone in the mansion, except for one or two of her women.

In truth he did find everything deserted as the abode of the dead, as he went into the house; while Calais, like a body from which the life-blood is ebbing away, was gathering all her force for a final struggle at the spot where fighting was in progress.

Lord Wentworth, gloomy, savage, and in a measure drunken with despair, went directly to the apartments occupied by Madame de Castro.

He did not send in his name, as his custom had been, but entered brusquely, like a master, the room where she was sitting with one of the maids who had been furnished her.

Without any salutation to the wondering Diane, he said imperiously to the maid,—

"Leave the room at once! The French will be in the city this evening, and I have neither the time nor the power to protect you. Go and find your father; your place is with him. Go at once, and tell the two or three women who are left in the house that I wish them to do the same without loss of time."

"But, my Lord—" the maid remonstrated.

"Ah!" returned the governor, stamping his foot angrily; "did you not hear what I said? I wish it!"

"But, my Lord—" Diane began.

"I have said, 'I wish it!' Madame," replied Lord Wentworth, with a gesture of inflexible determination. The maid left the room in terror.

"Truly, I should not have known you, my Lord," said Diane, after an agonizing silence.

"It is because you have never before seen me in the guise of a vanquished man, Madame," rejoined Lord Wentworth, with a bitter smile. "You have been a farseeing prophet of ruin and disaster for me; and I was in truth an insensate fool not to believe you. I am beaten, absolutely beaten, beyond resource and beyond hope. So you may rejoice."

"Is the success of the French at this point really beyond question?" asked Diane, who could with difficulty conceal her pleasure.

"How can it be otherwise, Madame? The Nieullay and Risbank forts and the Old Château are in their power. They have the city between three fires, and Calais is theirs beyond cavil. So you may rejoice."

"Oh!" Diane rejoined, "with such a foe as you, my Lord, victory is never certain; and in spite of myself,—yes, I confess, and you will understand me,—in spite of myself I still am incredulous."

"But Madame," cried Lord Wentworth, "do you not see that I have left the field; that after having taken part in the battle to the very last, I could not make up my mind to witness the final catastrophe, and that is why I am here? Lord Derby will surrender in an hour and a half. In that time, Madame, the French will enter Calais in triumph, and Vicomte d'Exmès with them. So you may rejoice."

"You say that in such a strange way, my Lord, that I do not know whether I ought to believe you or not," said Diane, who was beginning to hope nevertheless; so that her expression and her involuntary smile were illumined by the thought of deliverance.

"In order to persuade you, then, Madame," rejoined Lord Wentworth,—"for I mean to persuade you,—I will adopt another manner of speaking, and I will say to you: Madame, in an hour and a half the French will enter the city in triumph, and Vicomte d'Exmès with them. Tremble!"

"What do you mean?" cried Diane, as the color fled from her cheeks.

"What! Am I not sufficiently explicit?" said Lord Wentworth, approaching Diane with a laugh of sinister meaning. "I say to you: In an hour and a half, Madame, our rôles will be changed,—you will be free, and

I a prisoner; Vicomte d'Exmès will come to restore you to liberty and love and happiness, and to cast me into a dungeon. Tremble!"

"Why, pray, should I tremble?" Diane responded, retreating as far as the walls would allow from the sombre yet burning gaze of this man.

"*Mon Dieu*! it is very easy to understand," said Lord Wentworth. "At this moment I am master; but in an hour and a half I shall be a slave,—in an hour and a quarter rather, for the minutes are flying. In an hour and a quarter I shall be in your power; now you are in mine. In an hour Vicomte d'Exmès will be here; but now I am here. So rejoice and tremble, Madame!"

"My Lord, my Lord!" cried poor Diane, repulsing Lord Wentworth, with rapidly beating heart. "What do you want of me?"

"What do I want of you!—of you!" said the governor in a hollow voice.

"Don't come near me, or I will cry out; I will call for help, and dishonor you, villain!" exclaimed Diane, in an ecstasy of terror.

"Cry out and call for help as much as you choose; it's all the same to me," Lord Wentworth rejoined with ominous tranquillity. "The house is deserted, and so are the streets; no one will answer your cries for at least an hour. Look! I have not even taken the trouble to close the doors and windows, so sure am I that no one will come in less than an hour."

"But they will at the end of that time," Diane retorted; "and then I will accuse and denounce you, and my deliverers will kill you."

"No," said Lord Wentworth, coldly, "for it is I who will kill myself. Do you imagine that I have any desire to survive the fall of Calais? In an hour I shall kill myself; I have made up my mind beyond recall. But before that I choose to give full play to my passion, and to satisfy my vengeance and my love in this last supreme hour. Come, my fair one, your resistance and your contempt are out of season now,—for I no longer beg, but command; I no longer implore, but demand."

"And I die!" cried Diane, drawing a knife from her bosom.

Before she had time to strike, Lord Wentworth sprang toward her, seized her weak little hands in his powerful ones, tore the knife from her grasp, and threw it far away.

"Not yet!" he cried, with a smile of terrible import; "I do not choose, Madame, that you should turn your hand against yourself yet. Afterward you may do as you choose; and if you prefer to die with me rather than live with him, you will be quite at liberty to do so. But this last hour,—for there is only an hour left now,—this last hour of your life belongs to me; I have but this hour in which to make amends to myself for the eternity of hell to come hereafter; so be very sure that I will not renounce my right."

He attempted to lay hold of her. Thereupon fainting, and feeling that her strength was forsaking her, she threw herself at his feet.

"Mercy, my Lord!" she cried, "mercy, I ask mercy and forgiveness on my knees! By the memory of your mother, remember that you are a gentleman."

"A gentleman!" retorted Lord Wentworth, shaking his head; "yes, I was a gentleman, and I so bore myself, I think, so long as I triumphed and hoped,—yes, so long as I lived. But now I am no longer a gentleman; I am simply a man,—a man who is about to die, and proposes first to be revenged."

He raised Madame de Castro, kneeling at his feet, and held her close in a passionate embrace. She tried to pray, or to cry out, but she could not.

At this moment a great uproar was heard in the street.

"Ah!" Diane succeeded in ejaculating, her eye kindling once more with a ray of hope.

"Good!" said Wentworth, with a demoniac laugh; "it seems that the people are beginning to plunder on their own account while waiting for the enemy. So be it! They are doing quite right, upon my word! It is for the governor to set the example."

"Mercy!" she managed to say once more.

"No, no!" was Lord Wentworth's response. "You are too beautiful."

She swooned.

But the governor had not even had time to kiss Diane's colorless lips, when the uproar came nearer.

Vicomte d'Exmès, the two Peuquoys, and three or four French archers burst violently through the doorway and appeared upon the threshold.

Gabriel fairly leaped upon Lord Wentworth, sword in hand, with a terrible cry.

"Villain!"

Lord Wentworth, with clenched teeth, also seized his sword which was lying upon a chair.

"Stand back!" said Gabriel to his companions, who were about to intervene. "It is my pleasure to punish the infamous scoundrel with my own hand."

Without another sound the two adversaries furiously crossed weapons.

Pierre and Jean Peuquoy and their companions took up positions so as to give them ample space, and remained silent but by no means indifferent spectators of this deadly combat.

Diane was still lying unconscious upon the couch.

Let us tell in a few words how this providential succor had come to the defenceless prisoner so much sooner than Lord Wentworth had anticipated.

Pierre Peuquoy, during the two preceding days, had, as he had promised Gabriel, aroused and armed all those who were in secret devoted to the French cause. The ultimate victory being no longer doubtful, this class had naturally become much more numerous. They were for the most part circumspect and cautious burghers, who were unanimous in thinking that since they no longer had any means of offering resistance, the best course was to arrange for capitulation on the most favorable terms that could be obtained.

The armorer, who did not want to strike the final blow until it was perfectly safe to do so, waited until his strength was sufficiently great, and the siege far enough advanced, to run no risk of uselessly exposing the lives of those who relied on him. As soon as the Old Château was taken, he determined to act. But it took him some time to assemble his fellow-conspirators, who were scattered all over the city; and it was just as Lord Wentworth left the breach, that the movement within the city made itself felt.

But it was the more irresistible in proportion as it had been slow of development.

In the first place, the penetrating blast of Pierre Peuquoy's horn had brought, as if by magic, Vicomte d'Exmès, Jean, and half of their men, rushing out of the Risbank fort. The feeble detachment which kept the walls at that point was speedily disarmed, and the gate opened to the French.

Thereupon the whole Peuquoy faction, increased by this reinforcement, and emboldened by their first easily won success, hastened to the breach, where Lord Derby was trying to make as gallant a struggle as possible.

When this sort of revolt thus left Lord Wentworth's lieutenant between two fires, what was there for him to do? The French flag had already been brought into Calais by Vicomte d'Exmès. The city militia had risen, and were threatening to open the gates to the besiegers. Lord Derby preferred to yield at once. It was only to anticipate the governor's orders by a few moments, and to avoid another hour and a half of profitless resistance, even if this resistance should not become impossible, which would make the defeat no less complete, and might lead to more cruel reprisals.

Lord Derby sent a flag of truce to the Duc de Guise.

That was all that Gabriel and the Peuquoys asked for the nonce. They remarked the absence of Lord Wentworth, and were alarmed at it. So they left, where a few dropping shots were still to be heard, and spurred on by a presentiment of evil, they hastened to the governor's residence, with two or three trusty soldiers.

All the doors were open, and they found no difficulty in making their way to Madame de Castro's apartments, whither Gabriel hurried them on.

It was full time; and the sword of Diane's lover came most opportunely to protect the daughter of Henri II. from a most base and cowardly assault.

The duel between Gabriel and the governor was of short duration. The two combatants seemed to be equally expert swordsmen. Both showed equal coolness in a like state of fury. Their blades were entwined together like two serpents, and crossed and recrossed with the rapidity of lightning.

However, after two minutes fencing, Lord Wentworth's sword was struck from his hand by a vigorous counter on Gabriel's part.

In crouching to avoid the stroke, Lord Wentworth slipped upon the floor and fell.

Anger, scorn, hatred, and all the violent emotions which were struggling in Gabriel's heart left no room for generosity. There was no quarter for such a foe. In an instant he was upon him, with his sword at his breast.

There was not one of those who were present at the scene, inflamed as they were with indignation so lately aroused, who would have cared to stay the avenging hand.

But Diane de Castro while the fight was in progress had had time to recover from her swoon.

As she raised her heavy eyelids she saw and understood all, and rushed between Gabriel and Lord Wentworth.

Love Disdained.

By an extraordinary coincidence, the last word she had uttered as she fainted was the first upon her lips when she regained consciousness.

"Mercy!"

She prayed for mercy for the very man to whom she had herself prayed in vain.

Gabriel, at the sight of his idolized Diane, and the sound of her omnipotent voice, no longer was sensible of anything except her gentleness and his love for her. In his heart rage at once gave way to clemency.

"Do you wish him to live, Diane?" he asked his beloved.

"I beg it of you, Gabriel," said she; "for ought we not to give him time to repent?"

"So be it!" said the young man; "let the angel save the demon's life,—it is her proper role."

And still keeping Lord Wentworth, boiling with rage, under his knee, he said quietly to the Peuquoys and the archers,—

"Come here and bind this man while I hold him; then you can imprison him in his own dwelling until Monsieur de Guise determines his fate."

"No! kill me, kill me!" cried Lord Wentworth, struggling furiously.

"Do as I say!" said Gabriel, without loosing his hold. "I begin to think that life will be a greater burden to him than death."

Gabriel's orders were obeyed; and Lord Wentworth struggled and fumed and threatened in vain, for he was gagged and bound in an instant. Then two or three of the men took the ex-governor of Calais in their arms and carried him off, without ceremony.

Gabriel then turned to Jean Peuquoy, and said to him in his cousin's hearing,—

"My friend, I have already told Martin-Guerre the extraordinary story of his impersonation in your presence. You then deplored the cruel error which led to the punishment of an innocent man; and you asked for nothing better, I know, than to relieve as speedily as possible the terrible suffering he is at this moment undergoing for another. Do me a favor then—"

"I can guess what it is," brave Jean interrupted. "You desire me, do you not, to seek one Ambroise Paré, who may be able to save your poor squire? I fly to do it; and that he may be the better cared for, I will have him taken at once to our house, if it can be done without endangering his life."

Pierre Peuquoy, in a sort of stupefaction, listened to Gabriel and his cousin, and looked from one to the other, as if he was dreaming.

"Come, Pierre," said Jean, "you will help me in this. Oh! of course you are astonished, and do not understand; but I will explain everything to you as we go along, and I shall have no difficulty in making you see the matter as I now do; and then you will be the very first one—for I know you well—to wish to repair the wrong which you have unwittingly committed."

Thereupon, after saluting Diane and Gabriel, Jean left the room with Pierre, who had already begun to ask questions.

When Madame de Castro was left alone with Gabriel, she fell on her knees in the first impulse of pious gratitude, and raising her eyes and her hands toward heaven and to him who had been the instrument of her salvation,—

"I thank Thee, O God!" said she; "thrice over I thank Thee, for having saved me, and for having saved me by his hand!"

CHAPTER XXII
LOVE REQUITED

Then Diane threw herself into Gabriel's arms,—"And you, too, Gabriel," said she, "you, too, I must thank and bless. With my last conscious thought, I invoked my guardian angel, and you came to me. Thanks! oh, thanks!"

"Oh, Diane," he replied, "how I have suffered, and what a weary time it has been since I saw you last!"

"And I too have suffered, and have found the waiting weary," she cried.

They then began—at too great length to be dramatic, it must be confessed—to tell what each had endured and felt during their unhappy separation.

Calais, the Duc de Guise, vanquished and victors,—all were forgotten. All the strife and all the deadly passion which was rife about the two lovers did not reach them. Lost in their world of love and ecstasy, they no longer saw or heard the sights or sounds of the sad world around them.

When one has undergone so much grief and terror, the heart is enfeebled and softened to a certain extent by suffering, and though brave to overcome disaster, can no longer resist happiness. In this balmy atmosphere of chaste emotion, Diane and Gabriel gave themselves up without restraint to the sweet influences of peace and joy, to which they had so long been strangers.

To the scene of insane passion which we have described succeeded another similar, and yet widely different at the same time.

"How good it seems to be with you, my friend," said Diane. "Instead of the presence of that impious wretch whom I hated so, and whose love made me shudder, what ecstasy to have you near me, so reassuring, and so precious!"

"And I," rejoined Gabriel, "since our childhood, when we were happy without knowing it, do not remember, Diane, that I have ever known in my poor lonely, troubled life a single moment to be compared to this."

For a while they were silent, gazing in rapt enjoyment at each other.

Diane resumed:—

"Come and sit by me, Gabriel. Can you believe it, dear, this moment, which has united us once more in so unhoped-for a manner, I have nevertheless dreamed of and foreseen, even in my apparently hopeless captivity? I have always felt sure that my deliverance would come through you, and that in my supreme peril God would send you, my own knight, to rescue me."

"For my part, Diane," said Gabriel, "the thought of you has always led me on as a lover and guided my steps like a ray of light. Shall I make a confession to you and to my own conscience? Although many other potent motives might have urged me on, I never should have conceived the idea of taking Calais, Diane, which is mine alone, nor should I ever have had the courage to carry it out by resorting to such reckless expedients, had it not been that you were a prisoner here, and that my prophetic instinct of the danger which beset you encouraged and stimulated me. Except for my hope of rescuing you and the other holy purpose for which I live, Calais would still be in English hands. May God, in His mercy, not chastise me for having wished to do and having done what was right for selfish reasons only!"

Gabriel thought at that moment of the scene in the Rue St. Jacques, of the self-abnegation of Ambroise Paré, and the stern belief of the admiral that Heaven demands unstained hands to sustain a pure cause.

But Diane's beloved voice restored his confidence somewhat as she exclaimed,—

"God chastise you, Gabriel! God chastise you for being noble and generous!"

"Who knows?" said he, casting upward a look heavy with sad foreboding, as if he were asking the question of Heaven.

"*I* know," replied Diane, with a lovely smile.

She was so bewitching as she said it that Gabriel, in admiration of her beauty, and lost to every other thought, could not restrain the exclamation,—

"Oh, Diane, you are as beautiful as an angel!"

"And you as valiant as a hero, Gabriel," said Diane. They were seated side by side; their hands touched by accident and met in a fervent clasp. Darkness was beginning to fall.

Diane, with blushing cheeks, rose and walked away a few steps.

"Are you going, Diane? You are flying from me!" said the youth, sadly.

"Oh, no indeed!" said she eagerly, drawing near again. "With you it is very different; and I have no fear, dearest."

Diane was wrong; it was a different sort of danger that threatened her now, but danger nevertheless; and it might be that the friend was as much to be feared as the foe.

"That is right, Diane!" said Gabriel, taking the little hand, white and soft, which she surrendered to him once more; "that is as it should be. Let us enjoy a little happiness after all we have gone through. Let us give free play to our hearts to revel in their confidence and joy."

"Yes, indeed; it is so good to be near you, Gabriel!" Diane replied. "Let us forget the world and the uproar around us for a moment; let us enjoy to the full the unaccustomed sweetness of this hour. God, I think, will allow us to do so without anxiety or dread. You are right; else why have we suffered so?"

With a graceful movement which was common with her when she was a child, she laid her lovely head upon Gabriel's shoulder; her great velvety eyes slowly closed, and her hair brushed the lips of the ardent youth.

It was he then who rose, shuddering and bewildered.

"Well, what is it?" said Diane, opening her drooping eyes in wonder.

He fell on his knees before her, pale as a ghost, and threw his arms about her.

"Oh, Diane, Diane! I love you!" he cried from the bottom of his heart.

"And I love you, too, Gabriel," Diane replied, fearlessly, and as if in obedience to an irresistible impulse of her heart.

How their faces came nearer together; how their lips met; how in that long, sweet kiss, their very souls were blended, God only knows; certain it is that they did not know themselves.

But suddenly Gabriel, who felt his reason trembling in the vertigo of happiness, tore himself away from Diane.

"Diane, leave me!" he almost shrieked, with a note of horror in his voice, "let me fly!"

"Fly! and why, pray?" she asked wonderingly.

"Oh, Diane, Diane! if you should turn out to be my sister!" replied Gabriel, beside himself.

"Your sister!" echoed Diane, overwhelmed, paralyzed. Gabriel checked himself, dismayed and like one stunned by his own words; drawing his hand across his burning brow, he asked in a loud voice,—

"What did I say?"

"What did you say, really?" said Diane. "Must I believe it to be literally true, that fearful word? What is the key to this terrible mystery? Can I really be your sister? Oh, *mon Dieu*!"

"My sister? Did I tell you that you were my sister?" said Gabriel.

"Ah, it is true, then!" cried Diane, gasping for breath.

"No; it is not, cannot be true! I do not know it, and who can know it? Besides, I ought not to have said a word of all this to you. It is a secret involving life and death which I have sworn to keep. Ah, Heaven have pity upon me! I have preserved my self-control and my reason amid suffering and misfortune; must it be that the first drop of happiness which passes my lips should intoxicate me even to insanity and forgetfulness of my oath!"

"Gabriel," rejoined Madame de Castro, gravely, "God knows that it is no vain and purposeless curiosity which moves my words; but you have said either too much or too little for my peace of mind. Now you must finish."

"Impossible, impossible!" cried Gabriel in terror.

"And why impossible?" said Diane. "Something in my heart assures me that these dread secrets concern me quite as nearly as yourself, and that you have no right to conceal them from me."

"That is very true," Gabriel rejoined, "and you have certainly as much right as I to this suffering. But since the burden bears upon me alone, ask me not to share it with you."

"But I do ask it, and desire, nay, I demand my rightful share of your burdens," Diane returned; "and to go still further, Gabriel, I implore you! Will you refuse me?"

"But I have sworn to the king!" exclaimed Gabriel anxiously.

"You have sworn?" rejoined Diane. "Very well, keep your oath loyally to strangers or to indifferent persons, nay, even to your friends, and it will be well done of you. But with me, who, as you admit, have as deep an interest as yourself in this mystery, can you, ought you, to preserve this baleful silence? No, Gabriel, not if you have any pity for me. My doubts and anxiety on this subject have already torn my heart enough. In this matter, if not, alas! in the other events of your life, I am, in a measure, your second self. Do you perjure yourself, pray, when you muse upon your secret in the solitude of your own conscience? Do you think that my loyal and sincere heart, tried by so many bitter tests, will not be as steadfast as yours to retain and hold in trust the secret of joy or sorrow confided to it, and which belongs to it as much as to you?"

The soft and soothing tones of Diane's voice flowed on, moving the young man's inmost soul, as if it were an instrument obedient to her words.

"And then, Gabriel, since fate forbids our being bound together by the ties of happy love, how can you have the heart to deny me the only communion of feeling which is permissible for us,—that of sorrow? Shall we not suffer less if we suffer together? Is it not, then, very sad to think that the only bond which can unite us still keeps us apart?"

Feeling that Gabriel, though half convinced, was still in doubt, she resumed,—

"Besides, you must beware! If you persist in your silence, why should I not adopt the same language with you which caused you so much terror and anguish just now,—why, I know not,—but which you yourself, after all, long ago taught my lips and my heart? Surely your betrothed has the right to tell you over and over again that she loves you, and none but you. Your promised wife in God's sight may surely, with a chaste caress, put her head upon your shoulder and her lips to your forehead thus—"

But Gabriel, with a sinking heart, again put Diane aside, with a shudder.

"No!" he cried, "have pity on my reason, Diane, I implore you. So you really wish to know the terrible secret in all its details? Well, in the face of a possible crime, I allow it to pass my lips. Yes, Diane, you must take in their literal meaning the words which I let bill in my agony a moment ago. Diane, it is possible that you are the daughter of the Comte de Montgommery, my father; it is possible that you are my sister."

"Holy Virgin!" murmured Madame de Castro, overwhelmed by this revelation. "But how can it be?" she added.

"I should have preferred," said Gabriel, "that your pure and peaceful life should never have come to know aught of this mystery, so full of terror and crime. But I am confident, alas! that in the end my strength alone would not have been sufficient to prevail against my love. So you must assist me against yourself, Diane, and I will tell you all."

"I listen, Gabriel, in terrible dread, but with attention," said Diane.

Gabriel then narrated everything to her: how his father had loved Madame de Poitiers, and in the eyes of all the court had seemed to be favored by her; how the dauphin, the present king, had become his rival; how the Comte de Montgommery had disappeared one day, and how Aloyse had come to know, and had revealed to his son what had taken place. But that was the extent of the nurse's information; and since Madame de Poitiers obstinately refused to speak, the Comte de Montgommery alone, if he were still living, could tell the secret of Diane's birth.

When Gabriel had finished the lugubrious history, Diane cried,—

"This is indeed frightful! But whatever be the issue, my friend, there is misery in store for us. If I am the Comte de Montgommery's daughter, you are my brother Gabriel; if I am the king's daughter, you are the rightfully outraged enemy of my father. So that in either event we must be parted."

"No, Diane," Gabriel replied, "our wretchedness, thank God, is not altogether hopeless. Since I have begun to tell you the whole story, I will go on to the end. I feel, too, that you were in the right; it has encouraged me to confide in you; and my secret, after all, has only left my heart to be shared by yours."

Gabriel then told Madame de Castro of the strange and perilous bargain he had made with Henri II., and the king's solemn promise to restore the Comte de Montgommery to freedom if the Vicomte de Montgommery, after having defended St. Quentin against the Spaniards, should wrest Calais from the English.

Now Calais had been for an hour a French city, and Gabriel thought that he might say with all modesty that he had had a large share in bringing about that glorious result.

As he continued, the light of hope began to chase away the gloom from Diane's face as the light of dawn dissipates the darkness.

When Gabriel had finished, she remained silent for a moment in deep thought; then she said firmly, holding out her hand to him,—

"Poor Gabriel! doubtless we have as much to think about and suffer in the future as we have had in the past. But let us not stop there, my friend. We must not allow ourselves to become weak and timid. For my part, I will do my best to be strong and brave like you and with you. The important thing now is to set to work and unravel our fate one way or the other. Our agony is drawing to a close, I believe. You have now kept and more than kept your promise to the king, and he, I trust, will redeem his to you. It is upon that expectation that we must henceforth base all our thoughts and hopes. What do you mean to do now?"

"Monsieur le Duc de Guise," replied Gabriel, "was my illustrious confidant, and was accessory to all that I undertook to do here. I know that, except for him, I could have done nothing; but he knows as well that he could have done nothing without me. He, only, can and ought to bear witness to the king of the part I have taken in this new conquest. I have so much the more reason to expect this act of justice from him because he promised me solemnly, for the second time, within a few days, to give that testimony. Now I am going at once to remind Monsieur de Guise of his undertaking, also to request from him a letter to his Majesty, and since my presence here is no longer essential, to start at once for Paris—"

Gabriel was still speaking eagerly, and Diane listening with her eyes beaming with hope, when the door opened, and Jean Peuquoy appeared, discomposed, and in apparent consternation.

"Well, what is it?" asked Gabriel, anxiously. "Is Martin-Guerre worse?"

"No, Monsieur le Vicomte," replied Jean. "Martin-Guerre has been taken to our house by my efforts, and Master Ambroise Paré has already seen him. Although amputation of the leg was deemed necessary, Master Paré thinks that we may be sure that your gallant squire will survive the operation."

"Splendid news!" said Gabriel. "Ambroise Paré is doubtless with him still?"

"Monseigneur," replied the burgher, sadly, "he was obliged to leave him to attend another wounded man, more illustrious and more hopeless."

"Who is it, pray?" asked Gabriel, changing color. "Maréchal Strozzi, Monsieur de Nevers—?"

"Monsieur le Duc de Guise, who lies dying at this moment," said Jean.

Gabriel and Diane simultaneously uttered a cry of grief.

"And I was just saying that we were nearing the end of our agony," said Madame de Castro, after a moment's silence. "Oh, *Mon Dieu*! *mon Dieu*!"

"Call not upon God, Madame," said Gabriel, with a sad smile. "God is just, and justly chastises my selfishness. I took Calais only for my father's sake and yours. It is God's will that I should have taken it for the good of France."

CHAPTER XXIII
LE BALAFRÉ

Nevertheless, hope was not yet dead for Gabriel and Diane, since the Duc de Guise was breathing still. The unhappy creatures seized eagerly at the least chance, as the drowning man clutches at a straw.

Vicomte d'Exmès left Diane's side to go and ascertain for himself the extent of this catastrophe which had befallen them just when continued ill-fortune had seemed to be relaxing its rigorous severity.

Jean Peuquoy, who accompanied him, related to him on the way what had happened.

Lord Derby, being summoned by the mutinous citizens to capitulate before the time fixed by Lord Wentworth, had sent a flag of truce to the Duc de Guise to arrange the preliminaries.

Nevertheless, fighting still continued at several points, and was made still more desperate during these final struggles, by the wrath of the vanquished and the impatience of the victors.

François de Lorraine, who was as daring a soldier as he was a skilful general, appeared in person at the spot where the affray seemed to be hottest and most dangerous.

It was at a breach already half carried on the other side of a ditch, which was completely filled with débris.

The Duc de Guise on horseback, and a shining mark for the missiles which were aimed at him from all sides, calmly urged on his men by his words and his example.

Suddenly he saw above the breach the white flag of truce.

A haughty smile spread over his noble features; for it was the definitive assurance of his victory that he saw approaching.

"Hold!" he cried in the midst of the mêlée to those who surrounded him. "Calais surrenders! Down with your arms!"

He raised the visor of his helmet, and putting spurs to his horse, rode forward a few paces with his eyes fixed on the white flag, the symbol of his triumph and of peace.

Darkness, moreover, was beginning to fall, and the uproar had not ceased.

An English man-at-arms, who probably had not seen the flag of truce nor heard amid the din the Duc de Guise's order to his men, sprang at his horse's rein, and threw him back upon his haunches; and as the absorbed duke, without so much as noticing the obstacle which thus arrested his progress, drove the spurs in again, the trooper struck him in the face with his lance.

"I was not able to learn," continued Jean, "what part of Monsieur de Guise's face was struck; but it is certain that it is a terrible wound. The handle of the lance broke off, and the iron remained in the wound. The duke, without a word, fell forward upon the pommel of his saddle. It seems that the Englishman who dealt the fatal blow was torn to pieces by the furious French soldiers; but alas! that could not help Monsieur de Guise. He was carried from the field like one dead. Since then he has not regained consciousness."

"So that Calais is not ours?" asked Gabriel.

"Oh, indeed it is!" replied Jean. "Monsieur le Duc de Nevers received the flag of truce, and imposed most advantageous conditions, like a conqueror. But the gain of such a city will hardly compensate France for the loss of such a hero."

"*Mon Dieu*! Do you look upon him as already beyond help, then?" said Gabriel, shuddering.

"Alas! alas!" was the weaver's only reply, with a sorrowful shake of the head.

"Whither are you leading me at this pace?" continued Gabriel. "Do you know where they have taken him?"

"To the guard-house of the Château-Neuf, so Master Ambroise Paré was told by the man who brought him the terrible news. Master Paré was anxious to go to him at once, so Pierre went to show him the way, and I came to tell you. I foresaw that it would be a very important matter for you, and that under the circumstances there would doubtless be something for you to do."

"I have only to grieve like the others,—yes, even more than the others," said Gabriel. "But," added he, "as well as I can distinguish objects in the darkness, I should say we were near our destination."

"This is the Château-Neuf," said Jean.

Citizens and soldiers, an enormous, excited crowd eager and muttering, filled all the approaches to the guard-house whither the Duc de Guise had been carried. Questions, conjectures, and remarks of all sorts were passing from mouth to mouth among the restless groups, like the rustling wind among the echoing shades of a forest.

Gabriel and Jean Peuquoy had great difficulty in making their way through this closely packed crowd as far as the steps of the guard-house, the entrance to which was guarded by a strong party of pikemen and halberdiers. Some of them held lighted torches, which cast their lurid rays upon the moving mass of people.

Gabriel started as he saw by the flickering light of the torches Ambroise Paré standing at the foot of the steps, motionless, with contracted brows, and convulsively pressing his folded arms against his heaving chest. Tears of grief and rage were glistening in his handsome eyes.

Behind him stood Pierre Peuquoy, as gloomy and cast down as he.

"You here, Master Paré!" cried Gabriel. "What are you doing here, pray? If Monsieur le Duc de Guise has still a breath of life in his body, your place is at his side."

"Ah! you must not say so to me, Monsieur d'Exmès," retorted the surgeon, quickly, when raising his eyes he recognized Gabriel. "Tell me if you have any authority over these stupid guards."

"What! Do they refuse to let you pass?" asked Gabriel.

"They will not listen to a word," rejoined Ambroise Paré. "Oh, to think that God should make so precious an existence depend upon such paltry distinctions!"

"But you must go in," said Gabriel. "Your presence is indispensable there."

"We begged at first," said Peuquoy, interposing, "and then we threatened. They replied to our prayers with laughter, and to our threats with blows. Master Paré tried to force his way in, but was forcibly repulsed, and wounded by the handle of a halberd, I think."

"It's easily understood," said Ambroise Paré, bitterly. "I have no gold collar or spurs; I have nothing but a keen glance and a sure hand."

"Wait," said Gabriel, "I will soon make them admit you."

He walked toward the steps of the guard-house, but a pikeman bowing respectfully as he saw him, barred his way.

"Pardon me," said he with deference, "but we have received orders to allow no one whatever to go in."

"Blackguard!" said Gabriel, still keeping command over himself, however; "do your orders apply to Vicomte d'Exmès, captain of his Majesty's Guards, and Monsieur de Guise's friend? Where is your leader that I may speak to him?"

"Monseigneur, he is on guard at the inner door," replied the pikeman, still more humbly.

"I will go to him, then," rejoined Gabriel, haughtily; "Come, Master Paré, follow me."

"Monseigneur, you may pass, since you demand it," said the soldier; "but this man cannot pass."

"Why so?" asked Gabriel. "Why cannot the surgeon be admitted to the wounded man?"

"All the surgeons, doctors, and quacks," replied the pikeman, "all those at least who are recognized and licensed, have already been summoned to Monseigneur's bedside. Not one is missing, so we are informed."

"Ah, that is just what alarms me!" said Ambroise Paré, with contemptuous irony.

"This man has no license in his pocket," the soldier continued. "I know him well. He has saved more than one poor fellow's life in the camp, it is true; but he is not the man for dukes."

"Less talk!" cried Gabriel, stamping his foot angrily. "It is my desire that Master Paré should go in with me."

"Impossible, Monsieur le Vicomte."

"I have said that it is my desire, blackguard!"

"Pray remember," the soldier replied, "that my orders compel me to disobey you."

"Ah," cried Ambroise, sadly, "the duke may be dying while this absurd discussion is going on!"

This cry would have scattered all Gabriel's hesitation to the winds, even if the impetuous youth had found it possible to hesitate longer at such a crisis.

"So you really wish that I should treat you as if you were Englishmen!" he cried to the halberdiers. "So much the worse for you, then! Monsieur de Guise's life is worth twenty such lives as yours, after all. We will see if your pikes will dare to cross with my sword."

The blade flashed from the scabbard like a ray of light, and drawing Ambroise Paré after him, he ascended the steps of the guard-house.

There was so much of menace in his whole look and bearing; there was so much force in the physician's calm and determined demeanor; and the mere personality, to say nothing of the expressed will of a man of gentle birth, had so much prestige at that epoch,—that the guards were subdued, and stood aside with their weapons lowered, less in deference to the viscount's sword than to his name.

"Let him pass!" cried a voice among the populace. "They have the appearance of having been sent by God to save the Duc de Guise."

Gabriel and Ambroise Paré reached the door of the guard-house without further hindrance.

In the narrow porch through which they had to pass to reach the main hall, the lieutenant in command of the men outside was stationed, with three or four soldiers.

Vicomte d'Exmès, without stopping, said to him briefly and in a tone which called for no reply,—

"I am bringing another surgeon to see Monseigneur."

The lieutenant bowed, and allowed him to pass without the least objection.

Gabriel and Paré entered the hall.

The attention of all present was too deeply absorbed in the sad business in hand to notice their arrival.

It was truly a harrowing and fearful sight which was presented to their gaze.

In the centre of the hall, oil a camp bed, lay the Duc de Guise, motionless and unconscious, the blood streaming from his head.

His face was pierced from side to side; the iron head of the lance, having entered the cheek beneath the right eye, had passed through his head to that portion of the neck immediately below the left ear, and the broken fragment projected half a foot from the gaping wound, which was frightful to look upon.

Around the bed were grouped some ten or twelve physicians and surgeons, utterly bewildered amid the general despair.

They were doing nothing whatever beyond looking on and talking.

Just as Gabriel came in with Ambroise Paré, one of them was saying aloud,—

"Thus, having consulted together, we are under the painful necessity of announcing our unanimous opinion that Monsieur le Duc de Guise is mortally wounded, beyond hope of recovery: for in order to afford any chance of saving his life, the fragment of the lance must be withdrawn from the wound, and to extract it would be to kill Monseigneur beyond peradventure."

"So, then, you prefer to let him die!" rang out the determined voice of Ambroise Paré from behind the foremost lookers-on. He had from that distance seen with a glance the really almost hopeless condition of the illustrious patient.

The surgeon who had spoken raised his head to discover his bold critic, and failing to do so, he resumed,—

"Who would be so rash as to venture to lay his impious hands upon that august face, and run the risk, without chance of success, of causing the death of such a sufferer?"

"I!" said Ambroise Paré, stepping forward with head erect into the group of surgeons.

And without paying any further attention to those who surrounded him, or to the exclamations of surprise elicited by his word, he leaned over the duke to get a nearer view of the wound.

"Ah! It is Master Ambroise Paré," said the surgeon-in-chief, contemptuously, as he recognized the madman who dared to utter an opinion different from his. "Master Ambroise Paré forgets," he added, "that he has not the honor of being numbered among the surgeons of the Duc de Guise."

"Say rather," retorted Ambroise, "that I am his only surgeon, since his regular attendants all abandon him. Besides, the Duc de Guise, a few days since, after an operation which I performed successfully under his eyes, chose to say to me, and very seriously if not officially, that hereafter he should avail himself of my services in case of need. Monsieur le Vicomte d'Exmès, who was present, can bear me out in what I say."

"I declare that what he says is true," said Gabriel.

Ambroise Paré had already turned his attention once more to the seemingly lifeless body of the duke, and was carefully examining the wound.

"Well," asked the surgeon-in-chief, with an ironical smile, "after your examination do you still persist in your desire to extract the iron from the wound?"

"Most certainly I do," said Ambroise Paré, resolutely.

"What wonderful instrument do you propose to use?"

"My hands, to be sure," replied Ambroise.

"I protest with all my force," cried the infuriated surgeon, "against any such profanation of Monseigneur's last hours."

"And we join in your protest," shouted all his associates.

"Have you any means of saving the prince's life to propose?" asked Ambroise Paré.

"No, it is impossible," was the unanimous chorus.

"He is mine, then," said Ambroise, extending his hands over the body as if to take formal possession of it.

"We withdraw, then," said the surgeon-in-chief, and he and his associates made a movement toward the door.

"What do you propose to do?" was the question put to Ambroise on all sides.

"The Duc de Guise is dead to all that transpires," he replied, "and I propose to act as if he were really dead."

With these words, he removed his doublet, and rolled up his sleeves.

"The idea of performing such experiments on Monseigneur, *tanquam in anima vili*," said an old physician, shocked at these preparations, and clasping his hands in horror.

"Yes," replied Ambroise, without raising his eyes from the sufferer. "I am going to treat him, not as a man, not even as a beast of the field, but as an inanimate thing. See!"

He placed his foot boldly upon the duke's chest.

A subdued sound of commingled terror, doubt, and menace ran through the assemblage.

"Take care, Master!" said Monsieur de Nevers, touching Ambroise Paré on the shoulder; "take care! If you fail I will not answer for the anger of the duke's friends and servants."

"Ah!" said Ambroise, with a sad smile, as he turned toward the speaker.

"Your head is in danger," said another.

Ambroise Paré looked up to Heaven as if for strength; then he rejoined with melancholy gravity,—

"So be it! I will endanger my own head in an attempt to save this one. But you can at least," he added, looking proudly around, "leave me to work in peace."

All stepped aside with a sort of respectful deference to the power of genius.

In the solemn silence no further sound was heard except the stertorous breathing of the wounded man.

Ambroise Paré placed his left knee upon the duke's chest; then, leaning over, he took the wooden part of the lance in his hands, as he had said, and moved it to and fro, gently at first, afterwards with more force.

The duke started as if in terrible pain.

The faces of all who were present were pallid with horror.

Ambroise himself stopped for a moment, as if afraid to proceed. The sweat of anguish moistened his forehead; but he set to work again almost immediately.

After a minute, which seemed more than an hour long, the iron at last came from the wound.

Ambroise Paré cast it away with a shudder, and quickly stooped over the yawning orifice.

When he rose, his features were illuminated with a joyous light. But in a moment his serious mood returned, and falling on his knees, he raised his hands to God, while a tear of happiness rolled down his cheek.

It was a sublime moment. Without a word from the great surgeon, every one understood that once more there was hope. The duke's attendants wept hot tears of joy, and some even kissed the skirt of Ambroise Paré's coat.

But no one spoke, waiting for him to say the first word.

He spoke at last, his grave voice trembling with emotion,—

"I will answer now for the life of Monseigneur de Guise."

In an hour, in truth, the duke had recovered consciousness, and even the power of speech.

Ambroise Paré finished dressing the wound; and Gabriel was standing beside the bed to which the surgeon had caused his august patient to be removed.

"So, Gabriel," said the duke, "I owe to you not only the taking of Calais, but my life as well; for it seems that you brought Master Paré to my bedside almost by force."

"Yes, Monseigneur," Ambroise interposed; "save for Monsieur d'Exmès's intervention, they would not have allowed me to come near you."

"God bless my two saviors!" said François de Lorraine.

"I implore you not to talk so much, Monseigneur," said the surgeon.

"Well, I will hold my peace; but just one word,—one question."

"What may it be, Monseigneur?"

"Do you think, Master Paré," asked the duke, "that the results of this horrible wound will be to affect my health or my reason?"

"I am sure not, Monseigneur," said Ambroise; "but I fear that a cicatrix will remain,—a scar (*balafré*)—"

"A scar!" cried the duke; "oh, that is nothing! It is an adornment to a warrior's features; and the sobriquet of *Balafré* is one that I should not object to in the least."

It is well known that his contemporaries and posterity were of the Duc de Guise's opinion, who from that time (as well as his son after him) was surnamed *Le Balafré* by his generation and by history.

CHAPTER XXIV
PARTIAL DÉNOUEMENT

We go forward to the 8th of January,—the day succeeding that on which Gabriel d'Exmès had finally restored to the King of France Calais, his fairest city, which had been lost to him for so many years, and the Duc de Guise, his greatest captain, who had been in imminent danger of death.

But we have no longer to deal with questions involving the future fate of nations; we are at present to occupy ourselves with matters of private and domestic import. From the breach in the walls of Calais and the sick bed of François de Lorraine we pass to the living-room in the dwelling of the Peuquoys.

It was in that room on the lower floor of the house that Jean had decided to lodge Martin, in order to avoid the fatigue of ascending the stairs; and it was there that Ambroise Paré had, the evening before, with his usual skill and success, performed upon the brave squire the amputation that he deemed necessary.

So that certainty had taken the place of what had before been only hope. Martin-Guerre was still in a state of great exhaustion, it is true; but his life was saved.

It would be impossible to describe the regret of Pierre Peuquoy—his remorse, rather—when he learned the truth from Jean. His stern but honest and loyal soul could not obtain its own forgiveness for such a bitter mistake. The honest armorer was constantly urging upon Martin-Guerre to ask or to accept all that he possessed,—his heart and his strong arm, his property and his life.

But we know already that Martin-Guerre had pardoned Pierre Peuquoy,—nay, more, had approved what he had done,—without waiting for him to express his sorrow therefor.

Thus they were on the best of terms; and we must not be surprised to find a sort of domestic council—similar to the one at which we have already been present during the bombardment—in progress at the bedside of Martin-Guerre, who was as one of the family thenceforth.

Vicomte d'Exmès, who was to start for Paris that same evening, was admitted to their deliberations, which were, all things considered, of a less painful nature to the gallant allies of the Risbank fort than on the previous occasion.

In truth, the reparation which was due to the honor of the Peuquoy name was not now beyond the bounds of possibility. The real Martin-Guerre was married; but there was nothing to indicate that Babette's seducer was, and it only remained to find the villain.

Thus it happened that Pierre's expression was calmer and more kindly, but Jean's was very sorrowful, while Babette seemed to be in the deepest dejection.

Gabriel looked from one to another in silence; and Martin-Guerre, stretched upon his bed of pain, was in despair at the thought that he could do nothing for his new-found friends, except furnish them with vague and unsatisfactory information as to the personal appearance of his double.

Pierre and Jean had just returned from the bedside of Monsieur de Guise; for the duke had refused to delay any longer the expression of his gratitude to the brave, patriotic burghers for the effective and glorious part they had taken in the surrender of the city; and Gabriel had introduced them to him at his urgent request.

Pierre was proudly and joyously describing to Babette the details of the presentation.

"Yes, my dear sister," he was saying, "when Monsieur d'Exmès had told the Duc de Guise of our co-operation in all this, in terms which were certainly too flattering and highly colored, the great man deigned to express his satisfaction to Jean and myself with a gracious consideration which I, for my part, shall never forget, though I should live for more than a hundred years. But he gladdened and touched my heart above all by adding that he was anxious to serve us in some way, and asking me in what way he could do so. Not that I was interested for myself, Babette,—you know me too well for that; but do you know what favor I mean to ask of him?"

"No, indeed I do not, my brother," murmured Babette.

"Well, dear sister," continued Pierre, "as soon as we have found the wretch who so basely betrayed you,—and we shall find him, never fear!—I will ask Monsieur de Guise to assist me with his influence in making him save your good name. We have ourselves neither power nor riches, and some such support as his may be necessary to help us to obtain justice."

"Suppose that you fail of obtaining justice, even with his support, cousin?" asked Jean.

"Thanks to my good right arm," Pierre replied energetically, "vengeance at least will not fail me. And yet," he added in a lower voice, and glancing timidly at Martin-Guerre, "I must confess that violence has been productive of but little good thus far."

For a moment he said no more, but was lost in thought. When he shook off his absorption, he was surprised to see that Babette was weeping.

"What makes you weep, pray, my sister?" he asked.

"Ah, I am very unhappy!" cried Babette, sobbing as if her heart would break.

"Unhappy, and why? I believe that in the future the clouds will break away, and—"

"No, they will grow even darker," she said.

"No, no, everything will come all right; make your mind easy," said Pierre. "There can be no hesitation between a reparation which brings nothing but pleasure in its train, and a terrible vengeance. Your lover will come back to you; you will be his wife—"

"But suppose I refuse to marry him?" cried Babette. Jean Peuquoy could not forbear a joyous movement, which did not escape Gabriel's notice.

"Refuse to marry him!" exclaimed Pierre, surprised beyond measure. "Why, you loved him!"

"Yes, I did love him," said Babette; "for he was suffering; besides he seemed to love me, and showed respect and tenderness for me. But the man who deceived me, who lied to me and abandoned me, who appropriated the language, the name, and perhaps the very clothes of another, to lay siege to and surprise a poor, trusting heart—ah, that man I hate and I despise!"

"But if he were willing to marry you?" said Pierre. "It would only be because he was driven to do it, or because he hoped for favors from the Duc de Guise. He would bestow his name upon me either from fear or avarice. No, no, I pray I may never see him again!"

"Babette," replied Pierre, sternly; "you have no right to say, 'I pray I may never see him again.'"

"My dear brother, for mercy's sake! for pity's sake!" cried Babette, weeping piteously, "do not force me to marry a man whom you have yourself called a villain and a coward."

"Babette, think of your dishonored name!"

"I prefer to blush a moment for my misplaced love rather than to blush for my husband all my life."

"Babette, think of your fatherless child!"

"It would be far better for him, I think, to be without a father who would detest him, than to lose his mother who will adore him; and his mother, if she marries that man, will surely die of shame and chagrin."

"So, Babette, you turn a deaf ear to all my remonstrances and entreaties?"

"I implore your affection and your pity, my brother."

"Very well, then," said Pierre, "my affection and my pity will reply to your words, sorrowfully but firmly. As it is necessary above all things, Babette, that you should possess the esteem of others and retain your good name, and as I prefer your unhappiness to your dishonor, since being dishonored your unhappiness will be twofold,—I, your elder brother, the head of your family, wish you to understand that you should marry, if he agrees, the man who betrayed you, and who alone has the power to-day to give you back the honor he has stolen. The law and our religion endow me with an authority over you, which I forewarn you I must use in case of need, to compel you to take a step which, to my mind, is required by your duty toward God, your family, your unborn child, and yourself."

"You condemn me to death, brother," replied Babette, in an altered voice. "It is well; and I bow to your will, since it is my fate and my punishment, and not a soul intercedes for me."

As she spoke, she looked at Gabriel and Jean Peuquoy, who were both silent,—the latter because he was suffering keenly, the other because he wished to see what course events would take.

But at Babette's direct appeal, Jean could no longer restrain himself; and addressing his words to her, but turning to Pierre, he rejoined with a bitter irony, which was hardly in accord with his character,—

"Why do you wish that any one should intercede for you, Babette? Is it because this thing that your brother demands of you is not altogether just and wise? His way of looking at the affair is indeed admirable. He has deeply at heart your honor and that of his family; and to maintain that honor intact, what does he do? He forces you to marry a forger. Truly it is marvellous! To be sure, this scoundrel when once he is taken into the family will probably bring everlasting dishonor upon it by his conduct. It is certain that Monsieur d'Exmès, now present, will not fail to demand from him, in the name of Martin-Guerre, a bitter reckoning for his basely false impersonation, and that this will probably lead to your having to go before the judges, Babette, as the wife of this low-lived appropriator of a name. But what does it matter? You will none the less belong to him by a valid title, and your child will none the less be the recognized and acknowledged son of the false Martin-Guerre. You will die perhaps of the disgrace of being his wife, but your maiden reputation will remain unsullied in everybody's eyes."

Jean Peuquoy uttered these sentiments with a degree of indignant warmth which surprised Babette herself.

"I should hardly have known you, Jean," exclaimed Pierre in amazement. "Is it really you, who speak thus?—you, who are generally so moderate and calm."

"It is just because of my moderation and calmness," replied Jean, "that I am able to view more dispassionately the situation into which you are inconsiderately plunging us to-day."

"Do you believe, pray," rejoined Pierre, "that I would accept with any better grace the infamy of my brother-in-law than my sister's shame? No; if we find Babette's betrayer, I am in hopes that, after all, his fraud may have done no harm except to ourselves and Martin-Guerre; and in that event I rely upon good Martin's friendship for us to cause him to desist from making a complaint, the result of which would fall upon the innocent equally with the guilty."

"Oh," said Martin-Guerre from his bed, "there is no vindictiveness in my nature, and I have no desire for the death of the sinner. If he but pays his debt to you, I will discharge him from any claim I have against him."

"All that is very fine so far as the past is concerned," retorted Jean, who seemed only moderately delighted over the squire's forgiving disposition. "But the future,—who will answer for the future?"

"I will be always on the watch," replied Pierre. "Babette's husband shall never be out of my sight, and it will be best for him to remain an honest man and walk in the straight path, or else—"

"You will inflict justice upon him yourself, will you not?" Jean interposed. "It will be full time. Babette, meanwhile, will have been sacrificed all the same."

"Very well; but you must remember, Jean," retorted Pierre, rather out of patience, "that if it is a difficult position, I simply am meeting it. I did not bring it about. Have you, who talk so finely, been able to devise any other plan than that which I suggest?"

"Yes, of course there is another resource," said Jean.

"What is it?" asked Pierre and Babette in one breath,—Pierre, it must be said, quite as eagerly as his sister.

Vicomte d'Exmès said not a word, but listened with redoubled intentness.

"Oh, well," said Jean, "may it not be possible to find some honest man, who, more moved than alarmed by Babette's ill-fortune, would agree to give her his name?"

Pierre shook his head incredulously,—

"We must not hope for that," said he. "Any one who would close his eyes to such a thing must be either in love or a coward. In either event, we should be obliged to admit strangers or indifferent friends into our sad secret; and although Monsieur d'Exmès and Martin are no doubt our most loyal friends, still I deeply regret that circumstances have made them acquainted with facts which ought never to have been known outside of the family."

Jean Peuquoy replied with an emotion which he tried in vain to hide,—

"I would not suggest a coward to Babette for her husband; but as to your other supposition, Pierre, may we not consider that, too? Suppose that some one were in love with my cousin; suppose that he, also, had been made acquainted by circumstances with her fault, but had learned of her repentance at the same time, and had resolved to assure himself a peaceful and happy future, to forget the past, which Babette surely would like well to efface by her virtue and goodness hereafter,—suppose all this were true; what would you say, Pierre; and you, Babette?"

"Oh, that cannot be! It is a dream!" cried Babette, whose eyes, nevertheless, were illumined with a ray of hope.

"Do you know such a man, Jean?" asked Pierre, in a matter-of-fact way; "or is it not a mere supposition on your part,—as Babette says, a dream?"

Jean Peuquoy, at this straightforward question, hesitated and stammered, and was very ill at ease.

He did not notice the silent, but deep and attentive interest with which Gabriel was following his every motion; he was entirely absorbed in observing Babette, who, breathing fast, and with eyes cast down, seemed to be battling with an emotion which the honest weaver, little skilled in such matters, knew not how to interpret.

He did not draw from it any deduction favorable to his hopes, for it was in a piteous sort of voice that he answered his cousin's direct interrogatory,—

"Alas, Pierre, it is only too probable! I confess that all that I have said is only a dream. In truth, it would not be sufficient for the fulfilment of my dream that Babette should be dearly loved; there must be a little love on her side as well, otherwise she would still be wretched. Now, the man who would be willing thus to buy his own happiness from Babette at the price of forgetfulness would doubtless have to make excuses for some disadvantages on his own side; he would probably not be young nor handsome,—in a word, not lovable. Thus there is no likelihood that Babette would consent to become his wife, and that is why all that I have said is, I fear, nought but idle dreaming."

"Yes, it was a dream," said Babette, sadly, "but not for the reasons that you give, my cousin. The man who would be generous enough to come to my rescue by such devotion, though he should be the most withered and ugly of his sex, ought to be young and beautiful in my sight; for his very act would show a freshness of soul which is not always to be found in the youth of twenty; nor can such kind and generous thoughts fail to leave the imprint of nobleness upon the features. I should find him worthy of my love, too, for he would have given me the greatest proof of his affection that woman could receive. My duty and my pleasure would be to love him all my life and with all my heart, and so that would be very easy. But the impossible and improbable part of your dream, my cousin, would be to find any one capable of such self-abnegation for a poor girl, without charm, and dishonored as I am. There may be men noble enough and kind-hearted enough to entertain for an instant the idea of such a sacrifice, and that is a great deal; but upon reflection, even they would hesitate, and withdraw at the last moment, and I should fall once more from hope to despair. Such, my good Jean, are the real reasons why what you said was nought but a dream."

"And what if it were the truth after all?" said Gabriel suddenly rising from his chair.

"What, what do you say?" cried Babette, completely bewildered.

"I say, Babette, that this devoted, generous heart does exist," replied Gabriel.

"Do you know the man?" asked Pierre, deeply moved.

"I do know him," replied the young man, smiling. "He loves you indeed, Babette, but with the affection of a father as well as of a lover,—an affection which longs to cherish and forgive you. Thus you may accept without reservation this sacrifice of his, in which is no possibility of error, and which is induced only by most tender compassion and most sincere devotion. Besides, you will give as much as you receive, Babette: you will receive honor, but you will bestow happiness; for he who loves you stands alone in the world, joyless, with no interests to make life sweet to him and nothing to hope for in the future. But you will bring him all these things; and if you consent, you will make him as happy to-day as he will make you some day hereafter. Do I not speak the truth, Jean Peuquoy?"

"But, Monsieur le Vicomte, I am ignorant," stammered Jean, trembling like a leaf.

"Very true, Jean," continued Gabriel, still smiling; "there is really one thing that you don't perhaps know; that is, that Babette feels for him by whom she is beloved, not only profound esteem and deep-seated gratitude, but a holy affection. Babette, although she has not guessed it, has felt a vague presentiment of this love of which she is the object, and was at first relieved in her own heart, then touched by it, and finally made happy by the thought of it. Her violent aversion for the villain who deceived her dates from that time. That is why she went on her knees to her brother a moment ago to implore him not to insist on her union with that wretch, whom she only thought that she loved, in the mistaken innocence of her pure, young heart, and whom she loathes to-day with all the force with which she loves him who holds out a hand to rescue her from shame. Am I wrong, Babette?"

"Really, Monseigneur, I don't know," said Babette, with a face as white as the driven snow.

"One doesn't know, and the other is ignorant," resumed Gabriel. "What, Babette, and you, Jean, do you know nothing of your own inmost hearts? Are you ignorant of your own dearest thoughts? Come, come, that isn't possible! I am not the first to make it clear to you, Babette, that Jean loves you. Surely, Jean, you suspected before I spoke, that you were beloved by Babette?"

"Oh, can it be so?" cried Pierre Peuquoy, in a perfect ecstasy of delight; "oh, no, it would be too much happiness!"

"But just look at them!" said Gabriel to him.

Babette and Jean were gazing at each other, still irresolute and half incredulous.

Then, Jean read in the eyes of Babette such fervent gratitude, and Babette so moving an appeal in those of Jean, that both were convinced and persuaded at the same moment.

Without knowing how it came about, they were locked in each other's arms.

Pierre Peuquoy was so entirely overcome that he could not utter a word; but he pressed Jean's hand with a fervor more eloquent than all the words of all the languages in the world.

As for Martin-Guerre, he sat up in bed, despite the risk, and with eyes swimming in tears of joy, clapped his hands with a will at this unexpected dénouement.

When the first transport of joy had somewhat subsided, Gabriel said,—

"Now we will arrange matters thus. Jean Peuquoy must marry Babette as soon as possible; but before finally taking up their abode with their brother, I insist that they pass a few months in my house at Paris. In that way Babette's secret, the sad cause of this happy marriage, will be buried forever in the five faithful hearts of those who are here present. There is a sixth, to be sure, who might betray the secret; but he, if he ever learns Babette's fate, which is not likely, will not have it in his power to annoy them for long—that I will answer for. So, my dear kind friends, you may live henceforth in perfect content and peace, and have no fear of the future."

"Ah, my noble, high-souled guest!" said Pierre, kissing Gabriel's hand.

"To you, and you alone," said Jean, "do we owe our happiness, even as the king owes Calais to you."

"And every morning and evening," added Babette, "we will pray fervently to God for the welfare of our savior."

"Yes, Babette," Gabriel replied, deeply moved, "yes, I thank you for that thought: pray God that your savior may now have the power to save himself."

CHAPTER XXV
HAPPY OMENS

"Why?" Babette Peuquoy replied to the melancholy and doubting tone of Gabriel's last words, "are you not successful in everything you undertake?—in the defence of St. Quentin and the capture of Calais as well as in arranging a happy marriage for poor Babette?"

"Yes, it is true," said Gabriel, with a sad smile; "God seems to have decreed that the most insuperable and most alarming obstacles in my path should vanish like magic at my approach; but, alas! that is no proof, my dear child, that I shall finally attain the end which I so earnestly desire."

"Ah," said Jean Peuquoy, "you have made too many others happy, not to be happy yourself at last."

"I accept the omen, Jean," replied Gabriel, "and there could be no more favorable augury of my own success than to leave my friends in Calais peaceful and happy. But you know that it is necessary that I should leave you now, perhaps to become immersed in sorrow and in tears—who can tell? Let us at all events leave no regrets behind, and let us arrange everything in which we are interested."

So they fixed a day for the wedding, which Gabriel, to his great regret, was not able to attend, and then agreed upon the day upon which Jean and Babette were to start for Paris.

"It may be," said Gabriel, sadly, "that you will not find me at home to welcome you. I hope that will not be the case, but I may perhaps be obliged to be absent from Paris and the court for a time. But let that make no difference about your coming. Aloyse, my good old nurse, will entertain you in my behalf as well as I myself could do. You and she must, however, give a thought now and then to your absent host."

Martin-Guerre had to remain at Calais, notwithstanding all his remonstrances and entreaties. Ambroise Paré declared that his convalescence would be very slow and tedious, and meanwhile he would require the most constant care and watchfulness. Therefore his choler was of no avail, and he was obliged to yield.

"But as soon as you are entirely well, my faithful fellow," said Vicomte d'Exmès, "come to Paris; and whatever may befall, I will fulfil my promise to you, never fear, and deliver you from your strange persecutor. Now I am doubly bound to do it."

"Oh, Monseigneur, think of yourself, not of me," said Martin-Guerre.

"Every obligation will be met," Gabriel resumed; "but I must say 'adieu,' my good friends, for it is time for me to return to Monsieur de Guise. I have asked certain favors of him in your presence, which he will accord me, I think, in consideration of the services I have been fortunate enough to render during these recent occurrences."

But the Peuquoys refused to take leave of Gabriel thus. They insisted upon meeting him at the Paris gate at three o'clock, to see him once more and say farewell to him there.

Martin-Guerre was the only one who had to say his last words to his master at this moment, and they were not uttered without regret and sorrow. But Gabriel comforted him somewhat with a few of the kind expressions which came so naturally to his lips.

A quarter of an hour later Vicomte d'Exmès was ushered into the presence of the Duc de Guise.

"Oh, there you are, my ambitious young friend!" said the duke, as he saw him come in.

"My only ambition has been to do my best to second your efforts, Monseigneur," said Gabriel.

"Oh, from that point of view you have shown no ambition at all," rejoined Le Balafré (we may henceforth give the duke that name, or, more properly speaking, that title). "I call you ambitious, Gabriel," he continued playfully, "because of the innumerable extravagant requests you have made upon me; and upon my word I am not sure that I can satisfy you."

"I based them rather upon what I knew of your benevolence than upon my own poor merits," said Gabriel.

"You have a very high opinion of my benevolence, then," said the Duc de Guise, with mild raillery. "I leave it to you, Monsieur de Vaudemont," he continued, turning to a gentleman seated beside his bed, who had just come to visit him,—"I leave it to you to say if any one should be allowed to present such paltry requests to a prince."

"Consider that I erred in what I said, then, Monseigneur," Gabriel responded, "and that I based my requests upon my own merits and not upon your benevolence."

"Another blunder!" cried the duke; "for your gallantry is a hundred times beyond my power to recompense. Now just listen for a moment, Monsieur de Vaudemont, and let me tell you of the unprecedented favors which Monsieur d'Exmès asks at my hands."

"I venture to predict, Monseigneur," said the Marquis de Vaudemont, "that they are sure to be absurdly small, both in proportion to his merit and your power. However, let me hear them."

"In the first place," continued the duke, "Monsieur d'Exmès asks me to take back to Paris with me the little band of volunteers whom he enlisted at his own expense and for his own purpose, but meanwhile to make such use as I please of them. He reserves only four men to serve as his own suite on his journey to Paris. And these brave fellows, whom he thus lends to me under pretense of recommending them to me, are no others, Monsieur de Vaudemont, than the incarnate fiends who accompanied him in that marvellous escalading expedition which ended in the capture of the impregnable Risbank fort. Well, which of us renders the other a service in this transaction, Monsieur d'Exmès or myself?"

"I must confess that Monsieur d'Exmès does," said the Marquis de Vaudemont.

"And by my faith, I accept this new obligation," resumed the duke, gayly. "I shall not allow your eight fellows to spoil in idleness, Gabriel. As soon as I can leave my bed I will take them with me on my expedition against Ham; for I do not propose to leave the English one foot of earth in our dear France. Malemort himself, the everlastingly wounded man, will be on hand, too; for Master Pare has promised that he shall be cured as soon I am."

"He will be very fortunate, Monseigneur," said Gabriel.

"So, then, there is your first request granted, and with no great effort on my part. In the second place, Monsieur d'Exmès reminds me that Madame Diane de Castro, the king's daughter, whom you know, Monsieur de Vaudemont, is here at Calais, where she has been held prisoner by the English. Vicomte d'Exmès, realizing how deeply I am engrossed with other matters, has very opportunely reminded me to assure this lady of the royal blood of the protection and respect which are her due. Does, or does not Monsieur d'Exmès render me a service in this matter also?"

"Without the slightest doubt," replied the Marquis de Vaudemont.

"The second point is settled, then," said the duke. "My orders are already given; and whilst I am reputed to be an indifferent courtier, I am altogether too sensible of my duty as a gentleman, to forget at this time the consideration which is due to the person and exalted rank of Madame de Castro; therefore, a suitable escort will be ready to accompany her to Paris, when and how she chooses."

Gabriel expressed his gratitude only by a deep inclination, fearing that he might betray the interest and importance which that promise had for him.

"In the third place," resumed the Duc de Guise, "Lord Wentworth, the English governor of this city, was taken prisoner by Monsieur d'Exmès. In the terms of capitulation granted to Lord Derby, we bound ourselves to admit him to ransom; but Monsieur d'Exmès, to whom both prisoner and ransom belong, permits us to show ourselves still more liberal. In fact, he asks for our authority to send Lord Wentworth to England without requiring him to pay any price for his freedom. Will not this action give great éclat to our courtesy, even beyond these narrow limits; and does not Monsieur d'Exmès thereby render us once more a service of real value?"

"Undoubtedly, as is demonstrated by Monseigneur's noble appreciation of it," said Monsieur de Vaudemont.

"Make your mind easy, Gabriel," said the duke; "Monsieur de Thermes has gone, on your behalf and mine, to set Lord Wentworth at liberty and return his sword to him. He may leave the city as soon as he desires."

"I thank you, Monseigneur," said Gabriel; "but do not give me credit for too much magnanimity. I am only requiting Lord Wentworth for various courtesies he extended to me when I was myself his prisoner, and giving him at the same time a lesson in fair dealing and probity; I doubt not he will understand the allusion and the implied reproof."

"You have more reason than any one else to deal sternly with him upon such questions," said the duke in all seriousness.

"Now, Monseigneur," said Gabriel, much disturbed to find the principal object of his solicitude ignored by the Duc de Guise, "allow me to remind you of the promise you were good enough to make me in my tent on the eve of the capture of the Risbank fort."

"Wait one moment, I beg, O most impatient youth!" said Le Balafré. "In consideration of these three eminent services which I have rendered you, which Monsieur de Vaudemont has verified, I have well earned the right to demand a favor at your hands. I ask you then, as you are about to start so soon for Paris, to take with you and present to the king the keys of the city of Calais—"

"Oh, Monseigneur!" Gabriel interrupted, in an outburst of gratitude.

"You will not find that a very burdensome duty, I fancy," said the duke. "Besides, you are used to commissions of this sort, for you know I intrusted to your care the flags captured in our Italian campaign."

"Ah, how well you understand the art of doubling the force of your kind deeds by your manner of performing them!" cried the enraptured Gabriel.

"Further than that," continued the duke, "you will hand to his Majesty at the same time a copy of the capitulation, and this letter, which I wrote this morning from beginning to end with my own hand despite the orders of Master Ambroise Paré. But you see," he added significantly, "no one could possibly have done you justice, Gabriel, or asked that justice be done you by others, with so much assurance as myself. Now I trust you will be satisfied with me, and that the result of what I have done will be that you will have nothing with which to reproach the king. Here, my friend, are the keys and the letter. I have no need to charge you to take care of them."

"And I, Monseigneur, have no need to say that I am yours in life and death," said Gabriel, in a voice choked with emotion.

He took the little box of carved wood and the sealed letter which the duke handed him. They were the priceless talismans which might perhaps be the means of procuring for him his father's freedom and his own happiness.

"Now I will not detain you longer," said the Duc de Guise. "You are probably in haste to be on your way; and I, less fortunate than you, find myself, after this morning of excitement, in a state of weariness, which enjoins rest upon me even more imperiously than Master Ambroise Paré."

"Adieu, then; and once more, Monseigneur, accept my heartfelt thanks," said Vicomte d'Exmès.

At this moment Monsieur de Thermes, whom the Duc de Guise had sent to Lord Wentworth, hurried into the room in a state of great excitement.

"Ah," said the duke to Gabriel, "our ambassador to the victor need not set out without an interview with our ambassador to the vanquished. But how's this," he added, "what's the matter, De Thermes? You seem to be greatly distressed."

"So I am, indeed, Monseigneur," said Monsieur de Thermes.

"Why, what has happened?" asked Le Balafré. "Has Lord Wentworth—"

"Lord Wentworth, to whom, Monseigneur, in accordance with your commands, I announced his release and returned his sword, accepted the act of grace coldly and without a word. I was just leaving him in amazement at such discourteous behavior, when I heard a loud cry, which made me hasten back. The first use he had made of his freedom was to run himself through the body with the sword he had just received at my hands. He had killed himself instantly, and I found only his dead body."

"Ah," cried the Duc de Guise, "it must have been the despair caused by his defeat which drove him to that extremity. Do you not think so, Gabriel? It is a real misfortune!"

"No, Monseigneur," replied Gabriel, with sorrowful gravity; "no, Lord Wentworth did not die because he had been beaten."

"How's that! what was the reason, then?" asked Le Balafré.

"I beg you to allow me to say nothing as to the real reason," replied Gabriel. "I would have kept the secret if Lord Wentworth had lived, and I must guard it even more carefully now he is no more. However," continued Gabriel, lowering his voice, "in view of this proud act of his, I may confide to you, Monseigneur, that in his place I would have done just as he has. Yes, Lord Wentworth did well; for even if he had had no cause to blush before me, still the conscience of a true gentleman is a sufficiently troublesome creditor to induce one to impose silence upon it at any cost; and when one has the honor to belong to the nobility of a noble country, there are irreparable faults the effects of which can only be avoided by falling-dead as he has done."

"I understand you, Gabriel," said the Duc de Guise. "It only remains for us to pay Lord Wentworth the last honors."

"He is worthy of them," returned Gabriel; "and while I deeply deplore this necessary end of his career, I am glad, nevertheless, that I can still think with esteem and regret, as Intake leave of him on earth, of the man whose guest I was in this city."

When he said farewell to the Duc de Guise a few moments later with renewed acknowledgments, Gabriel went at once to the governor's former residence, where Madame de Castro was still living.

He had not seen Diane since the evening before; but she had quickly learned, in common with all Calais, of Ambroise Paré's fortunate intervention and the safety of the Duc de Guise; so Gabriel found her calm and reassured.

Lovers are always superstitious, and the peace of mind of his well-beloved had a cheering effect upon him.

Diane was naturally still better pleased when Gabriel told her what had taken place between the Duc de Guise and himself, and showed her the letter and the box which had been intrusted to him because of his unremitting labor and his defiance of so many dangers.

But even amid so many causes for gratulation she felt the regret of a Christian at Lord Wentworth's sad end; for though he had, to be sure, abused and insulted her for an hour or two, he had protected and treated her with all due respect for three months.

"May God pardon him as I do!" she said.

Gabriel went on to speak of Martin-Guerre and the Peuquoys, and of the escort which Monsieur de Guise had promised her, Diane, and referred to all her surroundings.

Indeed, he would have been only too glad to find a thousand other subjects of conversation to afford him an excuse for remaining; and yet the engrossing idea which called him to Paris still absorbed his thoughts to a great degree. He longed both to go and to stay; he was at once happy and anxious.

At last, as the hours passed by, Gabriel was obliged to say that he could only postpone his departure for a few moments longer.

"Are you going, Gabrieli Well, it is much better that you should for many reasons," said Diane. "I have not had the courage to speak to you of your departure; and yet by not deferring it you will give me the greatest proof of your affection that it would be possible for me to receive. Yes, my friend, go, so that I may have a shorter time to wait and suffer. Go, so that our fate may be decided as speedily as possible."

"May God bless you for your brave words, which go so far to sustain my courage!" said Gabriel.

"At this very moment," said Diane, "I feel while I am listening to you, as I know you must while speaking to me, an indefinable anxiety. We have been talking of a hundred things, and yet we have not dared to touch upon the matter which really lies nearest to our hearts and our lives. But since you are going in a very few moments, we may now revert without fear to the only subject in which we are really interested."

"Ah, you read my own heart and yours at a single glance!" said Gabriel.

"Listen a moment," said Diane. "Besides the letter you are to deliver to the king from the Duc de Guise, you will give his Majesty this other one from me which I wrote last night. In it I have told him how you saved me and set me free. Thus it will be made clear to him and to all others that you have restored his city to the king, and his daughter to the father. I speak thus; for I fervently trust that Henri II.'s affection for me is not deceptive, and that I have a right to call him my father."

"Dear Diane, God grant that you augur truly!" cried Gabriel.

"I envy you, Gabriel," continued Diane, "because you will lift the veil, and learn our destiny before I shall. However, I shall soon follow you, dear. Since Monsieur de Guise is so kindly disposed towards me, I will ask for an escort to-morrow; and although I shall be forced to travel more leisurely than you, I shall be at Paris a very few days after you."

"Oh, yes, do come soon!" said Gabriel, "for it seems to me as if your presence would bring me good fortune."

"In any event," Diane replied, "I do not want to be entirely separated from you; but I desire that there should be some one to remind you of me from time to time. Since you will be obliged to leave your faithful squire, Martin-Guerre, here, take with you the French page whom Lord Wentworth gave me. André is only a child, scarcely sixteen, and perhaps still younger in disposition than in years; but he is devoted and loyal, and will do you good service. Accept him from me. Amidst the less congenial companions of your suite, he will be a pleasanter and more agreeable attendant for you, and I shall be glad to know that he is always at your side."

"Oh, thanks for such thoughtful consideration," said Gabriel; "but you know that I must depart in a very few moments—"

"André knows my purpose," said Diane. "Oh, if you knew how proud he is to be in your service. He must be all ready now, and I have only a few last instructions to give him. If you go now and take your leave of the good Peuquoys, André will be with you before you quit Calais."

"I will take him with very great pleasure," said Gabriel; "I shall at least have some one with whom I can sometimes converse about you."

"I thought of that," said Madame de Castro, with a slight blush. "But now, adieu," she said earnestly; "we must say adieu."

"Oh, not 'adieu,'" replied Gabriel; "not that sad word which means a long separation; not 'adieu,' but *au revoir*!"

"Alas!" said Diane, "when and under what circumstances shall we meet again! If the riddle of our destiny be solved contrary to our wishes, will it not be better that we should never see each other more?"

"Oh, don't say so, Diane!" cried Gabriel; "don't say so! Besides, who but myself can inform you of the result, whether it be disastrous or happy?"

"Ah, *Dieu*!" Diane replied with a shudder, "it seems to me as if, whether it were happy or disastrous, I should die of joy or grief simply upon hearing your lips speak the words."

"But how shall I let you know?" asked Gabriel.

"Wait one moment," replied Diane.

She drew a gold ring from her huger, and took from a chest the nun's veil which she had worn at the Benedictine convent at St. Quentin.

"Listen, Gabriel," said she, in a tone of deep solemnity as she gave them to him; "as it is probable that everything will be settled before I reach Paris, send André to meet me. If God declares himself for us, he will bring back this wedding-ring to the Vicomtesse de Montgommery; but if our hopes are blighted, let him bring this nun's veil to Sister Bénie."

"Oh, let me fall at your feet and adore you as one of the angels from heaven!" cried the young man, touched to the very soul by this affecting proof of her great love.

"No, Gabriel, no, rise from your knees," Diane replied; "let us be steadfast and dignified in God's sight. Press upon my lips a pure brotherly kiss, as I will a sisterly one upon yours, thereby endowing you with faith and strength, so far as my power can go."

In silence they exchanged a sacred, sorrowful kiss.

"And now, my dear," continued Diane, "let us part, for it is time; not saying adieu, since you dread the word, but *au revoir,* to meet again in this world or the next!"

"*Au revoir, au revoir*!" murmured Gabriel.

He clasped Diane to his breast in a close embrace, and fastened a long, yearning gaze upon her, as if to draw from her lovely eyes the strength of which he was so much in need.

At last, upon a sorrowful but expressive motion which she made to him, he released her; and placing the ring on his finger and the veil in his bosom, he said once more in a stifled voice,—

"*Au revoir*, Diane!"

"Gabriel, *au revoir*!" Diane replied, with a hopeful gesture.

Gabriel fled as if he were a madman.

Half an hour later, with renewed tranquillity, he left behind him the fair city of Calais, which it had been his good fortune to restore to the kingdom of France.

He was on horseback, accompanied by the young page André, who had overtaken him, and by four of his volunteers.

One of these last was Ambrosio, who was very glad to find an opportunity of taking back to Paris with him certain English small wares, which he expected to dispose of to advantage to the habitués of the court.

Another was Pilletrousse, who, in a conquered city, where he was one of the masters and victors, was afraid that he might yield to temptation and recur to his former habits.

Yvonnet was also among them: he had not been able to find in provincial Calais a single tailor worthy his patronage; and his costume had been too seriously injured by the hard usage it had experienced to be presentable,—it could not be replaced suitably except at Paris.

Lactance was the last of the four; he had asked leave to accompany his master so that he might receive his confessor's assurance that his exploits had not exceeded his penances, and that his assets in the shape of self-inflicted austerities would suffice to meet the liabilities he had incurred by his feats of arms.

Pierre and Jean Peuquoy, with Babette, accompanied the five horsemen on foot as far as what was called the Paris gate.

There they were compelled to part. Gabriel said a last farewell to his kind friends, and gave them a warm clasp of his hand; while they, with tears in their eyes, wished him all happiness and showered benedictions upon him.

But the Peuquoys soon lost sight of the little band, who set off at a trot, and disappeared at a turn in the road. The good burghers returned with sad hearts to Martin-Guerre.

Gabriel felt grave and preoccupied, but not sorrowful.

He was hopeful!

Once before Gabriel had left Calais to seek at Paris the solution of the mystery surrounding his destiny. But on that occasion circumstances wore a much less favorable appearance. He was concerned about Martin-Guerre, Babette, and the Peuquoys, and anxious, about Diane, whom he had left behind, a prisoner in the hands of Lord Wentworth, who was in love with her. Then, too, his vague presentiments of the future were but slightly tinged with hope; for he had, after all, done nothing more than prolong the resistance of a town, which was in the end obliged to surrender. Surely, that was hardly an achievement great enough to deserve so great a reward.

But to-day he left behind him no cause for gloomy thoughts. The two wounded men, both so dear to him, his general and his squire, were both saved, and Ambroise Paré guaranteed their recovery; Babette Peuquoy was to marry a man whom she loved, and by whom she was beloved, her honor as well as her future happiness being assured; Madame de Castro was free, and treated like a queen in a French city, and no later than the next day would follow him to Paris.

Last of all, our hero had struggled so long with Fortune that he might well hope that he had at last tired her out; the undertaking which he had carried through triumphantly to its close—conceiving the idea of taking Calais, as well as furnishing the means to accomplish it—was not one of those the value of which admits of discussion or haggling. The key of France restored to the possession of the King of France! Such an exploit most certainly justified the most lofty ambition; and the Vicomte d'Exmès's ambition was no more than a just and holy one.

He was hopeful. The persuasive encouragement and soothing promises of Diane were still ringing in his ears with the last good wishes of the Peuquoys. Gabriel saw about him André—whose presence reminded him of his beloved—and the gallant and devoted soldiers of his escort; before his eyes, firmly attached to the pommel of his saddle, he saw the box which contained the keys of Calais; in his doublet he could feel the precious copy of the capitulation and the still more precious letters of the Duc de Guise and Madame de Castro; Diane's gold ring shone upon his finger,—ever present and eloquent pledges of good fortune.

The very sky, beautifully blue and cloudless, seemed to speak of hope; the pure and bracing air made the blood run warm in his veins; the thousand sounds to be heard in the country in the twilight were eloquent of peace and tranquillity; and the sun, which was setting in a glory of purple and gold on Gabriel's left hand, was a most comforting sight to his eyes and his heart.

It was impossible to set out toward a coveted goal under happier auspices.

We shall see in due time what came of it.

CHAPTER XXVI
A QUATRAIN

On the evening of Jan. 12, 1558, Queen Catherine de Médicis was holding at the Louvre one of the periodical receptions of which we have previously spoken, at which all the princes and nobles of the realm were wont to assemble.

This particular occasion was an exceptionally brilliant and lively one, although a large part of the nobility were absent at the seat of war, in the north, with the Duc de Guise's army.

Among the ladies present besides Catherine, the queen *de jure,* were Madame Diane de Poitiers, the queen *de facto,* the young queen-dauphine, Mary Stuart, and the melancholy Élisabeth, afterward Queen of Spain, whose very beauty, already so admired, was fated to cause her so much misery.

The distinguished assembly included the man who was at that time the head of the House of Bourbon, Antoine, the titular king of Navarre,—a weak and vacillating prince, who had been sent to the French court by his virile-hearted wife, Jeanne d'Albret, to try and obtain by the intervention of Henri II. the restitution of his kingdom of Navarre, which had been confiscated by Spain.

But Antoine de Navarre was already inclining to the Calvinistic doctrines, and was not looked upon with a very favorable eye at a court which was in the habit of burning heretics at the stake.

His brother, Louis de Bourbon, Prince de Condé, was likewise present. His was a character to inspire more respect if not more affection. He was, however, a more pronounced Calvinist than the King of Navarre, and was generally considered to be the secret leader of the rebellious spirits. He possessed the power to make himself a great favorite with the people, being not only a bold rider but very skilful with the sword and dagger, although in stature he was quite short, and had decidedly disproportionate shoulders. Besides, he was a great gallant, very clever, and passionately devoted to the ladies. A popular chanson of the day spoke thus of him:—

"Ce petit homme tant joli,
Toujours cause et toujours rit,
Et toujours baise sa mignonne.
Dieu gard' de mal le petit homme." [2]

The gentlemen who, openly or secretly, advocated the principles of the Reformed religion were naturally grouped around the King of Navarre and the Prince de Condé,—among them being Admiral de Coligny, La Renaudie, and the Baron de Castelnau, who, having but recently arrived from Touraine, his native province, had been presented at court that day for the first time.

The assemblage, despite the absence of many great seigneurs, was numerous and distinguished; but amid all the confusion, excitement, and enjoyment, two men remained absorbed by grave and apparently unpleasant reflections.

These two men, whose abstraction was caused by widely different reasons, were the king and the Constable de Montmorency.

Henri II. was at the Louvre corporeally, but his thoughts were all at Calais.

During the three weeks since the departure of the Duc de Guise, he had been thinking unceasingly, night and day, of that perilous expedition, the object of which was to drive the English out of the kingdom forever, but which was quite as likely to seriously endanger the welfare of France.

Henri had more than once blamed himself for having allowed Monsieur de Guise to attempt so hazardous a stroke.

If the undertaking should prove abortive, what a disgrace for France in the eyes of all Europe! what superhuman efforts must be made to repair such a failure! The disastrous day of St. Laurent would be a mere bagatelle beside that. The constable had undergone defeat, but François de Lorraine had actually gone in search of it.

The king, who had had no intelligence from the besieging army for three days, was preoccupied with gloomy forebodings, and paid but little heed to the encouraging assurances of the Cardinal de Lorraine, who, standing near the king's couch, was vainly trying to restore his courage.

Diane de Poitiers was quick to remark the gloomy humor of her royal lover; but as she observed Monsieur de Montmorency in another part of the room, apparently in quite as great dejection as the king, she directed her steps toward him.

It was the siege of Calais which was the cause of his downheartedness, but, as we have said, for a very different reason.

The king was afraid of failure, while the constable dreaded success much more.

For success in that enterprise would definitely establish the Duc de Guise in the first rank, and relegate him to the second. The salvation of France would be the ruin of the poor constable, and we must confess that his selfishness had always taken precedence of his patriotism.

So he was very uncourteous to the beautiful favorite who advanced smilingly toward him.

Our readers will remember the inexplicable and depraved passion which the mistress of the most courtly and gallant king in Christendom entertained for this brutal veteran.

"What is the trouble with my old soldier to-day?" she asked in her most winning tones.

"Ah, so you mock me too, do you, Madame?" said Montmorency, sharply.

"I mock you, my friend! You don't realize what you are saying."

"I was thinking of what you said yourself," rejoined the constable, with a muttered curse. "You called me your old soldier. Old? yes, that is true; I am no longer a beau of twenty years. Soldier? no. You can see plainly that I am no longer considered good for anything except to show myself with my parade sword in the halls of the Louvre."

"Do not speak so," said the favorite, with an affectionate smile. "Are you not still the *constable*?"

"What does a constable amount to, when there is a lieutenant-general of the kingdom?"

"The latter title expires with the circumstances which called it into existence, while yours, being attached, with no power of revocation, to the highest military dignity in the kingdom, will last as long as your life."

"But I am already dead and buried," said the constable, with a bitter laugh.

"Why do you say that, my friend?" replied Madame de Poitiers. "You have not ceased to be as powerful and as formidable to the nation's enemies without as to your personal enemies within."

"Let us talk seriously, Diane, and not try to flatter or deceive each other with empty words."

"If I deceive you, it is only because I myself am deceived," Diane rejoined. "Give me proofs that I am wrong, and I will not only acknowledge my error on the spot, but I will do all I can to rectify it."

"Very well," said the constable; "in the first place, you speak of the enemies without trembling before me. Those are very comforting words; but, in reality, who is sent against these enemies?—a general who is younger and doubtless more fortunate than myself, but who may some day turn this good fortune of his to his own private advantage."

"What makes you think that the Duc de Guise will succeed?" asked Diane, with most subtle flattery.

"His failure," replied the constable, hypocritically, "would be a terrible misfortune for France, which I should bitterly deplore for my country's sake; but his success would perhaps be an even more terrible misfortune, which I should dread for the sake of my sovereign."

"Do you believe then," said Diane, "that the ambition of Monsieur de Guise—"

"I have probed it, and it is very deep," replied the jealous courtier. "If by any chance there should be a change of reign, have you considered what that ambition, assisted by the influence of Mary Stuart, might be able to effect upon the mind of a young and inexperienced king! My devotion to your interests has completely alienated Queen Catherine from me. The Guises will be more sovereign than the sovereign himself."

"Such a catastrophe is, thank God, very improbable and very far distant," returned Diane, who could not avoid the reflection that her friend of sixty years was rather free with his conjectures as to the prospects of the early demise of a king who was but forty.

"There are other chances against us much nearer at hand and almost as terrible," said Montmorency, shaking his head very gravely.

"What are they, my friend?"

"Have you lost your memory, Diane, or do you only pretend to forget who went to Calais with the Duc de Guise; who, apparently, was the one who first breathed a suggestion of this foolhardy enterprise into his ear, and who will return in triumph with him, if he does triumph, and will no doubt succeed in receiving credit for some share in the victory?"

"Are you speaking of Vicomte d'Exmès?" asked Diane.

"Of whom else, Madame? Even though you may have forgotten his extravagant undertaking, he will remember it, never fear! And more than that, fortune is so capricious that he is quite capable of having kept his promise, and of loudly calling upon the king to redeem his."

"Impossible!" exclaimed Diane.

"What is it that seems impossible to you, Madame,—that Monsieur d'Exmès should keep his word, or that the king should be true to his?"

"Either supposition is absurd and insane, and the second even more so than the first."

"If, however, the first should be realized, it may very well be that the second will follow; for the king is very weak on these questions of honor, and he would be quite capable, Madame, of priding himself upon his chivalrous loyalty, and of disclosing his secret and ours to a common foe."

"Once more I say it is a wild, impossible dream," cried Diane, turning pale, nevertheless.

"But, Diane, suppose you were to see this dream with your eyes, and touch it with your hands, what would you do!"

"Indeed I do not know, my good constable," said Madame de Valentinois; "we should have to consult and look around, and then act. Anything rather than that extremity! If the king abandons us, why, then, we must get along without him; and confidently anticipating that he will never dare to disavow what we have done after the event, we must exercise our own power and our personal influence and credit to the utmost."

"Ah, that is just what I expected you would say!" said the constable. "Our power! our personal influence! Speak of your own, Madame; but as for mine, it has sunk so low that in truth I look upon it as dead and gone. My enemies within, for whom just now you expressed so much pity, might have very pretty sport with me at this time. There is no gentleman at this court who hasn't more power than this pitiful constable. You can see yourself how I am avoided. It is very simple; for who would care to pay his court to a fallen star! It will be much safer, therefore, Madame, for you not to rely hereafter upon the support of a discredited, disgraced old servant, friendless and without influence, yes, even penniless."

"Penniless!" Diane echoed incredulously.

"Why yes, Madame,—penniless, by the Mass!" said the constable a second time, and angrily. "That is perhaps the most grievous part of it, at my age, and after all the services I have rendered. The last war ruined me; for my ransom and those of several of my people exhausted my last pecuniary resources. Those who abandon me know it very well. I shall be reduced one of these days to going about the streets asking for alms, like Belisarius, the Carthaginian general, I think it was, whom I have heard my nephew, the admiral, speak of."

"What! have your friends all left you, my constable?" asked Diane, smiling at her old lover's erudition, as well as at his covetousness.

"Yes," said the constable: "I have no friends, I tell you." He added, most pathetically,—"The unfortunate never have friends."

"I propose to prove you in the wrong," said Diane. "I can clearly see now the source of this sullen humor which has gained control of you. But why did you not tell me in the first place? Do you lack confidence in me, pray? It is sad, indeed, if you do. But no matter! I only intend to be revenged in a friendly way. Tell me, did not the king impose a new tax last week?"

"Yes, dear Diane," replied the constable, who had grown much calmer under the influence of Diane's words; "a very just tax, too, and heavy enough to defray all the expenses of the war."

"That will do very well," said Diane; "and I will show you that even a woman may be able to do more than repair fortune's cruel blows to such men as you. Henri seems to me to be in a very ill-humor to-day. But never mind! I will speak with him forthwith; and you will soon be forced to agree that I am a kind friend and faithful ally."

"Ah, Diane, you are as kind and good as you are beautiful! That I will always maintain," said Montmorency, gallantly.

"But when I have replenished the springs from which your influence and your favor flow, you will not abandon me, will you, my old lion? And you will not talk any more to your devoted friend of your powerlessness against her enemies and yours?"

"Why, my dear Diane, are not all that I am and all that I have at your service?" said the constable; "and if I sometimes grieve at the loss of my influence, is it not because I fear thereby to be less powerful to serve my beautiful sovereign mistress?"

"Very good!" said Diane, with her most seductive smile. She gave her lovely white hand to her superannuated lover, who imprinted upon it a tender kiss with his bearded lips; then, with a last encouraging glance, she moved away from him toward the king.

The Cardinal de Lorraine was still at Henri's side, watching over the interests of his absent brother, and doing his utmost to remove the king's fears as to the issue of the ill-considered expedition against Calais.

But Henri was paying more attention to his unquiet thoughts than to the cardinal's consoling words.

It was at this moment that Madame Diane approached them.

"I'll undertake to say, Messire," she began, addressing the cardinal with much warmth, "that your Eminence is saying to the king something unkind about poor Monsieur de Montmorency."

"Oh, Madame," retorted Charles de Lorraine, bewildered by this unexpected attack, "I venture to ask his Majesty to bear me witness that the name of Monsieur le Connétable has not been once uttered during our interview."

"That is true," said the king, carelessly.

"That is merely another way of doing him a disservice."

"But if I can neither speak nor keep silent about him, what am I to do, Madame, I beg?"

"You should say pleasant things about him," replied Diane.

"Very well, then," retorted the wily cardinal; "if I must do that, I will say (for the commands of beauty have never found me lacking in dutiful submission) that Monsieur de Montmorency is a great commander; that he won the battle of St. Laurent, and retrieved the fortunes of France; and that just at this time, to put the finishing touch to his work, he has assumed the offensive against our enemies, and is now engaged in attempting a memorable and glorious achievement under the walls of Calais."

"Calais! Calais!—ah, who will bring me news of Calais?" murmured the king, who had heard only that name in this war of words between the minister and the favorite.

"You have an admirable and Christian-like manner of awarding praise, Monsieur le Cardinal," Diane rejoined; "and I congratulate you upon your mastery of ironical compliment."

"Well, Madame," said Charles de Lorraine, "in truth, I do not see how else I could award praise to this poor Monsieur de Montmorency, as you called him just now."

"You are not honest in your search, Messire," replied Diane. "Might you not, for instance, do more justice to the zeal with which the constable organized means of defence at Paris, and brought the few troops who were left here to a state of efficiency, while others were jeopardizing and compromising the vital forces of the kingdom in rash and foolhardy enterprises?"

"Oh-ho!" exclaimed the cardinal.

"Alas!" sighed the king, who heard nothing except what bore directly upon the subject of his solicitude.

"Might we not say, further," added Diane, "that although chance has not been friendly to Monsieur de Montmorency's magnificent efforts, and fortune has declared against him, he is at least entirely without personal ambition; he recognizes no other interest save that of his country, in whose cause he has sacrificed everything,—his life, which he was among the first to put in jeopardy; his liberty, of which he was so long deprived; and his property, which is all gone."

"Indeed!" said Charles de Lorraine, with an air of amazement.

"Yes, your Eminence," Diane repeated; "there is no doubt about that,—Monsieur de Montmorency is ruined."

"Ruined! Do you mean it?" said the cardinal.

"He is so entirely without means," continued the unblushing favorite, "that I was just on the point of appealing to his Majesty to aid this loyal servant in his distress."

The king made no reply, so absorbed was he.

"Yes, Sire," Diane said, addressing him directly in order to attract his attention, "I most earnestly beg you to come to the assistance of your faithful constable, whose pecuniary resources have been exhausted to the last sou by the price of his ransom and the great expense of the war contracted in your Majesty's service. Sire, are you listening to me?"

"Excuse me, Madame," said Henri; "I seem hardly able this evening to fix my attention upon any subject. The thought of a possible disaster at Calais occupies my mind entirely, as you can well understand."

"That is just the reason," Diane replied, "why your Majesty, in my opinion, ought to treat gently and befriend the man who has done his best beforehand to minimize the effects of this calamity, if it must befall."

"But we are as much in need of money ourselves as the constable," said the king.

"How about this new tax which has been levied?" asked Diane.

"The funds produced by that," said the cardinal, "are to be appropriated to the payment and maintenance of the troops."

"In that event," was Diane's rejoinder, "the better part of them should go to the leader of the troops."

"Very well, the leader is at Calais?" replied the cardinal.

"No, indeed, he is here in Paris, at the Louvre," retorted Diane.

"Pray, Madame, do you desire that failure and defeat should be rewarded?"

"That would be much better, Monsieur le Cardinal, than that mad recklessness should be encouraged."

"Enough of this!" the king interposed; "do you not see that your quarrelling tires and annoys me? Do you know, Madame, and Monsieur de Lorraine, the quatrain which I came across recently in my book of Hours?"

"A quatrain?" Diane and Charles de Lorraine repeated with one breath.

"If my memory serves me," said Henri, "it was this:—"

"Sire, si vous laissez, comme Charles desire,
Comme Diane fait, par trop vous gouverner,
Fondre, pétrir, mollir, refondre et retourner,
Sire, vous n'êtes plus, vous n'êtes plus que cire.'" [3]

Diane did not lose her self-possession in the least.

"A pretty piece of foolery," said she; "but it credits me with much more influence over his Majesty's mind than I possess, alas!"

"Ah, Madame," rejoined the king, "you ought not to make a bad use of that influence just because you know that you possess it."

"But do I really possess it, Sire?" said Diane, in her most winning tones. "If it be so, your Majesty will grant what I ask in behalf of the constable."

"Very well," said the king, impatiently; "now I trust you will leave me to my gloomy forebodings and my anxiety."

The cardinal, in the face of such weakness, could only raise his eyes imploringly to heaven. Diane darted a triumphant glance at him.

"Thanks, your Majesty," she said to the king. "I obey you and withdraw; but pray dismiss your anxiety and dread, Sire, for victory loves the generous-hearted, and I firmly believe that you will be victorious."

"Ah, I accept the augury, Diane," replied Henri. "With what transports of joy would I receive information to that effect! For a long time I have not slept; I have hardly existed. *Mon Dieu,* how slight after all is the power of kings! To think that I have at this moment no means of knowing what is transpiring at Calais! You may well say, Monsieur le Cardinal, that your brother's silence is most alarming. Ah, for news from Calais! Who will bring it to me? In God's name, who?"

An usher entered, and bowing low before the king as the last word fell from his lips, announced in a loud voice,—

"A messenger from Monsieur de Guise has arrived from Calais, and solicits the honor of an audience of his Majesty."

"A messenger from Calais!" echoed the king, rising to his feet, with gleaming eye, and almost beside himself.

"At last!" said the cardinal, trembling between joy and fear.

"Introduce Monsieur de Guise's messenger; introduce him at once," added the king, eagerly.

It need not be said that every voice was hushed, every heart beating high, and that all eyes were turned toward the door.

Gabriel entered amid a profound silence.

[2] "He's such a bewitching little man.
And he's talking and laughing the livelong day,
And kissing his sweetheart whene'er he can.
God keep little Louis from all harm's way!"

[3] "Oh, Sire, be careful; for if you allow,
As Charles ever longs to, and Diane does now,
The one or the other, or both, to derange you,
To shape you and work you, remodel and change you,
By yielding too freely to all their demands,
Soon you'll be like the softest of wax in their hands."

CHAPTER XXVII
THE VICOMTE DE MONTGOMMERY

Gabriel was attended as he had been on his return from Italy by four of his people,—Ambroise, Lactance, Yvonnet, and Pilletrousse,—who bore the English flags; but they came no farther than the threshold.

The youth himself held in both hands a velvet cushion, upon which were two letters and the keys of the city.

At this sight Henri's countenance assumed an expression of joy and fear curiously blended.

He thought that he understood the welcome message, but the stern messenger made him anxious.

"Vicomte d'Exmès!" he muttered, as he saw Gabriel slowly approaching him.

Madame de Poitiers and the constable, exchanging looks of consternation, also faltered beneath their breath.

"Vicomte d'Exmès!"

Gabriel, meanwhile, with a grave and solemn mien, kneeled before the king, and said with a firm, clear voice,—

"Sire, here are the keys of the city of Calais, which was surrendered to Monsieur de Guise by the English, after a siege of seven days and three fierce assaults, and which Monsieur has made haste to deliver to your Majesty."

"Calais is ours?" asked the king, although he had heard and understood perfectly.

"Calais is yours, Sire," Gabriel repeated.

"*Vive le roi*!" with one accord cried all who were present, with the possible exception of the Constable de Montmorency.

Henri II., who could think of nothing now but his vanished fears and the glorious triumph of his arms, saluted the excited assemblage with radiant face.

"Thanks, Messieurs, thanks!" said he; "I accept your congratulations in the name of France. But they should not be addressed to me alone; it is but fair that the better part of them should be reserved for the gallant leader of the undertaking,—my noble cousin, Monsieur de Guise."

Murmurs of approbation were heard throughout the assemblage; but the time had not yet arrived when any one dared to cry, "Vive le Duc de Guise," in the king's presence.

"In our dear cousin's absence," continued Henri, "we are happy in being able to address our thanks and congratulations to you who represent him here, Monsieur le Cardinal de Lorraine, and to you, Monsieur le Vicomte d'Exmès, whom he has intrusted with this glorious and honorable commission."

"Sire," said Gabriel, respectfully but firmly, as he inclined his head in acknowledgment of the king's words, "Sire, your pardon, but I am no longer called Vicomte d'Exmès."

"What!" exclaimed Henri, with a frown.

"Sire," Gabriel continued, "since the day that Calais fell, I have felt justified in assuming my real name and my true title,—Vicomte de Montgommery."

At that name, which for so many years had not been pronounced at court save in whispers, there was a veritable explosion of surprise among the bystanders. This youth styled himself Vicomte de Montgommery; then the Comte de Montgommery, his father, doubtless must still be alive! What was the significance of the revival of that name, once so renowned, after so long a disappearance?

The king did not hear these comments, which were quite inaudible, but he had no difficulty in divining their import; he had become paler than his Italian strawberries, and his lips were trembling with impatience and indignation.

Madame de Poitiers was also in a tremor; and the constable in his corner had emerged from his gloomy impassiveness, and his roving look had become fixed.

"What do you mean, Monsieur?" returned the king, in a tone which he found great difficulty in keeping within bounds. "What is this name which you venture to assume, and whence do you derive so much imprudence?"

"The name is mine, Sire," said Gabriel, calmly; "and what your Majesty regards as imprudence is only confidence."

It was evident that Gabriel had determined to enter boldly upon the course he had adopted, to risk all that he might gain all, and to make all hesitation or avoidance of the issue impossible for the king as well as for himself.

Henri understood his words in that sense; but he dreaded the consequences of his own wrath, and so he replied, in order to postpone the outburst which he feared,—

"Your personal affairs may be attended to later, Monsieur; but at present be good enough to remember that you are the messenger of Monsieur de Guise. I think you have not yet fully executed your commission."

"That is true," said Gabriel, with a low bow. "I have still to present to your Majesty the flags conquered from the English. Behold them, Sire! Furthermore, Monsieur le Duc de Guise sends this letter to the king."

He presented Le Balafré's letter upon the cushion. The king took it, broke the seal, tore open the envelope, and said to the cardinal as he passed the letter to him,—

"To you, Monsieur le Cardinal, rightly belongs the pleasure of reading aloud your brother's letter. It is not addressed to the king, but to France."

"What, Sire!" said the cardinal, "does your Majesty really wish—"

"It is my desire, Monsieur le Cardinal, that you should accept the honor which is your due."

Charles de Lorraine bowed, and took the letter respectfully from the king's hands, unfolded it, and amid profound silence read what follows:—

> "SIRE,—Calais is in our power; we have wrested in one week from the English a city which cost them a year's siege two centuries ago.
>
> "Guines and Ham, the last two posts which are still in their possession in France, can now hold out but a short time; and I venture to promise your Majesty that within a fortnight our hereditary enemies will have been definitely expelled from the kingdom.
>
> "I thought it my duty to be generous to the conquered. They gave up their artillery and their supplies; but the terms of

capitulation to which I gave my assent allowed all such inhabitants of Calais as might so desire to withdraw", with their property, to England. Indeed, perhaps it would have been hazardous to leave so potent an element of discord in a newly-captured city.

> "The number of dead and wounded is very small, thanks to the rapidity with which the place was carried.
>
> "Time and leisure fail me, Sire, to furnish your Majesty with more ample details to-day. Being myself seriously wounded—"

At this point the cardinal turned pale, and ceased to read.

"What, our cousin wounded!" cried the king, feigning anxiety.

"Your Majesty and your Eminence may be reassured," said Gabriel. "Monsieur le Duc de Guise's wound will have no serious results, thank God! At present there remains of its effects nought but a noble scar upon his face and the glorious surname of *Le Balafré*."

The cardinal had meanwhile read a few lines in advance, and convinced himself that what Gabriel said was true, and with renewed calmness resumed his reading as follows:—

> "Being myself seriously wounded the very day of our entry into Calais, I was saved by the prompt assistance and marvellous skill of a young surgeon, Master Ambroise Paré; but I am still very weak, and consequently obliged to forego the pleasure of writing more at length to your Majesty.
>
> "You will be able to learn further details from him who brings to you with this letter the keys of the city, along with the English flags, and of whom I must say a word to your Majesty before I close.
>
> "For it is not to me, Sire, by any means, that all the honor of this marvellous capture of Calais belongs. I have striven to contribute to it with all my power with the aid of our gallant troops; but we owe the first conception of it, as well as the means of execution and its final success, to the bearer of this letter, Monsieur le Vicomte d'Exmès—"

"It would appear, Monsieur," the king interposed, addressing Gabriel, "that our cousin does not yet know you under your new name."

"Sire," replied Gabriel, "I should not have presumed to assume it for the first time except in your Majesty's presence."

At a sign from the king, the cardinal continued,—

> "In fact, I must admit that I had never dreamed of this hold stroke when Monsieur d'Exmès sought me out at the Louvre, laid bare to me his sublime project, answered my objections and did away with my doubts, and finally induced me to undertake this unprecedented exploit, which would be sufficient of itself, Sire, to make a reign glorious.
>
> "But that is not all. The risks of such a momentous undertaking were not to be lightly incurred; it was essential that the counsel of long experience should give its sanction to the dream of ardent courage. Monsieur d'Exmès provided the means of introducing Monsieur le Maréchal Strozzi into Calais in disguise, and thus of obtaining accurate information as to the opportunities of attack and means of defence. Beyond that, he gave us an exact detailed plan of the ramparts and fortified positions, so that we made our approaches to Calais with as much confidence as if the walls had been of glass.
>
> "Before the walls of the city, and in all the assaults, at the Nieullay fort and the Old Château,—everywhere, in fact, Vicomte d'Exmès, at the head of a small band, raised at his own expense, performed prodigies of valor. But on those occasions he was only on a level with many of our gallant captains, who cannot, in my humble opinion, be surpassed. Therefore I touch but lightly upon the proofs of gallantry which he afforded on every occasion, to confine myself to those deeds in which he stands alone, and without a compeer.
>
> "Thus, the Risbank fort, which at once protected from attack and afforded free entrance to Calais on the ocean side, would have made it possible for strong reinforcements from England to be thrown into the city. In that event we should have been lost,—nay, exterminated; our gigantic enterprise

> would have proved a failure, and made us the laughing-stock of all Europe. The question then was how, without ships, we could carry a fort which was defended by the ocean? Very well! Vicomte d'Exmès performed that miracle. In the night-time, alone with his volunteers upon a little boat, aided by a secret understanding with certain parties within the walls, he succeeded, after a hazardous voyage and an escalading feat terrible to think of, in planting the French flag upon that impregnable fort."

At this point, notwithstanding the king's presence, the reading was interrupted for a moment by a murmur of admiration which nothing could restrain, and which burst from that assemblage of illustrious and valiant men as if it were the irresistible expression of the feeling of all hearts.

Gabriel's bearing, as he stood with lowered eyes, calm and dignified and modest, two or three paces from the king, added to the favorable impression caused by the narration of his exploit, and attracted the admiration of the young women and the old soldiers at once.

The king, too, was touched; and the glance which he gave the hero of this glorious adventure showed signs of a softer feeling for him. Madame de Poitiers alone bit her colorless lips, while Monsieur de Montmorency knit his thick eyebrows savagely.

The cardinal, after this brief interruption, resumed the reading of his brother's letter.

> "The Risbank fort once won, the city was ours. The English men-of-war did not dare to risk a hopeless attack. Three days after, we entered Calais in triumph, sustained even then by a well-planned diversion by Monsieur d'Exmès's allies in the city, and by a vigorous sortie which he himself led.
>
> "It was in this final struggle, Sire, that I received the terrible wound which almost cost me my life; and if I may be allowed to call attention to a service personal to myself amid so many public services, I will add that Monsieur d'Exmès, almost by force, brought to what nearly proved to be my death-bed Master Paré, the surgeon who saved my life."

"Oh, Monsieur, let me thank you in my turn," said Charles de Lorraine, interrupting himself, with deep emotion.

Then he resumed with even more warmth and vigor of expression, as if it were his brother himself who was speaking.

> "Sire, the honor and credit of such brilliant success is commonly awarded to the one under whose leadership it has been achieved. Monsieur d'Exmès, first of all, as modest as he is great, would freely consent that his name should be lost to sight in favor of mine. Nevertheless, I have deemed it proper to apprise your Majesty that the youth who hands you this letter has in fact been both the head and the arm of our enterprise, and that, except for him, Calais, where I am at this moment writing, would still be an English city. Monsieur d'Exmès has requested me to make this declaration, if I were willing, to the king's ear alone,—but to be sure to make it to him. It is that which I now do, in a voice loud with gratitude and joy.
>
> "It was no more than my duty to give Monsieur d'Exmès this honorable certificate. The rest is for you, Sire. It is a right which I envy you, but which I cannot usurp, nor do I wish to do so. It seems to me that the gift of a reconquered city and the assurance of the integrity of a kingdom can hardly be paid for with presents.
>
> "It would appear, however, from what Monsieur d'Exmès has told me, that your Majesty has in your hands a prize worthy of his achievement. I can well believe it, Sire; but none but a king—yea, none but a great king like your Majesty—can bestow upon such a kingly exploit any reward approximate to its value.
>
> "With this, Sire, I pray God to grant you a long life and a happy reign.
>
> "And I am your Majesty's
>
> "Most humble and obedient servant and subject,
>
> "FRANÇOIS DE LORRAINE.
>
> "*Given at Calais, this 8th January*, 1558."

When Charles de Lorraine had finished his reading and restored the letter to the king's hands, the movement of approbation, which expressed the restrained congratulation of the whole court, manifested itself anew, and once more made Gabriel's heart leap with joy, mightily moved as he was despite his apparent calmness. If respect for the king's presence had not imposed bounds upon their enthusiasm, the young conqueror would doubtless have been welcomed most warmly and with unstinted applause.

The king instinctively felt this general impulse; moreover, he partook of it to some extent, and he could not refrain from saying to Gabriel, as if he had been the interpreter of the unexpressed feeling of all,—

"It is well, Monsieur! You have done exceedingly well! I earnestly hope that, as Monsieur de Guise gives me to understand, it may really be in our power to recompense you in a manner worthy of yourself and of me."

"Sire," replied Gabriel, "I have but one ambition, and your Majesty well knows what that—"

But as Henri made an expressive gesture, he hastened to add,—

"Pardon me, Sire, but my commissions are not yet fully executed."

"What remains for you to do?" asked the king.

"Sire, a letter from Madame de Castro for your Majesty."

"From Madame de Castro?" repeated Henri, eagerly.

With a quick and impulsive movement, he rose from his seat, and descended the steps which led to the royal platform, took Diane's letter with his own hands, and said in a low tone to Gabriel,—

"It is true, Monsieur, you not only restore a daughter to the king, but a child to her father. I am doubly indebted to you. But let me read the letter."

As the courtiers, still motionless and mute, were respectfully awaiting the king's commands, Henri, feeling annoyed by this observant silence, added aloud,—

"Let me not restrain the expression of your gratification, Messieurs. I have no further news to give you; what remains is a private matter between myself and the messenger of our cousin De Guise. So you have only to discuss the glad intelligence, and congratulate yourselves upon it; and you are quite free now to do so, Messieurs."

The royal permission was quickly accepted; the party separated into groups and began to converse, and soon nothing was to be heard but the indistinct and confused buzzing which is always the combined result of a hundred different conversations in the same room.

Madame de Poitiers and the constable still thought of nothing but keeping watch upon the king and Gabriel.

With an interchange of speaking glances, they had communicated their mutual dread to one another; and Diane, by a slight and almost imperceptible movement, had drawn near her royal lover.

Henri did not notice the jealous couple, being entirely absorbed by his daughter's letter.

"Dear Diane! Poor dear Diane!" he was whispering, deeply moved.

When he had read the letter to the end, carried away by his kingly nature, whose first, spontaneous impulse was certainly liberal and just, he said to Gabriel, almost aloud, "Madame de Castro also commends her liberator to me, and it is just that she should. She tells me, Monsieur, that you not only rescued her from captivity, but that you have also saved her honor."

"Oh, I but did my duty, Sire!" said Gabriel.

"Then must I not fail in mine," returned Henri, warmly. "It is for you to speak now, Monsieur. Tell me what you desire at our hands, *Monsieur le Vicomte de Montgommery*!"

CHAPTER XXVIII
JOY AND ANGUISH

Monsieur le Vicomte de Montgommery! At that name which, when pronounced by the king, seemed to promise all that he wanted, Gabriel's heart fairly leaped for joy.

Henri clearly intended to pardon his father.

"See! he gives way," said Madame de Poitiers, beneath her breath to the constable, who had come to her side.

"Let us wait our opportunity," said Monsieur de Montmorency, without losing his self-possession.

"Sire," Gabriel was saying to the king, more easily moved as his custom was by hope than by fear, "Sire, it cannot be necessary for me to repeat to your Majesty what favor it is that I venture to ask of your kindness, your benevolence,—I may say, of your sense of justice. Having, I trust, accomplished what your Majesty asked of me, may I hope that your Majesty will condescend to grant my request! Have you forgotten your promise, or do you choose to redeem it?"

"Yes, Monsieur, I will redeem it, upon the condition that silence is to be maintained as we agreed," Henri replied, without hesitation.

"That condition, Sire, shall be exactly and rigorously observed; to that I pledge my honor anew," said Gabriel.

"Come hither, then, Monsieur," said the king.

Gabriel approached him. The Cardinal de Lorraine discreetly stepped aside; but Madame de Poitiers, who was seated by Henri's side, did not stir, and was doubtless able to hear what was said, although the king lowered his voice so that it might reach Gabriel's ear alone.

However, this watchful surveillance did not disturb the king's determination, it must be confessed; for he continued firmly,—

"Monsieur le Vicomte de Montgommery, you are a valiant subject whom I esteem and honor. Even when you are in possession of what you crave and have so nobly earned, we shall still be far from having discharged our indebtedness to you. However, take this ring, and present it to the governor of the Châtelet at eight o'clock to-morrow morning. He will be advised of your coming, and will deliver to you on the spot the object of your sublime and holy quest."

Gabriel, who felt as if his knees were tottering from excess of joy, could restrain himself no longer, but fell at the king's feet.

"Ah, Sire!" said he, his breast heaving with emotion and his eyes wet with tears of happiness, "all the force and energy of which I may claim to have given proof I hereby devote to your Majesty's service for the rest of my life, as I would have devoted them to the service of my hatred if you had said 'no.'"

"Really?" said the king, smiling good-humoredly.

"Yes, Sire, I confess it; and you ought to understand me, since you have pardoned my father. Yes, I believe I would have haunted your Majesty and your Majesty's children, as I will now defend and protect you and love you in them. Before God, who punishes all false swearing sooner or later, I will keep my oath of fidelity just as I would have kept my oath of vengeance."

"Well, we shall see! Rise, Monsieur," said the king, still smiling. "Calm yourself; and to restore your self-control, tell me some details of this unhoped-for success at Calais, of which it seems to me I shall never tire of hearing and speaking."

By this means Henri retained Gabriel by his side more than an hour, asking questions and listening, and making him repeat everything, even to the most minute details, a hundred times without seeming to grow weary.

Then he handed the young hero over to the tender mercies of the ladies, who were eager to have their turn at questioning him.

But in the first place the Cardinal de Lorraine, who was quite without information as to Gabriel's antecedents, and saw in him only his brother's friend and protégé, insisted upon presenting him to the queen.

Catherine de Médicis, in the presence of the whole court, was obliged to extend her thanks and congratulations to the man who had won so glorious a victory for the king. But she did it with noticeable coldness and reserve; and the stern and contemptuous glance of her gray eyes gave the lie in a great measure to the words which fell from her lips, but which did not express the sentiments of her heart.

Gabriel, while thanking Catherine in respectful terms, was conscious of a freezing sensation at his heart when he heard her lying compliments, beneath which he seemed to discern, as he recalled the past, an ironical and hidden threat.

As he turned to withdraw after paying his respects to Catherine de Médicis, he saw a sight which was quite sufficient to justify his presentiment of evil.

He chanced to look toward the king, and saw with terror that Diane de Poitiers was conversing in whispers with him, with her wicked, sardonic smile. The more Henri II. seemed to remonstrate, the more persistent she seemed to become.

Finally, she called the constable, who also talked with the king with much earnestness for a long time.

Gabriel saw all this from a distance. Not one of his enemies' movements escaped him, and he suffered the torments of the damned.

But just when his heart was being thus torn by conflicting emotions, the young queen-dauphine, Mary Stuart, approached him gayly, and overwhelmed him with compliments and questions.

Gabriel, despite his anxiety, exerted all his powers to reply to her.

"Why, it's magnificent!" said Mary, enthusiastically, "is it not, my dear Dauphin?" she added, addressing François, her youthful husband, who joined cordially in his wife's friendly words.

"What would one not do to deserve such kind words?" said Gabriel, whose distraught eyes never left the group composed of the king, Diane, and the constable.

"When I felt attracted to you by a strangely sympathetic feeling some time ago," continued Mary Stuart, with the charming grace that was peculiar to her, "it was doubtless because my heart foresaw that you would contribute this marvellous achievement to the glory of my dear uncle De Guise. Ah, I would that I, like the king, had the power of rewarding you! But a woman, alas! has neither titles nor honors at her disposal."

"Oh, but I really have all that I could ask for in the world!" said Gabriel. At the same time he was thinking to himself, "The king no longer replies, he listens simply."

"Well, then," rejoined Mary Stuart, "if I had the power, I would create desires in you so that I might gratify them. But at this moment, see, I have nothing but this bunch of violets which the gardener at the Tournelles just sent me as a great rarity after the late frost. With the permission of Monseigneur le Dauphin, I will give you these flowers as a memento of the day. Will you accept them?"

"Oh, Madame!" cried Gabriel, kissing respectfully the fair hand that offered them.

"Flowers," continued Mary Stuart, dreamily, "offer us their sweet odor when we are glad, and comfort us in times of sorrow. I may be very unhappy some day, but I shall never be altogether so as long as I am allowed to have flowers near me. It is understood of course, Monsieur d'Exmès, that to you, in this hour of good fortune and triumph, I offer them only for their perfume."

"Who knows," said Gabriel, shaking his head sadly,—"who knows if I, triumphant and fortunate as you say, do not need them rather to comfort and console me?"

His gaze, even while he was speaking, was still fastened upon the king, who for the moment seemed to be thinking deeply, and yielding to the arguments always more and more earnest of Madame de Poitiers and the constable.

Gabriel could but tremble at the thought that the favorite must have overheard the king's promise, and that his father and himself were undoubtedly the subject of their conversation.

The young queen-dauphine left him, with some gentle raillery upon his preoccupation.

At this moment Admiral de Coligny came up to him, and, in his turn, offered his hearty felicitations upon his success in maintaining and surpassing at Calais the renown he had won at St. Quentin.

The poor fellow had never seemed to be so petted by fate or more worthy of envy than when he was enduring such tortures as he had never before imagined.

"You are quite as successful," said the admiral, "in gaining victories as in minimizing the effects of defeat. I am more than proud to have foreseen your extraordinary merit, and my only regret is that I was not present to share with you the dangers of this noble feat of arms, so fortunate for you and so glorious for France."

"Other occasions will not be lacking, Monsieur l'Amiral," said Gabriel.

"I am much inclined to doubt it," said Coligny, with some sadness. "May God grant that if we do ever meet again upon a battle-field, it may not be on opposing sides!"

"May Heaven forefend, indeed!" exclaimed Gabriel, earnestly; "what mean you by those words, Monsieur l'Amiral?"

"Four adherents of the Religion have been burned alive during the last month," replied Coligny. "The Reformers, who are growing every day in numbers and in power, will eventually grow weary of this hateful and iniquitous persecution. Even now two armies might be formed, I fear, from the two parties into which France is divided."

"'Well?" said Gabriel, inquiringly.

"Well, Monsieur d'Exmès, despite the walk which we took together to the Rue St. Jacques, you retained your freedom of action, and only bound yourself at your own discretion. But now you seem to me to be too high in favor at court, and justly so, not to be enrolled in the king's army, as against the heresy, as it is called."

"I think that you are mistaken, Monsieur l'Amiral," said Gabriel, whose eyes never left the king. "I have every reason to think, on the other hand, that I shall very soon have the right to march in the ranks of the oppressed against the oppressors."

"What! What do you mean?" asked the admiral. "You are pale, Gabriel, and your voice falters. Pray, what is the matter?"

"Oh, nothing, nothing, Monsieur l'Amiral! But I must leave you. *Au revoir*! We shall soon meet again."

Gabriel had observed an acquiescent gesture made by the king; whereupon Monsieur de Montmorency had left the room at once, darting a triumphant glance at Diane as he went.

However, the reception came to an end a few moments later; and Gabriel, as he was bowing to the king on taking his leave, ventured to say,—

"Sire, until to-morrow."

"Until to-morrow, Monsieur," the king replied.

But as he spoke Henri avoided Gabriel's eye; he even turned away, nor did he smile any longer, while Madame de Poitiers's face was beaming.

Gabriel, whom every one thought to see radiant with joy and hope, withdrew with grief and terror at his heart.

All the evening he haunted the neighborhood of the Châtelet.

He regained his courage to some slight extent when time passed without his seeing Monsieur de Montmorency leave the prison.

Then he felt the royal signet on his finger, and recalled the solemn words of Henri II., which left no chance for doubt, and which could not conceal a deception,—"The object of your sublime and holy ambition shall be restored to you."

Courage! The night which still separated Gabriel from the decisive moment seemed more than a year long.

CHAPTER XXIX
PRECAUTIONARY MEASURES

What Gabriel thought and what he suffered during those mortal hours God only knows; for when he returned to his own house he said nothing to his retainers, nor even to his nurse. From that moment began an absorbed and concentrated dumb life, so to speak,—a life all action, and very sparing of words, to which he devoted himself strictly from this time on, as if he had tacitly taken vows of silence.

Consequently, the disappointed hopes, energetic resolutions, projects of love or vengeance,—everything, in short, that Gabriel thought or dreamed, or vowed in his own heart that night remained a secret between his noble heart and his God.

Not till eight o'clock could he present himself at the Châtelet, with the ring given him by the king,—the talisman which was to open all the doors, not to him alone, but to his father.

Until six in the morning Gabriel remained alone in his room, and refused to speak with any person.

At that hour he descended to the first floor, all clad and equipped as if for a long journey. He had asked the nurse the night before to give him all the money she could get together.

The people of his household were most earnest in offering their services to him. The four volunteers who had come in his suite from Calais were foremost in placing themselves at his disposal; but he thanked them most heartily, and dismissed them, retaining only the page André, the latest comer, and his nurse Aloyse.

"My good Aloyse," he began, "I am expecting from day to day the arrival of two guests, friends of mine, from Calais,—Jean Peuquoy and his wife Babette. It may be, Aloyse, that I shall not be here to receive them; but even in my absence,—nay, especially in my absence,—I beg you, Aloyse, to make them welcome, and treat them as if they were my brother and sister.

Babette already knows you well from having heard me speak of you a hundred times. She will trust in you as a daughter in her mother; so I entreat you, in the name of your affection for me, to show her a mother's tenderness and indulgence."

"I promise you I will, Monseigneur," said the kind-hearted nurse, simply; "and you know that from me those words are sufficient. Have no anxiety about your guests, for they shall want for nothing in the way of bodily comfort."

"Thanks, Aloyse," said Gabriel, pressing her hand. "Now for you, André!" said he to the page whom Madame Diane de Castro had given him. "I have certain last commissions of grave importance which I must confide to a trusty hand, and I have selected you, André, to execute them, because you take the place of my faithful Martin-Guerre."

"I am at your command, Monseigneur," said André.

"Listen carefully to what I say," continued Gabriel. "In an hour I shall leave this house alone; if I return in a short time, you will have nothing to do,—or rather, I shall have different orders to give you. But it is possible that I may not return,—not to-day, that is, nor to-morrow, nor for a long time to come—"

The nurse, in despair, raised her clasped hands heavenward imploringly. André interrupted his master.

"Pardon, Monseigneur! you say that you may not return here for a long time?"

"Yes, André."

"And am I not to accompany you?—and perhaps not to see you again for a long while?" added André, who seemed both sorrowful and embarrassed at this information.

"That may well be, no doubt," said Gabriel.

"But Madame de Castro," rejoined the page, "before I quitted her intrusted to my care a message, a letter for Monseigneur—"

"And you have never yet given it to me, André?" said Gabriel, warmly.

"Pardon me, Monseigneur," André replied; "I was instructed not to deliver it unless you were to return from the Louvre either very sorrowful or in a state of angry excitement. Only in such case Madame Diane told me to give Monsieur d'Exmès the letter, which contained what might be a warning to him and perhaps a consolation."

"Give it me, quickly, give it me!" cried Gabriel. "Advice and consolation could not arrive more opportunely, I fear."

André drew from his doublet a letter very carefully wrapped up, and handed it to his new master; Gabriel hurriedly broke the seal, and withdrew to a window recess to read it.

This is what he read:—

> MY FRIEND,—Amid all the anguish and all the dreams of this last night, which separates me from you, perhaps forever, the most terrible thought which has torn my heart is this:—
>
> It may be that, in carrying out the momentous and formidable duty which you are about to undertake with such brave heart, you may come in contact, nay, even in conflict, with the king. It may be that the unforeseen issue of your struggle will force you to hate the king, or even incite you to visit your wrath upon him.
>
> Gabriel, I do not yet know if he is my father, but I do know that he has until now cherished me as his child. The mere dread of your vengeance makes me shudder while I write, and its accomplishment would be my death-blow.
>
> And yet the duty which depends upon my own birth may perhaps compel me to think as you do; perhaps I, like you, may have to avenge him whom I shall hereafter know as my father upon him who has hitherto been a father to me,—frightful thought!
>
> But while doubt and darkness still hide the solution of this terrible enigma from my sight, while I am still ignorant on which side my hatred belongs and on which my love, Gabriel, I implore you,—and if you have loved me, you will obey me, Gabriel,—respect the person of the king.
>
> I can reason now, without passion at least, if not without emotion; and I feel, yes, I am sure, that it is not for man to punish man, but for God.

> So, dear friend, whatever happens, do not try to take from the hands of God the prerogative of chastisement, even to strike a criminal.
>
> If he whom I have until now called my father is guilty, and being only human, he may be, do not be his judge, far less his executioner. Have no fear; the Lord will judge him, and the Lord will avenge you more terribly than you could do yourself. Leave your cause fearlessly to His justice.
>
> Unless God makes you the involuntary and, in some sort, fatal instrument of His pitiless justice; unless He makes use of your hand in your own despite; unless you strike the blow unwillingly and without wishing it,—Gabriel, do not constitute yourself his judge, and above all things do not with your own hand carry out the sentence.
>
> Do this for love of me, my friend. In mercy's name I ask it; and it is the last prayer and the last despairing cry to your heart from
>
> DIANE DE CASTRO.

Gabriel read the letter twice from beginning to end; but meanwhile, André and the nurse could detect no sign of emotion on his pale face save the mournful smile which had become so familiar there.

When he had refolded Diane's letter and hidden it in his breast, he remained silent for a time, with bent head and in deep thought.

Then, as if awaking from a dream,—

"It is well," he said aloud. "The orders I have to give you, André, are not changed; and if, as I was saying, I do not soon return, whether you learn anything about me, or whether you do not hear my name mentioned, whatever happens or does not happen, remember my words,—this is what you are to do."

"I am listening, Monseigneur," said André, "and I will obey you in every detail; for I love you, and am your devoted servant."

"Madame de Castro," said Gabriel, "will be at Paris within a few days. Make arrangements to be informed of her arrival as soon as possible."

"It will be very easy to do that, Monseigneur."

"Go to her at once if you can," continued Gabriel, "and deliver this sealed package from me. Take especial care not to lose it, André, although it contains nothing of value to any one else,—a lady's veil, nothing more. But no matter! Do you yourself deliver this veil to her in person, and say to her—"

"What shall I say, Monseigneur?" asked André, seeing that his master was hesitating.

"No, say nothing to her," Gabriel resumed, "except that she is free, and that I give back to her all her promises, even that of which this veil is the pledge."

"Is that all, Monseigneur?" asked the page.

"That is all," said Gabriel. "But, André, if nothing has been heard of me, and you see that Madame de Castro is a little anxious, you may add—But for what good? No, add nothing, André. Ask her, if you choose, to take you back into her service. Otherwise, come back here and await my return."

"That is to say, Monseigneur, that you will surely come back?" asked the nurse, with tears in her eyes. "But when you said that perhaps we should not hear any more of you—"

"Perhaps that would be best, dear Mother," said Gabriel, "that you should hear nothing of me. In any event, hope for the best, and await my return."

"Hope, when you have disappeared from all eyes, even from those of your poor nurse! Ah, it is very hard to hope!" replied Aloyse.

"But who said that I should disappear?" returned Gabriel. "Ought I not to provide for every contingency? For my own part, never fear; whatever precautions I may take I rely upon embracing you again very soon, Aloyse, with all the gratitude of my heart. That is most probable; for Providence is a kind and loving mother to him who implores her protection. Did I not begin, too, by saying to André that all my injunctions to him would probably be useless and void in the almost certain event of my return to-day?"

"May God bless you for those dear words, Monseigneur!" cried poor Aloyse, moved beyond expression.

"Have you no other orders to give, Monseigneur, to be executed during your absence?—which may God make of brief duration!" asked André.

"Wait a moment," said Gabriel, as a thought seemed suddenly to occur to him. Seating himself at a table, he wrote the following letter to Coligny:—

> MONSIEUR L'AMIRAL,—I propose to instruct myself in the principles of your religion, and you may count me as one of you after to-day.
>
> Whatever may be the instrument of my conversion, whether your persuasive words or some other motive, I, nevertheless, devote irrevocably to your cause and that of the oppressed religion my heart, my life, and my sword.
>
> Your very humble companion and good friend,
>
> GABRIEL DE MONTGOMMERY.

"Deliver this as well, if I fail to return," said Gabriel, handing the letter sealed to André. "And now, my dear friends, I must say adieu, and leave you. The time has come."

Half an hour later Gabriel knocked with trembling hand at the great door of the Châtelet.

CHAPTER XXX
THE SECRET PRISONER

Monsieur de Salvoison, the governor of the Châtelet who had received Gabriel at his first visit, had recently died, and the new governor was Monsieur de Sazerac.

It was to him that the young man was escorted. Anxiety, with its iron hand, had seized poor Gabriel's throat so tightly that he could not utter a single word; but he silently presented the ring which the king had given him to the governor.

Monsieur de Sazerac bowed gravely.

"I was expecting you, Monsieur," he said; "I received an hour ago the order in which you are interested. My instructions are, upon presentation of this ring, and without asking any other explanation from you, to deliver to you the nameless prisoner who has been detained for many years in the Châtelet under the designation of Number 21. Am I right, Monsieur?"

"Yes, yes, Monsieur," replied Gabriel, eagerly; for hope returning had restored his voice. "And this order, Monsieur le Gouverneur?"

"I am ready to execute, Monsieur."

"Oh, oh! Can it really be?" said Gabriel, shaking from head to foot.

"It surely is so," replied Monsieur de Sazerac, with an accent in which an indifferent person might have detected a shade of sadness and bitterness.

But Gabriel was too distracted and excited by his joy. "Ah, it is true, then!" cried he. "I do not dream. My eyes are open. My insane terrors were dreams; and you are really going to deliver this prisoner to me, Monsieur? Oh, I thank thee, my God! And thanks to thee, Sire! But come, let us go quickly, Monsieur, I beseech you."

He took two or three steps as if to lead the way before Monsieur de Sazerac; but his strength, so vigorous and inexhaustible in the face of suffering and danger, failed him in the excess of his joy. He was obliged to stop for a moment, for his heart was beating so violently and so fast that he thought he should suffocate.

Poor human nature was too weak to undergo such a tumult of conflicting emotions.

The almost despaired-of realization of such far-off hopes and the end and aim of his whole life,—the goal of his superhuman efforts suddenly attained; gratitude to the loyal king and the just God; filial love at last to be satisfied; another passion, still more ardent, to be at last decided for better or worse,—such a multitude of feelings, all aroused and excited at the same moment, made poor Gabriel's heart overflow.

But amid this inexpressible whirl of emotions and almost insane happiness, his least confused thoughts framed themselves into something like a hymn of thanksgiving to Henri II., to whom he owed this delirium of joy.

Gabriel repeated over and over again in his grateful heart his oath to devote his whole life to this truehearted king and his children. How, in God's name, could he for one moment have doubted so noble and excellent a monarch!

But at last, shaking off his ecstatic mood, he said to the governor, who had stopped beside him,—

"Pardon, Monsieur! Pardon this weakness which overcame me for a moment. Joy, you see, is sometimes too heavy a load to carry."

"Oh, do not apologize, Monsieur, I beg!" replied the governor, in a deep voice.

This time Gabriel noticed the tone in which he spoke, and fixed his eyes upon him.

Nowhere could a more kindly, open, and honest face be found. Everything about this prison-governor indicated sincerity and kindness of heart.

Strangely enough, the emotion which at that moment was depicted upon the good man's features, while he observed Gabriel's exuberant happiness, was heartfelt compassion.

Gabriel caught the singular expression, and every vestige of color fled from his cheeks as a presentiment of evil laid hold upon his heart.

But such was his nature that this ill-defined dread, suddenly intruding upon his happiness, served only to impart renewed energy to his valiant soul y and standing proudly erect, he said to the governor,—

"Come, Monsieur, let us go. I am strong again now, and quite ready."

Gabriel and Monsieur de Sazerac thereupon went down into the prison, preceded by a valet carrying a torch.

Gabriel found gloomy souvenirs at every step, and recognized at the windings of the corridors and on the staircases the dark walls which he had seen before, and the sombre impressions which he had experienced on his former visit without being able to explain them.

When they reached the iron door of the dungeon in which he had, with so strange a feeling at his heart, visited the haggard, dumb prisoner, he stopped abruptly.

"He is there," said he, with beating heart.

But Monsieur de Sazerac sorrowfully shook his head.

"No," he replied, "he is no longer there."

"What!" ejaculated Gabriel. "No longer there! Are you mocking me, Monsieur?"

"Oh, Monsieur!" said the governor, in mild reproach.

A cold sweat moistened Gabriel's brow.

"Pardon, pardon," he murmured. "But what do your words imply? Oh, tell me; speak quickly!"

"I am very much grieved to inform you, Monsieur, that last evening the secret prisoner confined here was transferred to a floor below this."

"Ah!" said Gabriel, bewildered. "Why was that, pray?"

"He had been warned, Monsieur, as I think you know, that if he should so much as make an attempt to speak to any person whatsoever, if he uttered the slightest exclamation, and muttered a name, even in response to a question, he would be immediately transferred to a deeper and more terrible and deadly dungeon than his own."

"I know all that," muttered Gabriel, in so low a tone that it did not reach the governor's ear.

"Once before, Monsieur," continued Monsieur de Sazerac, "the prisoner had ventured to disobey that order, and it was then that he was transferred to this dungeon which is before us, and which you have seen,—harsh and cruel enough, God knows. It seems, Monsieur, or so I have been told, that you were informed when you visited the prison before of the doom of eternal silence which he was compelled to undergo, even though alive."

"Yes, yes," said Gabriel, almost insane with impatient dread. "Well, Monsieur?"

"Yesterday evening," continued Monsieur de Sazerac, with sorrow and commiseration in his tones, "just before the outer doors were closed for the night, a man came to the Châtelet,—a man of eminence, whose name I cannot mention."

"No matter; go on!" exclaimed Gabriel.

"This man," pursued the governor, "gave orders that he should be taken to the cell of Number 21. I accompanied him alone. He spoke to the prisoner without at first obtaining a reply, and I hoped that the old man would come out triumphantly from this ordeal; for full half an hour he maintained an immovable silence in the face of all the importunities and provocations that were showered upon him."

Gabriel breathed a deep sigh, and raised his eyes to heaven, but said not a word to interrupt the governor's dolorous recital.

"Unfortunately, the prisoner at last, upon something which was whispered in his ear, rose to a sitting posture, tears gushed from his stony eyes, and he spoke, Monsieur. I was instructed to narrate all these particulars to you, so that you might the more readily believe my word as a gentleman when I add, 'The prisoner spoke.' I declare to you, with sorrow, but upon my honor, that I myself heard him."

"And then?" asked Gabriel, brokenly.

"Thereupon," replied Monsieur de Sazerac, "I was required, in spite of my earnest remonstrances and my entreaties, to fulfil the inhuman duty which my office imposed upon me,—to obey a power higher than mine, and which would have been at no loss to find more willing instruments had I refused,—and to cause the prisoner to be transferred by his dumb jailer to the dungeon beneath this."

"The dungeon beneath this!" cried Gabriel. "Ah, let us go quickly, for I am bringing him deliverance at last!"

The governor sadly shook his head; but Gabriel saw not the motion, for he was already rushing down the slippery and dilapidated steps which led to the lowest depths of the gloomy prison.

Monsieur de Sazerac took the torch from the hands of the attendant, whom he dismissed with a motion, of his hand, and followed Gabriel, with his handkerchief over his mouth.

At every step the air grew fouler and more suffocating. When they reached the foot of the staircase they were fairly gasping for breath, and the feeling was instinctive that nothing could live more than a few moments in that atmosphere, save the unclean creatures they were crushing beneath their feet.

But Gabriel never thought of that. He took from the governor's trembling hands the rusty key that he handed him, and opening the heavy, worm-eaten door, rushed headlong into the dungeon.

By the light of the torch a form could be distinguished in a corner stretched upon a heap of foul straw.

Gabriel threw himself upon the body, drew it from the corner, and tried to restore it to life, crying,—

"Father, father!"

Monsieur de Sazerac fairly shook with horror at that cry.

The arms and the head of the old man fell back inert and lifeless under Gabriel's caressing hands.

CHAPTER XXXI
THE COMTE DE MONTGOMMERY

Gabriel, still kneeling beside the lifeless mass, raised his pale, bewildered countenance, and cast a glance of ominous tranquillity around him. He seemed to be questioning himself and pondering deeply; and his almost unnatural calm touched and alarmed Monsieur de Sazerac more than all the outcry and sobbing in the world would have done.

Suddenly, as if the idea that life might not be extinct had just occurred to him, he hurriedly placed his hand over the heart of the corpse.

For a moment or two he felt and listened eagerly.

"Nothing!" he then said in a firm but gentle voice, which was terrible for those very qualities; "nothing!—the heart no longer beats, but the flesh is still warm."

"What a marvellously strong constitution!" the governor muttered; "he might have lived for a long time to come."

All this time the eyes had remained open. Gabriel leaned over and closed them with reverent touch. Then he imprinted a respectful and loving kiss, the first and the last, upon the poor wasted lids, which had been wet with so many bitter tears.

"Monsieur," observed Monsieur de Sazerac, hoping to divert Gabriel from his terrifying contemplation of the inert body before him, "if the deceased was dear to you—"

"Dear to me, Monsieur!" Gabriel interrupted; "why, yes,—he was my father."

"Very well, Monsieur, if you desire to pay the last sad honors to his memory, I am directed to allow you to remove the body from this place."

"Ah, indeed!" replied Gabriel, with the same terrible calmness. "He is strictly just with me, then, and is keeping his word to me with great exactitude, I must confess. You must know, Monsieur le Gouverneur, that he swore to restore my father to me. He is restored to me: behold him! I recognize the fact that there was no undertaking to restore him to me alive."

He laughed a harsh, unpleasant laugh.

"Come, courage!" rejoined Monsieur de Sazerac. "It is time now to say adieu to him for whom you weep."

"I am doing so, as you see, Monsieur."

"Yes, but I mean that you really must leave this place at once. The air that we breathe here is not fit for human lungs, and a longer stay in this poisonous miasma might be very dangerous."

"Here is a proof of it before our eyes," said Gabriel, pointing to the body of his father.

"Come, come, we must be going!" replied the governor, taking the poor fellow's arm to force him away.

"Yes, yes, I will follow you," said Gabriel; "but for God's sake, leave me here a few moments longer!"

Monsieur de Sazerac made a sign of assent, and withdrew as far as the door, where the air was less noxious and heavy.

Gabriel, on his knees by the side of the dead man, and with head bent and hands hanging at his side, remained mute and motionless for some moments, praying or dreaming.

What said he to his dead father? Did he ask those lips, which Death's pitiless finger had closed too soon, for the solution of the enigma he was trying to unravel? Did he swear to the sainted victim that he would avenge him in this world, independently of God's vengeance in the world to come? Did he scan those already decomposing features, to conjecture what sort of man had been this father of his whom he now saw for the second time, and to dream of the peaceful and happy life that might have been in store for him under his watchful care? Did his thoughts dwell upon the past or the future; upon the affairs of this world, or the divine power of the Lord; upon vengeance or forgiveness?

The subject of this sombre communion between a dead father and his son remained forever a secret between Gabriel and his God.

Four or five minutes had passed; and breathing had become a painful and laborious task to these two men who had descended to these pestilential depths,—one in the performance of a holy duty, and the other led by an instinct of humanity.

"Again, I beg you to come away," said the kind-hearted governor to Gabriel. "It is full time that we should go up into the air."

"I am coming," said Gabriel, "I am coming."

He took his father's icy hand in his, and kissed it tenderly; he leaned over his damp and decomposing forehead, and left a kiss there, too.

All this passed without a tear. Alas! he could not weep.

"*Au revoir*!" said he; "*au revoir*!"

He rose with the same wonderfully calm and steadfast bearing and expression, whatever passions and emotions may have been rending his heart and soul.

He cast a last look at his father, and wafted a last caress to him, then followed Monsieur de Sazerac with slow and measured step.

On their way to the upper regions he asked to be shown the dark, cold cell where the prisoner had passed so many years of sorrow and despair, and which he, Gabriel, had once entered without embracing his father.

He spent a few moments there of silent meditation, and eager, though hopeless, interest.

When he and the governor had ascended to light and life once more, Monsieur de Sazerac could not repress a shudder of horror and pity as the daylight fell upon the features of the young man, whom he invited to his own room; for his chestnut locks had become silvery white.

After a short interval he said to him, in a voice trembling with emotion,—

"Is there nothing I can do for you now, Monsieur? You have but to ask, and I shall be more than happy to gratify any wish of yours with which my duties do not conflict."

"Monsieur," replied Gabriel, "you told me that I should be allowed to render the last honors to the dead. This evening I shall send some bearers here; and if you will kindly have the body placed in a coffin, and allow them to take it away, they will see that the prisoner is interred in the tomb of his ancestors."

"It shall be done, Monsieur," replied Monsieur de Sazerac; "but I must warn you that one condition was imposed upon the granting of this privilege."

"What was that, Monsieur?" asked Gabriel, coldly.

"That you should, in accordance with your agreement, cause no scandal or disturbance."

"I will keep that promise, too," said Gabriel. "The men will come by night, and without any knowledge as to the burden they are carrying will transport the body to the Rue des Jardins St. Paul, to the funeral vault of the counts of—"

"Pardon, Monsieur!" the governor interposed hurriedly; "I do not know the prisoner's name, nor is it my wish or my duty to know it. I have been compelled by the obligations of my office and the word I have given to maintain silence with you upon many matters; and you should be quite as reserved with me."

"But I for my part have nothing to conceal," replied Gabriel, proudly. "It is only the guilty who wish to cover their tracks."

"While you are only one of the unfortunates," said the governor. "After all, that is not much better, is it?"

"Besides," continued Gabriel, "I have already surmised the matters about which you have kept silence; indeed, I could tell you myself. For instance, this powerful individual who came here last evening, and who wished to talk with the prisoner so that he might make him speak—well, I could tell you almost the exact words of the talisman which finally induced my father to break silence,—the silence whereon depended the feeble remnant of his life, for which he had up to that time struggled bravely with his murderers."

"What! you say that you know?" said Monsieur de Sazerac, in amazement.

"I am sure of it," was Gabriel's reply. "The individual in question said to the poor old man, 'Your son lives!' or, perhaps, 'Your son has covered himself with renown!' or, again, 'Your son is coming to set you free!' He spoke to him of his son, at all events—the villain!"

The governor let fall an exclamation of astonishment.

"And at the mention of his son," continued Gabriel, "the wretched father, who had up to that time succeeded in restraining himself even before his most implacable foe, could not overcome a joyful impulse, and though he had remained dumb under all the provocation of his hatred, cried for joy when his love was awakened. Tell me, Monsieur, do I say truly?"

The governor bent his head without replying.

"It must be true, since you deny it not," Gabriel continued. "You can see how fruitless was your endeavor to conceal from me what this influential man said to the wretched captive. And as for the name of this all-powerful person, it was in vain also for you to pass that over in silence. Do you wish that I should name him to you?"

"Oh, Monsieur, Monsieur!" cried Monsieur de Sazerac, earnestly. "We are alone, it is true, but be careful. Are you not afraid?"

"I have already told you," said Gabriel, "that I have nothing to fear. Well, then, Monsieur, this man's name was Monsieur le Connétable, Duc de Montmorency. The executioner's mask has fallen off, you see."

"Oh, Monsieur!" ejaculated the governor, looking fearfully around.

"As to the prisoner's name and mine," pursued Gabriel, calmly, "those you do not know. But there is no reason why I should not tell them to you. Moreover, you may have already met me, and may meet me again during your life; then, too, you have been kind and considerate in this supreme moment of my existence; and when you hear my name in men's mouths, as may very well be the case within a few months, it will be well that you should know that he of whom they are talking is the same whom you have made your debtor to-day."

"I shall be most happy," said Monsieur de Sazerac, "to learn that fate has not continued to be so relentless toward you."

"Oh, such questions have no more interest for me!" said Gabriel, gravely. "But, in any event, let me tell you that since my father's death last night in this prison I am the Comte de Montgommery."

The governor of the Châtelet stood as if turned to stone, and could find no word to say.

"And now, adieu, Monsieur," added Gabriel; "adieu. Accept my warmest thanks; may God protect you!"

He saluted Monsieur de Sazerac, and left the gloomy precincts of the prison with a firm step.

But when the fresh air and the bright light of day recalled him to himself, he stayed his steps a moment, dizzy and tottering. The actuality of life came too suddenly upon him as he emerged from that hell.

However, as the passers-by began to look askance at him, he asserted his will, and walked away from the deathly spot.

In the first place he bent his steps to a lonely corner of the Place de Grève. There he took out his tablets, and wrote these words to his nurse:—

> MY GOOD ALOYSE,—Do not expect me, for I shall not return to-day. I must be alone for a time, to move about, and think, and wait. But have no anxiety about me; I shall surely see you again.

This evening arrange matters so that everything will be quiet in the house at an early hour. You alone must sit up, and open the door to four men who will knock at the great door a little before midnight, when the street is deserted.

I ask you personally to conduct these men, laden as they will be with a sorrowful but priceless burden, to the family burial-vault; point out to them the open tomb in which they must place him whom they will have in charge, and watch carefully the preparations for the interment; then, when they are at an end, give each of the men four golden crowns, guide them back to the door without noise, and return at once to the tomb to kneel and pray as you would for your master and your father.

I will pray also at the same hour, but far away from the spot. It must be so. I feel that the sight of that tomb might excite me to reckless and violent deeds, and I must ask counsel rather from God in solitude.

Au revoir, dear Aloyse, *au revoir*. Remind André of his commission to Madame de Castro, and do not yourself forget my guests, Jean and Babette Peuquoy. *Au revoir*, and God be with you!

GABRIEL DE M.

Having written this letter, Gabriel sought and found four men of the people,—laborers, that is to say.

He gave each of them four crowns in advance, and promised them as many more. In order to earn their wages, one of them was to take a letter to its address immediately; then, all four were to present themselves at the Châtelet a little before ten that same evening, to receive at the governor's hands a coffin, and convey it secretly and silently to the Rue des Jardins St. Paul, to the same house to which the letter was addressed.

The poor workmen overwhelmed Gabriel with their gratitude, and as they left him, in high glee over the windfall, they promised to fulfil his orders to the letter.

"Well, I have at least made four honest fellows happy," said Gabriel, with sorrowful pleasure, if we may be allowed the expression.

Then he pursued a course which led him out of the city, and on his way he passed the Louvre. Wrapped in his cloak, and with arms folded upon his breast, he stood for some moments gazing at the royal abode.

"Now it is for us two to settle our account," he muttered, with a glance of defiance. He resumed his journey, and as he went along there recurred to his memory the horoscope which Master Nostradamus had written long ago for the Comte de Montgommery, and which, in the master's own words, he had found by a remarkable coincidence to be exactly appropriate for his son, according to the laws of astrology,—

> "En joûte, en amour, cettuy touchera
> Le front du roy,
> Et cornes ou bien trou sanglant mettra
> Au front du roy.
> Mais le veuille ou non, toujours blessera
> Le front du roy.
> Enfin, l'aimera, puis, las! le tuera
> Dame du roy."

Gabriel reflected that curious prediction had already been fulfilled from point to point in his father's case; for the Comte de Montgommery in his youth had wounded King François I. in the face with a burning brand, and had afterward been King Henri's rival in love, and had been slain only the evening before by that very "lady of the king," who had loved him.

Up to that time Gabriel also had been loved by a queen,—Catherine de Médicis.

Would his destiny too be realized to the end? Would his vengeance or his fate decree that he should overthrow and wound the king "in the tilting-field?"

If that should happen, it would be a matter of indifference to Gabriel whether the king's lady who had loved him should slay him sooner or later.

CHAPTER XXXII
THE KNIGHT-ERRANT

Poor Aloyse, whose life for many years had been passed in waiting, in solitude, and in suffering, again sat two or three endless hours at the window, to see if she could not catch a glimpse of her beloved young master.

When the laborer to whom Gabriel had intrusted the letter knocked at the door, Aloyse rushed to open it. "News at last!" she thought.

News at last, indeed, and terrible news! Aloyse, after the first few lines, felt a mist coming before her eyes, and to conceal her emotion hastened to return to her own room, where she finished with much difficulty the perusal of the fatal missive, the tears streaming from her eyes the while.

However, hers was a stout heart and a valiant soul; so she collected her energies, wiped away her tears, and left her room to say to the messenger,—

"It is well! Until this evening, when I shall expect you and your companions."

André the page questioned her anxiously, but she bade him wait till the following day for answers to his questions. Until then she had enough to think of and to do.

When evening had fallen, she sent the people of the household to bed in good season.

"The master will surely not return to-night," she told them.

But when she was left alone she thought,—

"Ah! the master will return; but, alas! it will be the old master, not the young one,—it will be the dead, and not the living. For what body would he command me to see entombed in the vault of the counts of Montgommery, unless it were that of the Comte de Montgommery himself? Oh, my noble lord, for whom my poor Perrot died, have you at last gone to join your faithful servant? But have you carried your secret with you to the tomb? Oh, mystery of mysteries!—mystery and terror everywhere! But no matter!

Though I know and understand nothing, though I hope not, still will I obey; it is my duty, and I will do it. Oh, my God!"

Aloyse's sorrowful revery ended in a fervent prayer. It is the habit of the human soul, when the burden of life becomes too heavy to bear, to seek help and shelter in God's bosom.

About eleven o'clock, the streets being then entirely deserted, a loud knocking was heard at the great door. Aloyse started and turned pale, but summoning all her fortitude, she took a torch in her hand, and descended to admit the men who bore the sad burden. She received with a deep and respectful salute the master who thus returned to his own house after such a long absence. Then she said to the bearers, "Follow me with as little noise as possible. I will show you the way." Going in advance with her light, she led them to the funeral vault.

When they had reached the spot, the bearers placed the coffin in one of the open tombs, and put the cover of black marble in place; then the poor fellows, who had been taught by suffering to look with holy awe upon death, removed their caps, and falling on their knees, offered a short prayer for the soul of the unknown dead.

When they had risen, the nurse led them back in silence, and on the threshold slipped into the hand of one of them the sum Gabriel had promised; whereupon they vanished like dumb spectres, without having uttered a single word.

Aloyse returned to the tomb, and passed the rest of the night on her knees, praying and weeping.

The next morning André found her pale but calm; she said to him simply,—

"My child, we must never lose hope; but it is useless for us to expect Monsieur le Vicomte d'Exmès any longer. So you must set about executing the commissions with which he charged you in case he did not return at once."

"Very well," said the page, sorrowfully. "I will start at once then to go and meet Madame de Castro."

"In the name of your absent master, I thank you for your zeal, André," said Aloyse.

The boy did as he promised, and set out the same day. He inquired for the noble traveller he was seeking at every halting-place on the road, but did not meet her until he reached Amiens.

Diane de Castro had but just arrived at that city, with the escort with which the Duc de Guise had furnished her as the daughter of Henri II. She had stopped to rest a few hours at the house of Monsieur de Thuré, the governor of the place.

As soon as Diane espied the page, she changed color; but controlling herself with an effort, she made a sign to him to follow her into the next room. When they were alone, she asked him,—

"Well, André, what have you for me?"

"Nothing but this, Madame," the page replied, handing her the package containing the veil.

"Ah, it is not the ring!" cried Diane.

That was as far as her observation went at first; but she soon collected herself somewhat, and a prey to that insatiable curiosity which makes the unfortunate eager to anticipate the extremity of their sorrow, she eagerly interrogated André.

"Did Monsieur d'Exmès intrust you, besides this, with no writing for me?"

"No, Madame."

"But surely you must have some verbal message to give me?"

"Alas!" the page replied, shaking his head, "Monsieur d'Exmès said only that he gave you back all your promises, Madame, even to that of which this veil is the pledge; he added nothing to that."

"But under what circumstances did he send you to me? Had you given him my letter? What said he after reading it? When he put this package in your hands, what did he say? Speak, André! You are devoted and faithful, I know, and my whole future depends on your answers; the very least word may serve as a guide and consolation to me in the darkness which surrounds me."

"Madame," said André, "I will tell you all that I know; but that all is very little."

"Oh, go on, speak, pray speak!" cried Madame de Castro.

André thereupon told her faithfully—omitting nothing, for Gabriel had not enjoined secrecy upon him—all that his master before his departure had charged Aloyse and himself to do, in the event that his absence were prolonged. He told of the young man's hesitation and his bitter suffering; that after reading Diane's letter he had seemed at first to be on the point of speaking, but had ended by saying nothing except a few vague and indefinite words. In fact, André kept his promise, and forgot nothing,—not a gesture, or a half-uttered word, or a failure to speak. But he had said truly that he knew scarcely anything, and his story only contributed to Diane's doubt and uncertainty.

She looked mournfully at the black veil, the lone messenger from her lover, and the true symbol of her destiny. It seemed as if she were questioning its sombre folds, and seeking help and counsel from them.

"One of two things must have happened," she said to herself. "Either Gabriel has learned that he is really my brother, or he has lost all hope of ever penetrating the fatal mystery. I have only to choose between these two calamities. Yes, it must be so, and I have no more illusions on which I can feed my hope. But ought not Gabriel to have spared me this cruel uncertainty? He gives me back my word; but why? Oh, why does he not confide to me what is going to become of him, and what he means to do? Ah, this silence terrifies me more than all the anger and all the threats in the world!"

Diane questioned her very soul to know whether she would do better to follow her first plan, and enter some convent in Paris or the Provinces, never to leave its walls again; or whether it was not her duty to return to court, try to see Gabriel once more, and beg him to tell her the truth as to what had occurred and as to his future plans, and whatever happened, to watch over the life of the king, her father, which might perhaps be in danger.

Of her father? But was Henri II. her father? Might she not prove herself to be the impious and guilty daughter of her real father in trying to impede the righteous vengeance which strove to punish or even to slay the king? A frightful alternative!

But Diane was a woman, and an affectionate and noble-hearted woman. She said to herself that in any event there might be repentance for anger, but that no one could repent of having forgiven; and so, carried away by her naturally kindly disposition, she determined to return to Paris, and until she should have reassuring news of Gabriel and his designs, to remain by the king's side to safeguard and defend him. Even Gabriel himself might have need of her intervention, who could say? When she should have saved the two beings who were dearest of all on earth to her, it would be time to take refuge in God's bosom.

Having determined upon this course, Diane, the brave-hearted, hesitated no longer, but continued her journey to Paris.

She reached her destination three days later, and went at once to the Louvre, where she was welcomed by Henri with unfeigned delight and a wealth of affection truly paternal.

But, in spite of all her endeavors, she could not force herself to adopt any except a sorrowful and cold demeanor in receiving these proofs of fondness; and the king himself, remembering Diane's affection for Gabriel, oftentimes felt embarrassed and moved in his daughter's presence. She reminded him of certain matters which he would have much preferred to forget.

Thus he no longer dared to mention her alliance to François de Montmorency, which had been formerly projected, and so Madame de Castro's mind was at rest upon that point at least.

She had, however, many other subjects of anxiety. Neither at the Montgommery mansion, nor at the Louvre, nor in fact anywhere, was any definite news of Gabriel to be had.

The young man had in a certain sense disappeared.

Days and weeks and whole months rolled by, and Diane in vain made inquiries directly and indirectly; no one could say what had become of Gabriel.

Some persons thought that they had met him, always sombre and gloomy. But no one had spoken to him; the suffering soul which they had taken for Gabriel had always shunned them, and vanished at their first attempt to approach him. Moreover, no two agreed as to the locality where they had encountered Vicomte d'Exmès. Some said at St. Germain, some at Fontainebleau, others at Vincennes, and some even located him in Paris. What reliance could be placed upon such contradictory reports?

Yet many of them were right. For Gabriel, spurred on by a terrible remembrance and by still more terrible thoughts, could not remain two days in the same place. A never-ending need of action and movement drove him from a locality as soon as he arrived there. On foot or in the saddle, in town or country, he must always be in motion, pale and forbidding in appearance, and like Orestes of old haunted by the Furies.

His wanderings, too, kept him always out-of-doors; and he never entered within the walls of a house except when driven by absolute necessity.

On one occasion, however, Master Ambroise Paré, who had come back to Paris, his patients being all cured, and hostilities somewhat relaxed in the North, was surprised by a visit at his own house from his old acquaintance Vicomte d'Exmès. He received him with the deference due to one of gentle birth and the cordiality with which one welcomes a friend.

Gabriel, like a man newly returned from foreign lands, interrogated the surgeon upon matters which everybody knew all about.

Having in the first place asked him about Martin-Guerre, who, thoroughly cured, was probably on his way to Paris at that time, he questioned him about the Duc de Guise and the army. In that quarter matters had progressed marvellously. Le Balafré was before Thionville; Maréchal de Thermes had taken Dunkirk; Gaspard de Tavannes had taken possession of Guines and the province of Oie. In fact, the English no longer held one foot of ground in the whole kingdom, as François de Lorraine had sworn should be the case.

Gabriel listened with grave face, and apparently with little interest, to this good news.

"I am obliged to you, Master," he said to Ambroise Paré; "I rejoice to learn that our enterprise at Calais will not be without enduring results for France, at all events. Nevertheless it was not curiosity to hear of these matters which was my principal reason for coming to you. Master, long before I came to admire you for your great skill at the bedside of the wounded, I remember that certain words I heard you speak moved me deeply; it was one day last year in the little house on the Rue St. Jacques. Master, I have come to talk with you about these matters of religion, which your keen insight has penetrated so to the core. You have definitively embraced the cause of the Reformed religion, I suppose?"

"Yes, Monsieur d'Exmès," said Ambroise Paré, firmly. "The correspondence which the great Calvin was kind enough to enter into with me has removed my last doubts and my last scruples. I am now the most thoroughly devoted reformer of them all."

"Well, then, Master," said Gabriel, "will you not share your knowledge with a neophyte of the best intentions? I speak of myself. Will you not strengthen my doubting faith, as you would put in place a broken limb?"

"It is my duty to comfort and relieve the souls of my fellow-creatures as well as their bodies, when I can do so," said Ambroise Paré. "I am quite at your service, Monsieur d'Exmès."

For more than two hours they talked together, Ambroise ardent and eloquent, Gabriel calm and sorrowful, but a docile pupil.

At the end of that time Gabriel rose, and said to him, as he warmly pressed his hand,—

"Thanks! This conversation has done me much good. Unfortunately The time has not yet come when I can openly declare myself one of your number. It is necessary that I should wait yet a little while, even in the best interests of the Religion itself. Otherwise my conversion might well expose your holy cause to persecution some day, or to calumny at least. I know what I am saying. But now I understand, thanks to you, Master, that you and your fellows are really marching in the right path, and from this moment, believe that I am with you in heart, if not bodily. Adieu! Master Ambroise, adieu! We shall soon meet again."

Gabriel, without further elucidation of his words, took his leave of the surgeon-philosopher, and left the house.

In the early days of the following month,—May, 1558,—he appeared for the first time since his mysterious departure at his own home in the Rue des Jardins St. Paul.

There were new-comers there. Martin-Guerre had returned a fortnight previously, and Jean Peuquoy and his wife Babette had been living there for three months.

But God had not decreed that Jean's devotion should be put to the final test, nor perhaps that Babette's fault should go wholly unpunished. A few days before, she had been prematurely delivered of a dead child.

The poor mother had wept bitterly, but had bowed her head in humble acceptance of a grief which seemed like an expiation to her repentant heart; and as Jean Peuquoy had generously offered his sacrifice to her, so she in her turn for his sake resigned herself to the hand of God.

Moreover, the comforting affection of her husband and Aloyse's motherly encouragement did not fail the sweet child in her affliction.

Martin-Guerre, with his wonted good-humor, did his best to console her.

One day, as the four were sitting in friendly converse together, the door opened, and to their great amazement and still greater joy the master of the house, Vicomte d'Exmès himself, suddenly appeared, walking slowly and with a grave and sober face.

Four exclamations were heard as one; and Gabriel was quickly surrounded by his two guests, his squire, and his nurse.

When their first transports of delight had subsided, Aloyse began eagerly to question him whom in words she called her lord and master, but who was always her child in the language of her faithful heart.

What had become of him during his long absence? What did he mean to do now? Did he not intend at last to remain among those who loved him so dearly?

Gabriel laid a finger on his lips, and with a mournful but firm glance, imposed silence upon Aloyse's loving anxiety.

It was clear that he did not choose to explain his movements in the past or in the future, or that he could not.

But he took his turn at asking questions of Jean and Babette about their own affairs. Had they wanted for anything? Had they any recent intelligence of their good brother Pierre at Calais?

He tenderly expressed his sympathy for Babette, and tried to comfort her so far as it is possible to comfort a mother who is weeping for her child.

Thus Gabriel passed the remainder of the day amid his friends and his retainers, always kind and affectionate toward them, but never for an instant shaking, off the melancholy which overshadowed him like a black pall.

As for Martin-Guerre, who never once took his eyes off his dear master, found again at last, Gabriel spoke with him and inquired about his health with much interest. But throughout the whole day he never breathed a word of the promise he had made him months before, and seemed to have forgotten the engagement he had entered into to punish the wretch who had stolen his name and his honor, and had persecuted poor Martin with impunity for so long.

Martin himself was too respectful and too unselfish to direct his master's mind to the subject.

But when it was evening Gabriel rose, and said in a tone which admitted neither contradiction nor remonstrance, "I am obliged to leave you now."

Then turning to Martin-Guerre, he added,—

"My good Martin, I have been busy in your behalf during my travels, and unknown as I was, I have inquired and investigated; and I believe that I have at last found traces of the real truth of the matter in which you are interested; for I have not forgotten my engagement with you, Martin."

"Oh, Monseigneur!" cried the squire, overjoyed and embarrassed at the same time.

Gabriel continued, "I say again, I have collected sufficient proofs to justify me in believing that I am on the right track. But now I must have your assistance, my friend. At the end of this week, start for your own province, but do not go directly there. Be at Lyons one month from to-day. I will meet you there at that time, and we will take measures for acting together."

"I will do as you say, Monseigneur," said Martin-Guerre; "but shall I not see you again, meanwhile?"

"No, no, I must be alone henceforth," Gabriel replied, vigorously. "I am going away again now; and do not try to hinder me, for it would simply cause me needless pain. Adieu, my dear friends. Martin, remember,—at Lyons, a month hence."

"I will await you there, Monseigneur," said the squire.

Gabriel took leave with great warmth of Jean Peuquoy and his wife, pressed Aloyse's hands in his, and without seeming to notice the good soul's grief, set out once more to resume that wandering life to which he seemed to have condemned himself.

CHAPTER XXXIII
IN WHICH ARNAULD DU THILL APPEARS ONCE MORE

Six weeks later than the events last described, on the 15th of June, 1558, the green vine which clung to the brown walls of the finest house in the village of Artigues, near Rieux, served as a background for a picture of rural domesticity which while somewhat homely in character was not entirely without significance.

A man who, to judge from his dusty boots, had been walking quite a considerable distance, was sitting upon a wooden bench, carelessly holding his feet toward a woman who was on her knees before him busily unlacing his boots.

The man was frowning, the woman smiling.

"Haven't you finished yet, Bertrande?" said he, crossly. "You are so clumsy and slow that you almost drive me out of my wits."

"There, it's all done, Martin," said the woman, softly.

"There, it's all done, is it?" growled the pretended Martin. "Now where are my other boots? I'll wager that you didn't even think to bring them to me, you fool. So I shall have to go barefoot until you fetch them."

Bertrande disappeared within the house, and in less than a second returned with another pair of boots, which she hastened with her own hands to draw on her lord and master's feet.

Doubtless these individuals have been recognized as Arnauld du Thill, still masquerading under the name of Martin-Guerre, and now as always domineering and brutal, and Bertrande de Rolles, infinitely softened and brought to her senses by bitter experience.

"Where is my glass of beer?" asked Martin, in the same surly tone.

"It is all ready, dear," said Bertrande, timidly, "and I am just going to get it for you."

"I always have to wait," said the other, stamping with impatience. "Come, be quick about it, or I'll—"

An expressive gesture completed his sentence. Bertrande went and came again with the swiftness of light. Martin took from her hands a brimming glass of beer, which he swallowed in one draught with evident satisfaction. "That's good," he condescended to say as he handed the empty glass to his wife.

"My poor love, are you warm?" she ventured to ask, wiping her rough-spoken spouse's forehead with her handkerchief. "Here, put on your hat, for fear of the draught. You are very tired, aren't you?"

"What!" growled Martin; "don't I have to fall in with the customs of this idiotic neighborhood, and on every anniversary of our wedding go round among all the villages hereabout to ask a pack of accursed relatives to dinner? Upon my word, I had forgotten this absurd custom, if you had not reminded me of it yesterday, Bertrande! However, I have made the rounds, and in two hours the whole tribe of hungry kinsfolk will be upon us."

"Thanks, dear," said Bertrande. "You are quite right; it is an absurd custom, but a peremptory one, to which we must submit, if we would not be looked upon as arrogant and scornful."

"Well reasoned," replied Martin, ironically. "And have you done your part, sluggard? Is the table laid in the orchard?"

"Yes, Martin, as you ordered."

"Have you been to invite the judge also?" asked the affectionate spouse.

"Yes, Martin; and he said that he would do his best to be present at the feast."

"Do his best!" cried Martin, angrily. "That isn't enough; he *must* come! You must have given the invitation wrong. I count upon gaining some influence over this judge, as you know perfectly well; but you always try to displease me. His presence was the only thing which reconciled me in the least to this tedious custom and the useless expense of this ridiculous anniversary."

"Ridiculous to celebrate the anniversary of our wedding!" rejoined Bertrande, while her eyes filled with tears. "Ah, Martin, to be sure, you are a learned man now; you have travelled much, and seen many things, and can afford to despise the old usages of the province; but no matter. This anniversary reminds me of a time when you were less harsh and more loving to your poor wife."

"Yes," said Martin, with a sardonic smile; "and when my wife was less loving and more of a termagant to me; when she even forgot herself so far sometimes as to—"

"Oh, Martin, Martin!" cried Bertrande, "do not recall those times; for they make me blush, and I find it hard now to explain my own actions."

"And so do I. When I think that I could ever have been such an ass as to put up with—Ah, ah! let us leave the subject! My disposition is much changed, and yours as well,—I am glad to do you that justice. As you say, Bertrande, I have seen a good deal since those days. Your unbearable temper, which drove me out into the world to get rid of you, also compelled me to gain experience; and when I returned here last year, I succeeded in rearranging matters in their proper order. To effect that result, I had only to bring with me another Martin, called 'Martin Club.' So now everything goes along to my satisfaction, and we certainly have a most united household."

"That is true, thank God!" said Bertrande.

"Bertrande!"

"Martin!"

"Go at once," said he, with the tone of an absolute master,—"go back at once to the judge of Artigues, renew your invitation, and obtain his formal promise to be present at our feast; if he does not come, remember that I will wreak my disappointment on you alone."

"I will go at once," said Bertrande, suiting the action to the word.

Arnauld du Thill followed her retreating form for a moment with a satisfied expression; then, being left alone, he stretched himself lazily on the bench, drinking in the fresh air, and blinking with the selfish and disdainful comfort of a man happy in having nothing to fear and nothing to wish for.

He did not notice a man, apparently a traveller, who with the aid of a cane was walking laboriously along the road,—which was quite deserted, that being the hottest hour of the day. As the traveller saw Arnauld, he stopped in front of him.

"Pardon me, my friend," said the stranger. "Is there not, pray, in this village of yours an inn where I may rest and dine?"

"No, there is not," replied Arnauld, without moving; "you will have to go to Rieux, two leagues from here, before you will come across an innkeeper's signpost."

"Two leagues more!" exclaimed the wayfarer; "and I am quite exhausted now. I would willingly give a pistole for a chance to lie down, and for something to eat at this moment."

"A pistole!" said Arnauld, ever on the alert, as of old, when money was to be had. "Well, my good fellow, we can give you, if you wish, a bed in a corner here; and as for dinner,—why, we are going to have an anniversary feast to-day, and one guest more will make no difference. How does that suit you?"

"Perfectly," replied the stranger; "for, as I told you, I am almost fainting with fatigue and hunger."

"Very well; it's a bargain, then," said Arnauld; "you may remain here for a pistole."

"I will pay in advance," said the traveller.

Arnauld du Thill sat up to take the money, and at the same time raised his hat, which had concealed his eyes and his face.

The stranger was then able to see his features; and at the first glance he cried, recoiling in amazement,—

"My nephew, Arnauld du Thill!"

Arnauld looked carefully at him, and turned pale; but he soon collected himself.

"Your nephew?" said he. "Why, I don't know you! Who are you?"

"You don't know me, Arnauld?" exclaimed the stranger; "you don't know your old uncle, your mother's own brother, Carbon Barreau, to whom you have been the source of so much trouble,—as indeed you have been to the whole family?"

"By my faith, no!" said Arnauld, with an insolent laugh.

"What! do you deny me and yourself as well?" rejoined Carbon Barreau. "Tell me, do you mean to say that you did not cause your mother, who was my sister, to die of grief,—a poor, lone widow, whom you abandoned at Sagias ten years ago? Ah! you may not recognize me, hard heart; but I know you well."

"I have no idea what you mean," replied Arnauld, brazenly, entirely cool and collected. "My name is not Arnauld, but Martin-Guerre; and I am not from Sagias, but belong in Artigues. The old men in the neighborhood have known me from my birth, and will swear to my identity; and if you want to be laughed at, you have only to repeat your statement before my wife, Bertrande de Rolles, and all my kinsfolk."

"Your wife! your kinsfolk!" said Carbon Barreau, in bewilderment. "Pardon! Is it possible that I am mistaken? No; it cannot be! Such a resemblance—"

"At the end of ten years it is hard to verify," Arnauld interrupted. "Come, your sight is growing dim, my good friend! My real uncles and relatives you can see and talk with yourself very soon."

"Oh, very well! In that case," replied Carbon Barreau, who began to be convinced, "you may well boast of your resemblance to my nephew, Arnauld du Thill."

"I never heard of him except from you," said Arnauld, sneeringly, "and I never have boasted of it yet."

"Ah, when I said that you might boast of it," returned the good man, "I did not mean that there was any cause for pride in resembling such a rascal, far from it! I am in a position to say, since I am one of the family, that my nephew was the most infernal blackguard imaginable. And indeed when I reflect, it seems very improbable that he should still be alive, for the villain must have been hung long before this."

"Do you think so?" retorted Arnauld, not without bitterness.

"I am sure of it, Monsieur Martin-Guerre," said Carbon Barreau, with an air of conviction. "However, it doesn't offend you, does it, to have me speak in such terms of the scoundrel, since you are not he, my good host?"

"Not in the least," said Arnauld, decidedly ill at ease, however.

"Ah, Monsieur," continued the uncle, who was rather inclined to chatter, "how many times have I congratulated myself, in speaking to his poor weeping mother, on having remained unmarried, and having had no children to dishonor my name and ruin my life, as that vile good-for-nothing did for her."

"Let me see; that is true," said Arnauld to himself. "Uncle Carbon had no children,—no heirs, that is to say."

"What are you thinking, Master Martin?" asked the stranger.

"I was thinking," Arnauld replied in his sweetest tones, "that in spite of your assertions to the contrary, Messire Carbon Barreau, you would be very happy to-day if you had a son, or even, in default of a son, this same evil-disposed nephew, whom you seem to regret so little, but who would at least be something for you to love, and somebody to whom you could hand down your property when you die."

"My property?" said Carbon Barreau.

"Yes, to be sure, your property," replied Arnauld. "You who scatter pistoles around with so lavish a hand cannot be poor; and this Arnauld, whom I resemble, would be your heir, I suppose. *Pardieu*! I am inclined to regret to a certain extent that I am not he."

"Arnauld du Thill, if he is not hung, would really be my heir," returned Carbon Barreau, gravely. "But he will derive no great advantage from that fact, for I am not rich. I offer a pistole for the privilege of resting a while and for a little refreshment, because I am overborne with weariness and hunger; but that does not prevent my purse from being light,—too light, alas!"

"Hum!" said Arnauld, incredulously.

"Don't you believe me, Master Martin-Guerre? As you please. It is no less true that I am now on my way to Lyons, to see the President of the Parliament, where I acted as usher for twenty years, who offers me shelter and sustenance for the rest of my days. He sent me twenty-five pistoles to pay my few small debts, and the expenses of the journey, large-hearted man that he is! But what I have left of that sum is all that I own in the world. Therefore my heritage is too trifling a matter for Arnauld du Thill, even were he alive, to take the trouble to claim it. That is why—"

"Enough of this, dotard!" Arnauld du Thill rudely interrupted him, in high ill-humor. "Do you suppose I have time to listen forever to your twaddle? Just give me your pistole and go into the house, if you choose. You shall dine in an hour's time, and can sleep after that, and then we shall be quits. That does not require so much talk."

"But it was you who questioned me," said Carbon Barreau.

"Come, come! Do you propose to go in, fellows or not? See, some of my guests are already arriving, and with your leave I will quit you to receive them. Go in. I treat you without ceremony, and do not escort you."

"So I see," said Carbon Barreau, as he entered the house, grumbling at his host's sudden changes of humor.

Three hours later the company was still at the table under the elms. The number of the guests was complete, and the judge of Artigues, whose favor Arnauld meant to win, had the place of honor.

Good wine and pleasant talk were circulating. The younger people talked of the future and the graybeards of the past, while Uncle Carbon Barreau had been able to make sure that his host was really called Martin-Guerre, and was recognized and treated by all the inhabitants of Artigues as one of themselves.

"Do you remember, Martin-Guerre," said one of them, "the Augustinian monk, Brother Chrysostom, who taught us both to read?"

"Yes, I remember him," said Arnauld.

"Do you remember, Cousin Martin," asked another, "that it was on your wedding-day that cannon were first fired at a merry-making in the province?"

"Yes, I remember," replied Arnauld.

And, as if to refresh his memory, he embraced his wife, who was sitting at his side, the picture of happy pride.

"Since your memory is so exceedingly good, my good Master," suddenly exclaimed a clear, firm voice behind the guests, addressing Arnauld du Thill, "since you remember so many things, perhaps you may remember me, as well!"

CHAPTER XXXIV
JUSTICE IN A QUANDARY

He who spoke thus, in a commanding tone, cast aside the dark cloak of ample dimensions which hid his person; and Arnauld du Thill's guests, who had turned at the sound of his voice, could see a young cavalier of haughty bearing and richly dressed.

At a little distance a servant was holding by their bridles the two horses on which he and his master had ridden.

All rose respectfully, greatly surprised and very curious.

Arnauld du Thill turned as white as a dead man,

"Monsieur le Vicomte d'Exmès," he muttered in his fright.

"Well," continued Gabriel, in a voice of thunder, addressing him,—"well! you recognize me, do you?"

Arnauld, after hesitating a moment, had quickly reckoned up his chances, and decided upon the course he should take.

"To be sure," said he, in a trembling voice which he struggled to control,—"to be sure I recognize Monsieur le Vicomte d'Exmès, from having sometimes seen him at the Louvre when I was in the service of Monsieur de Montmorency; but I cannot believe that Monseigneur would recognize me, the poor and obscure servant of the constable."

"You forget," said Gabriel, "that you have been my servant as well."

"What, I?" cried Arnauld, feigning the most extreme amazement. "Oh, pardon, Monseigneur is surely mistaken!"

"I am so certain that I am not mistaken," retorted Gabriel, calmly, "that I without hesitation call upon the judge of Artigues, here present, to cause your immediate arrest and imprisonment. Is that sufficiently clear?"

There was a movement of affright among the guests. The wondering judge drew near. Arnauld alone retained his appearance of tranquillity.

"May I not at least know of what crime I am accused?" he asked.

"I accuse you," replied Gabriel, firmly, "of having wickedly substituted yourself for my squire, Martin-Guerre, and of having basely and treacherously stolen his name, his house, and his wife, by means of a resemblance so exact that it passes understanding."

Upon hearing this concisely stated accusation, the guests exchanged looks of stupefied bewilderment.

"What does this mean?" they whispered. "Martin-Guerre not Martin-Guerre? What diabolical sorcery is at the bottom of all this?"

Several of the good people crossed themselves, and repeated beneath their breath certain words designed to exorcise evil spirits. The majority began to look upon their host with something like terror.

Arnauld du Thill saw that it was time for him to strike some decisive blow to win back these timid and yielding creatures to his side; so turning to her whom he called his wife, he cried,—

"Bertrande, speak, I conjure you! Am I or am I not your husband?"

Poor Bertrande, terrified and gasping, thus far had simply, without uttering a word, watched first her husband and then Gabriel, with her great eyes open to their fullest extent.

But at Arnauld du Thill's imperious gesture and his threatening tone, she hesitated no longer, but threw herself into his arms with effusion.

"Dear Martin-Guerre!" she cried.

At these words the charm was broken, and the offensive murmurs were turned against Gabriel.

"Monsieur," said Arnauld du Thill, triumphantly, "in the face of my wife's testimony and that of all my friends and kinsmen, do you still persist in your strange accusation?"

"I do indeed," was Gabriel's reply.

"One moment!" cried Master Carbon Barreau, interposing. "I know very well, my host, that I am not losing my eyesight. If there is somewhere a person who resembles this man, feature for feature, then I declare that one of the two is my nephew, Arnauld du Thill, like myself a native of Sagias."

"Ah, what a fortunate reinforcement just at the right moment!" said Gabriel. "Master," he added, addressing the old man, "do you recognize this man as your nephew?"

"In truth," said Carbon Barreau, "I don't know how to tell whether it is he or the other one; but I would be willing to take my oath in advance that if there is any imposture, my nephew is the impostor, for he was always much addicted to that sort of thing."

"You hear, Monsieur le Juge," said Gabriel to the magistrate; "whichever be the culprit, there can no longer be any doubt about the crime."

"But where is this fellow who, to cheat me, claims to have been cheated himself?" cried Arnauld du Thill, boldly. "Am I not to be confronted with him! Is he in hiding? Let him come forward, and submit to judgment himself."

"Martin-Guerre, my squire," said Gabriel, "has already surrendered himself to the authorities at Rieux, in accordance with my command. Monsieur le Juge, I am the Comte de Montgommery, formerly captain of his Majesty's Guards. The accused himself recognizes me. I call upon you to order him to be arrested and confined, as his accuser has been. When they are both in the hands of justice I hope that I shall be able easily to prove on which side is the truth, and on which the imposture."

"That is very clear, Monseigneur," said the confused judge to Gabriel. "Let Martin-Guerre be taken to prison."

"I give myself up," said Arnauld, "strong as I am in my innocence. My dear, kind friends," he added, addressing the throng, whom he judged it prudent to keep in his interest, "I rely upon your loyal testimony to aid me in this extremity. All of you who have known me heretofore recognize me, do you not?"

"Yes, yes, never fear, Martin!" replied all the friends and kinsfolk, touched by his appeal to them.

As for Bertrande, she had taken occasion to swoon.

Eight days later the hearing of the cause began before the court at Rieux.

Surely it was a curious case, and one difficult to decide. It certainly deserved to be handed down as a cause célèbre to our own days, three hundred years later, as it has been.

If Gabriel de Montgommery had not been somewhat involved in it, it is quite probable that the good judges of Rieux, to whom the cause was submitted, would never have been able to decide it.

What Gabriel was most earnest in asking was that the two adversaries should not be allowed to meet under any pretext until otherwise ordered.

They were interrogated and confronted with the witnesses separately, and Martin, as well as Arnauld du Thill, was kept in most rigorous seclusion.

Martin-Guerre, wrapped in a heavy cloak, was confronted one by one with his wife and all his neighbors and friends, all of whom recognized him. It was his face and his figure, and they could not be mistaken.

But all of them were equally positive in their recognition of Arnauld du Thill when he was shown to them.

Carbon Barreau, on the other hand, was equally positive in his recognition of each of them as his nephew, Arnauld du Thill.

They were all excited and terrified, and there seemed to be not the slightest guide by which the truth might be made to appear.

How was it possible to distinguish between two who were such exact counterparts as Arnauld du Thill and Martin-Guerre?

"The Evil One himself would be at his wit's end," said Carbon Barreau, in his confusion between his two nephews.

But in unravelling this unprecedented and extraordinary freak of Nature, the most reliable guides for Gabriel and the judges, failing material differences, would be contradictions in matters of fact and divergent characteristics.

In the story of their early years, Martin and Arnauld du Thill, each in his turn, told exactly the same facts, remembered the same dates, and mentioned the same names, with remarkable unanimity.

In support of his statements, Arnauld produced Bertrande's letters, the family papers, and the ring which was blessed on his wedding day.

But Martin explained it by telling how Arnauld, after having given him up to be hung at Noyon, had had an opportunity to steal all the papers and his wedding-ring.

Thus nothing removed the perplexity of the judges, and their uncertainty never grew less. The appearances and indications were as strong and convincing on one side as on the other; and the allegations of the two accused seemed equally sincere.

Fresh proofs and additional testimony were needed to untie so complicated a knot. Gabriel undertook to find and produce them.

In the first place, the presiding judge propounded this question anew to Martin and to Arnauld du Thill, separately as before.

"Where did you pass your time between your twelfth and your sixteenth year?"

The immediate answer of each of the accused was,—

"At St. Sébastien, in Biscaye, with my cousin Sanxi."

Sanxi was present, summoned as a witness, and testified to the truth of the fact.

Gabriel approached him, and whispered a word in his ear.

Sanxi laughed, and began to address Arnauld in the Basque tongue. Arnauld turned pale, and said not a word.

"What!" said Gabriel, "you passed four years at St. Sébastien, and yet do not understand the dialect of the province?"

"I have forgotten it," stammered Arnauld.

Martin-Guerre, when submitted to this test in his turn, chattered away in Basque for a quarter of an hour, to the great delight of Cousin Sanxi and the edification of the spectators and judges.

This first indication to throw light upon the truth was soon followed by another, which although similar to an experience of Ulysses was no less significant.

The inhabitants of Artigues who were contemporaries of Martin-Guerre still remembered with admiration not unmixed with envy his skill at tennis; but since his return the false Martin had always declined to play when it was suggested, on the plea of a wound in his right hand.

The true Martin-Guerre, on the other hand, took great delight in holding his own against the most expert tennis-players in the presence of the judges.

He played sitting down even, and always wrapped in his cloak. His partner did nothing but bring him the balls, which he hit with really marvellous dexterity.

From that moment public sympathy, so potent a factor on such occasions, was on Martin's side,—that is to say, as very seldom happens, on the side of right.

One more curious fact put the finishing touch to Arnauld du Thill's chances with the judges.

The two accused men were of precisely the same height; but Gabriel, always on the watch for the least sign, thought that he had discovered that his brave squire's foot, his only foot, alas! was much smaller than Arnauld du Thill's.

The old cobbler of Artigues appeared before the court with his old and new measurements.

"Yes," said the old fellow, "it is certain that Martin-Guerre used to wear nines, and I was greatly surprised when he returned to find that he wore twelves; but I took it to be the effect of his long journeys."

The true Martin-Guerre then proudly held out to the cobbler the only foot which Providence had left him, to aid doubtless in the grander triumph of the truth. The simple-minded old man, having taken its measure, recognized it, and declared it to be the identical foot he had shod in former days, and which had remained almost the same in spite of its long travels and the double service it had had to do.

After that decisive testimony everybody was unanimous for Martin's innocence and the guilt of Arnauld du Thill.

But these material proofs were not enough, and Gabriel desired to adduce moral certainty in addition.

He produced the peasant to whom Arnauld du Thill had intrusted the strange commission to announce Martin-Guerre's death by hanging at Noyon. The good man ingenuously told of his amazement at finding in the Rue des Jardins St. Paul the very man whom he had seen take the Lyons road. This was the circumstance which had aroused Gabriel's first suspicion of the real truth.

Then Bertrande de Rolles was examined anew.

Poor Bertrande, in spite of the general change of opinion, was still for him who aroused her fear.

Being asked if she had not noticed a change in her husband's disposition since his return, she replied,—

"Oh, yes, indeed! he came back much changed; but for the better, Messieurs," she hastened to add.

Being pressed to explain herself more clearly, she said naïvely, "Formerly, Martin was weaker and more good-natured than a sheep, and let me lead him about and cuff him till I was ashamed of him. But he came back a man, a master. He proved to me beyond a doubt that I was very wrong before, and that it is my duty as his wife to obey his word and his stick. Now he commands, and I wait upon him; he lifts his hand, and I kiss his feet. He brought back this air of authority from his travels, and since his return our relations have become what they should be. We are going in the right direction now, and I am very glad of it."

Others of the Artigues people testified that the old Martin-Guerre had always been as inoffensive and pious and kind as the new one was quarrelsome and blasphemous and niggardly.

Like the cobbler and Bertrande they had attributed these changes to his travels.

At last Comte Gabriel de Montgommery deigned to give evidence, amid the respectful silence of judges and spectators.

He told of the strange circumstances attending his having in his service the two Martin-Guerres, one after the other; how he had puzzled for a long while over the singular variations in the disposition and character of his double squire, and of the events which had finally led him to suspect the truth.

In short, Gabriel told everything that we have told heretofore,—Martin's frights and Arnauld du Thill's treason, the virtues of the one and the crimes of the other; he made the whole obscure and confused history as clear as day, and ended by demanding punishment of the culprit and restitution of his rights for the innocent man.

The justice of that day was less obliging and convenient for accused persons than that of the present time. Thus it was that Arnauld du Thill was still ignorant of the overwhelming evidence adduced against him. He had seen with much anxiety the tests of knowledge of the Basque patois and skill in the game of tennis result to his disadvantage; but he believed that he had, after all, given sufficiently plausible excuses. As for the episode of the old cobbler, he had understood nothing of it. Last of all, he did not know whether Martin-Guerre, who was persistently kept out of his sight, had come out any better than he himself had from the various examinations and ordeals.

Gabriel, moved by a just and generous feeling, had insisted that Arnauld du Thill should be allowed to be present when the speech summing up the charges should be made, and to reply to it if necessary. Martin was under no such necessity, and remained in his prison. But Arnauld was brought before the tribunal so that judgment might be passed after hearing both sides; and he lost not a word of Gabriel's forcible and convincing statement.

However, when Gabriel had finished, Arnauld du Thill, without yielding an inch to fear or discouragement, calmly rose and asked leave to speak in his own defence. The court would have refused; but Gabriel seconded his request, and he was allowed to speak.

He spoke admirably; the cunning blackguard was really eloquent by nature, and had a shrewd and clever mind.

Gabriel's principal endeavor had been to apply the evidence to dispelling the obscurity which hung about the adventures of the two Martins. Arnauld, on the other hand, devoted himself to twisting all the threads together again and to bringing the minds of the judges a second time into that state of confusion in which lay his only hope. He avowed that he himself could in nowise comprehend all the entanglements arising from these two existences, which were continually being mistaken for each other. It was not his affair to explain all the blunders for which they tried to hold him responsible. All he had to do was to answer for his own life and justify his own actions; and that he was ready to do.

He then repeated the logically arranged and compact story of his own acts and movements from his cradle down to that day. He spoke to his friends and kinsfolk, reminding them of circumstances which they had themselves forgotten, laughing at certain memories, and weeping at others.

He could not speak Basque, it is true, nor play tennis; but everybody had not the faculty of remembering languages, and he showed the scar on his hand. Even if his adversary had satisfied the court on those two points, nothing was easier when occasion demanded than to learn a patois and attain skill at a game by practice.

The Comte de Montgommery, certainly led astray by some mischief-maker, accused him of having stolen from his squire the papers which established his name and his identity; but there was no proof of that fact.

As for the peasant, who could say that he was not an accomplice of the *soi-disant* Martin?

Regarding the money for the Comte de Montgommery's ransom, which he. Martin-Guerre, was accused of having stolen, he could only say that he had returned to Artigues with a certain sum larger than that lost by the count; but he accounted for it by exhibiting the certificate of the very eminent and powerful nobleman, the Connétable Duc de Montmorency.

In his peroration, Arnauld with infinite address rung the changes upon the constable's mighty name in the ears of the bewildered judges. He insisted that they should send to make inquiries concerning him of his illustrious master, and he was confident that the result of such inquiries would be his speedy and decisive justification.

In short, the crafty rascal's speech was so clever and insidious, he expressed himself with so much warmth, and impudence sometimes so closely resembles innocence, that Gabriel saw that the judges were undecided and wavering once more.

It was necessary then to strike a decisive blow; and Gabriel, although it was much against his wish, determined to do it.

He spoke a single word in the president's ear; whereupon the latter ordered Arnauld du Thill to be remanded to prison and Martin-Guerre to be produced.